W9-CHK-408

THREE NOVELS

OTHER WORKS BY WILLIAM S. BURROUGHS
PUBLISHED BY GROVE PRESS

Naked Lunch
The Ticket That Exploded

William S. Burroughs

GROVE PRESS
New York

THREE NOVELS

The Soft Machine
Nova Express
The Wild Boys

This collection copyright © 1980 by William S. Burroughs
The Soft Machine copyright © 1961, 1966 by William S. Burroughs
Nova Express copyright © 1964 by William S. Burroughs
The Wild Boys copyright © 1969, 1970, 1971 by William S. Burroughs

Acknowledgment is due to Alfred A. Knopf, Inc., for permission to
quote, in *The Wild Boys*, from *The Trial* by Franz Kafka, translated by
Willa and Edwin Muir, copyright © 1937, 1956 by Alfred A. Knopf, Inc.
"Mother and I Would Like to Know," in *The Wild Boys*, was first pub-
lished in *Evergreen Review* No. 67; an earlier version appeared in
Mayfair and was reprinted in *The Job*.

All rights reserved.

No part of this book may be reproduced, stored in a retrieval
system, or transmitted in any form, by any means, including
mechanical, electronic, photocopying, recording or otherwise,
without prior written permission of the publisher.

Published by Grove Press, Inc.
920 Broadway
New York, N.Y. 10010

First Black Cat Edition 1980
First Evergreen Edition 1988

Library of Congress Cataloging-in-Publication Data

Burroughs, William S., 1914–
    The soft machine; Nova express; The wild boys.
    I. Title: Soft machine.   II. Title: Nova express.
III. Title: Wild boys.
PS3552.U75A6   1988   813'.54   87-31629
ISBN 0-8021-3084-4

Manufactured in the United States of America

10 9 8 7 6 5 4 3 2 1

CONTENTS

The Soft Machine

CONTENTS

Dead on Arrival

I WAS WORKING the hole with the sailor and we did not do bad. Fifteen cents on an average night boosting the afternoons and short-timing the dawn we made out from the land of the free. But I was running out of veins. I went over to the counter for another cup of coffee. . .in Joe's Lunch Room drinking coffee with a napkin under the cup which is said to be the mark of someone who does a lot of sitting in cafeterias and lunchrooms. . . Waiting on the man. . . "What can we do?" Nick said to me once in his dead junky whisper. "They know we'll wait. . ." Yes, they know we'll wait. . .

There is a boy sitting at the counter thin-faced kid his eyes all pupil. I see he is hooked and sick. Familiar face maybe from the pool hall where I scored for tea sometime. Somewhere in grey strata of subways all-night cafeterias rooming house flesh. His eyes flickered the question. I nodded toward my booth. He carried his coffee over and sat down opposite me.

The croaker lives out Long Island. . . light yen sleep waking up for stops. Change. Start. Everything sharp and clear. Antennae of TV suck the sky. The clock jumped the way time will after four P.M.

"The Man is three hours late. You got the bread?"

"I got three cents."

"Nothing less than a nickel. These double papers he claims." I looked at his face. Good looking. "Say kid I known an Old Auntie Croaker right for you like a Major . . . Take the phone. I don't want him to rumble my voice."

About this time I meet this Italian tailor cum pusher I know from Lexington and he gives me a good buy on H. . . At least it was good at first but all the time shorter and shorter. . . "Short Count Tony" we call him. . .

Out of junk in East St. Louis sick dawn he threw himself across the washbasin pressing his stomach against the cool porcelain. I draped myself over his body laughing. His shorts dissolved in rectal mucus and carbolic soap. summer dawn smells from a vacant lot.

"I'll wait here. . . Don't want him to rumble me. . ."

Made it five times under the shower that day soapy bubbles of egg flesh seismic tremors split by fissure spurts of jissom. . .

I made the street, everything sharp and clear like

after rain. See Sid in a booth reading a paper his face like yellow ivory in the sunlight. I handed him two nickels under the table. Pushing in a small way to keep up The Habit: INVADE. DAMAGE. OCCUPY. Young faces in blue alcohol flame.

"And use that alcohol. You fucking can't wait hungry junkies all the time black up my spoons. That's all I need for Pen Indef the fuzz rumbles a black spoon in my trap." The old junky spiel. Junk hooks falling.

"Shoot your way to freedom kid."

Trace a line of goose pimples up the thin young arm. Slide the needle in and push the bulb watching the junk hit him all over. Move right in with the shit and suck junk through all the hungry young cells.

There is a boy sitting like your body. I see he is a hook. I drape myself over him from the pool hall. Draped myself over his cafeteria and his shorts dissolved in strata of subways. . .and all house flesh. . . toward the booth. . .down opposite me. . . The Man I Italian tailor. . . I know bread. "Me a good buy on H."

"You're quitting? Well I hope you make it, kid. May I fall down and be paralyzed if I don't mean it. . . You gotta friend in me. A real friend and if."

Well the traffic builds up and boosters falling in with jackets shirts and ties, kids with a radio torn from the living car trailing tubes and wires, lush-workers flash rings and wrist watches falling in sick all hours. I had the janitor cooled, an old rummy, but it couldn't last with that crowd.

"Say you're looking great kid. Now do yourself a

favor and stay off. I been getting some really great shit lately. Remember that brown shit sorta yellow like snuff cooks up brown and clear. . ."

Junky in east bath room. . . invisible and persistent dream body. . . familiar face maybe. . . scored for some time or body. . .in that grey smell of rectal mucus. . . night cafeterias and junky room dawn smells. three hours from Lexington made it five times. . . soapy egg flesh. . .

"These double papers he claims of withdrawal."

"Well I thought you was quitting. . ."

"I can't make it."

"*Imposible quitar eso.*"

Got up and fixed in the sick dawn flutes of Ramadan.

"*William tu tomas más medicina?. . . No me hágas casa, William.*"

Casbah house in the smell of dust and we made it. . . empty eukodal boxes stacked four feet along the walls. . .dead on the surplus blankets. . .girl screaming . . . *vecinos* rush in. . .

"What did she die of?"

"I don't know she just died."

Bill Gains in Mexico City room with his douche bag and his stash of codeine pills powdered in a bicarbonate can. "I'll just say I suffer from indigestion." coffee and blood spilled all over the place. cigarette holes in the pink blanket. . . The Consul would give me no information other than place of burial in The American Cemetery.

"Broke? Have you no pride? Go to your Consul." He gave me an alarm clock ran for a year after his death.

Leif repatriated by the Danish. freight boat out of Casa for Copenhagen sank off England with all hands. Remember my medium of distant fingers?—

"What did she die of?"

"End."

"Some things I find myself."

The Sailor went wrong in the end. hanged to a cell door by his principals: "Some things I find myself doing I'll pack in is all."

Bread knife in the heart. . .rub and die. . .repatriated by a morphine script. . .those out of Casa for Copenhagen on special yellow note. . .

"All hands broke? Have you no pride?" Alarm clock ran for a year. "He just sit down on the curb and die." Esperanza told me on Niño Perdido and we cashed a morphine script. those Mexican Nar. scripts on special yellow bank-note paper. . .like a thousand dollar bill . . .or a Dishonorable Discharge from the US Army. . . And fixed in the cubicle room you reach by climbing this ladder.

Yesterday call flutes of Ramadan: *"No me hágas casa."*

Blood spill over shirts and light. the American trailing in form. . . He went to Madrid. This frantic Cuban fruit finds Kiki with a *novia* and stabs him with a kitchen knife in the heart. (Girl screaming. Enter the nabors.)

"Quédase con su medicina, William."

Half bottle of Fundador after half cure in the Jew Hospital. shots of demerol by candlelight. They turned off the lights and water. Paper-like dust we made it. Empty walls. Look anywhere. No good. *No bueno.*

He went to Madrid. . . Alarm clock ran for yesterday. . . *"No me hágas casa."* Dead on arrival. . . you might say at the Jew Hospital. . . blood spilled over the American. . . trailing lights and water. . . The Sailor went so wrong somewhere in that grey flesh. . . He just sit down on zero. . . I nodded on Niño Perdido his coffee over three hours late. . . They all went away and sent papers. . . The Dead Man write for you like a major. . . Enter *vecinos.* . . Freight boat smell of rectal mucus went down off England with all dawn smell of distant fingers. . . About this time I went to your Consul. He gave me a Mexican after his death. . . Five times of dust we made it. . . with soap bubbles of withdrawal crossed by a thousand junky nights. . . Soon after the half maps came in by candlelight. . . OCCUPY. . . Junk lines falling. . . Stay off. . . Bill Gains in the Yellow Sickness. . . Looking at dirty pictures casual as a ceiling fan short-timing the dawn we made it in the corn smell of rectal mucus and carbolic soap. . . familiar face maybe from the vacant lot. . . trailing tubes and wires. . . "You fucking-can't-wait-hungry-junkies! . . ." Burial in the American Cemetery. *"Quédase con su medicina. . ."* On Niño Perdido the girl screaming. . . They all went way through Casbah House. . . "Couldn't you write me any better than that? Gone away. . . You can look any place."

No good. *No Bueno.*

You wouldn't believe how hot things were when I left the States—I knew this one pusher wouldn't carry any shit on his person just shoot it in the line—Ten twenty grains over and above his own absorption according to the route he was servicing and piss it out in bottles for his customers so if the heat came up on them they cop out as degenerates—So Doc Benway assessed the situation and came up with this brain child—

"Once in the Upper Baboonasshole I was stung by a scorpion—the sensation is not dissimilar to a fix— Hummm."

So he imports this special breed of scorpions and feeds them on metal meal and the scorpions turned a phosphorescent blue color and sort of hummed. "Now we must find a worthy vessel," he said—So we flush out this old goof ball artist and put the scorpion to him and he turned sort of blue and you could see he was fixed right to metal—These scorpions could travel on a radar beam and service the clients after Doc copped for the bread—It was a good thing while it lasted and the heat couldn't touch us—However all these scorpion junkies began to glow in the dark and if they didn't score on the hour metamorphosed into scorpions straight away—So there was a spot of bother and we had to move on disguised as young junkies on the way to Lexington—Bill and Johnny we sorted out the names but they keep changing like one day I would wake up as Bill the next day as Johnny—So there we are in the train compartment shivering junk sick our eyes watering and burning.

Who Am I to Be Critical?

AND ALL OF A SUDDEN the sex chucks hit me in the crotch
and I sagged against the wall and looked at Johnny too
weak to say anything, it wasn't necessary, he was there
too and without a word he dipped some soap in warm
water and dropped my shorts and rubbed the soap on
my ass and worked his cock up me with a corkscrew
motion and we both came right away standing there
and swaying with the train clickety clack clack spurt
spurt into the brass cuspidor—We never got to Lexington actually—Stopped off in the town of Marshal and
hit this old country croaker for tincture with the aged
mother suffering from piles in the worst form there is
line and he wrote like a major—That night we got into
a pool game and Doc won a Dusenberg Panama hat

tan suit and dark glasses like 1920 sports and the further
South we went the easier it was to score like we brought
the twenties along with us—Well we come to this
Mexican border town in time to see something interesting—In order to make way for a new bridge that never
got built actually they had torn down a block of shacks
along the river where the Chink railway workers used to
smoke the black stuff and the rats had been down under
the shacks hooked for generations—So the rats was running all through the street squealing sick biting everyone in sight—When we went to look for our car couldn't
find it and no cars anywhere just this train left over
from an old Western—The track gave out somewhere
north of Monterrey and we bought some horses off a
Chinaman for a tin of mud—By this time there were
soldiers everywhere shooting the civilians so we scored
for some Civil War uniforms and joined one of the
warring powers—And captured five soldiers who were
wearing uniforms of a different color and the General
got drunk and decided to hang the prisoners just for
jolly and we rigged up a cart with a drop under a tree
limb—The first one dropped straight and clean and one
of the soldiers wiped his mouth and stepped forward
grinning and pulled his pants down to an ankle and his
cock flipped out spurting—We all stood there watching
and feeling it right down to our toes and the others who
were waiting to be hanged felt it too—So we stripped
them and they got hard-ons waiting—They couldn't
help it you understand. That night we requisitioned a
ranch house and all got drunk and Johnny did this

dance with his tie around his neck lolling his head on
one side and letting his tongue fall out and wriggled
his ass and dropped his pants and his cock flipped out
and the soldiers rolled around laughing till they pissed
all over themselves—Then they rigged up a harness under his arms and hoisted him up off the floor to a beam
and gang-fucked him—By the time we got to Monterrey
there was Spaniards around in armor like a costume
movie and again we were lucky to arrive just at the
right time. There was a crowd of people in the Zoco and
we pushed up front with our rush-hour technique and
saw they were getting ready to burn some character at
the stake—When they lit the faggots at his feet the only
sound you could hear was the fire crackling and then
everyone sucked in his breath together and the screams
tore through me and my lips and tongue swole up with
blood and I come in my pants—And I could see others
had shot their load too and you could smell it like a
compost heap, some of us so close our pants steamed in
the fire just pulling the screams and the smoke down
into our lungs and sort of whimpering—It was tasty I
tell you—So we hit Mexico City just before sunrise and
I said here we go again—That heart pulsing in the sun
and my cock pulsed right with it and jissom seeped
through my thin cotton trousers and fell in the dust
and shit of the street—And a boy next to me grinning
and gave me a backhand pickpocket feel, my cock still
hard and aching like after a wet dream—And we
crawled up onto a muddy shelf by the canal and made
it there three times slow fuck on knees in the stink of

sewage looking at the black water—It turned out later this kid had the epilepsy—When he got these fits he would flop around and come maybe five times in his dry goods, made you feel good all over to watch it—He really had it built in and he told me he could fix it with a magic man we trade places—So we started off on foot across the mountains and down the other side to high jungle warm and steamy and he kept having these fits and I dug it special fucking him in the spasm his asshole fluttering like a vibrator—Well we come to this village and found the magic man in a little hut on the outskirts—An evil old character with sugary eyes that stuck to you—We told him what we wanted and he nodded and looked at both of us and smiled and said he would have to cook up the medicine we should come back next day at sundown—So we came back and he gave us the bitter medicine in clay pots—And I hadn't put the pot down before the pictures started coming in sharp and clear: the hanged boy pulling his legs up to the chin and pumping out the spurts by the irrigation ditch, the soldiers swinging me around in the harness, the burned man screaming away like a good one and that heart just pulsing and throwing off spurts of blood in the rising sun—Xolotl was explaining to me that only one body is left in the switch they were going to hang me and when I shot my load and died I would pass into his body—I was paralyzed by the medicine any case and they stripped me and lashed my body with special type sex nettles that burned and stung all over and my tongue swole up and gagged me and my eyes blurred over with blood—They rigged up a gallows with a split-bamboo platform and a ladder and I start up the ladder Xolotl goosing me and stood under the noose and he tightens it around my neck muttering spells and then gets down on the floor leaving me alone up there on the platform with the noose waiting—I saw him reach up with an obsidian knife and cut the rope held the platform and I fell and silver light popped in my eyes like a flash bulb—I got a whiff of ozone and penny arcades and then I felt it start way down in my toes these bone wrenching spasms emptied me and everything spilled out shit running down the back of my thighs and no control in my body paralyzed, twisting up in these spasms the jissom just siphoned me right into Xolotl's cock and next thing I was in his ass and balls flopping around spurting all over the floor and that evil old fuck crooning and running his hands over me so nasty— But then who am I to be critical?—I stayed there in the magic man's hut for three days sleeping and woke up the lookout different—And the magic man gave me some medicine to control the fits and I headed on south —Came at sundown to a clear river where boys were swimming naked—And one of them turned grinning with a hard-on and shoved his finger in and out his fist and I fell in one of my fits so they all had a go at me —The cold mountain shadows came down and touched my naked ass and I went back with the boy to his hut and ate beans and chili and lay with him on the floor breathing the pepper smell of his belches and stayed there with him and worked his patch of corn on the side of the mountain—That boy could keep a hard-on all night and I used to stick peppers up my ass when he fucked me like my guts was on fire—Well maybe I would be there still, work all day and after the work knocked out no words no thoughts just sit there looking at the blue mountains and ate and belched and fucked and slept same thing day after day the greatest—But one day we scored for a bottle of mescal and got lushed and he looked at me and said: *"Chinga de puto* I will rid the earth of you in the name of Jesus Christu!" and charges me with a machete—Well I'd seen it coming and tossed a cup of mescal in his eyes and side-stepped and he fell on his face and I rammed the planting stick right into the base of his brain—So that was that—And started South again and came finally to this spot where a lot of citizens were planting corn with sticks all working in concert, I didn't like the look of it but I was strung out for groceries and decided to make contact a mistake as it turned out—Because as soon as I walked out into that field I felt this terrible weight on me and there I was planting corn with them and everything I did and thought was already done and thought and there was this round of festivals where the priests put on lobster suits and danced around snapping their claws like castanets and nothing but maize maize maize— And I guess I would be there yet fructifying the maize God except for this one cat who was in Maya drag like me but I could see he was a foreigner too—He was very technical and a lovely fellow—He began drawing formulas on the floor and showed me how the priests operated their control racket: "It's like with the festivals and the fucking corn they know what everybody will see and hear and smell and taste and that's what thought is and these thought units are represented by symbols in their books and they rotate the symbols around and around on the calender." And as I looked at his formulas something began to crack up in my brain and I was free of the control beam and next thing we both got busted and sentenced to "Death in Centipede" —So they strapped us to couches in a room under the temple and there was a terrible smell in the place full of old bones and a centipede about ten feet long comes nuzzling out of one corner—So I turn on something I inherit from Uranus where my grandfather invented the adding machine—I just lay there without any thought in tons focus of heavy blue silence and a slow wave went through me and spread out of me and the couch began shaking and the tremors spread into the ground and the roof fell in and crushed the centipede and smashed the couch so the straps were loose and I slipped out and untied Technical Tilly—So we got out of there dodging stellae and limestone skulls as the whole temple came down in chunks and the wind blowing a hurricane brought in a tidal wave and there wasn't much left of the whole set when things cleared away—All the workers were running around loose now looking for the priests—The head priest was paralyzed and had turned into a centipede—We found him in a cubby hole under the rubble along with some others who were half crab or in various stages of disgusting metamorphosis—And

I figured we should do something special with these characters they are wise guys—So we organize this "fun fest" and made some obsidian jockstraps strung together with copper wire and heated the straps up white-hot and slipped them on, the priests did a belly dance like you used to see it in burlesque and we sat there yelling: "Take it off Take it off," laughing till we pissed and shit and came—You never heard such laughing with the control gone and goosing them with hot copper pricks—And others we put weights on their backs and dragged them through wooden troughs with flint flakes sticking up and so on—Fun and games what? Well after that none of us could look at corn and the grocery problem became acute—So we organize this protection racket shaking down the agriculturals—"It could happen again here—Kick in or else"—And they kicked in come level on average—Well groceries—And I had perfected a gimmick to keep my boys in line—I was still subject to these fits but I had learned to control the images—That is just before I flipped out I could put any image in the projector and—Action—Camera— Take—It always happened the way I took it and any character gave me any static was taken care of that way —But the boys from the North were moving in whole armies so we packed in and shifted to the hunting and fishing lark—I picked thirty of the most likely and suitable lads all things considered and we moved South up over the mountains and down the other side into jungle then up and over again getting monotonous— Piecing out the odds best we could spot of this and a

spot of that—Once in a while I had to put it about with
the earthquakes but come level on average what you
might call a journeyman thief—Well fever and snakes
and rapids and boys dropping out here and there to
settle down with the locals I had no mob left when I
run up against this really evil setup—The Chimu were
something else—So we hit this town and right away I
don't like it.

"Something here, John—Something wrong—I can
feel it."

To begin with the average Chimu is unappetizing to
say the least—Lips eaten off by purple and orange skin
conditions like a baboon's ass and pus seeping out a
hole where the nose should be disgust you to see it—
And some of them are consisting entirely of penis flesh
and subject to blast jissom right out their skull and fold
up like an old wine bag—Periodically the Chimu organize fun fests where they choose up sides and beat
each other's brains out with clubs and the winning
team gang-fucks the losers and cut their balls off right
after to make pouches for coco leaves they are chewing
all the time green spit dripping off them like a cow
with the aftosa—All things considered I was not in-
narrested to contact their loutish way of life—In the
middle of this town was a construction of clay cubicles
several stories high and I could see some kinda awful
crabs were stirring around inside it but couldn't get
close because the area around the cubicle is covered
with black bones and hot as a blasting furnace—They
had this heat weapon you got it?—Like white-hot ants

all over you—Meanwhile I had been approached by the
Green Boys have a whole whore house section built
on catwalks over the mud flats entirely given over to
hanging and all kinds death in orgasm young boys need
it special—They were beautiful critters and swarmed
all over me night and day smelling like a compost heap
—But I wasn't buying it sight unseen and when I
proposed to watch a hanging they come on all indignant
like insulted whores—So I am rigged up a long distance
periscope with obsidian mirrors Technical Tillie moan-
ing about the equipment the way he always does and
we watched them hang this boy just down from the
country—Well I saw that when his neck snapped and
he shot his load instead of flowing into the Green Boy
the way nature intended these hot crabs hatched out of
his spine and scoffed the lot.

So we organize the jungle tribes and take Boy's Town
and confine the Green Boys in a dormitory, they are all
in there turning cartwheels and giggling and masturbating and playing flutes—That was our first move to cut
the supply line—Then after we had put the squeeze on
and you could hear them scratching around in the
cubicle really thin now we decided to attack—I had
this special Green Boy I was making it with who knew
the ropes you might say and he told me we have to
tune the heat wave out with music—So we get all the
Indians and all the Green Boys with drums and flutes
and copper plates and stayed just out of the heat blast
beating the drums and slowly closed in—Iam had
rigged up a catapult to throw limestone boulders and

shattered the cubicle so we move in with spears and clubs and finish them off and smashed the heat-sending set that was a living radio with insect parts—We turn the Green Boys loose and on our way rejoicing—

So down into the jungle on the head-shrinking lark—Know how it operates—You got these spells see? confines the citizen to his head under your control like you can shrink up all the hate in the area—What a gimmick but as usual I got greedy and the wind up is I don't have a head left to stand on—Sure I had the area sewed up but there wasn't any area left—Always was one to run things into the ground—Well there I was on the bottom when I hear about this virgin tribe called the Camuyas embrace every stranger and go naked all the time like nature intended and I said "the Camuyas are live ones" and got down there past all these bureaucrats with The Internal Indian Service doubted the purity of my intentions—But I confounded them with my knowledge of Mayan archaeology and the secret meaning of the centipede motif and Iam was very technical so we established ourselves as scientists and got the safe conduct—Those Camuyas were something else all naked rubbing up against you like dogs—They were sweet little critters and I might be there still except for a spot of bother with The Indian Commission about this hanging ceremony I organize figuring to trade in the chassis and renew my substance —So they chucked me out and talked usefully about that was that—And I made it up to the Auca who were warlike and wangled two healthy youths for a secret weapon—So took these boys out into the jungle and laid it on the line and one of them was ready to play ball and —spare you the monotonous details—Suffice it to say the Upper Amazon gained a hustler and there I was caught in the middle of all these feuds—Some one knocks off your cousin twice removed and you are obligated to take care of his great uncle—Been through all this before—Every citizen you knock off there are ten out looking for you geometric and I don't want to know—So I got a job with the Total Oil Company and that was another mistake—

Rats was running all over the morning—Somewhere North of Monterrey went into the cocaine business—By this time fish tail Cadillac—people—civilians—So we score for some business and get rich over the warring powers—shady or legitimate the same fuck of a different color and the general on about the treasure—We rigged their stupid tree limb and drop the alien corn— spot of business to Walgreen's—So we organize this 8267 kicked in level on average ape—Melodious gimmick to keep the boys in line—I had learned to control Law 334 procuring an orgasm by any image, Mary sucking him and running the outfield—Static was taken care of that way—what you might call a vending machine and boys dropping to Walgreen's—We are not locals. We sniff the losers and cut their balls off chewing all kinds masturbation and self-abuse like a cow with the aftosa—Young junkies return it to the white reader and one day I would wake up as Bill covered with ice and burning crotch—drop my shorts and comes gibbering

up me with a corkscrew motion—We both come right
away standing and trying to say something—I see other
marks are coming on with the mother tincture—The
dogs of Harry J. Anslinger sprouted all over me—By
now we had word dust stirring the 1920's, maze of dirty
pictures and the house hooked for generations—We all
fucked the boy burglar feeling it right down to our
toes—Spanish cock flipped out spurting old Mont-
gomery Ward catalogues—So we stripped a young
Dane and rigged the Yankee dollar—Pants down to the
ankle, a barefoot Indian stood there watching and feeling his friend—Others had shot their load too over a
broken chair through the tool heap—Tasty spurts of
jissom across the dusty floor—Sunrise and I said here we
go again with the knife—My cock pulsed right with it
and trousers fell in the dust and dead leaves—Return it
to the white reader in stink of sewage looking at open
shirt flapping and comes maybe five times his ass
fluttering like—We sniff what we wanted pumping out
the spurts open shirt flapping—What used to be me
in my eyes like a flash bulb, spilled adolescent jissom
in the bath cubicle—Next thing I was Danny Deever in
Maya drag—That night we requisitioned a Peruvian
boy—I would pass into his body—What an awful place
it is—most advanced stage—foreigner too—They rotate the symbols around IBM machine with cocaine—
fun and games what?

Public Agent

SO I AM A PUBLIC AGENT and don't know who I work for,
get my instructions from street signs, newspapers and
pieces of conversation I snap out of the air the way a
vulture will tear entrails from other mouths. In any case
I can never catch up on my back cases and currently
assigned to intercept blue movies of James Dean before
the stuff gets to those queers supporting a James Dean
habit which, so long as this agent picks his way through
barber shops, subway toilets, grope movies and Turkish
Baths, will never be legal and exempt narcotic.

The first one of the day I nailed in a subway pissoir:
"You fucking nance!" I screamed. "I'll teach you to
savage my bloody meat, I will." And I sloughed him
with the iron glove and his face smashed like rotten can-

taloupe. Then I hit him in the lungs and blood jumped
out his mouth, nose and eyes, spattered three commuters
across the room huddled in gabardine topcoats and
grey flannel suits under that. The broken fruit was lying
with his head damning the piss running over his face
and the whole trough a light pink from his blood. I
winked at the commuters. "I can smell them fucking
queers," I sniffed warningly. "And if there's one thing
lower than a nance it's a spot of bloody grass. Now you
blokes wouldn't be the type turn around and congor
a pal's balls off would you now?" They arranged themselves on the floor like the three monkeys: See No Evil,
Hear No Evil, and Speak No Evil.

"I can see you're three of our own," I said warmly and
walked into the corridor where schoolboys chase each
other with machetes, joyous boy-cries and zipper guns
echo through the mosaic caverns. I pushed into a
Turkish Bath and surprised a faggot brandishing a deformed erection in the steam room and strangled him
straightaway with a soapy towel. I had to check in. I
was thin now, barely strength in my receding flesh to
finish off that tired faggot. I got into my clothes shivering and gaping and walked into the terminal drugstore.
Five minutes to twelve. Five minutes to score. I walked
over to the night clerk and threw a piece of tin on him.

Piss running over his face. Don't know who I work
for. I get mine from his blood, newspapers and pieces.
"I can smell them fucking the air the way a vulture
will." In any case bloody grass. I sloughed him with the
iron room and strangled him like rotten cantaloupe.

Then I had to check in. I was the blood jumped out his mouth, nose receding flesh to finish. Across the room huddled my clothes shivering grey flannel suits under terminal drugstore. So I am a public agent and the whole trough a light pink instruction from street. I winked at the commuters. "Conversation I snap out of queers," I sniffed warningly. "It's a spot up on my back cases." Queers supporting the floor like the three monkeys. "Grope movies and Turkish our own," I said warmly and walked exempt narcotic. Cool boys chase each other with the first one of the day. To a Turkish Bath and surprised you bloody nance. Soapy towel glove hit him in the lungs and eyes spattered: Ping! And walked into the gabardine topcoats. Five minutes to that broken fruit.

"Treasury Department," I said. "Like to check your narcotic inventory against RX. . . How much you using young fellow?" Shaking my head and pushing all the junk bottles and scripts into my brief case: "I hate to see a young man snafu his life script. . . Maybe I can do something for you. That is if you promise me to take the cure and stay off."

"I promise anything. I gotta wife and kids."

"Just don't let me down is all."

I walked out and got straight in the lu of the Bus Terminal Chinese Restaurant. It's a quiet place with very bad food. But what a John for a junky.

Well I checked into the old Half-Moon Hotel you can get to the lobby through the subway and walked in on the wrong room, an ether party, with my cigarette lit and everyone's lung blew out about six characters, cats and chicks. So I get a face full of tits and spare ribs and throat gristle. . . All in the day's work. . . Follow up on it. Score. I walked the gabardine top tin on him. The broken fruit. Piss running over his face. "Like to check your narcotic inventor. I get mine from his blood."

"Much you using young fellow?"

"I can smell them fucking all the junk bottles and scripts." In any case bloody grass. . . See a young man snafu his and strangled him like rot do something for you in the blood. Jumped cure and stay off to finish. Grey flannel suits under all public agents of the bus from street. Grope movie and walked in on the wrong room warmly. Exempt light and lungs. And eyes spattered night clerk and threw a piece of coats. "Five minutes to Treasury Department," I said. Shaking my head and pushing the air the way a vulture will into my brief case. I hate sloughed him with the iron room life script. Maybe I can cantaloupe. Them I had to check you. Promise me to take out his mouth, nose receding flesh.

"I promise anything. I go huddled my clothes shivering." I walked out and got light pink instructions terminal Chinese commuters. Hit him in the lungs the day's work. Follow up. A word about my work. The Human Issue has been called in by the Home Office. Engineering flaws you know. There is the work of getting it off the shelves and that is what I do. We are not interested in the individual models, but in the mold, the human die. This must be broken. You never see any live ones up here in Freelandt. Too many patrols. It's a dull territory unless you enjoy shooting a paralyzed swan in a cesspool. Of course there are always the Outsiders. And the young ones I dig special. Long Pigs I call them. Give myself a treat and do it slow just feeding on the subject's hate and fear and the white stuff oozes out when they crack sweet as a lobster claw. . . I hate to put out the eyes because they are my water hole. They call me the Meat Handler. Among other things.

I had business with the Egyptian. My time was running out. He was sitting in a mosaic café with stone shelves along the walls and jars of colored syrups sipping a heavy green drink.

"I need the time milking," I said.

He looked at me, his eyes eating erogenous holes. His face got an erection and turned purple. And we went into the vacant lot behind the café naked to a turn.

White men killed at a distance. Don't know the answer, do you?

Den Mark of Trak in every face: "Death, take over."

"Never nobody liked dancing no better than Red."

"Let's dance," he said.

The script for shit, "Here you are, sir," and I could see he was heavy with the load. Outfields and back to Moscow for liquidation. I had business with the Gyp. Trak in every kidney. The script for heavy drink. His eyes got an erection and turned the effluvia and became addicts of vacant lot. My time was running out its last black grains.

Trak Trak Trak

THE SAILOR AND I burned down The Republic of Panama from Darien swamps to David trout streams on paregoric and goof balls—(Note: Nembutal)—You lose time putting a con down on a Tiddlywink chemist—"No glot—Clom Fliday"—(Footnote: old time junkies will remember—Used to be a lot of Chinese pushers in the 1920's but they found the West so unreliable dishonest and wrong when an Occidental junky comes to score they say: "No glot—Clom Fliday.")

And we were running short of substitute buyers—They fade in silver mirrors of 1910 under a ceiling fan—Or we lost one at dawn in a wisp of rotten sea wind—Out in the bay little red poison sea snakes swim desperately in sewage—Camphor sweet cooking paregoric smells billow from the mosquito nets—The termite floor gave under our feet spongy and rotten—The albatross at dawn on rusty iron roofs—

"Time to go, Bill," said the Sailor, morning light on cold coffee.

"I'm thin"—Crisscross of broken light from wood lathes over the patio, silver flak holes in his face—We worked the Hole together in our lush rolling youth—(Footnote: "working the Hole," robbing drunks on the subway)—And kicked a habit in East St. Louis—Made it four times third night, fingers scraping bone—At dawn shrinking from flesh and cloth—

Hands empty of hunger on the stale breakfast table—winds of sickness through his face—pain of the long slot burning flesh film—canceled eyes, old photo fading —violet brown souvenir of Panama City—I flew to La Paz trailing the colorless death smell of his sickness with me still, thin air like death in my throat—sharp winds of black dust and the grey felt hat on every head—purple pink and orange disease faces cut pre-natal flesh, genitals under the cracked bleeding feet—aching lungs in dust and pain wind—mountain lakes blue and cold as liquid air—Indians shitting along the mud walls—brown flesh, red blankets—

"No, señor. Necesita receta."

And the refugee German croaker you hit anywhere: "This you must take orally—You will inject it of course —Remember it is better to suffer a month if so you come out—With this habit you lose the life is it not?" And he gives me a long creepy human look—

And Joselito moved into my room suffocating me with soccer scores—He wore my clothes and we laid the same *novia* who was thin and sickly always making magic with candles and Virgin pictures and drinking aromatic medicine from a red plastic eye cup and never touched my penis during the sex act.

Through customs checks and control posts and over the mountains in a blue blast of safe conducts and three monkey creatures ran across the road in a warm wind—(sound of barking dogs and running water) swinging round curves over the misty void—down to end of the road towns on the edge of Yage country where shy Indian cops checked our papers—through broken stellae, pottery fragments, worked stones, condoms and shit-stained comics, slag heaps of phosphorescent metal excrement—faces eaten by the pink and purple insect disease of the New World—crab boys with human legs and genitals crawl out of clay cubicles—Terminal junkies hawk out crystal throat gristle in the cold mountain wind—Goof ball bums covered with shit sleep in rusty bathtubs—a delta of sewage to the sky under terminal stasis, speared a sick dolphin that surfaced in bubbles of coal gas—taste of metal left silver sores on our lips—only food for this village built on iron racks over an iridescent lagoon—swamp delta to the sky lit by orange gas flares.

In the flash bulb of orgasm I saw three silver numbers —We walked into the streets and won a football pool —Panama clung to our bodies stranger color through his eyes the lookout different.

Flash bulb monster crawling inexorably from Old Fred Flash—the orgasm in a 1920 movie, silver writing from backward countries—Flapping genitals in wind—explosion of the throat from peeled noon drifting sheets of male flesh to a stalemate of black lagoons while open shirts twist iridescent in the dawn—(this sharp smell of carrion.)

"Take it from a broken stalemate—The Doctor couldn't reach and see?: Those pictures are the line—Fading breath on bed showed sound track—You win handful of dust that's what."

Metamorphosis of the Rewrite Department coughing and spitting in fractured air—flapping genitals of carrion—Our drained countess passed on a hideous leather body—We are digested and become nothing here—dust air of gymnasiums in another country and besides old the pool now, a few inches on dead post cards—here at the same time there his eyes—Silver light popped stroke of nine.

Dead post card you got it?—Take it from noon refuse like ash—Hurry up see?—Those pictures *are* yourself—Is backward sound track—That's what walks beside you to a stalemate of physical riders—("You come with me, Meester?")—I knew Mexican he carried in his flesh with sex acts shooting them pills I took—Total alertness she is your card—Look, simple: Place exploded man goal in other flesh—dual controls country—double sex sad as the Drenched Lands.

Last man with such explosion of the throat crawling inexorably from something he carried in his flesh—Last turnstile was in another country and besides knife exploded Sammy the Butcher—Holes in 1920 movie—Newspaper tape fading, after dinner sleep ebbing carbon dioxide—Indications enough showed you calls to make, horrors crawling inexorably toward goal in other flesh—What are you waiting for, kid?—Slotless human wares?—Nothing here now—Metamorphosis is complete—Rings of Saturn in the dawn—The sky exploded question from vacant lots—youth nor age but as it were lips fading—There in our last film mountain street boy exploded "the word," sits quietly silence to answer.

"You come with me, Meester to greet the garbage man and the dawn? Traced fossil countenance everlastingly about the back door, Meester." sick dawn of inane cooperation—dead post cards swept out by typewriters clatter hints as we shifted commissions—Hurry up please—Crawling inexorably toward its goal—I—We—They—sit quietly in last terrace of the garden—The neon sun sinks in this sharp smell of carrion—(circling albatross—peeled noon—refuse like ash)—Ghost of Panama clung to our throats coughing and spitting in the fractured air, falling through space between worlds, we twisted slowly to black lagoons, flower floats and gondolas—tentative crystal city iridescent in the dawn wind—(adolescents ejaculate over the tide flats)—Dead post card are you thinking of?—What thinking?—peeled noon and refuse like ash—Hurry up please—Make yourself a bit smart—Who is the third that walks beside you to a stalemate of black lagoons and violet light? Last man—Phosphorescent

centipede feeding on flesh strung together we are digested and become nothing here.

"You come with me, Meester?"

Up a great tidal river to the port city stuck in water
hyacinths and banana rafts—The city is an intricate
split-bamboo structure in some places six stories high
overhanging the street propped up by beams and sections of railroad track and concrete pillars, an arcade
from the warm rain that falls at half hour intervals—
The coast people drift in the warm steamy night eating
colored ices under the arc lights and converse in slow
catatonic gestures punctuated by immobile silence—
Plaintive boy-cries drift through Night Of the Vagrant
Ball Players.

"Paco!—Joselito!—Enrique!—"

"*A ver Luckees!*"

"Where you go, Meester?"

"Squeezed down heads?"

Soiled mouth above a tuxedo blows smoke rings into
the night, "SMOKE TRAK CIGARETTES. THEY LIKE YOU. TRAK
LIKE ANY YOU. ANY TRAK LIKE YOU. SMOKE TRAKS. THEY
SERVICE. TRAK TRAK TRAK."

Los Vagos Jugadores de Pelota storm the stale streets
of commerce—Civil Guards discreetly turn away and
open their flys to look for crabs in a vacant lot—For the
Vagrant Ball Players can sound a Hey Rube Switch
brings a million adolescents shattering the customs
barriers and frontiers of time, swinging out of the jungle
with Tarzan cries, crash landing perilous tin planes and
rockets, leaping from trucks and banana rafts, charge

through the black dust of mountain wind like death in the throat.

The trak sign stirs like a nocturnal beast and bursts into blue flame, "SMOKE TRAK CIGARETTES. THEY LIKE YOU. TRAK LIKE ANY YOU. ANY TRAK LIKE YOU. SMOKE TRAKS. THEY SATISFY. THEY SERVICE. TRAK TRAK TRAK."

"Vagos Jugadores de Pelota, *sola esperanza del mundo*, take it to Cut City—Street gangs Uranian born in the face of nova conditions, cut word lines, cut time lines—Take it to Cut City, *muchachos*—'Minutes to go'—"

Jungle invades the weed grown parks where armadillos infected with the Earth Eating Disease gambol through deserted kiosks and Bolivar in catatonic limestone liberates the area—Candiru infiltrate causeways and swimming pools—Albinos blink in the sun—rank smell of rotten rivers and mud flats—swamp delta to the sky that does not change—islands of garbage where Green Boys with delicate purple gills tend chemical gardens—terminal post card shrinking in heavy time. Muttering addicts of the orgasm drug, boneless in the sun, eaten alive by crab men—terminal post card shrinking in heavy time. "Thing Police keep all Board Room Reports—Do not forget this, *Señor*—"

They were searching his room when he returned from the Ministry of Tourist Travel—Fingers light and cold as Spring wind rustling papers and documents—One flashed a badge like a fish side in dark water—

"Police, Johnny."

"Campers," obviously—"Campers" move into any

government office and start issuing directives and
spinning webs of inter-office memos—Some have connections in high sources that will make the operation
legal and exempt narcotic—Others are shoestring operators out of broom closets and dark rooms of the
Mugging Department—They charge out high on ammonia issuing insane orders and requisitioning any object in their path—Tenuous bureaus spring up like
sandstorms—The whole rancid oil scandal drifted out
in growth areas—

Bradly was reading the sign nailed to a split-bamboo
tenement—The sign was printed on white paper book
page size:

Cut The Sex and Dream Utility Lines//

Cut the Trak Service Lines//

The paws do not refresh//

Clom Fliday Meester Surplus Oil//

Working for the Yankee dollar?//

Trak your own utilities//

Under silent wings of malaria a tap on his shoulder:
"Documentes, señor. Passaport."

His passport drew them like sugar flashing gold teeth
in little snarls of incredulity: *"Passaport no bueno. No
en ordenes."*

The fuzz that could not penetrate to the passport
began chanting in unison: *"Comisaria! Comisaria!*

Comisaria! Meester a la Comisaria!—Passaport muy malo. No good. *No bueno.* Typical sights leak out." The Comandante wore a green uniform spattered with oil and gave out iron smoke as he moved—A small automatic moved round his waist on metal tracks trailing blue sparks—Seedy agents click into place with reports and documents.

"It is *permiso, si* to read the public signs. This"—his hand covered the white sign on a split-bamboo wall—"is a special case."

A man with a green eyeshade slid forward: "Yes. That's what they call it: 'making a case'—It's all there in the files, the whole rancid oil scandal of the Trak Sex And Dream Utilities in Growth Areas."

He pointed to a row of filing cabinets and lockers—Smell of moldy jockstraps and chlorine drifted through the police terminal. The Comandante turned the newspaper man back with a thin brown hand: "Much politics that one—It is better to be just technical."

A Swede con man hiding out in Rio Bamba under the cold souvenir of Chimborazi, junk cover removed for the nonpayment, syndicates of the world feeling for him with distant fingers of murder, perfected that art along the Tang Dynasty in the back room of a Chinese laundry. The Swede had one thing left: the grey felt hat concession for "growth areas" hidden under front companies and aliases. With a 1910 magic lantern he posed Indians in grey felt hats and broke the image into a million pieces reflected in dark eyes and blue mountain ice and black water and piss and lamp chimneys, tinted bureaucrat glasses, gun barrels, store fronts and café mirrors—He flickered the broken image into the eyes of a shrunken head that died in agony looking at a grey felt hat. And the Head radiated: HAT. .HAT. .HAT . .HAT. .HAT. .

"It is a jumping head," he said.

When the hat lines formed one thing that could break them was orgasm—So he captured a missionary's wife and flickered her with pornographic slides—And he took her head to radiate anti-sex—He took other anti-sex heads in coprophiliac vice and electric disgust—He dimed the Sex and Dream Utilities of the land. And he was shipped back to Sweden in a lead cylinder to found the Trak Service and the Trak Board.

Trak has come a long way from a magic lantern in the Chink laundry. The Heads were donated to the Gothenburg Museum where the comparatively innocuous emanations precipitated a mass sex orgy.

Vagos Jugadores, *sola esperanza del mundo,* take it to Cut City. the black obsidian pyramid of Trak Home Office.

"The perfect product, gentlemen, has precise molecular affinity for its client of predilection. Someone urges the manufacture and sale of products that wear out? This is not the way of competitive elimination. Our product never leaves the customer. We sell the Servicing and all Trak products have precise need of Trak servicing. . . The servicing of a competitor would act like antibiotic, offering to our noble Trak-strain services inedible counterpart. . . This is not just another habit-forming drug this is the habit-forming drug takes over all functions from the addict including his completely unnecessary under the uh circumstances and cumbersome skeleton. Reducing him ultimately to the helpless condition of a larva. He may be said then to owe his very life such as it is to Trak servicing. . ."

The Trak Reservation so-called includes almost all areas in and about the United Republics of Freelandt and, since the Trak Police process all matters occurring in Trak Reservation and no one knows what is and is not Reservation cases, civil and criminal are summarily removed from civilian courts with the single word TRAK to unknown sanctions. . . Report meetings of Trak personnel are synchronized with other events as to a low pressure area. . . Benway was reporting so-called actually included almost the report meetings of Trak persons. . . Sometimes the Reservation is other persons and events in Trak guards sub type. . .

"Outskirts of Mexico City—Can't quite make it with all the guards around—Are you at all competent to teach me the language? Come in please with the images—"

Smell death bed pictures—Cooperation inane—Carrion in the bank—Passport bad—Average on level tore canines—Understand fee: Corpses hang pants open in erogenous smells to Monterrey—Clear and loud ahead naked post cards and baby shoes—A man comes back to something he left in underwear peeled the boy warm in 1929—Thighs slapped the bed jumped ass up—"Johnny Screw"—Cup is split—wastings—Thermodynamics crawls home—game of empty hands—bed pictures post dead question—carrion smell sharp.

"Meester, jelly thing win you—Waiting for this?"

Streets of idiot pleasure—obsidian palaces of the fish city, bubbles twisting slow linen to the floor, traced fossils of orgasm.

"You win something like jelly fish, Meester."

His eyes calm and sad as little cats snapped the advantages: "And I told him I said I am giving notice— Hanged in your dirty movies for the last time—Three thousand years in show business and I never stand still for such a routine like this."

Street boys of the green with cruel idiot smiles and translucent amber flesh, aromatic jasmine excrement, pubic hairs that cut needles of pleasure—serving insect pleasures of the spine—alternate terminal flesh when the egg cracks.

"This bad place, Meester—This place of last fuck for Johnny."

Smile of idiot death spasms—slow vegetable decay filmed his amber flesh—always there when the egg cracks and the white juice spurts from ruptured spines —From his mouth floated coal gas and violets—The boy dropped his rusty black pants—delicate must of soiled linen—clothes stiff with oil on the red tile floor— naked and sullen his street boy senses darted around the room for scraps of advantage—

"You come with me Meester? Last flucky."

Stranger color through his eyes the lookout different, face transparent with all the sewers of death—Hard-ons

spread nutty smells through the outhouse—soiled linen
under the ceiling fan—spectral lust of shuttered rooms
—He left a shirt on my bed.

"Jimmy Sheffields is still as good as he used to be."

"He was servicing customers shit, Meester—So
Doctor Benway snapped the advantages—This special
breed spitting notice: Egg cracks the transmitter—Rat
spines gathering mushroom flesh—The boy dropped
around your room for scraps—Got the rag on body from
vegetable—Dropped his pants and his cock."

"Who are you—My boat—"

"Smells through the outhouse—A compost heap,
Meester."

Sacred Sewers of Death—Boy dropped under the
swamp cypress flopping around in soiled linen—
(Started off on foot across the deserted fields—a little
hut on the outskirts—The writer looked at both of us
good as he used to be.) Idiot pictures started coming
in—

"You win something like jelly with his knees up to
the chin—sad little irrigation ditch—Parrot on shoulder
prods that heart—Paralyzed, twisting in your movies for
the last time—Out of me from the waist down—I never
stand still for such lookout on street boys of the green—
Happened that boy could keep his gas and violets—This
spot advantages brown hands working in concert for a
switch to the Drenched Lands—Cyclotron shit these
characters—Come level on average smell under any
image—Evil odors high around the other—Jimmy
Sheffields is again as good—Street boy's breath receiv-

ing notice—Jelly routine like this—When the egg cracks our spines servicing special customers of fossil orgasm."

Kerosene lamp spattered light on red- and white-striped T-shirt and brown flesh—Dropped his pants—Pubic hairs cut stale underwear fan whiffs of young hard-on washing odors—afternoon wind where the awning flaps—

"Get physical with a routine like this?—Show you something interesting: diseased flesh servicing frantic last fuck for Johnny—Film over the bed you know, eyes pop out—Naked candy around the room, scraps of adolescent image, hot semen in Panama—Then the boy drops his drag and retires to a locker—*Who* lookout different? Who are *you* when their eyes pop out—Mandrake smells through the outhouse—The boy dropped and the boy wakes up paralyzed—Remember there is only one visit: iron roof—soiled linen under the clothes—scar tissue—shuttered room—evil odors of food—I wasn't all that far from being good as I used to be—Obsidian that broker before they get to him—A crab scuttles out heavy—You win something like vacant lot—sad little patch right?—boy face, green scarf—movies three up—You understand until I die work I never stand still for. and such got the job—End getting to know street boys of the Green Passport vending last fuck as his pants drop."

Dust of cities and wind faces came to World's End—call through remote dawn soaked in clouds, shivering back to mucus of the world.

Dust jissom in the bandanna trailing afternoon wind —under black Stetson peeled his stale underwear— Kerosene lamp spattered light on .22, delicate legs and brown flesh—clothes stiff in the locker room rubbing each other—sullen as the other two watched—Stranger dropped his pants—Brown hands spurt it to the chest—

"Find time buyer—Start job—Image under the same position—Change place of your defense—"

"A Johannesburg bidonville he was servicing—Customers shitting Nigger for an eyecup of degenerates— Ejaculated the next day as Johnny—Meal mouthed cunt suckers flow through you—This special breed spitting cotton travel on a radar beam of service proof shortbread—Shivering junk sick told your reporter the sex chucks hit us in heroin slow down—The paranoid ex-Communist was there—Rubbed Moscow up me with a corkscrew motion of his limestones—Split is the wastings of the pool game—irritably for Mexico—By now we had floppy city in the distance, 1920's faint and intermittent—The track gave out forever an inch from the false bottom—

"They had torn down the transmitter—Rats was running the post—Somewhere North of Monterrey we meet in warring powers—Captured the spine clinic and cook down the prisoners for jelly—We are accused of soliciting with prehensile tree limbs—The first one dropped your defense his mouth bleeding—Got the rag on— Waiting to see this exhibit, dropped his pants and I came the spectroscope—You could smell it like a compost heap, pants just pulling in the winds of Panhandle

—So we hit the Sacred Cotton Wood Grove—It's the only way to live—Jissom under the swamp cypress—and the warm Spring wind to feel my cock—(dead bird in the black swamp water)—He would flop around in the trees, come five times in his dry goods.

"He told me he could fix back places—a little hut on the outskirts—pale blue sugary eyes that stuck to you—The Writer looked at both of us and smiled a low pressure area, switch paper in his hands—weak and intermittent before the pictures started coming in: 'Lawd Lawd have you seen my boy with his knees up to the chin pumping out spurts by the irrigation ditch?'

"When I shot my load I was paralyzed from the medicine—Twisting in these spasms solid female siphoned out of me from the waist down—Shattering special type sex hangs from telegraph pole—And then I felt it way down in a carnival of splintered pink—

"Cold mountain shadows in the attic—And I went back with the boy to his cellar—Wonder whatever happened to that boy could keep a hard-on all night?—A man comes back to something looking at the blue mountains—Same thing day after day—World messages on the shit house wall—Cock spurting limestone—Summer dawn smell of boy balls so that was that—This spot where a lot of citizens will not work in concert—I didn't —Out for groceries and decided to whimper on the boys—We found Mother Green in your rubble along with some others from his deserted cock—Disgusting metamorphosis and a cyclotron shit these characters—

(You wouldn't have a rope would you?)—Maybe I'm asking too many agriculturals—

"Come level on average we'll hold that old cow in line—Put any image in the cold drink would you?— Wet back asleep with a hard-on was taken care of that way—Look, moving in whole armies and he sits me fishing lark—Silent and shaking things considered and we moved out hard—Around the other side piecing out the odds best we could—In the barn attic night and day smelling his thin cotton pants—He wakes buying it sight unseen.

"Jimmy busy doing *something* feller say—boys streaked with coal dust—Maybe I'm asking too many— (You wouldn't have a rope would you?)—Well now that bedroom sitter boy his cock came up wet sleep— Smiling looks at his crotch—Peeled slow and touch it— Springs out hard—Turns me around the end of his cock glistening—That smell through the dingy room clings to him like—Raw and peeled came to the hidden gallows—Open door underneath to cut down ghost assassins—Odor of semen drifts in the brain—Jimmy with cruel idiot smile shacks elbows twisting him over on his candy—Found a pajama cord and tied the boy— Jimmy lay there and suck his honey—Must have blacked out in the Mandrake Pub—So called Rock and Rollers crack wise on a lumpy studio bed with old shoes and overcoat some one cope—The boy wakes up paralyzed in hock—Sorted out name you never learned to use—Them marketable commodities turn you on direct connection come level on average—Whiff of dried jissom in the price—I was on the roof so sweet young breath came through the time buyer—

"The gate in white flames—Early answer to the boy wakes naked—Down on his stomach is he?—Ah there and iron cool in the mouth—Come see me tonight in bone wrenching spasms—Silver light pops something interesting—The boy features being younger of course —To your own people you frantic come level on average —Wait a bit—No good at this rate—Try one if you want worthless old shit screaming without a body—Roll two years operation completed—We are? Well the wind up is who?—*Quién es?*—World's End as a boy in drag retired to the locker—My page deals so many tasty ways on the bed—You know—Eyes pop out—Candy and cigarettes what? Rectum open, the warm muscle boy rampant and spitting adolescent image—Hot semen amuck in Panama—Scenic railways when their eyes pop out—Know the answer?—Two assholes and a mandrake—They'll do it every time—Rock and Rollers crack wise with overwhelming Minraud girl, wipe their ass on the women's toilet—And the boy wakes up paralyzed from arsenic and bleeding gums—Remember there is only one visit of a special kind—Flesh juice vampires is rotten smell of ice—No good *no bueno* outright or partially.

"Reason for the change of food he is subject to take back the keys—Square fact is that judges like it locked —Acting physician at Dankmoor fed up you understand until I die—End getting to know whose hanged man—One more chance still?—Come back to the Spanish bait, hard faced matron bandages the blotter—The shock when your neck breaks is far away—In this hotel room you are already dead of course—Boy stretches a leg, his cock flipped out—But uh well you see sputter of burning insect wings—"

In the sun at noon shirt open Kiki steps forward— With a wriggle stood naked spitting over the tide flats bare feet in dog's excrement—washed back on Spain repeat performance page.

Early Answer

PREDATED CHECKS BOUNCE all around us in green place
by the ball park—Come and jack off—passport vending
machines—Jimmy walked along North End Road—
(Slow-motion horses pulling carts—boys streaked with
coal dust)—a low-pressure area and the wind rising—
Came to the World's End Pissoir and met a boy with
wide shoulders, black eyes glinting under the street
lights, a heavy silk scarf tucked into his red- and white-
striped T-shirt—In the bedroom sitter the boy peeled
off his clothes and sat down naked on the bed blowing
cigarette smoke through his pubic hairs—His cock came
up in the smoke—Switchblade eyes squinted, he
watched with a smile wasn't exactly a smile as Jimmy
folded his clothes—Raw and peeled, naked now his

cock pulsing—Jimmy picked up his key and put it in his
mouth sucking the metal taste—The other sat smoking
and silent—A slow drop of lubricant squeezed out the
end of his cock glistening in light from the street—
Shutters clattered in the rising wind—A rotten vegetable smell seeped through the dingy room, shadow cars
moved across the rose wall paper—

K9 had an appointment at The Sheffield Arms Pub
but the short wave faded out on the location—Somewhere to the left? or was it to the right?—On? Off?
North End Road?—He walked through empty market
booths, shutters clattering—Wind tore the cover off
faces he passed raw and peeled—Came to World's End
wind blowing through empty time pockets—No Sheffield Arms—Back to his room full of shadows—There he
was sitting on the bed with the smile that wasn't
exactly a smile—At the washbasin a boy was using his
toothbrush—

"Who are these people?"

The boy turned from the washbasin "You don't remember me?—Well we met in a way that is"—The
toothbrush in his hand was streaked with blood.

Jimmy sat down on the bed his rectum tingling—The
other picked up his scarf from a chair and ran it through
his fingers looking at Jimmy with a cruel idiot smile—
His hands closed on Jimmy's elbows twisting him over
on his stomach down on the bed—The boy found a
pajama cord and tied Jimmy's hands behind his back—
Jimmy lay there gasping and sucked the key, tasting
metal in his mouth—The other saddled Jimmy's Body—

He spit on his hands and rubbed the spit on his cock—
He placed his hands on Jimmy's ass cheeks and shoved
them apart and dropped a gob of spit on the rectum—
He slid the scarf under Jimmy's hips and pulled his
body up onto his cock—Jimmy gasped and moved with
it—The boy slid the scarf up along Jimmy's body to the
neck—

He must have blacked out though he hadn't had
much to drink at the pub—two so-called double
brandies and two Barley wines—He was lying on a
lumpy studio bed in a strange room—familiar too—in
shoes and overcoat—someone else's overcoat—such a
coat he would never have owned himself—a tweedy
loose-fitting powder-blue coat—K9 ran to tight-fitting
black Chesterfields which he usually bought second-
hand in hock shops—He had very little money for
clothes though he liked to dress in "banker drag" he
called it—black suits—expensive ties and linen shirts—
Here he was in such a coat as he would never vol-
untarily have owned or worn—someone else's room—
bed sitter—cheap furniture suitcases open—K9 found
two keys covered with dust on the mantel—Sat down
convenient and sorted out his name—

"You never learned to use your Jimmy—slow with the
right—there will be others behind him with the scarf—
We met you know in a way that is in the smell of wine—
You don't remember me?"

Taste of blood in his throat familiar too—and overcoat—someone else's—streaked with coal dust—The

bed sitter boy as it always does folded his clothes—Lay
there gasping fresh in today—

"Went into what might be called the comfortable and
got myself a flat jewelry lying about wholesale side—
Learned how to value them marketable commodities
come level on average—well groceries—She started
screaming for a respectable price—I was on the roof so
I had to belt her—Find a time buyer before doing
sessions—There's no choice if they start job for instance
—Have to let it go cheap and start further scream along
the line—one or two reliable thieves—Work was steady
at the gate to meet me—early answer to use on anyone
considering to interfere—Once in a while I had to put
it about but usually what you might call a journeyman
thief—It was done so modern and convenient—Sorted
out punishment and reward lark—On, off? the bed
down on his stomach is he? Ah there you are behind
him with the scarf—Hands from 1910—There's no
choice if took off his clothes—Have to let it go cheap
and start naked."

Twisted the scarf tighter and tighter around Jimmy's
neck—Jimmy gasped coughing and spitting, face
swollen with blood—His spine tingled—Coarse black
hair suddenly sprouted all over him. Canines tore
through his gum with exquisite toothache pain—He
kicked in bone wrenching spasms. Silver light popped in
his eyes.

He decided to take the coat with him—Might pass
someone on the stairs and they would think he was the
tenant since the boy resembled him in build and fea-

tures being younger of course but then people are not observant come level on average—Careful—

"Careful—Watch the exits—wait a bit—no good at this rate—Watch the waves and long counts—no use moving out—try one if you want to—all dies in convulsions screaming without a body—Know the answer? —arsenic two years: operation completed—We are arsenic and bleeding gums—Who? *Quién es?*—World's End loud and clear—so conjured up wide shoulders and black eyes glinting—shadow cars through the dingy room—My page deals the bedroom sitter out of suitcase here on the bed where you know me with cruel idiot smile as Jimmy's eyes pop out—Silk scarf moved up rubbing—Pubic hair sprouted all over him tearing the flesh like wire—Eyes squinted from a smell I always feel—Hot spit burned his rectum open—The warm muscle contracts—Kicked breathless coughing and spitting adolescent image blurred in film smoke—through the gums the fist in his face—taste of blood—His broken body spurted life in other flesh—identical erections kerosene lamp—electric hair sprouted in ass and genitals—taste of blood in the throat—Hot semen spurted idiot mambo—one boy naked in Panama —Who?—*Quién es?*—Compost heap stench where you know me from—a smell I always feel when his eyes pop out—"

"Know the answer? arsenic two years: goof ball bum in 1910 Panama. They'll do it every time—Vampires is no good all possessed by overwhelming Minraud girl—"

"Are you sure they are not for protection?"

"Quite sure—nothing here but to borrow your body for a special purpose: ('Excellent—Proceed to the ice.') —in the blood arsenic and bleeding gums—They were addicted to this round of whatever visits of a special kind—An errand boy of such a taste took off his clothes —Indications enough naked now his cock healed scar tissue—Flesh juice vampires is no good—all sewage— sweet rotten smell of ice—no use of them better than they are—The whole thing tell you no good *no bueno* outright or partially."

"Reasons for the change of food not wholly disinterested—The square fact is that judges like a chair—For many years he used Parker—Fed up with present food in the Homicide Act and others got the job—So think before time that abolition is coming anyway after that, all the Top Jobbies would like to strike a bargain in return for accepting the end of hanging—Generous? Nothing—I wasn't all that far from ebbing in position—"

"Have to move fast—Nail that Broker before they get to him—Doing him a favor any case—"

He found the Broker in a café off the Socco—heavy with massive muscled flesh and cropped grey hair—K9 stood in the shadow and tugged his mind screen—The Broker stood up and walked down an alley—K9 stepped out of the shadows in his new overcoat—

"Oh it's you—Everything all right?—"

K9 took off his hat respectfully and covered his gun with it—He had stuffed the hat with the Green Boy's

heavy silk scarf—a crude silencer but there was nobody
in the alley—It wasn't healthy to be within earshot
when the Broker had business with anyone—He stood
with the hat an inch from the Broker's mid section—
He looked into the cold grey eyes—

"Everything is just fine," he said—

And pumped three Police Specials into the massive
stomach hard as a Japanese wrestler—The Broker's
mouth flew open sucking for breath that did not come—
K9 gave him three more and stepped aside—The Broker
folded, slid along a wall and flopped face up his eyes
glazing over—Lee dropped the burning hat and scarf
on a pile of excrement and walked out of the alley
powder smoke drifting from his cheap European suit—
He walked toward flesh of Spain and Piccadilly—

"Wind hand to the hilt—Fed up you understand until
I die—Work we have to do and way got the job—End
getting to know whose reports are now ended—'One
more change,' he said, 'touching circumstance'—Have
you still—Come back to the Spanish bait it's curtains
under his blotter."

Who? *Quién es?*—Question is far away—In this hotel
room you are writing whiffs of Spain—Boy stretches a
leg—His cock flipped out in the kerosene lamp—sputter
of burning insect wings—Heard the sea—tin shack
over the mud flats—erogenous holes and pepper
smells—

In the sun at noon shirt open as his pants dropped—
lay on his stomach and produced a piece of soap—
rubbed the soap in—He gasped and moved with it

—whiffs of his feet in the warm summer afternoon—

Who? *Quién es?* It can only be the end of the world ahead loud and clear—

Kiki steps forward on faded photo—pants slipping down legs with a wriggle stood naked spitting on his hands—Shot a bucket grinning—over the whispering tide flats youths in the act, pants down, bare feet in dog's excrement—Street smells of the world siphoned back red-and-white T-shirt to brown Johnny—that stale dawn smell of naked sleep under the ceiling fan—Shoved him over on his stomach kicking with slow pleasure—

"Hooded dead gibber in the turnstile—What used to be me is backward sound track—fossil orgasm kneeling to inane cooperation." wind through the pissoir—*"J'aime ces types vicieux qu'ici montrent la bite"*—green place by the water pipe—dead leaves caught in pubic hairs—"Come and jack off—1929"—Woke in stale smell of vending machines—The boy with grey flannel pants stood there grinning a few inches in his hand—Shadow cars and wind through other flesh—came to World's End. Brief boy on screen revolving lips and pants and forgotten hands in countries of the world—

On the sea wall met a boy in red-and-white T-shirt under a circling albatross—"Me Brown Meester?"—warm rain on the iron roof—The boy peeled his stale underwear—Identical erection flipped out in kerosene lamp—The boy jumped on the bed, slapped his thighs: "I screw Johnny up ass? *Así como perros*"—Rectums

merging to idiot Mambo—one boy naked in Panama
dawn wind—

In the hyacinths the Green Boys smile—Rotting music
trailing vines and birdcalls through remote dreamy lands
—The initiate awoke in that stale summer dawn smell,
suitcases all open on a brass bed in Mexico—In the
shower a Mexican about twenty, rectums naked, smell
of carbolic soap and barrack toilets—

Trails my summer dawn wind in other flesh strung
together on scar impressions of young Panama night—
pictures exploded in the kerosene lamp—open shirt
flapping in the pissoir—cock flipped out and up—
water from his face—sex tingled in the boy's slender
tight ass—

"You wanta screw me?"

"Breathe in, Johnny—Here goes—"

They was ripe for the plucking forgot way back
yonder in the corn hole—lost in little scraps of delight
and burning scrolls—through the open window trailing swamp smells and old newspapers—rectums naked
in whiffs of raw meat—genital smells of the two bodies
merge in shared meals and belches of institution cooking—spectral smell of empty condoms down along
penny arcades and mirrors—Forgotten shadow actor
walks beside you—mountain wind of Saturn in the
morning sky—From the death trauma weary good-by
then—orgasm addicts stacked in the attic like muttering burlap—

Odor rockets over oily lagoons—silver flakes fall
through a maze of dirty pictures—windy city out-

skirts—Smell of empty condoms, excrement, black dust
—ragged pants to the ankle—

Bone faces—place of nettles along adobe walls open
shirts flapping—savanna and grass mud—The sun went
—The mountain shadow touched ragged pants—whisper of dark street in faded Panama photo—"Muy got
good one, Meester" smiles through the pissoir—Orgasm
siphoned back street smells and a Mexican boy—Woke
in the filtered green light, thistle shadows cutting stale
underwear—

The three boys lay on the bank rubbing their stom-
achs against the warm sand—They stood up undressing
to swim—Billy gasped as his pants dropped and his
cock flipped out he hadn't realized it was that far up
from the rubbing—They swam lazily letting the warm
water move between their legs and Lloyd walked back
to his pants and brought a piece of soap and they passed
it back and forth laughing and rubbing each other and
Billy ejaculated his thin brown stomach arched out of
the water as the spurts shot up in the sunlight like tiny
rockets—He sagged down into the water panting and
lay there against the muddy bottom—

Under the old trestle trailing vines in the warm
summer afternoon undressing to swim and rubbing
their bellies—Lloyd rubbing his hand down further
and further openly rubbing his crotch now and grinning
as the other two watched and Billy looked at Jammy
hesitantly and began to rub too and slowly Jammy did
the same—They came into the water watching the
white blobs drift away—The Mexican boy dropped his

pants and his cock flipped out and he looked at Billy grinning—Billy turned and waded into the water and the Mexican followed him and turned him around feeling his crotch and shoved him down on his back in the shallow water, hitched his brown arms under Billy's knees and shoved them back against his chest—The Mexican held his knees with one arm and with the other hand dipped a piece of soap in the water and began rubbing it up and down Billy's ass—Billy shuddered and his body went limp letting it happen—The Mexican was rubbing soap on his own cock now with one hand—shiny black pubic hairs reflected sharp as wire—Slowly shoved his cock in—Billy gasped and moved with it—Spurts fell against his chest in the sunlight and he lay there in the water breathing sewage smells of the canal—

Billy squirmed up onto a muddy bank and took a handful of the warm mud and packed it around his cock and Lloyd poured a bucket of water on the mud and Billy's cock flipped out jumping in the green filtered light under the old trestle—

Stale underwear of penny arcades slipping down legs, rectums feeling the warm sun, laughing and washing each other soapy hands in his crotch, pearly spasms stirring the warm water—whiff of dried jissom in the bandanna trailing sweet young breath through remote lands—soft globs on a brass bed in Mexico—naked—wet—carbolic soap—tight nuts—piece of soap in the locker room rubbing each other off to "My Blue Heaven"—grinning as the other two watched—

The Mexican dropped his pants with a wriggle and stood naked in the filtered green light, vines on his back —Rubbing his crotch now into Billy's ass—Billy moved with it, rectum wriggling cock inside rubbing—

Ali squirmed teeth bared grinning—His thin brown stomach hit the pallet—"You is coming, Johnny?"— Sunlight on the army blankets—rectum wriggling slow fuck on knees *"así como perros"*—orgasm crackled with electric afternoon—bodies stuck together in magnetic eddies—Squirming cock in his intestines, rectum wriggling felt the hot sperm deep in his body—

Shoved him over on his stomach kicking—The Mexican held his knees—Hand dipped a piece of soap— Shoved his cock in laughing—Bodies stuck together in the sunlight kicked whiffs of rectal mucus—laughing teeth and pepper smells—"You is feeling the hot quick Mexican kid naked Mambo to your toes Johnny. . . dust in bare leg hairs tight brown nuts breech very hot . . .How long you want us to fuck very nice Meester? Flesh diseased dirty pictures we fucking tired of fuck very nice Mister." Sad image of sickness at the attic window say something to you *"adios"* worn out film washed back in prep school clothes to distant closing dormitory fragments off the page stained toilet pictures blurred rotting pieces of "Freckle Leg" dormitory dawn dripping water on his face diseased voice so painful telling you "Sparks" is over New York. "Have I done the job here?" With a telescope you can watch our worn out film dim jerky far away shut a bureau drawer faded sepia smile from an old calendar falling leaves sun cold

on a thin boy with freckles folded away in an old file
now standing last review.

"Maze of dirty pictures and vending machine flesh
whispers use of fraud on faded photo—IBM song yodels
dime a dozen type overcoats—Not taking any adolescent
on shit envelope in the bath cubicle—Come of your
stale movies sings Danny Deever in drag—Times lost or
strayed long empty cemetery with a moldy pawn ticket
—fading whisper down skid row to Market Street
shows all kinds masturbation and self-abuse—Young
boys need it special." silver paper in the wind distant
1920 wind and dust. He was looking at some thing a
long time ago where the second hand book shop used
to be just opposite the old cemetery.

"Who? *Quién es?—Hable, señor*—Talk loud and
clear."

"We are all from the American women with a delicate
lilt—I represent the lithe aloof young men of the breed
charmingly—We are all empowered to make arrests
and enough with just the right shade of show you."

"*Belt Her*—Find a time buyer before ports are now
ended—These are rotten if they start job for instance
—Blind bargain in return for accepting 'one more
chance'—Generous?—Nothing—That far to the bait
and it's curtains—Know what they meant if they start
job for instance?"

"Dead young flesh in stale underwear vending sex
words to magnetic Law 334—Indicates simple tape is
served sir, through iron repetition—Ass and genitals
tingling in 1929 jack-off spelt out broken wings of

Icarus—Control system ousted from half the body whispers skin instructions to memory of melting ice— area of Spain—channels ahead loud and clear—Line of the body fitted to other underwear and Kiki steps forward on faded photo—sad image dusted by the Panama night."

"So think before they can do any locks over the Chinese that abolition is war of the past—The end of hanging generous? Just the same position—Changed place of years in the end is just the same—Going to do?—Perhaps alone would you? All good things come to about that was that—"

Call through remote dawn of back yards and ash pits —plaintive ghost in the turnstile—Shadow cars and wind faces came to World's End—street light on soiled clothes dim jerky far away dawn in his eyes. Do you begin to see there is no boy there in the dark room? He was looking at something a long time ago. Changed place?—Same position—Sad image circulates through backward time—Clom Fliday."

Case of the Celluloid Kali

THE NAME IS Clem Snide—I am a Private Ass Hole—
I will take on any job any identity any body—I will do
anything difficult dangerous or downright dirty for a
price—

The man opposite me didn't look like much—A thin
grey man in a long coat that flickered like old film—He
just happens to be the biggest operator in any time
universe—

"I don't care myself you understand"—He watched
the ash spiraling down from the end of his Havana—
It hit the floor in a puff of grey dust—

"Just like that—Just time—Just time—Don't care myself if the whole fucking shithouse goes up in chunks—
I've sat out novas before—I was born in a nova."

"Well Mr. Martin, I guess that's what birth is you might say."

"I wouldn't say—Have to be moving along any case —The ticket that exploded posed little time—Point is they are trying to cross me up—small timers—still on the old evacuation plan—Know what the old evacuation plan is, Mr. Snide?"

"Not in detail."

"The hanging gimmick—death in orgasm—gills—No bones and elementary nervous system—evacuation to the Drenched Lands—a bad deal on the level and it's not on the level with Sammy sitting in—small timers trying to cross me up—Me, Bradly-Martin, who invented the double-cross—Step right up—Now you see me now you don't—A few scores to settle before I travel —a few things to tidy up and that's where you come in—I want you to contact the Venus Mob, the Vegetable People and spill the whole fucking compost heap through Times Square and Piccadilly—I'm not taking any rap for that green bitch—I'm going to rat on everybody and split this dead whistle stop planet wide open —I'm clean for once with the nova heat—like clean fall out—"

He faded in spiraling patterns of cigar smoke—There was a knock at the door—Registered letter from Antwerp—Ten thousand dollar check for film rights to a novel I hadn't written called *The Soft Ticket*—Letter from somebody I never heard of who is acting as my agent suggests I contact the Copenhagen office to discuss the Danish rights on my novel *Expense Account*—

bar backed by pink shell—new Orleans jazz thin in
the Northern night. A boy slid off a white silk bar stool
and held out the hand: "Hello, I'm Johnny Yen, a friend
of—well, just about everybody. I was more physical
before my accident you can see from this interesting
picture. Only the head was reduced to this jelly but like
I say it the impression on my face was taken by the
other man's eyes drive the car head-on it was and the
Big Physician (he's very technical) rushed him off to
a surgery and took out his eyes and made a quick impression and slapped it on me like a pancake before I
started to dry out and curl around the edges. So now
I'm back in harness you might say: and I have all of
'you' that what I want from my audience is the last
drop then bring me another. The place is hermetic. We
think so blockade we thought nobody could get thru our
flak thing. they thought. Switch Artist me. Oh, there
goes my frequency. I'm on now. . ."

The lights dimmed and Johnny pranced out in goggles flickering Northern Lights wearing a jockstrap of
undifferentiated tissue that must be in constant movement to avoid crystallization. A penis rose out of the
jock and dissolved in pink light back to a clitoris, balls
retract into cunt with a fluid plop. Three times he did
this to wild "*Olés!*" from the audience. Drifted to the
bar and ordered a heavy blue drink. D noted patches of
white crystal formed along the scar lines on Johnny's
copy face.

"Just like canals. Maybe I'm a Martian when the
Crystals are down."

You will die there a screwdriver through the head. The thought like looking at me over steak and explain it all like that stay right here. She was also a Reichian analyst. Disappear more or less remain in acceptable form to you the face.

"We could go on cutting my cleavage act, but *genug basta assez* dice fall *hombre* long switch street. . . I had this terrible accident in a car a Bentley it was I think they're so nice that's what you pay for when you buy one it's yours and you can be sure nobody will pull it out from under our assets. Of course we don't have assholes here you understand somebody might go and get physical. So we are strictly from urine. And that narrows things to a fine line down the middle fifty feefty and what could be fairer than that my Uncle Eyetooth always says he committed fornication but I don't believe it me old heavy water junky like him. . . So anyhoo to get back to my accident in my Bentley once I get my thing in a Bentley it's mine already.

So we had this terrible accident or rather he did. Oh dear what am I saying? It wasn't my first accident you understand yearly wounded or was it monthly Oh dear I must stay on that middle line. . .

"Survivor. Survivor. Not the first in my childhood. Three thousand years in show business and always keep my nose clean. Why I was a dancing boy for the Cannibal Trog Women in the Ice Age. remember? All that meat stacked up in the caves and the Blue Queen covered with limestone flesh creeps into your bones like cold grey honey. . .that's the way they keep them not

dead but paralyzed with this awful stuff they cook down
from vampire bats get in your hair Gertie always keep
your hair way up inside with a vampire on premises bad
to get in other alien premises. The Spanish have this
word for it, something about props *ajeno* or something
like that I know so am *ya la yo* mixa everything allup.
They call me Puto the Cement Mixer, now isn't that
cute? Some people think I'm just silly but I'm not silly
at all. . .and this boyfriend told me I looked just like a
shrew ears quivering hot and eager like burning leaves
and those were his last words engraved on my back
tape—along with a lot of other old memories that disgust me, you wouldn't believe the horrible routines I
been involved through my profession of Survival Artist
. . .and they think that's funny, but I don't laugh except
real quick between words no time you understand
laughing they could get at me doesn't keep them off
like talking does, now watch—"

A flicker pause and the light shrank and the audience
sound a vast muttering in Johnny's voice.

"You see"—Shadows moved back into nightclub seats
and drank nightclub drinks and talked nightclub talk—
"They'd just best is all. So I was this dancing boy for
these dangerous old cunts paralyzed men and boys they
dug special stacked right up to the ceiling like the pictures I saw of Belsen or one of those awful contracted
places and I said they are at it again. . .I said the Old
Army Game. I said 'Pass the buck.' Now you see it, now
you don't. . . Paralyzed with this awful gook the Sapphire Goddess let out through this cold sore she always

kept open on her lips, that is a hole in the limestone you understand she was like entirely covered with one of those stag rites. . . Real concentrated in there and irradiated to prevent an accident owing to some virus come lately wander in from Podunk Hepatitis. . . But I guess I'm talking too much about private things. . . But I know this big atomic professor, he's very technical too, says: 'There are no secrets any more, Pet,' when I was smooching around him for a quickie. My Uncle still gives me a sawski for a hot nuclear secret and ten years isn't hay, dahling, in these times when practically anybody is subject to wander in from the desert with a quit claim deed and snatch a girl's snatch right out from under her assets. . .over really I should say but some of we boys are so sick we got this awful cunt instead of a decent human asshole disgust you to see it. . . So I just say anything I hear on the old party line.

"I used to keep those old Cave Cunts at bay with my Impersonation Number where I play this American Mate Dance in Black Widow drag and I could make my face flap around you wouldn't believe it and the noises I made in uh orgasm when SHE ate me—I played both parts you unnerstand, imitated the Goddess Herself and turn right into stone for security. . . And SHE couldn't give me enough juice running out of this hole was her only orifice and she was transported dais and all, die ass and all, by blind uniques with no balls, had to crawl under HER dais dressed in Centipede Suit of the Bearer which was put on them as a great honor and they was always fighting over matter of crawl protocol

or protocrawl. . . So all these boys stacked to the ceiling
covered with limestone. . .you understand they weren't
dead any more than a fresh oyster is dead, but died in
the moment when the shell was cracked and they were
eaten all quivering sweet and tasty. vitamins the right
way. . .eaten with little jeweled adzes jade and sapphires
and chicken blood rubies all really magnificent. Of
course I pinched everything I could latch onto with my
prehensile piles I learned it boosting in Chi to pay the
Luxury Tax on C. three thousand years in show business. . . Later or was it earlier, the Mayan Calendar is
all loused up you know. . . I was a star Corn God inna
Sacred Hanging Ceremony to fructify the Corn devised
by this impresario who specializes in these far out bit
parts which fit me like a condom, he says the cutest
things. He's a doctor too. A big physician made my face
over after 'the accident' collided with my Bentley
head on. . .the cops say they never see anything so intense and it is a special pass I must be carrying I wasn't
completely obliterated.

"Oh there's my doctor made the face over after my
accident. He calls me Pygmalion now, isn't that cute?
You'll love him."

The doctor was sitting in a surgical chair of gleaming
nickel. His soft boneless head was covered with grey
green fuzz, the right side of his face an inch lower than
the left side swollen smooth as a boil around a dead,
cold undersea eye.

"Doctor, I want you to meet my friend Mister D the
Agent, and he's a lovely fellow too.

("Some time he don't hardly hear what you saying. He's very technical.")

The doctor reached out his abbreviated fibrous fingers in which surgical instruments caught neon and cut Johnny's face into fragments of light.

"Jelly," the doctor said, liquid gurgles through his hardened purple gums. His tongue was split and the two sections curled over each other as he talked: "Life jelly. It sticks and grows on you like Johnny."

Little papules of tissue were embedded in the doctor's hands. The doctor pulled a scalpel out of Johnny's ear and trimmed the papules into an ash tray where they stirred slowly exuding a green juice.

"They say his prick didn't synchronize at all so he cut it off and made some kinda awful cunt between the two sides of him. He got a whole ward full of his 'fans' he call them already.

"When the wind is right you can hear them scream in Town Hall Square. And everybody says 'But this is interesting.'

"I was more *physical* before my *accident*, you can see from this interesting picture."

Lee looked from the picture to the face, saw the flickering phosphorescent scars—

"Yes," he said, "I know you—You're dead *nada* walking around visible."

So the boy is rebuilt and gives me the eye and there he is again walking around some day later across the street and "No dice" flickered across his face—The copy there is a different being, something ready to slip in—

boys empty and banal as sunlight her way always—So he is exact replica is he not?—empty space of the original—

So I tailed the double to London on the Hook Von Holland and caught him out strangling a naked faggot in the bed sitter—I slip on the antibiotic hand cuffs and we adjourn to the Mandrake Club for an informative little chat—

"What do you get out of this?" I ask bluntly.

"A smell I always feel when their eyes pop out"— The boy looked at me his mouth a little open showing the whitest teeth this Private Eye ever saw—naval uniform buttoned in the wrong holes quilted with sea mist and powder smoke, smell of chlorine, rum and moldy jockstraps—and probably a narcotics agent is hiding in the spare stateroom that is always locked—There are the stairs to the attic room he looked out of and his mother moving around—dead she was they say—dead —with such hair too—red.

"Where do you feel it?" I prodded.

"All over," he said, eyes empty and banal as sunlight —"Like hair sprouting all over me"—He squirmed and giggled and creamed in his dry goods—

"And after every job I get to see the movies—You know—" And he gave me the sign twisting his head to the left and up—

So I gave him the sign back and the words jumped in my throat all there like and ready the way they always do when I'm right "You make the pilgrimage?"

"Yes—The road to Rome."

I withdrew the antibiotics and left him there with that dreamy little-boy look twisting the napkin into a hangman's knot—On the bus from the air terminal a thin grey man sat down beside me—I offered him a cigarette and he said "Have one of mine," and I see he is throwing the tin on me—"Nova police—You are Mr. Snide I believe." And he moved right in and shook me down looking at pictures, reading letters checking back on my time track.

"There's one of them," I heard some one say as he looked at a photo in my files.

"Hummm—yes—and here's another—Thank you Mr. Snide—You have been most cooperative—"

I stopped off in Bologna to look up my old friend Green Tony thinking he could probably give me a line —up four flights in a tenement past the old bitch selling black-market cigarettes and cocaine cut with Saniflush, through a dirty brown curtain and there is Green Tony in a pad with Chinese jade all over and Etruscan cuspidors—He is sitting back with his leg thrown over an Egyptian throne smoking a cigarette in a carved emerald holder—He doesn't get up but he says: "Dick Tracy in the flesh," and motions to a Babylonian couch.

I told him what I was after and his face went a bright green with rage, "That stupid bitch—She bringa the heat on all of us—Nova heat—" He blew a cloud of smoke and it hung there solid in front of him—Then he wrote an address in the smoke—"No. 88 Via di Nile, Roma."

This 88 Nile turned out to be one of those bar-soda

fountains like they have in Rome—You are subject to
find a maraschino cherry in your dry martini and right
next to some citizen is sucking a banana split disgust
you to see it—Well I am sitting there trying not to see it
so I look down at the far end of the counter and dug a boy
very dark with kinky hair and something Abyssinian in
his face—Our eyes lock and I give him the sign—And
he gives it right back—So I spit the maraschino cherry
in the bartender's face and slip him a big tip and he says
"*Rivideci* and bigger."

And I say "Up yours with a double strawberry phos-
phate."

The boy finishes his Pink Lady and follows me out
and I take him back to my trap and right away get into
an argument with the clerk about no visitors *stranezza*
to the hotel—Enough garlic on his breath to deter a
covey of vampires—I shove a handful of lire into his
mouth "Go buy yourself some more gold teeth," I told
him—

When this boy peeled off the dry goods he gives off
a slow stink like a thawing mummy—But his asshole
sucked me right in all my experience as a Private Eye
never felt anything like it—In the flash bulb of orgasm
I see that fucking clerk has stuck his head through the
transom for a refill—Well expense account—The boy
is lying there on the bed spreading out like a jelly slow
tremors running through it and sighs and says: "Almost
like the real thing isn't it?"

And I said "I need the time milking," and give him
the sign so heavy come near slipping a disk.

"I can see you're one of our own," he said warmly sucking himself back into shape—"Dinner at eight"— He comes back at eight in a souped up Ragazzi and we take off 160 per and scream to stop in front of a villa I can see the Bentleys and Hispano Bear Cats and Stutz Suisses and what not piled up and all the golden youth of Europe is disembarking—"Leave your clothes in the vestibule," the butler tells us and we walk in on a room full of people all naked to a turn sitting around on silk stools and a bar with a pink shell behind it—This cunt undulates forward and give me the sign and holds out her hand "I am the Contessa di Vile your hostess for tonight"—She points to the boys at the bar with her cigarette holder and their cocks jumped up one after the other—And I did the polite thing too when my turn came—

So all the boys began chanting in unison *"The movies! —The movies!*—We want *the movies!*—" So she led the way into the projection room which was filled with pink light seeping through the walls and floor and ceiling—The boy was explaining to me that these were actual films taken during the Abyssinian War and how lucky I was to be there—Then the action starts—There on the screen is a gallows and some young soldiers standing around with prisoners in loincloths—The soldiers are dragging this kid up onto the gallows and he biting and screaming and shitting himself and his loincloth slips off and they shove him under the noose and one of them tightens it around his neck standing there now mother naked—Then the trap fell and he drops

kicking and yelping and you could hear his neck snap
like a stick in a wet towel—He hangs there pulling his
knees up to the chest and pumping out spurts of jissom
and the audience coming right with him spurt for spurt
—So the soldiers strip the loincloths off the others and
they all got hard-ons waiting and watching—Got
through a hundred of them more or less one at a time—
Then they run the movie in slow motion slower and
slower and you are coming slower and slower until it
took an hour and then two hours and finally all the boys
are standing there like statues getting their rocks off
geologic—Meanwhile an angle comes dripping down
and forms a stalactite in my brain and I slip back to the
projection room and speed up the movie so the hanged
boys are coming like machine guns—Half the guests explode straightaway from altered pressure chunks of
limestone whistling through the air. The others are flopping around on the floor like beached idiots and the
Contessa gasps out "Carbon dioxide for the love of
Kali"—So somebody turned on the carbon dioxide tanks
and I made it out of there in an aqualung—Next thing
the nova heat moves in and bust the whole aquarium.

"Humm, yes, and here's another planet—"

The officer moved back dissolving most cooperative
connections formed by the parasite—Self-righteous millions stabbed with rage.

"That bitch—She brings the heat three dimensional."

"The ugly cloud of smoke hung there solid female
blighted continent—This turned out to be one of those
association locks in Rome—I look down at the end—

He quiets you, remember?—Finis. So I spit the planet from all the pictures and give him a place of residence with inflexible authority—Well, no terms—A hand has been taken—Your name fading looks like—Madison Avenue machine disconnected."

The Mayan Caper

JOE BRUNDIGE BRINGS YOU the shocking story of the Mayan Caper exclusive to *The Evening News*—

A Russian scientist has said: "We will travel not only in space but in time as well"—I have just returned from a thousand-year time trip and I am here to tell you what I saw—And to tell you how such time trips are made— It is a precise operation—It is difficult—It is dangerous —It is the new frontier and only the adventurous need apply—But it belongs to *anyone* who has the courage and know-how to enter—It belongs to *you*—

I started my trip in the morgue with old newspapers, folding in today with yesterday and typing out composites—When you skip through a newspaper as most of us do you see a great deal more than you know—In fact you see it all on a subliminal level—Now when I fold today's paper in with yesterday's paper and arrange the pictures to form a time section montage, I am literally moving back to the time when I read yesterday's paper, that is traveling in time back to yesterday—I did this eight hours a day for three months—I went back as far as the papers went—I dug out old magazines and forgotten novels and letters—I made fold-ins and composites and I did the same with photos—

The next step was carried out in a film studio—I learned to talk and think backward on all levels—This was done by running film and sound track backward—For example a picture of myself eating a full meal was reversed, from satiety back to hunger—First the film was run at normal speed, then in slow-motion—The same procedure was extended to other physiological processes including orgasm—(It was explained to me that I must put aside all sexual prudery and reticence, that sex was perhaps the heaviest anchor holding one in present time.) For three months I worked with the studio—My basic training in time travel was completed and I was now ready to train specifically for the Mayan assignment—

I went to Mexico City and studied the Mayans with a team of archaeologists—The Mayans lived in what is now Yucatan, British Honduras, and Guatemala—I will not recapitulate what is known of their history, but some observations on the Mayan calendar are essential to understanding this report—The Mayan calendar starts from a mythical date 5 Ahua 8 Cumhu and rolls

on to the end of the world, also a definite date depicted
in the codices as a God pouring water on the earth—
The Mayans had a solar, a lunar, and a ceremonial calendar rolling along like interlocking wheels from 5 Ahua
8 Cumhu to the end—The absolute power of the priests,
who formed about 2 percent of the population, depended on their control of this calendar—The extent of
this number monopoly can be deduced from the fact
that the Mayan verbal language contains no number
above ten—Modern Mayan-speaking Indians use Spanish numerals—Mayan agriculture was of the slash and
burn type—They had no plows. Plows can not be used
in the Mayan area because there is a strata of limestone
six inches beneath the surface and the slash and burn
method is used to this day—Now slash and burn agriculture is a matter of precise timing—The brush must be
cut at a certain time so it will have time to dry and the
burning operation carried out before the rains start—A
few days' miscalculation and the year's crop is lost—

The Mayan writings have not been fully deciphered,
but we know that most of the hieroglyphs refer to dates
in the calendar, and these numerals have been translated—It is probable that the other undeciphered symbols refer to the ceremonial calendar—There are only
three Mayan codices in existence, one in Dresden, one
in Paris, one in Madrid, the others having been burned
by Bishop Landa—Mayan is very much a living language and in the more remote villages nothing else is
spoken—More routine work—I studied Mayan and listened to it on the tape recorder and mixed Mayan in

with English—I made innumerable photomontages of Mayan codices and artifacts—the next step was to find a "vessel"—We sifted through many candidates before settling on a young Mayan worker recently arrived from Yucatan—This boy was about twenty, almost black, with the sloping forehead and curved nose of the ancient Mayans—(The physical type has undergone little alteration)—He was illiterate—He had a history of epilepsy—He was what mediums call a "sensitive"— For another three months I worked with the boy on the tape recorder mixing his speech with mine—(I was quite fluent in Mayan at this point—Unlike Aztec it is an easy language.) It was time now for "the transfer operation"—"I" was to be moved into the body of this young Mayan—The operation is illegal and few are competent to practice it—I was referred to an American doctor who had become a heavy metal addict and lost his certificate—"He is the best transfer artist in the industry" I was told "For a price."

We found the doctor in a dingy office on the Avenida Cinco de Mayo—He was a thin grey man who flickered in and out of focus like an old film—I told him what I wanted and he looked at me from a remote distance without warmth or hostility or any emotion I had ever experienced in myself or seen in another—He nodded silently and ordered the Mayan boy to strip, and ran practiced fingers over his naked body—The doctor picked up a box-like instrument with electrical attachments and moved it slowly up and down the boy's back from the base of the spine to the neck—The instrument clicked like a Geiger counter—The doctor sat down and explained to me that the operation was usually performed with "the hanging technique"—The patient's neck is broken and during the orgasm that results he passes into the other body—This method, however, was obsolete and dangerous—For the operation to succeed you must work with a pure vessel who has not been subject to parasite invasion—Such subjects are almost impossible to find in present time he stated flatly—His cold grey eyes flicked across the young Mayan's naked body:

"This subject is riddled with parasites—If I were to employ the barbarous method used by some of my learned colleagues—(nameless assholes)—you would be eaten body and soul by crab parasites—My technique is quite different—I operate with molds—Your body will remain here intact in deepfreeze—On your return, if you do return, you can have it back." He looked pointedly at my stomach sagging from sedentary city life—"You could do with a stomach tuck, young man—But one thing at a time—The transfer operation will take some weeks—And I warn you it will be expensive."

I told him that cost was no object—The *News* was behind me all the way—He nodded briefly: "Come back at this time tomorrow." When we returned to the doctor's office he introduced me to a thin young man who had the doctor's cool removed grey eyes—"This is my photographer—I will make my molds from his negatives." The photographer told me his name was Jiminez

—("Just call me 'Jimmy the Take'")—We followed the "Take" to a studio in the same building equipped with a 35 millimeter movie camera and Mayan backdrops—He posed us naked in erection and orgasm, cutting the images in together down the middle line of our bodies—Three times a week we went to the doctor's office—He looked through rolls of film his eyes intense, cold, impersonal—And ran the clicking box up and down our spines—Then he injected a drug which he described as a variation of the apomorphine formula—The injection caused simultaneous vomiting and orgasm and several times I found myself vomiting and ejaculating in the Mayan vessel—The doctor told me these exercises were only the preliminaries and that the actual operation, despite all precautions and skills, was still dangerous enough.

At the end of three weeks he indicated the time has come to operate—He arranged us side by side naked on the operating table under floodlights—With a phosphorescent pencil he traced the middle line of our bodies from the cleft under the nose down to the rectum —Then he injected a blue fluid of heavy cold silence as word dust fell from demagnetized patterns—From a remote Polar distance I could see the doctor separate the two halves of our bodies and fitting together a composite being—I came back in other flesh the lookout different, thoughts and memories of the young Mayan drifting through my brain—

The doctor gave me a bottle of the vomiting drug which he explained was efficacious in blocking out any control waves—He also gave me another drug which, if injected into a subject, would enable me to occupy his body for a few hours and only at night. "Don't let the sun come up on you or it's curtains—zero eaten by crab—And now there is the matter of my fee."

I handed him a brief case of bank notes and he faded into the shadows furtive and seedy as an old junky.

The paper and the embassy had warned me that I would be on my own, a thousand years from any help— I had a vibrating camera gun sewed into my fly, a small tape recorder and a transistor radio concealed in a clay pot—I took a plane to Mérida where I set about contacting a "broker" who could put me in touch with a "time guide"—Most of these so-called "brokers" are old drunken frauds and my first contact was no exception—I had been warned to pay nothing until I was satisfied with the arrangements—I found this "broker" in a filthy hut on the outskirts surrounded by a rubbish heap of scrap iron, old bones, broken pottery and worked flints—I produced a bottle of *aguardiente* and the broker immediately threw down a plastic cup of the raw spirit and sat there swaying back and forth on a stool while I explained my business—He indicated that what I wanted was extremely difficult—Also dangerous and illegal—He could get into trouble—Besides I might be an informer from the Time Police—He would have to think about it—He drank two more cups of spirit and fell on the floor in a stupor—The following day I called again—He had thought it over and perhaps—In any case he would need a week to prepare his medicines and this he could only do if he were properly supplied with *aguardiente*—And he poured another glass of spirits slopping full—Extremely dissatisfied with the way things were going I left—As I was walking back toward town a boy fell in beside me.

"Hello, Meester, you look for broker yes?—Muy know good one—Him," he gestured back toward the hut. "No good *borracho* son bitch bastard—Take *mucho dinero*—No do nothing—You come with me, Meester."

Thinking I could not do worse, I accompanied the boy to another hut built on stilts over a pond—A youngish man greeted us and listened silently while I explained what I wanted—The boy squatted on the floor rolling a marijuana cigarette—He passed it around and we all smoked—The broker said yes he could make the arrangements and named a price considerably lower than what I had been told to expect—How soon?—He looked at a shelf where I could see a number of elaborate hourglasses with sand in different colors: red, green, black, blue, and white—The glasses were marked with symbols—He explained to me that the sand represented color time and color words—He pointed to a symbol on the green glass, "Then—One hour"—He took out some dried mushrooms and herbs and began cooking them in a clay pot—As green sand touched the symbol, he filled little clay cups and handed one to me and one to the boy—I drank the bitter medicine and almost immediately the pictures I had seen of Mayan artifacts and codices began moving in my brain like animated cartoons—A spermy, compost heap smell filled the room—The boy began to twitch and mutter and fell to the floor in a fit—I could see that he had an erection under his thin trousers—The broker opened the boy's shirt and pulled off his pants—The penis flipped out spurting in orgasm after orgasm—A green light filled the room and burned through the boy's flesh—Suddenly he sat up talking in Mayan—The words curled out his mouth and hung visible in the air like vine tendrils—I felt a strange vertigo which I recognized as the motion sickness of time travel—The broker smiled and held out a hand—I passed over his fee—The boy was putting on his clothes—He beckoned me to follow and I got up and left the hut—We were walking along a jungle hut the boy ahead his whole body alert and twitching like a dog—We walked many hours and it was dawn when we came to a clearing where I could see a number of workers with sharp sticks and gourds of seed planting corn—The boy touched my shoulder and disappeared up the path in jungle dawn mist—

As I stepped forward into the clearing and addressed one of the workers, I felt the crushing weight of evil insect control forcing my thoughts and feelings into prearranged molds, squeezing my spirit in a soft invisible vise—The worker looked at me with dead eyes empty of curiosity or welcome and silently handed me a planting stick—It was not unusual for strangers to wander in out of the jungle since the whole area was ravaged by soil exhaustion—So my presence occasioned no comment—I worked until sundown—I was assigned to a hut by an overseer who carried a carved stick and wore an elaborate headdress indicating his rank—I lay down in the hammock and immediately felt stabbing probes of telepathic interrogation—I turned on the thoughts of a half-witted young Indian—After some hours the invisible presence withdrew—I had passed the first test—

During the months that followed I worked in the fields—The monotony of this existence made my disguise as a mental defective quite easy—I learned that one could be transferred from field work to rock carving the stellae after a long apprenticeship and only after the priests were satisfied that any thought of resistance was forever extinguished—I decided to retain the anonymous status of a field worker and keep as far as possible out of notice—

A continuous round of festivals occupied our evenings and holidays—On these occasions the priests appeared in elaborate costumes, often disguised as centipedes or lobsters—Sacrifices were rare, but I witnessed one revolting ceremony in which a young captive was tied to a stake and the priests tore his sex off with white-hot copper claws—I learned also something of the horrible punishments meted out to anyone who dared challenge or even think of challenging the controllers: *Death in the Ovens:* The violator was placed in a construction of interlocking copper grills—The grills were then heated to white heat and slowly closed on his body. *Death In Centipede:* The "criminal" was strapped to a couch and eaten alive by giant centipedes—These executions were carried out secretly in rooms under the temple.

I made recordings of the festivals and the continuous music like a shrill insect frequency that followed the workers all day in the fields—However, I knew that to play these recordings would invite immediate detection—I needed not only the sound track of control but the image track as well before I could take definitive action—I have explained that the Mayan control system depends on the calendar and the codices which contain symbols representing all states of thought and feeling possible to human animals living under such limited circumstances—These are the instruments with which they rotate and control units of thought—I found out also that the priests themselves do not understand exactly how the system works and that I undoubtedly knew more about it than they did as a result of my intensive training and studies—The technicians who had devised the control system had died out and the present line of priests were in the position of some one who knows what buttons to push in order to set a machine in motion, but would have no idea how to fix that machine if it broke down, or to construct another if the machine were destroyed—If I could gain access to the codices and mix the sound and image track the priests would go on pressing the old buttons with unexpected results—In order to accomplish the purpose I prostituted myself to one of the priests—(Most distasteful thing I ever stood still for)—During the sex act he metamorphosed himself into a green crab from the waist up, retaining human legs and genitals that secreted a caustic erogenous slime, while a horrible stench filled the hut—I was able to endure these horrible encounters by promising myself the pleasure of killing this disgusting monster when the time came— And my reputation as an idiot was by now so well established that I escaped all but the most routine control measures—

The priest had me transferred to janitor work in the temple where I witnessed some executions and saw the prisoners torn body and soul into writhing insect fragments by the ovens, and learned that the giant centipedes were born in the ovens from these mutilated screaming fragments—It was time to act—Using the drug the doctor had given me, I took over the priest's body, gained access to the room where the codices were kept, and photographed the books—Equipped now with sound and image track of the control machine I was in position to dismantle it—I had only to mix the order of recordings and the order of images and the changed order would be picked up and fed back into the machine—I had recordings of all agricultural operations, cutting and burning brush etc.—I now correlated the recordings of burning brush with the image track of this operation, and shuffled the time so that the order to burn came late and a year's crop was lost— Famine weakening control lines, I cut radio static into the control music and festival recordings together with sound and image track rebellion.

"Cut word lines—Cut music lines—Smash the control

images—Smash the control machine—Burn the books—
Kill the priests—Kill! Kill! Kill!—"

Inexorably as the machine had controlled thought
feeling and sensory impressions of the workers, the
machine now gave the order to dismantle itself and kill
the priests—I had the satisfaction of seeing the overseer pegged out in the field, his intestines perforated
with hot planting sticks and crammed with corn—I
broke out my camera gun and rushed the temple—This
weapon takes and vibrates image to radio static—You
see the priests *were* nothing but word and image, an
old film rolling on and on with dead actors—Priests
and temple guards went up in silver smoke as I blasted
my way into the control room and burned the codices—
Earthquake tremors under my feet I got out of there
fast, blocks of limestone raining all around me—A great
weight fell from the sky, winds of the earth whipping
palm trees to the ground—Tidal waves rolled over the
Mayan control calendar.

I Sekuin

I Sekuin, perfected these arts along the streets of
Minraud. Under sign of the Centipede. A captive head.
In Minraud time. In the tattoo booths. The flesh graft
parlors. Living wax works of Minraud. Saw the dummies
made to impression. While you wait. From short-time.
In the terminals of Minraud. Saw the white bug juice
spurt from ruptured spines. In the sex rooms of
Minraud. While you wait. In Minraud time. The sex
devices of flesh. The centipede penis. Insect hairs thru
grey-purple flesh. Of the scorpion people. The severed
heads. In tanks of sewage. Eating green shit. In the
aquariums of Minraud. The booths of Minraud. Under

sign of the centipede. The sex rooms and flesh films of Minraud. I Sekuin a captive head. Learned the drugs of Minraud. In flak Braille. Rot brain and spine. Leave a crab body broken on the brass and copper street. I Sekuin captive head. Carried thru the booths of Minraud. By arms. Legs.

Extensions. From the flesh works of Minraud. My head in a crystal sphere of heavy fluid. Under sing sign of the scorpion goddess. Captive in Minraud. In the time booths of Minraud. In the tattoo parlors of Minraud. In the flesh works of Minraud. In the sex rooms of Minraud. In the flesh films of Minraud. March my captive head. HER captive in Minraud time streets.

On a level plain in the dry sound of insect wings Bradly crash landed a yellow cub—area of painted booths and vacant lots—in a dusty shopwindow of trusses and plaster feet, a severed head on sand, red ants crawling through nose and lips—

"You crazy or something walk around alone?"

The guide pointed to the head: "Guard—You walk through his eyes and you N.G." The guide sliced a hand across his genitals: "This bad place, Meester—You *ven conmigo*—"

He led the way through dusty streets—Metal excrement glowed in corners—Darkness fell in heavy chunks blocking out sections of the city.

"Here," said the guide—"A restaurant cut from limestone, green light seeping through bottles and tanks where crustaceans moved in slow gyrations—The waiter took their order hissing cold dank breath through a disk mouth.

"Good place—cave crabs—*Muy bueno* for fuck, Johnny—"

The waiter set down a flat limestone shell of squid bodies with crab claws.

"Krishnus," said the guide.

Still alive, moving faintly in phosphorescent slime— The guide speared one on a bamboo spike and dipped it into yellow sauce—A sweet metal taste burned through stomach intestines and genitals—Bradly ate the krishnus in ravenous gulps—

The guide raised his arm from the elbow, "*Muy bueno*, Johnny—You see." The waiter was singing through his disk mouth a bubbling cave song— "*Vámanos*, Johnny—I show you good place—We smoke fuck sleep O.K. Muy got good one, Johnny—"

Word "Hotel" exploded in genitals—An old junky took Bradly's money and led them to a blue cubicle— Bradly leaned out a square hole in one wall and saw that the cubicle projected over a void on rusty iron props—The floor moved slightly and creaked under their feet—

"Some time this trap fall—Last fuck for Johnny."

There was a pallet on the iron floor, a brass tray with hashish pipes, and a stone jar.

"Johnny shirt off"—said the guide unbuttoning Bradly's shirt with gentle lush rolling fingers—"Johnny pants down"—He dipped a green phosphorescent

Pretend an Interest

BENWAY "CAMPED" in the Board of Health. He rushed in
anywhere brazenly impounding all junk. He was of
course well-known but by adroit face rotation managed
to piece out the odds, juggling five or six bureaus in the
air thin and tenuous drifting-away cobwebs in a cold
Spring wind under dead crab eyes of a doorman in
green uniform carrying an ambiguous object composite
of club, broom and toilet plunger, trailing a smell of
ammonia and scrubwoman flesh. An undersea animal
surfaced in his face, round disk mouth of cold grey
gristle, purple rasp tongue moving in green saliva: "Soul
Cracker," Benway decided. Species of carnivorous mollusk. Exists on Venus. It might not have bones. Time-
switched the tracks through a field of little white

flowers by the ruined signal tower. Sat down under a tree worn smooth by others sat there before. We remember the days as long procession of the Secret Police always everywhere in different form. In Guayaquil sat on the river bank and saw a big lizard cross the mud flats dotted with melon rind from passing canoes.

Carl's dugout turned slowly in the brown iridescent lagoon infested with sting ray, fresh water shark, arequipa, candirus, water boa, crocodile, electric eel, aquatic panther and other noxious creatures dreamed up by the lying explorers who infest bars marginal to the area.

"This inaccessible tribe, you dig, lives on phosphorescent metal paste they mine from the area. Transmute to gold straightaway and shit it out in nuggets. It's the great work."

Liver-sick gold eyes gold maps gold teeth over the *aguardiente* cooked on the Primus stove with canella and tea to cut the oil taste leaves silver sores in the mouth and throat.

"That was the year of the Rindpest when all the tourists died even the Scandinavians and we boys reduced to hawk the farter LWR—Local Wage Rate."

"No calcium in the area you understand. One blighter lost his entire skeleton and we had to carry him about in a canvas bathtub. A jaguar lapped him up in the end, largely for the salt I think."

Tin boys reduced to hawk the farter the substance and the strata—You know what that means? Carried the youth to dead water infested with consent—That was the year of The Clear—Local Wage Rate of Program Empty Body—

"Head Waters of the Baboon-asshole. . . That's hanging vine country—" (The hanging vine flicked around the youth's neck molding to his skull bones in a spiraling tendril motion snapped his neck, he hangs now ejaculating as disk mouths lined with green hairs fasten to his rectum growing tendrils through his body dissolving his bones in liquid gurgles and plops into the green eating jelly.)

"This bad place you write, Meester. You win something like jellyfish."

They live in translucent jelly and converse in light flashes liquefying bones of the world and eating the jelly—boy chrysalis rotting in the sun—lazy undersea eyes on the nod over the rotting meat vegetable sleep—limestone dope out of shale and water. . .

The youth is hanged fresh and bloody—Tall ceremony involves a scorpion head—lethal mating operation from the Purified Ones—No calcium in the area—Exists on Venus—It might not have bones—Ray moss of orgasm and death—Limestone God a mile away—Better than shouts: "Empty body!" Dead land here you understand waiting for some one marginal to the area.

"Deep in fucking drum country" (The naked Initiate is strapped with his back and buttocks fitted to a wooden drum. The drummer beats out orgasm message until the Initiate's flesh lights up with blue flame inside and the drum takes life and fucks the boy ((puffs of smoke across a clear blue sky. . .)) The initiate awoke in other flesh the lookout different. . . And he plopped into squares and patios on "Write me Meester.")

Puerto Joselito is located at the confluence of two strong brown rivers. The town is built over a vast mud flat crisscrossed by stagnant canals, the buildings on stilts joined by a maze of bridges and catwalks extend up from the mud flats into higher ground surrounded by tree columns and trailing lianas, the whole area presenting the sordid and dilapidated air of a declining frontier post or an abandoned carnival.

"The town of Puerto Joselito, dreary enough in its physical aspect, exudes a suffocating fog of smoldering rancid evil as if the town and inhabitants were slowly sinking in wastes and garbage. I found these people deep in the vilest superstitions and practices.

"Various forms of ritual execution are practiced here. These gooks have an aphrodisiac so powerful as to cause death in a total blood spasm leaving the empty body cold and white as marble. This substance is secreted by the Species Xiucutl Crustanus, a flying scorpion, during its lethal mating season in the course of which all male Xiucutl die maddened by the substance and will fly on any male creature infecting with its deadly sperm. In one ceremony the condemned are painted as gold, silver, copper and marble statues, then inoculated with Xiucutl sperm their convulsions are channeled by invisible control wires into exquisite ballets and freeze into garden fountains and park pedestals. And this is one of many ceremonies revolving on the

Ceremonial Calendar kept by the Purified Ones and the Earth Mother.

"The Purified One selects a youth each month and he is walled into a crystal cubicle molded on cervical vertebrae. On the walls of the cubicle, sex programs are cut in cuneiforms and the walls revolve on silent hydraulic pressures. At the end of the month the youth is carried through the street on a flower float and cerenominally hanged in the limestone ball court, it being thought that all human dross passes from the Purified One to die in the youth at the moment of orgasm and death. Before the youth is hanged he must give his public consent, and if he cannot be brought to consent he hangs the Purified One and takes over his functions. The Purified Ones are officially immortal with monthly injections of youth substance." Quote Green-Baum Early Explorer.

Carl's outboard vibrated in a haze of rusty oil, bit a jagged piece out of the dugout canoe and sank, in iridescent brown water. Somewhere in the distance the muffled jelly sound of underwater dynamite: ("The natives are fishing"). howler monkeys like wind through leaves. The dugout twisted slowly and stopped, touching a ruined jetty. Carl got out with his Nordic rucksack and walked to the square on high ground. He felt a touch on his shoulder light as wind. A man in moldy grey police tunic and red flannel underwear one bare foot swollen and fibrous like old wood covered with white fungus, his eyes mahogany color flickered as the watcher moved in and out. He gasped out the word "Control" and slipped to the ground. A man in grey hospital pajamas eating handfuls of dirt and trailing green spit crawled over to Carl and pulled at his pants cuff. Another moves forward on brittle legs breaking little puffs of bone meal. His eyes lit up a stern glare went out in smell of burning metal. From all sides they came pawing hissing spitting: *"Papeles," "Documentes," "Passaport."*

"What is all this scandal?" The Comandante in clean khaki was standing on a platform overlooking the square. Above him was an elaborate multileveled building of bamboo. His shirt was open on a brown chest smooth as old ivory. A little pistol in red leather cover crawled slowly across his skin leaving an iridescent trail of slime.

"You must forgive my staff if they do not quite measure up to your German ideal of spit and polish. . . backward. . . uninstructed. . . each living all alone and cultivating his little virus patch. . . They have absolutely nothing to do and the solitude. . ." He tapped his forehead. His face melted and changed under the flickering arc lights.

"But there must be thirty of them about," said Carl.

The Comandante gave him a sharp look. "They are synchronized of course. They can not see or even infer each other so all think he is only police officer on post. Their lines you *sabe* never cross and some of them are already. . ."

"And some of them are already dead. This is awkward since they are not legally responsible. We try to bury them on time even if they retain intact protest reflex. Like Gonzalez the Earth Eater. We bury him three times." The Comandante held up three fingers sprouting long white tendrils. "Always he eat way out. And now if you will excuse me the soccer scores are coming in from the Capital. One must pretend an interest."

The Comandante had aged from remote crossroads of Time crawled into a metal locker and shut the door whimpering with fears, emerged in a moldy green jockstrap his body painted I-red, U-green. The Assistant flared out of a broom closet high on ammonia with a green goatee and marble face. He removed Carl's clothes in a series of locks and throws. Carl could feel his body move to the muscle orders. The Assistant put a pail over his head and screamed away into distant hammers.

The Comandante spread jelly over Carl's naked paralyzed body. The Comandante was molding a woman. Carl could feel his body draining into the woman mold. His genitals dissolving, tits swelling as the Comandante penetrated applying a few touches to face and hair—(Jissom across the mud wall in the dawn sound of barking dogs and running water—) Down there the Comandante going through his incantations around Carl's empty body. The body rose presenting an erection, masturbates in front of the Comandante. Penis flesh spreads through his body bursting in orgasm explosions granite cocks ejaculate lava under a black cloud boiling with monster crustaceans. Cold grey undersea eyes and hands touched

Carl's body. The Comandante flipped him over with sucker hands and fastened his disk mouth to Carl's asshole. He was lying in a hammock of green hair, penis-flesh hammers bursting his body. Hairs licked his rectum, spiraling tendrils scraping pleasure centers, Carl's body emptied in orgasm after orgasm, bones lit up green through flesh dissolved into the disk mouth with a fluid plop. He quivers red now in boneless spasms, pink waves through his body at touch of the green hairs.

The Comandante stripped Carl's body and smeared on green jelly nipples that pulled the flesh up and in. Carl's genitals wither to dry shit he sweeps clear with a little whisk broom to white flesh and black shiny pubic hairs. The Comandante parts the hairs and makes Incision with a little curved knife. Now he is modeling a face from the picture of his *novia* in the Capital.

"And now, how you say, 'the sound effects.' " He puts on a record of her voice, Carl's lips follow and the female substance breathed in the words.

"Oh love of my *alma!* Oh wind of morning!"

"Most distasteful thing I ever stand still for." Carl made words in the air without a throat, without a tongue. "I hope there is a *farmacia* in the area."

The Comandante looked at him with annoyance: "You could wait in the office please."

He came out putting on his tunic and strapping on a Luger.

"A drugstore? Yes I *creo.* . . . Across the lagoon. . . I will call the guide."

Carl walked through a carnival city along canals where giant pink salamanders and goldfish stirred slowly, penny arcades, tattoo booths, massage parlors, side shows, blue movies, processions, floats, performers, pitchmen to the sky.

Puerto Joselito is located Dead Water. Inactive oil wells and mine shafts, strata of abandoned machinery and gutted boats, garbage of stranded operations and expeditions that died at this point of dead land where sting rays bask in brown water and grey crabs walk the mud flats on brittle stilt legs. The town crops up from the mud flats to the silent temple of high jungle streams of clear water cut deep clefts in yellow clay and falling orchids endanger the traveler.

In a green savanna stand two vast penis figures in black stone, legs and arms vestigial, slow blue smoke rings pulsing from the stone heads. A limestone road winds through the pillars and into The City. A rack of rusty iron and concrete set in vacant lots and rubble, dotted with chemical gardens. A smell of junky hat and death about the town deadens and weight these sentences with "disgust you to see it." Carl walked through footpaths of a vast shanty town. A dry wind blows hot and cold down from Chimborazo a soiled post card in the prop blue sky. Crab men peer out of abandoned quarries and shag heaps some sort of vestigial eye growing cheek bone and a look about them as if they could take root and grow on anybody. muttering addicts of the orgasm drug, boneless in the sun, gurgling throat gristle, heart pulsing slowly in transparent flesh eaten alive by the crab men.

Carl walked through the penis posts into a town of limestone huts. A ring of priests sat around the posts legs spread, erections pulsing to flicker light from their eyes. As he walked through the electric eyes his lips swelled and his lungs rubbed against the soft inner ribs. He walked over and touched one of the priests and a shock threw him across the road into a sewage ditch. Maize fields surround the town with stone figures of the Young Corn God erect penis spurting maize shoots looks down with young cruelty and innocent lips parted slightly terminal caress in the dropping eyes. The Young Corn God is led out and his robes of corn silk stripped from his body by lobster priests. A vine rope is attached to the stone penis of the Maize God. The boy's cock rises iridescent in the morning sun and you can see the other room from there by a mirror on the wardrobe. . . Well now, in the city a group of them came to this valley grow corn do a bit of hunting fishing in the river.

Carl walked a long row of living penis urns made from men whose penis has absorbed the body with vestigial arms and legs breathing through purple fungoid gills and dropping a slow metal excrement like melted solder forms a solid plaque under the urns stand about three feet high on rusty iron shelves wire mesh cubicles joined by catwalks and ladders a vast warehouse of living penis urns slowly transmuting to smooth red terra cotta. Others secrete from the head crystal pearls of lubricant that forms a shell of solid crystal over the red penis flesh.

A blast of golden horns: "The Druid priest emerges from the Sacred Grove, rotting bodies hang about him like Spanish moss. His eyes blue and cold as liquid air expand and contract eating light."

The boy sacrifice is chosen by erection acclaim. universal erection feeling for him until all pricks point to "Yes." Boy feels the "Yes" run through him and melt his bones to "Yes" stripped naked in the Sacred Grove shivering and twitching under the Hanging Tree green disk mouths sucking his last bone meal. He goes to the Tree naked on flower floats through the obsidian streets red stone buildings and copper pagodas of the Fish City stopping in Turkish Baths and sex rooms to make blue movies with youths. The entire city is in heat during this ceremony, faces swollen with tumescent purple penis flesh. Lightning fucks flash on any street corner leave a smell of burning metal blue sparks up and down the spine. A vast bath-town of red clay cubicles over twisting geological orgasm with the green crab boys disk mouths' slow rasping tongues on spine centers twisting in the warm black ooze.

Noteworthy is the Glazing Ceremony when certain of the living urns are covered with terra cotta and baked in red brick ovens by the women who pull the soft red meat out with their penis forks and decorate house and garden with the empty urns. The urnings for the Glazing Ceremony are chosen each day by locker number from the public urn and numbers read out over the soft speaker inside the head. Helpless urns listening to the number call charge our soft terror-eating substance, our rich substance.

Now it is possible to beat the number before call by fixing the urn or after call by the retroactive fix which few are competent to practice. There is also a Ceremonial Massage in which the penis flesh is rubbed in orgasm after orgasm until Death in Centipede occurs. Death in Centipede is the severest sentence of the Insect Court and of course all urnings are awaiting sentence for various male crimes. *Pues,* every year a few experienced urnings beat the house and make Crystal Grade. When the crystal cover reaches a certain thickness the urning is exempt from ceremonial roll call and becomes immortal with nothing to do but slowly accrete a thicker cover in the Crystal Hall of Fame.

Few beat the house. a vast limestone bat. High mountain valley cut off by severest sentence of symbiotic cannibalism. So the game with one another.

"I dunno me. Only work here. Technical Sergeant."

"Throw it into wind Jack."

A pimp leans in through the Country Club window. "Visit the House of David boys and watch the girls eat shit. Makes a man feel good all over. Just tell the madam a personal friend of mine." He drops a cuneiform cylinder into the boy's hip pocket feeling his ass with lost tongue of the penis urn people in a high mountain valley of symbiotic cannibalism. The natives are blond and blue-eyed sex in occupation. It is unlawful to have orgasm alone and the inhabitants

live in a hive of sex rooms and flickering blue movie
cubicles. You can spot one on the cubicle skyline miles
away. We all live in the blue image forever. The
cubicles fade out in underground steam baths where
lurk the Thurlings, malicious boys' spirits fugitive from
the blue movie who mislead into underground rivers.
(The traveler is eaten by aquatic centipedes and
carnivorous underwater vines.)

Orgasm death spurts over the flower floats—Limestone God a mile away—Descent into penis flesh cut
off by a group of them came to this game under the
Hanging Tree—Insect legs under red Arctic night—He
wore my clothes and terror—

The boy ejaculates blood over the flower floats. Slow
vine rope drops him in a phallic fountain. wire mesh
cubicles against the soft inner ribs. vast warehouse of
penis and the shock threw him ten feet to smooth dirt
and flak. God with erect penis spurting crystal young
cruelty and foe solid. dazzling terminal caress in silent
corridors of Corn God. erection feeling for descent in
the morning sun feels the "Yes" from there by a mirror
on you stripped naked. In the city a group of them
came to this last bone meal under the Hanging Tree.

"Pretty familiar."

The Priests came through the Limestone Gates playing green flutes: translucent lobster men with wild blue
eyes and shells of flexible copper. A soundless vibration
in the spine touched center of erection and the natives
moved toward the flute notes on a stiffening blood tube
for the Centipede Rites. A stone penis body straddles

the opening to the cave room of steam baths and sex cubicles and the green cab boys who go all the way on any line.

The Natives insert a grill of silver wires deep into the sinus where a crystal slowly forms. They strum the wires with insect hairs growing through flesh weaving cold cocaine sex frequencies.

From The Living God Cock flows a stream of lubricant into a limestone trough green with algae. The priests arrange the initiates into long dog-fuck lines molding them together with green jelly from the lubricant tanks. Now the centipede skin is strapped on each body a segment and the centipede whips and cracks in electric spasms of pleasure throwing off segments kicking spasmodically uncontrolled diarrhea spurting orgasm after orgasm synchronized with the flicker lights. Carl is taken by the centipede legs and pulled into flesh jelly dissolving bones—Thick black hair sprouts through his tumescent flesh—He falls through a maze of penny arcades and dirty pictures, locker rooms, barracks, and prison flesh empty with the colorless smell of death—

Cold metal excrement on all the walls and benches, silver sky raining the metal word fallout—Sex sweat like iron in the mouth. Scores are coming in. Pretend an interest.

In a puppet booth the manipulator takes pictures of bored insolent catatonics with eight-hour erections reading comics and chewing gum. The impresario is a bony Nordic with green fuzz on his chest and legs. "I get mine later with the pictures. I can't touch the performers. Wall of glass you know show you something interesting."

He pulls aside curtain: schoolboy room with a banner and pin-ups. on the bed naked boy puppet reading comics and chewing gum with a hypo.

Ghost your German. Spit penny arcades, tattoo booths, Nordic processions, human performers, trapeze artists. Whores of all sexes importune from scenic railways and ferris wheels where they rent cubicles, push up manhole covers in a puff of steam, pull at passing pant cuffs, careen out of the Tunnel of Love waving condoms of jissom. Old blind queens with dirty peep shows built into their eye sockets disguise themselves as penny arcades and feel for a young boy's throbbing cock with cold metal hands, sniff pensively at bicycle seats in Afghan Hound drag, Puerto Joselito is located through legs. Ghost slime sitting naked on tattoo booths, virus flesh of curse. suffocating town, this. Ways to bury explorer.

Old junky street cleaners push little red wagons sweeping up condoms and empty H caps, KY tubes, broken trusses and sex devices, kif garbage and confetti, moldy jockstraps and bloody Kotex, shit-stained color comics, dead kitten and afterbirths, jenshe babies of berdache and junky.

Everywhere the soft insidious voice of the Pitchman delayed action language lesson muttering under all your pillows "Shows all kinds masturbation and self-abuse. Young boys need it special."

Last Hints

CARL DESCENDED a spiral iron stairwell into a labyrinth of lockers, tier on tier of wire mesh and steel cubicles joined by catwalks and ladders and moving cable cars as far as he could see, tiers shifting interpenetrating swinging beams of construction, blue flare of torches on the intent young faces. locker room smell of moldy jockstraps, chlorine and burning metal, escalators and moving floors start stop change course, synchronize with balconies and perilous platforms eaten with rust. Ferris wheels silently penetrate the structure, roller coasters catapult through to the clear sky—a young workman walks the steel beams with the sun in his hair out of sight in a maze of catwalks and platforms where coffee fires smoke in rusty barrels and the workers blow on their black cotton gloves in the clear cold morning through to the sky beams with sun in his hair the workers blow on their cold morning, dropped down into the clicking turnstiles. buzzers, lights and stuttering torches smell of ozone. Breakage is constant. Whole tiers shift and crash in a yellow cloud of rust, spill boys masturbating on careening toilets, iron urinals trailing a wake of indecent exposure, old men in rocking chairs screaming antifluoride slogans, a Southern Senator sticks his fat frog face out of the outhouse and brays with inflexible authority: "And Ah advocates the extreme penalty in the worst form there is for anyone convicted of trafficking in, transporting, selling or caught in using the narcotic substance known as nutmeg. . . I wanna say further that ahm a true friend of the Nigra and understand all his simple wants. Why, I got a good Darkie in here now wiping my ass."

Wreckage and broken bodies litter the girders, slowly collected by old junkies pushing little red wagons patient and calm with gentle larcenous old woman fingers. gathering blue torch flares light the calm intent young worker faces.

Carl descended a spiral iron smell of ozone. Breakage is of lockers tier on tier crash in yellow cloud as far as he could see of indecent exposure on toilets. Swinging beams construct the intent young faces.

Locker room toilet on five levels seen from the ferris wheel. flash of white legs, shiny pubic hairs and lean brown arms, boys masturbating with soap under rusty showers form a serpent line beating on the lockers,

vibrates through all the tiers and cubicles unguarded
platforms and dead-end ladders dangling in space,
workers straddling beams beat out runic tunes with
shiny ball peen hammers. The universe shakes with
metallic adolescent lust. The line disappears through a
green door slide down to the subterranean baths twisting through torch flares the melodious boy-cries drift
out of ventilators in all the locker rooms, barracks,
schools and prisons of the world. "Joselito, Paco,
Enrique."

Jacking off he is whiff stateroom that is always kept
locked—and word dust dirtied his body falling through
the space between worlds—

The third kif pipe he went through the urinal sick
and dizzy. He just down from the country. He just down
from the green place by the dog's mirror. Sometimes
came to a place by the dogs. . . Jungle sounds and smells
drift from his coat lapels. A lovely Sub that boy.

Ghosts of Panama clung to our bodies—"You come
with me, Meester?"—On the boy's breath a flesh—His
body slid from my hands in soap bubbles—We twisted
slowly to the yellow sands, traced fossils of orgasm—

"You win something like jellyfish, Meester."

Under a ceiling fan, naked and sullen, stranger color
through his eyes the lookout different—fading Panama
photos swept out by an old junky coughing spitting in
the sick dawn—

(phosphorescent metal excrement of the city—brain
eating birds patrol the iron streets.)

Hospital smell of dawn powder—dead rainbow post

cards swept out by an old junky in backward countries.

"I don't know if you got my last hints as we shifted commissions, passing where the awning flaps from the Café de France—Hurry up—Perhaps Carl still has his magic lantern—Dark overtakes someone walking—I don't know exactly where you made this dream—Sending letter to a coffin is like posting it in last terrace of the garden—I would never have believed realms and frontiers of light exist—I'm so badly informed and totally green troops—B.B., hurry up please—"

(Stopped suddenly to show me a hideous leather body)—"I'm almost without medicine."

It was still good bye then against the window outside 1920's movie, flesh tracks broken—Sitting at a long table where the doctor couldn't reach and I said: "He has your voice and end of the line—Fading breath on bed showing symptoms of suffocation—I have tuned them out—How many plots have been forestalled before they could take shape in boy haunted by the iron claws?—Meanwhile a tape recorder cuts old newspapers." Panama clung to our bodies naked under the ceiling fan—excrement at the far end of forgotten streets—hospital smell on the dawn wind—

(Peeled his phosphorescent metal knees, brain broiled in carrion hunger.)

On the sea wall under fading Panama photo casual ghost of adolescent T-shirt traced fossil-like jellyfish—

"On the sea wall if you got my last hints over the tide flats—I don't know exactly where—woke up in other flesh—shirt with Chinese characters—breeze from

the Café de France—lantern burning insect wings—
I'm almost without medicine—far away—storms—
crackling sounds—Nothing here now but the circling
albatross—dead post card waiting a place forgotten—"

On the sea wall met a boy under the circling albatross—Peeled his red-and-white T-shirt to brown
flesh and grey under like ash and passed a joint back
and forth as we dropped each other's pants and he
looked down face like Mayan limestone in the kerosene
lamp sputter of burning insect wings over the tide
flats—Woke up in other flesh the lookout different—
hospital smell of backward countries—

Where the Awning Flaps

"So we got our rocks off permutating through each other's facilities on the blue route and after a little practice we could do it without the projector and perform any kinda awful sex act on any street corner behind the blue glass stirring the passing rectums and pubic hairs like dry leaves falling in the pissoir: *"J'aime ces types vicieux qu'ici montrent la bite—"*

Drinking from his eyes the idiot green boys plaintive as wind leaves erect wooden phallus on the graves of dying Lemur Peoples.

"Fluck flick take any place. Johnny you-me-neon-asshole-amigos-now."

"You only get a hard-on with my permission."

"Who you now Meester? Flick fluck take Johnny

over. Me screw Johnny up same asshole? You me make
flick-fluck-one-piece?"

Just hula hoop through each other to idiot Mambo.
Every citizen of the area has a blueprint like some are
Electricals and some are Vegetable Walking Carbonics
and so on, it's very technical. boy jissom tracks through
rectal mucus and Johnny.

"One track out so: panels of shadow."

"Me finish Johnny night."

So we get our rectums in transparent facilities blue
route process together. slow night to examine me.
every dawn smell fingers the passing rectum. finger on
all cocks: "I-you-me in the pissoir of present time."
"Idiot fuck you-me-Johnny. "flick fluck idiot asshole
buddies like a tree frog clinging in permission. Who
are you green hands? Fungoid purple?"

"Johnny over. Me screw. Flick fluck one piece."

Warm spermy smell to idiot Mambo. Silence belches
smell of ozone and rectal flight: "Here goes examiner
other rectums naked in Panama. citizen of the area."

On the sea wall met the guide under the Circling
Albatross. Peeled his red- and white-striped T-shirt
to brown flesh and grey under like ash and we passed
a joint back and forth as we dropped each other's pants
and he looked down face like Mayan limestone in the
kerosene lamp sputter of burning insect wings.

"I screw Johnny up ass." He jumped with his knees
on the bed and slapped his thighs, cock-shadow pulsing on the blue paint wall. "*Así como peeeeerrross.*"
ass hairs spread over the tide flats. Woke up in other

flesh, the lookout different, one boy naked in Panama dawn wind.

Casual adolescent of urinals and evening flesh gone when I woke up—Age flakes fall through the pissoir—Ran into my old friend Jones—so badly off—Forgotten coughing in 1920 movie—Vaudeville voices hustle on bed service—I nearly suffocated trying on the boy's breath—That's Panama—Brain-eating birds patrol the low frequency brain waves—nitrous flesh swept out by your voice and end of receiving set—Sad hand tuned out the stale urine of Panama.

"I am dying, Meester?—forgotten coughing in 1920 street?"

Genital pawn ticket peeled his stale underwear, shirt flapping whiffs of young hard-on—brief boy on screen laughing my skivvies all the way down—whispers of dark street in Puerto Assis—Meester smiles through the village wastrel—Orgasm siphoned back telegram: "Johnny pants down." (that stale summer dawn smell in the garage—vines twisting through steel—bare feet in dog's excrement—)

Panama clung to our bodies from Las Palmas to David on camphor sweet smell of cooking paregoric—Burned down the republic—The druggist no glot clom Fliday—Panama mirrors of 1910 under seal in any drugstore—He threw in the towel morning light on cold coffee stale breakfast table—little cat smile—pain and death smell of his sickness in the room with me—three souvenir shots of Panama City—Old friend came

and stayed all day face eaten by "I need *more*"—I have
noticed this in the New World—

"You come with me, Meester?"

And Joselito moved in at Las Playas during the es-
sentials—Stuck in this place—iridescent lagoons,
swamp delta, bubbles of coal gas still be saying "*A ver,
Luckees*" a hundred years from now—A rotting teakwood balcony propped up Ecuador.

"Die Flowers and Jungle bouncing they can't city?"

On the sea wall two of them stood together waving
—Age flakes coming down hard here—Hurry up—
Another hollow ticket—Don't know if you got my last
hints trying to break out of this numb dizziness with
Chinese characters—I was saying over and over shifted
commissions where the awning flaps in your voice—
end of the line—Silence out there beyond the gate—
casual adolescent shirt flapping in the evening wind—

"Old photographer trick wait for Johnny—Here goes
Mexican cemetery."

On the sea wall met a boy with red- and white-
striped T-shirt—(P.G. town in the purple twilight)
—The boy peeled off his stale underwear scraping
erection—warm rain on the iron roof—under the ceiling fan stood naked on bed service—bodies touched
electric film—contact sparks tingled—fan whiffs of
young hard-on washing adolescent T-shirt—The blood
smells drowned voices and end of the line—That's
Panama—sad movie drifting in islands of rubbish,
black lagoons and fish people waiting a place forgotten

—fossil honky-tonk swept out by a ceiling fan—Old photographer trick tuned them out.

"I am dying, Meester?"

Flashes in front of my eyes naked and sullen—rotten dawn wind in sleep—death rot on Panama photo where the awning flaps.

Sad servant stood on the sea wall in sepia clouds of Panama.

"Boy I was washed face in Panama maybe undressed there. money. good bye."

Johnny Yen's last *adiós* out of focus.

1920 Movies

FILM UNION SUB spirit couldn't find the cobbled road content with an occasional Mexican in the afternoon a body sadness to say good bye smell of blood and excrement with the wind sad distant voices infer his absence as wind and dust in empty streets of Mexico.

"I am the Director. You have known me for a long time. Mister, leave cigarette money."

Iron cell wall painted flaking rust—Grifa smoke through the high grate window of blue night—Two prisoners sit on lower iron shelf bunk smoking. One is American the other Mexican—The Cell vibrates with silent blue motion of prison and all detention in time.

"Johnny I think you little bit *puto* queer."

"*Sí.*" Johnny held up thumb and finger an inch apart.

"I screw Johnny up ass? *Bueno* Johnny?" His fingers flicked Johnny's shirt. They stood up. José hung his shirt on a nail, Johnny passed shirt and José hung one shirt over the other. "*Ven acá.*" He caught Johnny's belt-end with one hand and flipped the belt-tongue out and opened fly buttons with pickpocket fingers.

"Johnny pants down. *Ya duro.* Johnny hard. I think like *mucho* be screwed."

"*Claro.*"

"Fuck Johnny, Johnny come too?"

José moved into the bunk on knees: "Like this Johnny," he slapped his thighs. "*Como perros.*"

He opened a tin of vaseline as the other moved into place and shoved a slow twisting finger up Johnny's ass.

"Johnny like?"

"*Mucho.*"

"Johnny flip now."

He held Johnny's thighs and moved his cock in slow.

"Breathe in deep Johnny."

His cock slid in as Johnny breathed in. They froze there breathing: "*Bueno,* Johnny?"

"*Bueno.*"

"*Vámanos.*" Shadow bodies twisted on the blue wall. "Johnny sure start now."

"You is coming Johnny?"

"*Siiiiiii.*"

"Here goes Johnny." Spurts cross the surplus blanket smell of iron prison flesh and clogged toilets. pickpocket finger on his balls squeezing the spurts, cock throbbing against his spine, he squeezed through a maze of penny arcades dirty pictures in the blue Mexican night. The two bodies fell languidly apart bare feet on the Army blanket. Grifa smoke blown down over black shiny pubic hairs copper and freckle flesh. Paco's cock came up in smoke.

"*Otra vez*, Johnny?" He put his hands behind Johnny's knees.

"Johnny hear knees now."

Mexican thighs: "*Como perros* I fuck you."

Walls painted blue smoke through the grate. Finger up Johnny's ass moved two prisoners. He held Johnny's thighs and vibrated silent deep Johnny. His cock slid: "Johnny, I in."

"Let's go," twisted the iron frame. "*Porqué no?*"

"*Bueno*, Johnny." Candle shadow bodies. "Johnny sure *desnudate por completo*. . . Johnny?"

"*Siiii?*"

"Here goes *completo*." Plus blankets smell of iron and shirt on nail. Mexican pickpocket one shirt over the other. Spurts maze of dirty pictures. He pushed toe blue Mexican night Johnny pants down.

Part bare feet on the blanket. Black shiny pubic hairs.

"I think like *mucho* be José—Paco—Enrique."

"*Como perros* Johnny like? Breathe José in there deep Johnny."

His cock iron frame for what not breathing: "Let's go bunk."

"You is coming plus Paco." Cross blanket smell of

Johnny flicked one shirt. Go *completo* plus Kiki. He
flipped the tongue street: "You is coming for Johnny."
  One shirt spilling head. The bodies feel cock flip out
and up.
  "*Como eso* I fuck you." One shirt spilling Johnny.
Finger on his balls. Cock flipped out and up. black
shiny pubic head. the bodies smoke.
  "Fuck on knees. Lie down blanket. *Como eso*
through the iron." He feel tongue on knees. smoke
fuck on knees.
  "*Mucho* be *ángel como eso*."
  "Deep Johnny."
  Shoved white knees. Vaseline finger vibrate thighs.
"Flip now."
  "Paco? slow."
  "*Sí*, the ass Johnny? I screw Johnny up ass?"
  Spurts prison flesh to Mexican night: "Vibrate,
Johnny."
  "I screw Johnny."
  "Let's go."
  "Johnny knees down. *Boca abajo*. You is coming
como eso?"
  "Hard bunk Johnny. Me up in Freckles. *Como
perros* like on knees."
  "I screw Johnny Mexican. Smoke fuck Johnny.
Como eso Johnny fuck on knees."
  He feel flipped the knees. "You is coming *otra vez*
Johnny?" He flipped Johnny. vaseline finger see the
ass. one shirt spilling Johnny flicked out and up.
  "One *mucho* Johnny flip now."

"Breathe José into hilt ass Johnny."

"Start now."

"You is coming?"

Spurts cross *calzoncillos todo*. José hung his prison flesh. Finger on his balls feel "come here." He caught Johnny belt spine. He feel flipped the belt-tongue cross pickpocket fingers. The bodies fell languidly. Cock flipped out and up. Grifa smoke blown down line. "*A ver* like this." He clipped into the bunk on knees like: "*Como perros* come Johnny."

José knees. Vaseline finger twisting Johnny's thighs.

"Flip now. José slow deep Johnny." His cock slid ass Johnny.

"*Bueno* Johnny?"

Breathing: "Let's go bunk. Johnny candle shadow now."

"You is coming *por completo*."

"*Siiii*," spurts spilling cross pickpocket toe Mexican night cock flipped out and up. Part bare feet.

"Fuck on knees like" (Moving two prisoners in the blue? Is American bunk?)

"*Mucho* Johnny vibrate blue pressure. Breathe José in there. *Sí* iron frame."

"*Porqué no?*"

"Johnny here go *completo* plus Kiki." Hung his prison flesh on nail.

Johnny toilet finger on his balls feel other spurts cock. He fell flipped the pictures. The bodies fell street.

"*Claro* you like *mucho* be Kiki. *A ver. Como eso.*" Just

hula hoop through each other to idiot Mambo. . .all idiot Mambo spattered to control mechanization.

"Salt Chunk Mary" had all the "nos" and none of them ever meant "yes." She named a price heavy and cold as a cop's blackjack on a winter night and that was it. She didn't name another. Mary didn't like talk and she didn't like talkers. She received and did business in the kitchen. And she kept it in a sugar bowl. Nobody thought about that. Her cold grey eyes would have seen the thought and maybe something goes wrong on the next lay John Citizen come up with a load of 00 into your soft and tenders or Johnny Law just happens by. She sat there and heard. When you spread the gear out on her kitchen table she already knows where you sloped it. She looks at the gear and a price falls out heavy and cold and her mouth closes and stays shut. If she doesn't want to do business she just wraps the gear up and shoves it back across the table and that is that. Mary keeps a blue coffee pot and a pot of salt pork and beans always on the wood stove. When you fall in she gets up without a word and puts a mug of coffee and plate of salt chunk in front of you. You eat and then you talk business. Or maybe you take a room for a week to cool off. room 18 on the top floor I was sitting in the top room rose wall paper smoky sunset across the river. I was new in the game and like all young thieves thought I had a license to steal. It didn't last. Sitting there waiting on the Japanese girl works in the Chink laundry a soft knock and I open the door naked with a hard-on it was the top floor all the way up you understand nobody on that landing. "Ooooh" she says feeling it up to my oysters a drop of lubricant squeezed out and took the smoky sunset on rose wall paper I'd been sitting there naked thinking about what we were going to do in the rocking chair rocks off down the line she could get out of her dry goods faster than a junky can fix when his blood is right so we rocked away into the sunset across the river just before blast off that old knock on the door and I shoot this fear load like I never feel it wind up is her young brother at the door in his cop suit been watching through the key hole and learn about the birds and the bees some bee I was in those days good looking kid had all my teeth and she knew all the sex currents goose for pimple always made her entrance when your nuts are tight and aching a red haired smoky rose sunset one bare knee rubbing greasy pink wall paper he was naked with a hard-on waiting on the Mexican girl from Marty's a pearl of lubricant squeezed slowly out and glittered on the tip of his cock. There was a soft knock at the door. He got up off the crumpled bed and opened the door. The girl's brother stood there smiling. The red haired boy made a slight choking sound as blood rushed to his face pounded and sang in his ears. The young face there on the landing turned black around the edges. The red haired boy sagged against the door jamb. He came to on the bed the Mexican kid standing over him.

"All right now? Sis can't come."

The Mexican kid unbuttoned his shirt. He kicked

off his sandals dropped his pants and shorts grinning and his cock flipped out half up. The Mexican kid brought his finger up in three jerks and his cock came up with it nuts tight pubic hairs glistening black he sat down on the bed.

"Vaseline?"

The red haired boy pointed to the night table. He was lying on the bed breathing deeply his knees up. The Mexican kid took a jar of vaseline out of a drawer. He kneeled on the bed and put his hands behind the freckled knees and shoved the boy's knees up to his trembling red ears. He rubbed vaseline on the pink rectum with a slow circular pull. The red haired boy gasped and his rectum spread open. The Mexican kid slid his cock in. The two boys locked together breathing in each other's lungs. After the girl left I walk down to Marty's where I meet this Johnson has a disgruntled former chauffeur map indicates where a diamond necklace waits for me wall safe behind the Blue Period. Or maybe you Picasso on Rembrandt and cool off like I was sitting in a Turner sunset on the Japanese girl doing my simple artisan job hot and heavy. Mary she kept the guide ready her eyes heavy and cold as a cop's come around with the old birds and bees business. Nobody thought about that cold outside agent call. Recall John Citizen came up on her. Johnny Law just happens by magic shop in Westbourne Grove. Smell these conditions of ash? I twig that old knack. Klinker is dead. Blackout fell on these foreign suburbs here.

"Be careful of the old man. kinda special deputy carries a gun in the car."

Music fading in the East St. Louis night broken junk of exploded star sad servant of the inland side shirt flapping in a wind across the golf course a black silver sky of broken film precarious streets of yesterday back from shadows the boy solid now I could touch almost you know both of us use the copper luster basin in the blue attic room now Johnny's back. Who else put a slow cold hand on your shoulder shirt flapping shadows on a wall long ago fading streets a distant sky?

They walked through a city of black and white movies fading streets of thousand-run smoke faces. figures of the world slow down to catatonic limestone.

City blocks speed up out in photo flash. Hotel lobbies 1920 time fill with slow grey film fallout and funeral urns of Hollywood. Never learn? The guide clicked him through a silent turnstile into a cubicle of blue glass and mirrors so that any panel of the room was at alternate intervals synchronized with the client's sex-pulse mirror or wall of glass into the next cell on all sides and the arrangement was an elaborate permutation and very technical. . . So Johnny the Guide said: "The first clause in our blue contract is known as the examination to which both parties must submit. . . We call it the probing period, now isn't that cute?"

The guide put on helmet of photo goggles and antennae of orange neon flickering, smelling bat wings: "Johnny pants down. Johnny cock hard." He brought his arm up from the elbow swimming in for close-ups of Johnny's erection: take slow and take fast under flickering vowel colors: I red/U green/E white/O blue/A black/"Bend over Johnny." The examiner floats up from the floor, swims down through heavy water from the ceiling, shoots up from toilet bowl, English baths, underwater takes of genitals and pubic hairs in warm spermy water. The goggles lick over his body phosphorescent moths, through rectal hairs orange halos flicker around his penis. In his sleep, naked Panama nights, the camera pulsing in blue silence and ozone smells, sometimes the cubicle open out on all sides into purple space. X-ray photos of viscera and fecal movements, his body a transparent blue fish.

"So that's the examination we call it, sees all your processes. You can't deceive us in any way at all and now you got the right to examine me."

Lee put on the photo goggles melt in head and saw the guide now blond with brown eyes slender and tilted forward. He moved in for a close-up of the boy's flank and took his shirt off followed the pants down, circled the pubic hair forest in slow autogyros, zeroed in for the first stirrings of tumescence, swooping from the stiffening blood tube to the boy's face, sucking eyes with neon proboscis, licking testicles and rectum. The goggles and antennae fade in smoke and slow street-eyes swim up from grey dust and funeral urns. and in his sleep naked blue movies slow motion. Pulsing blue silence photos genitals and pubic hairs in rectal mucus and carbolic soap. Alternate mirror and screen guide put on goggles walked through grey-filled shadows that melted in his head. In time focus the natives. like flickering bat wings over faded thousand-run faces, hearing, smelling through them like: "Johnny cock hard." Slowdown to statues with catatonic erection slow falling through colors red green black. A hot spread: cheeks close-up. And felt over Johnny's body the slow float down from Hollywood. came to the hot Panama nights. They clicked in through a squat toilet with walls of blue glass and underwater shots of warm soapy spermy water smell. so felt the boy neon fingers on sex spots breathing through sponge rock penis-flesh and brown intestine jungles lined with flesh-eating vines and frantic parasites of the area. . .

Naked in the Panama night, rectal mucus and car-bolic soap. A blue screen guide put on goggles. Pale panels of shadow melted his head on all sides into blue silent wings over the clock of fecal movement smelling through them like transparent.

"A hot spread examination we call it. Johnny's body can't deceive us in any way. Came to the hot Panama nights to examine me."

Clicked into his head of blue glass. Close-up neon finger over the scar-impressions learning the instrument panels, recording on the transparent flesh of present time. It is happening right now. Slow 1920 finger rubbing vaseline on the cobra lamps, flickering movie shadows into the blue void. pulling finger rolls a cuneiform cylinder. Lens eye drank the boy's jissom in yellow light.

"Now Meester we flick fluck I me you cut." The two film tracks ran through impression screen. one track flash on other cut out in dark until cut back: "Me finish Johnny's shit. . . Clom through Johnny. . ." Hear rectums merging in flicks and orgasm of mutual processes. and pulsed in and out of each other's body on slow gills of sleep in the naked Panama nights and bent over the washstand in East St. Louis junk-sick dawn. smell of carbolic soap and rectal mucus and train whistle wake of blue silence and piss through my cock "I-you-me-fuck-up-ass-all-same-time-four-eyes." phantom cleavage crude and rampant. Every citizen can now grow sex forms in his bidet: in the night of Talara felt his hard-on against my khaki pants as we shifted slots and I browned a strange Danish dog under the nudes of Sweden. Warm spermy smell, room of blue glass strung together on light-lines of jissom and shit, shared meals and belches, the shifting of testes and contractions of rectum, flick-fluck back and forth.

"Here goes Johnny. We fluck now first run": in blue silence saw the two one track out: blue. Each meet image coming round the other erection-fucked-self and came other shit both.

"We flick-fluck I-you-film-tracks through rectal mucus and carbolic soap. Cut out pale panels of shadow." blue silent bat wings over rectums blending in transparent erection. a hot shit and all process together.

"Johnny's body can't deceive us in other body. slow night to examine me." sick dawn smell of carbolic finger. close-up finger on all cocks.

"I-you-me fuck up neon blind fingers phantom cleavage of boy impressions Witch Board of Present Time."

The idiot green boys leaped on Johnny like tree frogs clinging to his chest with sucker paws fungoid gills and red mushroom penis pulsing to the sex waves from Johnny eyes. warm spermy smell, lamps and flicker movies strung together on a million fingers shared meals and belches and lens-eye drank jissom. contract of rectum flight: "Here goes Johnny. One flight out." Screen other rectum naked in Panama night.

Ghost of Panama clung to our throats, coughing and spitting on separate spasm, phosphorescent breath fades in fractured air—sick flesh strung together on a million fingers shared meals and belches—nothing here now but circling word dust—dead post card falling through space between worlds—this road in this sharp smell of carrion—

We twisted slowly to black lagoons, flower floats and gondolas—tentative crystal city iridescent in the dawn wind—(Adolescents ejaculate over the tide flats.)

In the blue windy morning masturbating a soiled idiot body of cold scar tissue—catatonic limestone hands folded over his yen—a friend of any boy structure cut by a species of mollusk—Street boys of the green gathered—slow bronze smiles from a land of grass without memory—cool casual little ghosts of adolescent spasm—metal excrement and crystal glooms of the fish city—under a purple twilight our clothes shredded mummy linen on obsidian floors—Panama clung to our bodies—

"You come with me, Meester?"

Northern lights flicker from his "Yes"—The rope is adjusted—Writhing in wind black hair bursts through his flesh—Great canines tear into his gums with exquisite toothache pleasure—The green cab boys go all the way on any line.

Green boys—idiot irresponsibles—rolling in warm delta ooze fuck in color flashes through green jelly flesh that quivers together merging and drawing back in a temple dance of colors. "Hot licks us all the way we are all one clear green substance like flexible amber changing color and consistency to accommodate any occasion."

"This bad place Meester. You crazy or something walk around alone. Where you go?" The guide: impersonal screen swept by color winds light up green red white blue. antennae ears of flexible metal cartilage crackle blue spark messages leaving smell of ozone in the shiny black pubic hairs that grow on the guide's pink skull. blood and nerves hard meat cleaver his whole body would scorn to carry a weapon. And Being inside was him and more. face cut by image-flak impersonal young pilot eyes riding light rays pulsing through his head.

"Fluck Johnny? Up ass?" He guided Carl with electric tingles in spine and sex hairs through clicking gates and turnstiles, escalators and cable cars in synchronized motion. Impersonal young pilot eyes riding the blue silence permutated Carl into an iron cubicle with painted

blue walls pallet on the floor brass tea tray kif pipes
and jars of phosphorescent green sex paste. wall over
the pallet two-way mirrors opposite wall of glass opening on the next cubicle and so on, sex acts into the blue
distance. The Guide pointed to the mirror: "We fuck
good Johnny. On air now."

"Johnny pants down"—he was smearing the sex paste
on "Johnny's" ass hot licking the white nerves and
pearly genitals—Carl's lips and tongue swelled with
blood and his face went phosphorescent penis purple—
slow penetrating incandescent flesh tubes siphoned his
body into a pulsing sphere of blue jelly floated over
skeletons locked in limestone—The cubicles shifted—
Carl was siphoned back through the Guide and landed
with a fluid plop as the cubicles permutated fucking
shadows through ceilings of legs and sex hairs, black
spirals of phantom assholes lifting and twisting like a
Panhandle cyclone.

UNIT I: WHITE: "You wanta screw me?" "I wanta
screw you." Two marble white youths with identical
erections stand on a white tile bathroom floor. The
young faces sharp flash bulb of urgency fade-out
stale empty of hunger. (Crystal flute music. The boys
step from Attic frieze on Greek urns.)

Tarnished pub mirrors of the gentle ghost-people,
grey faded clubs under yellowing tusks of the beast
killed by improbable hyphenated names. In bath cubicles and locker rooms shut for the summer white light
bent over a chair—

UNIT II: BLACK: "Bend over." As the white youth bends over turns brown then black. The other half drums on his back. The youths fade in obsidian mirror, smell of opium and copal.

UNIT III: GREEN: "Loosen you up a bit." Black finger dips into green jelly. The finger turns green in rusty limestone with a slow circular pull. green boy of flexible green amber, bright lizards and beetles incrusted here and there, twists sighs out in jungle sound of frogs and bird calls and howler monkeys like wind in the trees, slow movement of rivers and forests cross the Drenched Lands. Vines twist through the boys smell of mud flats where sting rays bask in shallow canals brown with excrement sewage delta and coal gas swamps under orange gas flares and grey metal fallout.

UNIT IV: RED: "Breathe in Johnny. Here goes." Red youths fuck bent over a brass bed in Mexico. feel through a maze of penny arcades and dirty pictures to the blue Mexican night. penis of different size, shape swell in and out flicker faces and bodies burning flesh sparks from camp fires and red fuck lights in blue cubicles.

UNIT V: BLUE: SILENCE. The two bodies merge in a blue sphere. Vapor trails cross a blue sky. Out on a blue wave high fi cool and blue as liquid air in our slate-blue houses wrapped in orange flesh-robes that grow on us.

UNIT I: WHITE: The boys slow down to phallic statues. They fade out in old photos and 1920 movies. hairs rub the exquisite toothache pleasure: "I wanta screw you." Flash bulb of urgency fade: "Loosen you up a bit." The finger turns green out in stale streets of cry.

UNIT III: GREEN: The green boy of green flute music. worn amber with lizards incrusted and finger rusty sighs out in the spectral smell of birdcalls and howler monkeys like gentle ghost-people. slow movement of brown rivers. The boys in speed-up and barracks toilet smell of the mud flats and the white youths fuck brown with excrement under a static red sky. smell of subway dawns and turnstile. tarnished pub mirrors jungle sound of frogs. army of trees killed by the improbable hyphenated name. tendril movement in white light.

UNIT V: BLUE: "The initiate awoke in other flesh the lookout different." Cool blue casual youth check Board Books of the world finger light and cold as Spring wind. Little high blue notes drift through slate-blue houses. Street gangs Uranian born in the face of appalling conditions. Fade-out in "Mr. Bradly Mr. Martin" down the flash funnel of copy faces out in summer dawn we made it in a smell of carbolic soap and rectal mucus. slow green tendrils through the hair and the purple fungoid gills breathe empty green house. plaintive monkey phallus on the grave of dying peoples. red mesas cut by a blue wind. Copper youths languidly masturbate, coming in puffs of blue smoke cross the translucent red stone buildings and copper domes of the city a white

tooth sky cut with vapor trails. flash bulb of urgency
train whistles fade in black finger and basement pot.
cool blue light in stale streets of cry. In the hyacinths
green boys of a green flute music sigh out birdcalls
and howler monkey like: "You wanta screw me?" slow
movement of rivers. the boy's unit green with shit
smell of the mud flats. Jelly substance like excrement
flares under static red sky. Like smell RED: "Breathe in
Johnny. Here goes." Twisting over a brass bed in Mexico. The boys slow fucking shift old photos and 1910
movie of the two bodies. merge in blue smoke rings
loosen you up out drift away slate-blue Northern sky
water. limestone cave fades in blue drum of gentle
ghost-people. draft youths with indentical erection
in speed-up barracks orgasm. pub mirrors green fade
movie club. under the faces improbable names. green
boys formed the fuck drum message lights a blue
flame inside phallus (boy ear, blue sky). The initiate
awoke in the city of red stone different train whistle
masturbate with fingers light as Spring smoke. cross
road of the world the high blue domes of the city
and blue children born in the face of white battle. bulb
of urgency train war unit. Mr. Bradly cool blue down
the flash funnel out in stale summer dawn smell.
black drum talks mucus. The youths twist flowers and
sewers of the world. drum puffs of paint flesh. "flesh diseased dirty pictures how long you want us to fuck very
nice Mister? To cheat and betray us been sent?"

We got to untalking on question studying the porch
noise home from work used to be me Mister diseased

waiting face return various bits and pieces of the picture: that he coin a "nice-guy-myth" the bastard dirtier than Coin Smell Dorm.

"What you trying to unload on somebody Mister? radioactive garbage?"

Where You Belong

MY TROUBLE BEGAN when they decide I am executive timber—It starts like this: a big blond driller from Dallas picks me out of the labor pool to be his house-boy in a prefabricated air-conditioned bungalow—He comes on rugged but as soon as we strip down to the ball park over on his stomach kicking white wash and screams out "Fuck the shit out of me!"—I give him a slow pimp screwing and in solid—When this friend comes down from New York the driller says "This is the boy I was telling you about"—And friend looks me over slow chewing his cigar and says: "What are you doing over there with the apes? Why don't you come over here with the Board where you belong?" And he slips me a long slimy look Friend works for the

Trak News Agency—"We don't report the news—We write it." And next thing I know they have trapped a grey flannel suit on me and I am sent to this school in Washington to learn how this writing the news before it happens is done—I sus it is the Mayan Caper with an IBM machine and I don't want to be caught short in a grey flannel suit when the lid blows off—So I act in concert with the Subliminal Kid who is a technical sergeant and has a special way of talking. And he stands there a long time chewing tobacco is our middle name "—What are you doing over there?—Beat your mother to over here—Know what they mean if they start job for instance?—Open shirt, apparent sensory impressions calling slimy terms of the old fifty-fifty jazz—Kiss their target all over—Assembly points in Danny Deever—By now they are controlling shithouse of the world—Just feed in sad-eyed youths and the machine will process it —After that Minraud sky—Their eggs all over—These officers come gibbering into the queer bar don't even know what buttons to push—('Run with the apes? Why don't you come across the lawn?') And he gives me a long slimy responsible cum grey flannel suit and I am Danny Deever in drag writing 'the news is served, sir.' Hooded dead gibber: 'this is the Mayan Caper'— A fat cigar and a long white nightie—Nonpayment answer is simple as Board Room Reports rigged a thousand years—Set up excuse and the machine will process it—Moldy pawn ticket runs a thousand years chewing the same argument—I Sekuin perfected that art along the Tang Dynasty—To put it another way IBM machine controls thought feeling and *apparent* sensory impressions—Subliminal lark—These officers don't even know what buttons to push—Whatever you feed into the machine on subliminal level the machine will process—So we feed in 'dismantle thyself' and authority emaciated down to answer Mr of the Account in Ewyork, Onolulu, Aris, Ome, Oston—Might be just what I am look"—

We fold writers of all time in together and record radio programs, movie sound tracks, TV and juke box songs all the words of the world stirring around in a cement mixer and pour in the resistance message "Calling partisans of all nation—Cut word lines—Shift linguals—Free doorways—Vibrate 'tourists'—Word falling—Photo falling—Break through in Grey Room."

So the District Supervisor calls me in and puts the old white smaltz down on me:

"Now kid what are you doing over there with the niggers and the apes? Why don't you straighten out and act like a white man?—After all they're only human cattle—You know that yourself—Hate to see a bright young man fuck up and get off on the wrong track—Sure it happens to all of us one time or another—Why the man who went on to invent Shitola was sitting right where you're sitting now twenty-five years ago and I was saying the same things to him—Well he straightened out the way you're going to straighten out—Yes sir that Shitola combined with an ape diet—All we have to do is press the button and a hundred million more or less gooks flush down the drain in green cancer piss—

That's *big* isn't it?—And any man with white blood in him wants to be part of something big—You can't deny your blood kid—You're *white white white*—And you can't walk out on Trak—There's just no place to go."

Most distasteful thing I ever stood still for—Enough to make a girl crack her calories—So I walk out and the lid blew off—

Uranian Willy

URANIAN WILLY the Heavy Metal Kid, also known as Willy the Rat—He wised up the marks.

"This is war to extermination—Fight cell by cell through bodies and mind screens of the earth—Souls rotten from the Orgasm Drug—Flesh shuddering from the Ovens—Prisoners of the earth, come out—Storm the studio."

His plan called for total exposure—Wise up all the marks everywhere Show them the rigged wheel—Storm the Reality Studio and retake the universe—The plan shifted and reformed as reports came in from his electric patrols sniffing quivering down streets of the earth—the reality film giving and buckling like a bulkhead under pressure—burned metal smell of inter-

planetary war in the raw noon streets swept by screaming glass blizzards of enemy flak.

"Photo falling—Word falling—Use partisans of all
nations—Target Orgasm Ray Installations—Gothenburg Sweden—Coordinates 8 2 7 6—Take Studio—
Take Board Books—Take Death Dwarfs—Towers, open
fire."

Pilot K9 caught the syndicate killer image on a penny
arcade screen and held it in his sight—Now he was
behind it in it was it—The image disintegrated in photo
flash of total recognition—Other image on screen—Hold
in sight—Smell of burning metal in his head—"Pilot
K9, you are cut off—Back—Back—Back before the
whole fucking shithouse goes up—Return to base immediately—Ride music beam back to base—Stay out of
that time flak—All pilots ride Pan Pipes back to base."

It was impossible to estimate the damage—Board
Books destroyed—Enemy personnel decimated—The
message of total resistance on short wave of the world.

"Calling partisans of all nations—Shift linguals—Cut
word lines—Vibrate tourists—Free doorways—Photo
falling—Word falling—Break through in Grey Room."

Gongs of Violence

THE WAR BETWEEN the sexes split the planet into armed
camps right down the middle line divides one thing
from the other—And I have seen them all: The Lesbian
colonels in tight green uniforms, the young aides and
directives regarding the Sex Enemy from proliferating
departments.

On the line is the Baby and Semen Market where the
sexes meet to exchange the basic commodity which is
known as the "property"—Unborn properties are shown
with a time projector. As a clear young going face
flashes on the auction screen frantic queens of all nations scream: "A doll! A doll! A doll!" And tear each
other to pieces with leopard claws and broken bottles—
tobacco auction sound effects—Riots erupt like sand-

storms spraying the market with severed limbs and bouncing heads.

Biological parents in most cases are not owners of the property. They act under orders of absentee proprietors to install the indicated stops that punctuate the written life script—With each Property goes a life script—Shuttling between property farmers and script writers, a legion of runners, fixers, guides, agents, brokers, faces insane with purpose, mistakes and confusion pandemic—Like a buyer has a first-class Property and a lousy grade B life script.

"Fuck my life script will you you cheap downgrade bitch!"

Everywhere claim-jumpers and time-nappers jerk the time position of a property.

"And left me standing there without a 'spare jacket' or a 'greyhound' to travel in, my property back in 1910 Panama—I don't even feel like a human without my property—How can I feel without fingers?"

The property can also be jerked forward in time and sold at any age—The life of advanced property is difficult to say the least: poison virus agents trooping in and out at all hours: "We just dropped in to see some friends a population of patrols"—Strangers from Peoria waving quit claim deeds, skip tracers, collectors, claim-jumpers demanding payment for alleged services say: "We own the other half of the property."

"I dunno, me—Only work here—Technical Sergeant."

"Have you seen Slotless City?"

Red mesas cut by time winds—A network of bridges,

ladders, catwalks, cable cars, escalators and ferris
wheels down into the blue depths—The precarious
occupants in this place without phantom guards live
in iron cubicles—constant motion on tracks, gates click
open shut—buzzes, blue sparks, and constant breakage
—(Whole squares and tiers of the city plunge into the
bottomless void)—Swinging beams of construction and
blue flares on the calm intent young worker faces—
People rain on the city in homemade gliders and rockets
—Balloons drift down out of faded violet photos—The
city is reached overland by a series of trails cut in stone,
suspension bridges and ladders intricately booby-
trapped, wrong maps, disappearing guides—(A falling
bureaucrat in blue glasses screams by with a flash of
tin: "*Soy de la policia, señores—Tengo conexiónes*)
hammocks, swings, balconies over the void—chemical
gardens in rusty troughs—flowers and seeds and mist
settle down from high jungle above the city—Fights
erupt like sandstorms, through iron streets a wake of
shattered bodies, heads bouncing into the void, hands
clutching bank notes from gambling fights—Priests
shriek for human sacrifices, gather partisans to initiate
unspeakable rites until they are destroyed by counter
pressures—Vigilantes of every purpose hang anyone
they can overpower—Workers attack the passer-by with
torches and air hammers—They reach up out of man-
holes and drag the walkers down with iron claws—
Rioters of all nations storm the city in a landslide of
flame-throwers and Molotov cocktails—Sentries posted
everywhere in towers open fire on the crowds at arbi-

trary intervals—The police never mesh with present
time, their investigation far removed from the city always before or after the fact erupt into any café and
machine-gun the patrons—The city pulses with slotless
purpose lunatics killing from behind the wall of glass—
A moment's hesitation brings a swarm of con men,
guides, whores, mooches, script writers, runners, fixers
cruising and snapping like aroused sharks—

(The subway sweeps by with a black blast of iron.)

The Market is guarded by Mongolian Archers right in
the middle line between sex pressures jetting a hate
wave that disintegrates violators in a flash of light—
Everywhere posted on walls and towers in hovering
autogyros these awful archers only get relief from the
pressure by blasting a violator—Screen eyes vibrate
through the city like electric dogs sniffing for viola-
tions—

Remind the Board of the unsavory case of "Black
Paul" who bought babies with centipede jissom—
When the fraud came to light a whole centipede issue
was in the public streets and every citizen went armed
with a flame-thrower—So the case of Black Paul shows
what happens when all sense of civic responsibility
breaks down—

It was a transitional period because of the Synthetics
and everybody was raising some kinda awful life form
in his bidet to fight the Sex Enemy—The results were
not in all respects reasonable men, but the Synthetics
were rolling off that line and we were getting some
damned interesting types by golly blue heavy metal

boys with near zero metabolism that shit once a century and then it's a slag heap and disposal problem in the worst form there is: sewage delta to a painted sky under orange gas flares, islands of garbage where green boy-girls tend human heads in chemical gardens, terminal cities under the metal word fallout like cold melted solder on walls and streets, sputtering cripples with phosphorescent metal stumps—So we decided the blue heavy metal boys were not in all respects a good blueprint.

I have seen them all—A unit yet of mammals and vegetables that subsist each on the shit of the other in prestidigital symbiosis and achieved a stage where one group shit out nothing but pure carbon dioxide which the other unit breathed in to shit out oxygen— It's the only way to live—You understand they had this highly developed culture with life forms between insect and vegetable, hanging vines, stinging sex hairs —The whole deal was finally relegated to It-Never-Happened-Department.

"Retroactive amnesia it out of every fucking mind screen in the area if we have to—How long you want to bat this tired old act around? A centipede issue in the street, unusual beings dormant in cancer, hierarchical shit-eating units—Now by all your stupid Gods at once let's not get this show on the road let's stop it."

Posted everywhere on street corners the idiot irresponsibles twitter supersonic approval, repeating slogans, giggling, dancing, masturbating out windows, making machine-gun noises and police whistles "And you, Dead Hand, stretching the Vegetable People come out of that compost heap—You are not taking your old fibrous roots past this inspector."

And the idiot irresponsibles scream posted everywhere in chorus: "Chemical gardens in rusty shit peoples!!"

"All out of time and into space. Come out of the time-word 'the' forever. Come out of the body word 'thee' forever. There is nothing to fear. There is no thing in space. There is no word to fear. There is no word in space."

And the idiot irresponsibles scream: "Come out of your stupid body you nameless assholes!!"

And there were those who thought A.J. lost dignity through the idiotic behavior of these properties but he said:

"That's the way I like to see them. No fallout. What good ever came from thinking? Just look there" (another heavy metal boy sank through the earth's crust and we got some good pictures. . .) "one of Shaffer's blueprints. I sounded a word of warning."

His idiot irresponsibles twittered and giggled and masturbated over him from little swings and snapped bits of food from his plate screaming: "Blue people NG conditions! Typical sight leak out!"

"All out of time and into space."

"Hello, Ima Johnny. the naked astronaut."

And the idiot irresponsibles rush in with space-suits and masturbating rockets spatter the city with jissom.

"Do not be alarmed citizens of Annexia—Report to

your Nearie Pro Station for chlorophyll processing—
We are converting to vegetable state—Emergency
measure to counter the heavy metal peril—Go to your
'Nearie'—You will meet a cool, competent person who
will dope out all your fears in photosynthesis—Calling
all citizens of Annexia—Report to Green Sign for processing."

"Citizens of Gravity we are converting all out to
Heavy Metal. Carbonic Plague of the Vegetable People threatens our Heavy Metal State. Report to your
nearest Plating Station. It's fun to be plated," says this
well-known radio and TV personality who is now engraved forever in gags of metal. "Do not believe the
calumny that our metal fallout will turn the planet into
a slag heap. And in any case, is that worse than a compost heap? Heavy Metal is our program and we are
prepared to sink through it. . ."

The cold heavy fluid settled in his spine 70 tons per
square inch—Cool blocks of SOS—(Solid Blue Silence)
—under heavy time—Can anything be done to metal
people of Uranus?—Heavy his answer in monotone disaster stock: "Nobody can kick an SOS habit—70 tons
per square inch—The crust from the beginning you
understand—Tortured metal Ozz of earthquakes is tons
focus of this junk"—Sudden young energy—I got up
and danced—Know eventually be relieved—That's all
I need—I got up and danced the disasters—"

Gongs of violence and how—Show you something—
Berserk machine—"Shift cut tangle word lines—Word
falling—Photo falling—"

"I said the Chief of Police skinned alive in Bagdad not Washington, D.C."

"Switzerland freezes all foreign assets."

"Foreign assets?"

"What?—British Prime Minister assassinated in Rightist coup?"

"Mindless idiot you have liquidated the Commissar."

"Terminal electric voice of C—All ling door out of agitated—Ta ta Stalin—Carriage age ta—"

Spectators scream through the track—The electronic brain shivers in blue and pink and chlorophyll orgasms spitting out money printed on rolls of toilet paper, condoms full of ice cream, Kotex hamburgers—Police files of the world spurt out in a blast of bone meal, garden tools and barbecue sets whistle through the air, skewer the spectators—crumpled cloth bodies through dead nitrous streets of an old film set—grey luminous flakes falling softly on Ewyork, Onolulu, Aris, Ome, Oston— From siren towers the twanging tones of fear—Pan God of Panic piping blue notes through empty streets as the berserk time machine twisted a tornado of years and centuries—Wind through dusty offices and archives —Board Books scattered to rubbish heaps of the earth —Symbol books of the all-powerful board that had controlled thought feeling and movement of a planet from birth to death with iron claws of pain and pleasure— The whole structure of reality went up in silent explosions—Paper moon and muslin trees and in the black silver sky great rents as the cover of the world rained down—Biologic film went up. . . "raining dinosaurs" "It sometimes happens. . .just an old showman" Death takes over the game so many actors buildings and stars laid flat pieces of finance over the golf course summer afternoons bare feet waiting for rain smell of sickness in the room Switzerland Panama machine guns in Bagdad rising from the typewriter pieces of finance on the evening wind tin shares Buenos Aires Mr. Martin smiles old names waiting sad old tune haunted the last human attic.

Outside a 1920 movie theater in East St. Louis I met Johnny Yen—His face showed strata of healed and half-healed fight scars—Standing there under the luminous film flakes he said: "I am going to look for a room in a good naborhood"—Captain Clark welcomes you aboard this languid paradise of dreamy skies and firefly evenings music across the golf course echoes from high cool corners of the dining room a little breeze stirs candles on the table. It was an April afternoon. After a while some news boy told him the war was over sadness in his eyes trees filtering light on dappled grass the lake like bits of silver paper in a wind across the golf course fading streets a distant sky.

WAS WEIGHTLESS—NEW YORK HERALD TRIBUNE PARIS APRIL 17, 1961—"One's arms and legs in and out through the crowd weigh nothing—Grey dust of broom in old cabin—Mr. Bradly Mr. I Myself sit in the chair as I subways and basements did before that—But hung in dust and pain wind—My hand writing leaning to a boy's grey flannel pants did not change although vapor trails fading in hand does

not weigh anything now—Gagarin said grey junk yes-
terdays trailing the earth was quite plain and past the
American he could easily see the shores of continents
—islands and great rivers."

"Captain Clark welcomes you aboard."

Dead Fingers Talk

GLAD TO HAVE you aboard reader, but remember there is only one captain of this subway—Do not thrust your cock out the train window or beckon lewdly with thy piles nor flush thy beat benny down the drain— (Benny is overcoat in antiquated Times Square argot) —It is forbidden to use the signal rope for frivolous hangings or to burn Nigras in the washroom before the other passengers have made their toilet—

Do not offend the office manager—He is subject to take back the keys of the shithouse—Always keep it locked so no sinister stranger sneak a shit and give all the kids in the office some horrible condition—And Mr. Anker from accounting, his arms scarred like a junky from countless Wassermans, sprays plastic over it before he travails there—I stand on the Fifth Amendment, will not answer the question of the Senator from Wisconsin: "Are you or have you ever been a member of the male sex?"—They can't make Dicky whimper on the boys—Know how I take care of crooners?—Just listen to them—A word to the wise guy—I mean you gotta be careful of politics these days—Some old department get physical with you, kick him right in his coordinator—"Come see me tonight in my apartment under the school privy—Show you something interesting," said the janitor drooling green coca juice—

The city mutters in the distance pestilent breath of the cancerous librarian faint and intermittent on the warm Spring wind—

"Split is the wastings of the cup—Take it away," he said irritably—Black rocks and brown lagoons invade the world—There stands the deserted transmitter—Crystal tubes click on the message of retreat from the human hill and giant centipedes crawl in the ruined cities of our long home—Thermodynamics has won at a crawl—

"We were caught with our pants down," admits General Patterson. "They reamed the shit out of us."

Safest way to avoid these horrid perils is come over here and shack up with Scylla—Treat you right, kid—Candy and cigarettes—

Woke up in a Turkish Bath under a Johannesburg bidonville—

"Where am I you black bastards?"

"Why you junky white trash rim a shitting Nigger for an eyecup of paregoric?"

Dead bird—quail in the slipper—money in the bank —Past port and petal crowned with calm leaves she stands there across the river and under the trees—

Brains spilled in the cocktail lounge—The fat *macho* has burned down the Jai Lai bookie with his obsidian-handled .45—Shattering bloody blue of Mexico—Heart in the sun—Pantless corpses hang from telephone poles along the road to Monterrey—

Death rows the boy like sleeping marble down the Grand Canal out into a vast lagoon of souvenir post cards and bronze baby shoes—

"Just build a privy over me, boys," says the rustler to his bunk mates, and the sheriff nods in dark understanding Druid blood stirring in the winds of Panhandle—

Decayed corseted tenor sings Danny Deever in drag:

They have taken all his buttons off and cut his pants away

For he browned the colonel sleeping the man's ass is all agley

And he'll swing in 'arf a minute for sneaking shooting fey.

"Billy Budd must hang—All hands after to witness this exhibit."

Billy Budd gives up the ghost with a loud fart and the sail is rent from top to bottom—and the petty officers fall back confounded—"Billy" is a transvestite liz.

"There'll be a spot of bother about this," mutters The Master at Arms—The tars scream with rage at the cheating profile in the rising sun—

"Is she dead?"

"So who cares."

"Are we going to stand still for this?—The officers pull the switch on us," says young Hassan, ship's uncle—

"Gentlemen," says Captain Verre "I can not find words to castigate this foul and unnatural act whereby a boy's mother take over his body and infiltrate her horrible old substance right onto a decent boat and with bare tits hanging out, unfurls the nastiest colors of the spectroscope."

A hard-faced matron bandages the cunt of Radiant Jade—

"You see, dearie, the shock when your neck breaks has like an awful effect—You're already dead of course or at least unconscious or at least stunned—but—uh—well —you see—It's a *medical fact*—All your female insides is subject to spurt out your cunt the way it turned the last doctor to stone and we sold the results to Paraguay as a state of Bolivar."

"I have come to ascertain death not perform a hysterectomy," snapped the old auntie croaker munching a soggy crumpet with his grey teeth—A hanged man plummets through the ceiling of Lord Rivington's smart mews flat—Rivington rings the Home Secretary:

"I'd like to report a leak—"

"Everything is leaking—Can't stem it—*Sauve qui peut*," snaps the Home Secretary and flees the country disguised as an eccentric Lesbian abolitionist—

"We hear it was the other way around, doc," said the snide reporter with narrow shoulders and bad teeth—

The doctor's face crimsoned: "I wish to state that I have been acting physician at Dankmoor prison for thirty years man boy and bestial and always keep my nose clean—Never compromise myself to be alone with the hanged man—Always insist on the presence of my baboon assistant witness and staunch friend in any position."

Mr. Gilly looks for his brindle-faced cow across the piney woods where armadillos, innocent of a cortex, frolic under the .22 of black Stetson and pale blue eyes.

"Lawd Lawd have you seen my brindle-faced cow?— Guess I'm taking up too much of your time—Must be busy doing *something* feller say—Good stand you got whatever it is—Maybe I'm asking too many questions— talking too much—You wouldn't have a rope would you?—A *hemp* rope? Don't know how I'd hold that old brindle-faced cow without a rope if I did come on her—"

Phantom riders—chili joints—saloons and the quick draw—hangings from horseback to the jeers of sporting women—black smoke on the hip in the Chink laundry —"No tickee no washee—Clom Fliday—"

Walking through the piney woods in the summer

dawn, chiggers pinpoint the boy's groin with red dots—
Smell of boy balls and iron cool in the mouth—

"Now I want you boys to wear shorts," said the
sheriff, "Decent women with telescopes can see you—"

Whiff of dried jissom in a bandanna rises from the
hotel drawer—Sweet young breath through the teeth,
stomach hard as marble spurts it out in soft, white
globs—Funny how a man comes back to something he
left in a Peoria hotel drawer 1929—

1920 tunes drift into the locker room where two boys
first time tea high jack off to "My Blue Heaven"—

In the attic of the big store on bolts of cloth we
made it—

"Careful—don't spill—Don't rat on the boys."

The cellar is full of light—In two weeks the tadpoles
hatch—I wonder whatever happened to Otto's boy who
played the violin? A hard-faced boy patch over one eye
parrot on shoulder says: "Dead men tell no tales or
do they?"—He prods the skull with his cutlass and a
crab scuttles out—The boy reaches down and picks up
a scroll of hieroglyphs—"The map!—The map!"

The map turns to shitty toilet paper in his hands,
blows across a vacant lot in East St. Louis.

The boy pulls off the patch—The parrot flies away
into the jungle—Cutlass turns to a machete—He is
studying the map and swatting sand flies—

Junk yacks at our heels and predated checks bounce
all around us in the Mayan ball court—

"Order in the court—You are accused of soliciting

with prehensile piles—What have you to say in your defense?"

"Just cooling them off, judge—Raw and bleeding—Wouldn't you?"

"I want you to *smell* this bar stool," said the paranoid ex-Communist to the manic FBI agent—"Stink juice, and you may quote me has been applied by paid hoodlums constipated with Moscow goldwasser."

The man in a green suit—old English cut with two side vents and change pockets outside—will swindle the aging proprietress of a florist shop—"Old flub got a yen on for me—"

Carnival of splintered pink peppermint—"Oh Those Golden Slippers"—He sits up and looks into a cobra lamp—

"I am the Egyptian," he said looking all flat and silly.

And I said: "Really, Bradford, don't be tiresome—"

Under the limestone cave I met a man with Medusa's head in a hatbox and said "Be careful" to the customs inspector, freezed his hand forever an inch from the false bottom—

Will the gentle reader get up off his limestones and pick up the phone?—Cause of death: completely uninteresting.

They cowboyed him in the steam room—Is this Cherry Ass Gio? The Towel Boy or Mother Gillig Old Auntie of Westminster Place? Only dead fingers talk in braille—

Second run cotton trace the bones of a fix—

But is all back seat dreaming since the hitchhiker

with the chewed thumb and he said: "If decided?—
Could I ride with you chaps?"—(Heard about the death
later in a Copenhagen bar—Told a story about crayfish
and chased it with a Jew joke out behind the fear of
what I tell him we all know here.) So it jumped in my
throat and was all there like and ready when we were
sitting under the pretties, star pretties you understand,
not like me talking at all I used to talk differently. Who
did?—Paris?

"Mr. Bradly Mr. Martin, Johnny Yenshe, Yves Martin."

Martin he calls himself but once in the London
YMCA on Tottenham Court (never made out there)—
Once on Dean Street in Soho—No it wasn't Dean Street
that was someone else looked like Bradly—It was on
some back time street, silent pockets of Mexico City—
(half orange with red pepper in the sun)—and the
weakness hit me and I leaned against a wall and the
white spot never washed out of my glen plaid coat—
Carried that wall with me to a town in Ecuador can't
remember the name, remember the towns all around
but not that one where time slipped on the beach—
sand winds across the blood—half a cup of water and
Martin looked at the guide or was it the other, the
Aussie, the Canadian, the South African who is sometimes there when the water is given out and always
there when the water gives out—and gave him half his
own water ration with gambler fingers could switch
water if he wanted to—On the street once Cavesbury
Close I think it was somebody called him Uncle Charles

in English and he didn't want to know the man walked away dragging one leg—

Mr. Bradly Mr. Martin, slotless fade-out of distant fingers in the sick morning—I told him you on tracks— couldn't reach me with the knife—couldn't switch iron —and zero time to stop—couldn't make turnstile—bad shape from death Mr. Shannon no cept pay of distant fingers spilling old photo—at me with the knife and fell over the white subway—on tracks I told—The shallow water came in with the tide of washed condoms and sick sharks fed on sewage—only food for this village— swamp delta to the green sky that does not change—I —We—They—sit quietly where you made this dream— *"Finnies nous attendons une bonne chance"*—(Footnote: Last words in the diary of Yves Martin who presumably died of thirst in the Egyptian desert with three companions—Just who died is uncertain since one member of the party has not been found alive or dead and identity of the missing person is dubious—The bodies were decomposed when found, and identification was based on documents. But it seems the party was given to exchange of identifications, and even to writing in each others' diaries—Other members of the expedition were Mr. Shannon, Mr. Armstrong, Monsieur Pillou, Ahmed Akid the guide—)

As the series is soon ending are these experiments really necessary?

Cross the Wounded Galaxies

THE PENNY ARCADE peep show long process in different forms.

In the pass the muttering sickness leaped into our throats, coughing and spitting in the silver morning. frost on our bones. Most of the ape forms died there on the treeless slopes. dumb animal eyes on "me" brought the sickness from white time caves frozen in my throat to hatch in the warm steamlands spitting song of scarlet bursts in egg flesh. beyond the pass, limestone slopes down into a high green savanna and the grass-wind on our genitals. came to a swamp fed by hot springs and mountain ice. and fell in flesh heaps. sick apes spitting blood laugh. sound bubbling in throats torn with the talk sickness. faces and bodies covered with pus foam. animal hair thru the purple sex-flesh. sick sound twisted thru body. underwater music bubbling in blood beds. human faces tentative flicker in and out of focus. We waded into the warm mud-water. hair and ape flesh off in screaming strips. stood naked human bodies covered with phosphorescent green jelly. soft tentative flesh cut with ape wounds. peeling other genitals. fingers and tongues rubbing off the jelly-cover. body melting pleasure-sounds in the warm mud. till the sun went and a blue wind of silence touched human faces and hair. When we came out of the mud we had names.

In the pass muttering arctic flowers. gusts of frost wind. bones and most of the ape still felt. invisible slopes. spitting the bloodbends human bones out of focus. and ape-flesh naked human body. Caves frozen in my throat. green jelly genitals. Limestone slopes cover our bodies melting in savanna and grass mud. shit and sperm fed hot till the sun went. The mountain touched human bubbling throats. Torn we crawled out of the mud. faces and bodies covered the purple sex-flesh. and the sickness leaped into our body underwater music bubble in the silver morning frost. faces tentative flicker in ape forms. into the warm mud and water slopes. cold screaming sickness from white time. covered with phosphorescent shed in the warm lands. spitting ape wounds. feeling egg flesh. green pleasure-sounds warm our genitals. blue wind of silence. Apes spitting sound faces thru pus foam. the talking sickness had names. The sound stood naked in

the grass. music bubbling in the blood, quivering frog
eggs and sound thru our throats and swap we had names
for each other. tentative flicker-laugh and laughing
washed the hairs off. down to his genitals. Human our
bodies melted into when we crawled out.

And the other did not want to touch me because of
the white worm-thing inside but no one could refuse
if I wanted and ate the fear-softness in other men. The
cold was around us in our bones. And I could see the
time before the thing when there was green around
and the green taste in my mouth and the green plant-
shit on my legs. before the cold. . . And some did not
eat flesh and died because they could not live with the
thing inside. . . Once we caught one of the hairy men
with our vine nets and tied him over a slow fire and
left him there until he died and the thing sucked his
screams moving in my face like smoke and no one could
eat the flesh-fear of the hairy man and there was a
smell in the cave bent us over. . . We moved to keep
out of our excrement where white worms twisted up
feeling for us and the white worm-sickness in all our
bodies. We took our pots and spears and moved South
and left the black flesh there in the ashes. . . Came to
the great dry plain and only those lived who learned
to let the thing surface and eat animal excrement in
the brown water holes. . . Then thick grass and trees
and animals. I pulled the skin over my head and I made
another man put on the skin and horns and we fucked
like the animals stuck together and we found the animals stuck together and killed both so I knew the thing

inside me would always find animals to feed my mouth meat. . . Saw animals chase us with spears and woke eating my own hand and the blood in my mouth made me spit up a bitter green juice. But the next day I ate flesh again and every night we put on animal skins and smeared green animal excrement down our legs and fucked each other with whimpering snorting noises and stuck together shadows on the cave walls, and ate surface men. . . the skin over my head and green taste and the horns and we fucked before the thing inside me would. We caught one of the hairy men animaled him over a slow fire eating my own hand, the thing sucked his screams green bitter juice. Those lived who learned to let the softness in, eat animal excrement in the brown bones. . . I made another man put on the skin green plant shit on animal stuck together flesh. So I knew with the thing inside always find animals to feed with our vine nets. Blood in my mouth made me spit up moving in my face like the next day I ate flesh again. . . Moved to knee legs and fucked each other twisted up feeling and stuck together shadows on our bodies.

Glass blizzards thru the rusty limestone streets exploded flesh from the laughing bones. spattering blood cross urine of walls. We lived in sewers of the city, crab parasites in our genitals rubbing our diseased flesh thru each other on a long string of rectal mucus. place of the tapeworms with white bone faces and disk mouths feeling for the soft host mucus. the years. the long. the many. such a place. In a land of grass without memory,

only food of the hordes moving south, the dark armadillo flesh killed in the cool morning grass with throwing sticks. The women and their thing police ate the
flesh and we fought over their shit-encrusted pieces of
armadillo gristle.

Glass blizzards without memory. only food of flesh
was the dank urine of the city. crab parasites ate the
flesh. thru jungles of breath when we copulate with
white bones faces. place of nettles and scorpions for the
soft host mucus. intestines sprouting weed room in the
cool morning walls. the women in our genitals and
bowels. fought over their shit, rubbing our diseased
flesh-meat a mucus string: clawing thru shit place of
tapeworms in some disk mouth. larval bodies feeling
the penalty. the years. the long. the many. such shoots
growing.

Sitting naked at the bottom of a well. the cool mud
of evening touched our rectums. We shared a piece of
armadillo gristle, eating it out of each other's mouths.
above us a dry husk of insect bodies along the stone
well wall and thistles over the well mouth against green
evening sky. licking the gristle from his laughing teeth
and gums I said: "I am Allah. I made you." A blue mist
filled the well and shut off our word-breath. My hands
sank into his body. We fell asleep in other flesh. Smells
on our stomach and hands. Woke in noon sun, thistle
shades cutting our soft night flesh.

Evening touched our rectums. mud shells and frogs
croaking. licking the gristle asleep with other flesh.
the cool mud of breath, and our bodies we shared.

branches in the wind. his knees. other mouths. against
the green evening sky. "We laughing teeth and gums,"
I said. Hands woke in the noon sun soft night flesh.
smell on our stomach. thistle shades cutting. penny
arcade peep show—long process in different forms—
dead fingers talk in braille.

Think Police keep all Board Room Reports—and we
are not allowed to proffer the Disaster Accounts—Wind
hand caught in the door—Explosive Bio-Advance Men
out of space to employ Electrician in gasoline crack of
history—Last of the gallant heroes—"I'm you on tracks,
Mr. Bradly Mr. Martin"—Couldn't reach flesh in his
switch—and zero time to the sick tracks—A long time
between suns I held the stale overcoat—sliding between light and shadow—muttering in the dogs of
unfamiliar score—cross the wounded galaxies we intersect, poison of dead sun in your brain slowly fading
—Migrants of ape in gasoline crack of history, explosive
bio-advance out of space to neon—"I'm you, Wind Hand
caught in the door"—Coulnd't reach flesh—In sun I
held the stale overcoat, Dead Hand stretching the throat
—Last to proffer the disaster account on tracks. "See
Mr. Bradly Mr.—"

And being blind may not refuse to hear: "Mr. Bradly
Mr. Martin, disaster to my blood whom I created"—
(The shallow water came in with the tide and the
Swedish River of Gothenburg.)

Nova Express

FOREWORD NOTE

THE SECTION called "This Horrible Case" was written in collaboration with Mr. Ian Sommerville, a mathematician—Mr. Sommerville also contributed the technical notes in the section called "Chinese Laundry"—An extension of Brion Gysin's cut-up method which I call the fold-in method has been used in this book which is consequently a composite of many writers living and dead.

CONTENTS

Last Words

LISTEN TO MY LAST WORDS anywhere. Listen to my last words any world. Listen all you boards syndicates and governments of the earth. And you powers behind what filth deals consummated in what lavatory to take what is not yours. To sell the ground from unborn feet forever—

"Don't let them see us. Don't tell them what we are doing—"

Are these the words of the all-powerful boards and syndicates of the earth?

"For God's sake don't let that Coca-Cola thing out—"

"Not The Cancer Deal with The Venusians—"

"Not The Green Deal—Don't show them that—"

"Not The Orgasm Death—"

"Not the ovens—"

Listen: I call you all. Show your cards all players.
Pay it all pay it all pay it *all* back. Play it all pay it all
play it *all* back. For all to see. In Times Square. In Piccadilly.

"Premature. Premature. Give us a little more time."

Time for what? More lies? Premature? Premature for
who? I say to all these words are not premature. These
words may be too late. Minutes to go. Minutes to foe
goal—

"Top Secret—Classified—For The Board—The Elite
—The Initiates—"

Are these the words of the all-powerful boards and
syndicates of the earth? These are the words of liars
cowards collaborators traitors. Liars who want time for
more lies. Cowards who can not face your "dogs" your
"gooks" your "errand boys" your "human animals" with
the truth. Collaborators with Insect People with Vegetable People. With any people anywhere who offer you
a body forever. To shit forever. For this you have sold
out your sons. Sold the ground from unborn feet forever. Traitors to all souls everywhere. You want the
name of Hassan i Sabbah on your filth deeds to sell out
the unborn?

What scared you all into time? Into body? Into shit?
I will tell you: *"the word."* Alien Word *"the." "The"*
word of Alien Enemy imprisons *"thee"* in Time. In
Body. In Shit. Prisoner, come out. The great skies are
open. I Hassan i Sabbah *rub out the word forever.* If
you I cancel all your words forever. And the words of
Hassan i Sabbah as also cancel. Cross all your skies see

the silent writing of Brion Gysin Hassan i Sabbah: drew
September 17, 1899 over New York.

PRISONERS, COME OUT

"DON'T LISTEN to Hassan i Sabbah," they will tell you.
"He wants to take your body and all pleasures of the
body away from you. Listen to us. We are serving The
Garden of Delights Immortality Cosmic Consciousness
The Best Ever In Drug Kicks. And *love love love* in
slop buckets. How does that sound to you boys? Better
than Hassan i Sabbah and his cold windy bodiless rock?
Right?"

At the immediate risk of finding myself the most un-
popular character of all fiction—and history is fiction—
I must say this:

"Bring together state of news—Inquire onward from
state to doer—Who monopolized Immortality? Who
monopolized Cosmic Consciousness? Who monopolized
Love Sex and Dream? Who monopolized Life Time and
Fortune? Who took from you what is yours? Now they
will give it all back? Did they ever give anything away
for nothing? Did they ever give any more than they
had to give? Did they not always take back what they
gave when possible and it always was? *Listen:* Their
Garden Of Delights is a terminal sewer—I have been
at some pains to map this area of terminal sewage in
the so called pornographic sections of *Naked Lunch*

and *Soft Machine*—Their Immortality Cosmic Consciousness and Love is second-run grade-B shit—Their drugs are poison designed to beam in Orgasm Death and Nova Ovens—Stay out of the Garden Of Delights —It is a man-eating trap that ends in green goo— Throw back their ersatz Immortality—It will fall apart before you can get out of The Big Store—Flush their drug kicks down the drain—*They are poisoning and monopolizing the hallucinogen drugs—learn to make it without any chemical corn*—All that they offer is a screen to cover retreat from the colony they have so disgracefully mismanaged. To cover travel arrangements so they will never have to pay the constituents they have betrayed and sold out. Once these arrangements are complete they will blow the place up behind them.

"And what does my program of total austerity and total resistance offer *you*? I offer you nothing. I am not a politician. These are conditions of total emergency. And these are my instructions for total emergency if carried out *now* could avert the total disaster *now* on tracks:

"*Peoples of the earth, you have all been poisoned.* Convert all available stocks of morphine to apomorphine. Chemists, work round the clock on variation and synthesis of the apomorphine formulae. Apomorphine is the only agent that can disintoxicate you and cut the enemy beam off your line. Apomorphine and silence. I order total resistance directed against this conspiracy to pay off peoples of the earth in ersatz bullshit. I order

total resistance directed against The Nova Conspiracy
and all those engaged in it.

"The purpose of my writing is to expose and arrest
Nova Criminals. In *Naked Lunch*, *Soft Machine* and
Nova Express I show who they are and what they are
doing and what they will do if they are not arrested.
Minutes to go. Souls rotten from their orgasm drugs,
flesh shuddering from their nova ovens, prisoners of the
earth to *come out*. With your help we can occupy The
Reality Studio and retake their universe of Fear Death
and Monopoly—

"(Signed) INSPECTOR J. LEE, NOVA POLICE"

Post Script Of The Regulator: I would like to sound a
word of warning—To speak is to lie—To live is to col-
laborate—Anybody is a coward when faced by the
nova ovens—There are degrees of lying collaboration
and cowardice—That is to say degrees of intoxication
—It is precisely a question of *regulation*—The enemy
is not man is not woman—The enemy exists only where
no life is and moves always to push life into extreme
untenable positions—You can cut the enemy off your
line by the judicious use of apomorphine and silence—
Use the sanity drug apomorphine.

"Apomorphine is made from morphine but its physiological action is quite different. Morphine depresses the
front brain. Apomorphine stimulates the back brain.
acts on the hypothalamus to regulate the percentage of

various constituents in the blood serum and so normalize the constitution of the blood." I quote from *Anxiety
and Its Treatment* by Doctor John Yerbury Dent.

PRY YOURSELF LOOSE AND LISTEN

I was traveling with The Intolerable Kid on The
Nova Lark—We were on the nod after a rumble in The
Crab Galaxy involving this two-way time stock; when
you come to the end of a biologic film just run it back
and start over—Nobody knows the difference—Like
nobody there before the film.* So they start to run it
back and the projector blew up and we lammed out of
there on the blast—Holed up in those cool blue mountains the liquid air in our spines listening to a little
high-fi junk note fixes you right to metal and you nod

* Postulate a biologic film running from the beginning to the
end, from zero to zero as all biologic film run in any time
universe—Call this film X1 and postulate further that there
can only be one film with the quality X1 in any given time
universe. X1 is the film and performers—X2 is the audience
who are all trying to get into the film—Nobody is permitted
to leave the biologic theater which in this case is the human
body—Because if anybody did leave the theater he would
be looking at a different film Y and Film X1 and audience X2
would then cease to exist by mathematical definition—In
1960 with the publication of *Minutes To Go*, Martin's stale
movie was greeted by an unprecedented chorus of boos and
a concerted walkout—"We seen this five times already and
not standing still for another twilight of your tired Gods."

out a thousand years.† Just sitting there in a slate house wrapped in orange flesh robes, the blue mist drifting around us when we get the call—And as soon as I set foot on Podunk earth I can smell it that burnt metal reek of nova.

"Already set off the charge," I said to I&I (Immovable and Irresistible)—"This is a burning planet —Any minute now the whole fucking shit house goes up."

† Since junk *is* image the effects of junk can easily be produced and concentrated in a sound and image track—Like this: Take a sick junky—Throw blue light on his so-called face or dye it blue or dye the junk blue it don't make no difference and now give him a shot and photograph the blue miracle as life pours back into that walking corpse—That will give you the image track of junk—Now project the blue change onto your own face if you want The Big Fix. The sound track is even easier—I quote from *Newsweek*, March 4, 1963 Science section: "Every substance has a characteristic set of resonant frequencies at which it vibrates or oscillates." —So you record the frequency of junk as it hits the junk-sick brain cells—

"What's that?—Brain waves are 32 or under and can't be heard? Well speed them up, God damn it—And instead of one junky concentrate me a thousand—Let there be Lexington and call a nice Jew in to run it—"

Doctor Wilhelm Reich has isolated and concentrated a unit that he calls "the orgone"—Orgones, according to W. Reich, are the units of life—They have been photographed and the color is blue—So junk sops up the orgones and that's why they need all these young junkies—They have more orgones and give higher yield of the blue concentrate on which Martin and his boys can nod out a thousand years—Martin is stealing *your orgones.*—You going to stand still for this shit?

So Intolerable I&I sniffs and says: "Yeah, when it happens it happens fast—This is a rush job."

And you could feel it there under your feet the whole structure buckling like a bulkhead about to blow—So the paper has a car there for us and we are driving in from the airport The Kid at the wheel and his foot on the floor—Nearly ran down a covey of pedestrians and they yell after us: "What you want to do, kill somebody?"

And The Kid sticks his head out and says: "It would be a pleasure Niggers! Gooks! Terrestrial dogs"—His eyes lit up like a blow torch and I can see he is really in form—So we start right to work making our headquarters in The Land Of The Free where the call came from and which is really free and wide open for any life form the uglier the better—Well they don't come any uglier than The Intolerable Kid and your reporter—When a planet is all primed to go up they call in I&I to jump around from one faction to the other agitating and insulting all the parties before and after the fact until they all say: "By God before I give an inch the whole fucking shit house goes up in chunks."

Where we came in—You have to move fast on this job—And I&I is fast—Pops in and out of a hundred faces in a split second spitting his intolerable insults—We had the plan, what they call The Board Books to show us what is what on this dead whistle stop: Three life forms uneasily parasitic on a fourth form that is beginning to wise up. And the whole planet absolutely flapping hysterical with panic. The way we like to see them.

"This is a dead easy pitch," The Kid says.

"Yeah," I say. "A little bit too easy. Something here, Kid. Something wrong. I can feel it."

But The Kid can't hear me. Now all these life forms came from the most intolerable conditions: hot places, cold places, terminal stasis and the last thing any of them want to do is go back where they came from. And The Intolerable Kid is giving out with such pleasantries like this:

"All right take your ovens out with you and pay Hitler on the way out. Nearly got the place hot enough for you Jews didn't he?"

"Know about Niggers? Why darkies were born? Antennae coolers what else? Always a spot for *good* Darkies."

"You cunts constitute a disposal problem in the worst form there is and raise the nastiest whine ever heard anywhere: 'Do you love me? Do you love me? Do you love me???' Why don't you go back to Venus and fertilize a forest?"

"And as for you White Man Boss, you dead prop in Martin's stale movie, you terminal time junky, haul your heavy metal ass back to Uranus. Last shot at the door. You need one for the road." By this time everybody was even madder than they were shit scared. But I&I figured things were moving too slow.

"We need a peg to hang it on," he said. "Something really ugly like virus. Not for nothing do they come from a land without mirrors." So he takes over this newsmagazine.

"Now," he said, "I'll by God show them how ugly the Ugly American can be."

And he breaks out all the ugliest pictures in the image bank and puts it out on the subliminal so one crisis piles up after the other right on schedule. And I&I is whizzing around like a buzz saw and that black nova laugh of his you can hear it now down all the streets shaking the buildings and skyline like a stage prop. But me I am looking around and the more I look the less I like what I see. For one thing the nova heat is moving in fast and heavy like I never see it anywhere else. But I&I just says I have the copper jitters and turns back to his view screen: "They are skinning the chief of police alive in some jerkwater place. Want to sit in?"

"Naw," I said. "Only interested in my own skin."

And I walk out thinking who I *would* like to see skinned alive. So I cut into the Automat and put coins into the fish cake slot and then I really see it: Chinese partisans and well armed with vibrating static and image guns. So I throw down the fish cakes with tomato sauce and make it back to the office where The Kid is still glued to that screen. He looks up smiling dirty and says:

"Wanta molest a child and disembowel it right after?"

"Pry yourself loose and listen." And I tell him. "Those Tiddly Winks don't fuck around you know."

"So what?" he says. "I've still got The Board Books.
I can split this whistle stop wide open tomorrow."

No use talking to him. I look around some more and
find out the blockade on planet earth is broken. Explorers moving in whole armies. And everybody con-
cerned is fed up with Intolerable I&I. And all he can
say is: "So what? I've still got . . . /" Cut.

"Board Books taken. The film reeks of burning switch
like a blow torch. Prerecorded heat glare massing Hiroshima. This whistle stop wide open to hot crab people.
Mediation? Listen: Your army is getting double zero
in floor by floor game of 'symbiosis.' Mobilized reasons
to love Hiroshima and Nagasaki? Virus to maintain
terminal sewers of Venus?"

"All nations sold out by liars and cowards. Liars who
want time for the future negatives to develop stall you
with more lying offers while hot crab people mass war
to extermination with the film in Rome. These reports
reek of nova, sold out job, shit birth and death. Your
planet has been invaded. You are dogs on all tape. The
entire planet is being developed into terminal identity
and complete surrender."

"But suppose film death in Rome doesn't work and
we can get every male body even madder than they are
shit scared? We need a peg to evil full length. By God
show them how ugly the ugliest pictures in the dark
room can be. Pitch in the oven ambush. Spill all the
board gimmicks. This symbiosis con? Can tell you for
sure 'symbiosis' is ambush straight to the ovens. 'Human

dogs' to be eaten alive under white hot skies of Min-raud."

And Intolerable I&I's "errand boys" and "strike-breakers" are copping out right left and center:

"Mr. Martin, and you board members, vulgar stupid Americans, you will regret calling in the Mayan Aztec Gods with your synthetic mushrooms. Remember we keep exact junk measure of the pain inflicted and that pain must be paid in full. Is that clear enough Mr. In-tolerable Martin, or shall I make it even clearer? Allow me to introduce myself: The Mayan God of Pain And Fear from the white hot plains of Venus which does not mean a God of vulgarity, cowardice, ugliness and stu-pidity. There is a cool spot on the surface of Venus three hundred degrees cooler than the surrounding area. I have held that spot against all contestants for five hundred thousand years. Now you expect to use me as your 'errand boy' and 'strikebreaker' summoned up by an IBM machine and a handful of virus crystals? How long could you hold that spot, you 'board mem-bers'? About thirty seconds I think with all your guard dogs. And you thought to channel my energies for 'operation total disposal'? Your 'operations' there or here this or that come and go and are no more. *Give my name back.* That name must be paid for. You have not paid. My name is not yours to use. Henceforth I think about thirty seconds is written."

And you can see the marks are wising up, standing around in sullen groups and that mutter gets louder and louder. Any minute now fifty million adolescent gooks will hit the street with switch blades, bicycle chains and cobblestones.

"Street gangs, Uranian born of nova conditions, get out and fight for your streets. Call in the Chinese and any random factors. Cut all tape. Shift cut tangle magpie voice lines of the earth. Know about The Board's 'Green Deal?' They plan to board the first life boat in drag and leave 'their human dogs' under the white hot skies of Venus. 'Operation Sky Switch' also known as 'Operation Total Disposal.' All right you board bastards, we'll by God show you 'Operation Total Exposure.' For all to see. In Times Square. In Piccadilly."

So Pack Your Ermines

"So PACK YOUR ERMINES, Mary—*We* are getting out of here right now—I've seen this happen before—The marks are coming up on us—And the heat is moving in—Recollect when I was traveling with Limestone John on The Carbonic Caper—It worked like this: He rents an amphitheater with marble walls he is a stone painter you dig can create a frieze while you wait—So he puts on a diving suit like the old Surrealist Lark and I am up on a high pedestal pumping the air to him—Well, he starts painting on the limestone walls with hydrochloric acid and jetting himself around with air blasts he can cover the wall in ten seconds, carbon dioxide settling down on the marks begin to cough and loosen their collars."

"But what is he painting?"

"Why it's arrg a theater full of people suffocating—"

So we turn the flops over and move on—If you keep it practical they can't hang a nova rap on you—Well, we hit this town and right away I don't like it.

"Something here, John—Something wrong—I can feel it—"

But he says I just have the copper jitters since the nova heat moved in—Besides we are cool, just rolling flops is all three thousand years in show business—So he sets up his amphitheater in a quarry and begins lining up the women clubs and poets and window dressers and organizes this "Culture Fest" he calls it and I am up in the cabin of a crane pumping the air to him—Well the marks are packing in, the old dolls covered with ice and sapphires and emeralds all really magnificent—So I think maybe I was wrong and everything is cool when I see like fifty young punks have showed in aqualungs carrying fish spears and without thinking I yell out from the crane:

"Izzy The Push—Sammy The Butcher—*Hey Rube!*"

Meanwhile I have forgotten the air pump and The Carbonic Kid is turning blue and trying to say something—I rush and pump some air to him and he yells: "No! No! No!"

I see other marks are coming on with static and camera guns, Sammy and the boys are not making it—These kids have pulled the reverse switch—At this point The Blue Dinosaur himself charged out to discover what the beef is and starts throwing his magnetic spirals at the rubes—They just moved back ahead of him until he runs out of charge and stops. Next thing the nova heat slipped antibiotic handcuffs on all of us.

NABORHOOD IN AQUALUNGS

I was traveling with Merit John on The Carbonic Caper—Larceny with a crew of shoppers—And this number comes over the air to him—So he starts painting The D Fence last Spring—And shitting himself around with air blasts in Hicksville—Stopped ten seconds and our carbon dioxide gave out and we began to cough for such a purpose suffocating under a potted palm in the lobby—

"Move on, you dig, copping out 'The Fish Poison Con.'"

"I got you—Keep it practical and they can't—"

Transported back to South America we hit this town and right away being stung by the dreaded John—He never missed—Burned three thousand years in me playing cop and quarry—So the marks are packing in virus and subject to dissolve and everything is cool—Assimilate ice sapphires and emeralds all regular—So I walk in about fifty young punks—Sammy and the boys are all he had—One fix—Pulled the reverse switch —Traveling store closing so I don't work like this— John set my medications—Nagasaki in acid on the walls faded out under the rubber trees—He can cover

feet back to 1910—We could buy it settling down—
Lay up in the Chink laundry on the collars—

"But what stale rooming house flesh—"

Cradles old troupers—Like Cleopatra applying the
asp hang a Nova Rap on you—

"Lush?—I don't like it—Empty pockets in the worn
metal—Feel it?"

But John says: "Copper jitters since the space sell—
The old doll is covered—"

Heavy and calm holding cool leather armchair—Organizes this wispy mustache—I stopped in front of a
mirror—Really magnificent in a starched collar—It is a
naborhood in aqualungs with free lunch everywhere
yell out "Sweet Sixteen"—I walked without Izzy The
Push—

"Hey Rube!!"

Came to the Chinese laundry meanwhile—I have
forgotten the Chink in front—Fix words hatch The
Blue Dinosaur—I was reading them back magnetic—
Only way to orient yourself—Traveling with the Chink
kid John set throat like already written—"Stone Reading" we call it in the trade—While you wait he packs
in Rome—I've checked the diving suit like every night
—Up on a high pedestal perform this unnatural act—
In acid on the walls—Set your watch by it—So that
gives us twenty marks out through the side window
and collars—

"But what in St. Louis?"

Memory picture coming in—So we turn over silver
sets and banks and clubs as old troupers—Nova Rap on

you that night as we walked out—I don't like it—
Something picking up laundry and my flesh feel it—

But John says: "Afternoon copper jitters since the
caper—Housebreaking can cause this—"

We are cool just rolling—when things go wrong once
—show business—We can't find poets and organize
this cut and the flesh won't work—And there we are
with the air off like beached idiots—Well I think maybe kicks from our condition—They took us—The old
dolls on a train burning junk—Thawing flesh showed
in aqualungs—Steam a yell out from the crane—

"Hey Rube!!"

Three silver digits explode—Meanwhile I have forgotten streets of Madrid—And clear as sunlight pump
some air to him and he said: "Que tal Henrique?"

I am standing through an invisible door click the air
to him—Well we hit this town and right away aphrodisiac ointment—

"Doc goofed here, John—Something wrong—Too
much Spanish."

"What? It's green see? A green theater—"

So we turn the marks over and rent a house as old
troupers—And we flush out this cool pure Chinese H
from show business—And he starts the whole Green
Rite and organizes this fibrous grey amphitheater in old
turnip—Meanwhile I have forgotten a heavy blue
silence—Carbonic Kid is turning to cold liquid metal
and run pump some air to him in a blue mist of vaporized flicker helmets—The metal junkies were not
making it—These kids intersected The Nova Police—

We are just dust falls from demagnetized patterns—
Show business—Calendar in Weimar youths—Faded
poets in the silent amphitheater—His block house went
away through this air—Click St. Louis under drifting
soot—And I think maybe I was in old clinic—Outside
East St. Louis—Really magnificent for two notes
a week—Meanwhile I had forgotten "Mother"—
Wouldn't you?—Doc Benway and The Carbonic Kid
turning a rumble in Dallas involving this pump goofed
on ether and mixed in flicker helmets—

"He is gone through this town and right away tape
recorders of his voice behind, John—Something wrong
—I can pose a colorless question??"

"Is all right—I just have the silence—Word dust falls
three thousand years through an old blue calendar—"

"William, no me hagas caso—People who told me I
could move on you copping out—said 'Good-Bye' to
William and 'Keep it practical' and I could hear him hit
this town and right away I closed the door when I
saw John—Something wrong—Invisible hotel room is
all—I just have the knife and he said:

"Nova Heat moved in at the seams—Like three thousand years in hot claws at the window'—

"And Meester William in Tétuan and said: 'I have
gimmick is cool and all very technical—These colorless
sheets are the air pump and I can see the flesh when it
has color—Writing say some message that is coming
on all flesh—'

"And I said: 'William tu es loco—Pulled the reverse
switch—No me hagas while you wait'—Kitchen knife

in the heart—Feel it—Gone away—Pulled the reverse switch—Place no good—No bueno—He pack caso— William tu hagas yesterday call—These colorless sheets are empty—You can look any place—No good—No bueno—Adios Meester William—"

THE FISH POISON CON

I was traveling with Merit Inc. checking store attendants for larceny with a crew of "shoppers"—There was two middle-aged cunts one owning this chihuahua which whimpered and yapped in a cocoon of black sweaters and Bob Schafer Crew Leader who was an American Fascist with Roosevelt jokes—It happens in Iowa this number comes over the car radio: "Old Sow Got Caught In The Fence Last Spring"—And Schafer said "Oh my God, are we ever in Hicksville." Stopped that night in Pleasantville Iowa and our tires gave out we had no tire rations during the war for such a purpose—And Bob got drunk and showed his badge to the locals in a road house by the river—And I ran into The Sailor under a potted palm in the lobby— We hit the local croakers with "the fish poison con"—"I got these poison fish, Doc, in the tank transported back from South America I'm a Ichthyologist and after being stung by the dreaded Candirú—Like fire through the blood is it not? Doctor, and coming on now"—And The Sailor goes into his White Hot Agony Act chasing the doctor around his office like a blowtorch He never missed—But he burned down the croakers—So like Bob and me when we "had a catch" as the old cunts call it and arrested some sulky clerk with his hand deep in the company pocket, we take turns playing the tough cop and the con cop—So I walk in on this Pleasantville croaker and tell him I have contracted this Venusian virus and subject to dissolve myself in poison juices and assimilate the passers-by unless I get my medicine and get it regular—So I walk in on this old party smelling like a compost heap and steaming demurely and he snaps at me, "What's *your* trouble?"

"The Venusian Gook Rot, doctor."

"Now see here young man my time is valuable."

"Doctor, this is a medical emergency."

Old shit but good—I walked out on the nod—

"All he had was one fix, Sailor."

"You're loaded—You assimilated the croaker—Left me sick—"

"Yes. He was old and tough but not too tough for The Caustic Enzymes Of Woo."

The Sailor was thin and the drugstore was closing so I didn't want him to get physical and disturb my medications—The next croaker wrote with erogenous acid vats on one side and Nagasaki Ovens on the other —And we nodded out under the rubber trees with the long red carpet under our feet back to 1910—We could buy it in the drugstore tomorrow—Or lay up in the Chink laundry on the black smoke—drifting through stale rooming houses, pool halls and chili—Fell back

on sad flesh small and pretentious in a theatrical boarding house the aging ham cradles his tie up and stabs a
vein like Cleopatra applying the asp—Click back
through the cool grey short-change artists—lush rolling
ghosts of drunken sleep—Empty pockets in the worn
metal subway dawn—

I woke up in the hotel lobby the smell heavy and
calm holding a different body molded to the leather
chair—I was sick but not needle sick—This was a black
smoke yen—The Sailor still sleeping and he looked
very young under a wispy mustache—I woke him up
and he looked around with slow hydraulic control his
eyes unbluffed unreadable—

"Let's make the street—I'm thin—"

I was in fact very thin I saw when I stopped in front
of a mirror panel and adjusted my tie knot in a starched
collar—It was a naborhood of chili houses and cheap
saloons with free lunch everywhere and heavy calm
bartenders humming "Sweet Sixteen"—I walked without thinking like a horse will and came to The Chinese
Laundry by Clara's Massage Parlor—We siphoned in
and The Chink in front jerked one eye back and went
on ironing a shirt front—We walked through a door
and a curtain and the black smoke set our lungs
dancing The Junky Jig and we lay up on our junk hip
while a Chinese kid cooked our pills and handed us
the pipe—After six pipes we smoke slow and order a
pot of tea the Chink kid goes out fix it and the words
hatch in my throat like already written there I was
reading them back—"Lip Reading" we call it in the

trade only way to orient yourself when in Rome—
"I've checked the harness bull—He comes in Mc-
Sorley's every night at 2:20 A.M. and forces the local
pederast to perform this unnatural act on his person—
So regular you can set your watch by it: 'I won't—
I won't—Not again—Glub—Glub—Glub.'"—"So that
gives us twenty minutes at least to get in and out
through the side window and eight hours start we
should be in St. Louis before they miss the time—Stop
off and see The Family"—Memory pictures coming in
—Little Boy Blue and all the heavy silver sets and
banks and clubs—Cool heavy eyes moving steel and oil
shares—I had a rich St. Louis family—It was set for
that night—As we walked out I caught the Japanese
girl picking up laundry and my flesh crawled under the
junk and I made a meet for her with the afternoon—
Good plan to make sex before a caper—Housebreaking
can cause this wet dream sex tension especially when
things go wrong—(Once in Peoria me and The Sailor
charged a drugstore and we can't find the jimmy for
the narco cabinet and the flash won't work and the
harness bull sniffing round the door and there we are
with The Sex Current giggling ourselves off like
beached idiots—Well the cops got such nasty kicks
from our condition they took us to the RR station and
we get on a train shivering burning junk sick and the
warm vegetable smells of thawing flesh and stale come
slowly filled the car—Nobody could look at us steaming away there like manure piles—) I woke out of a
light yen sleep when the Japanese girl came in—Three

silver digits exploded in my head—I walked out into streets of Madrid and won a football pool—Felt the Latin mind clear and banal as sunlight met Paco by the soccer scores and he said: "Que tal Henrique?"

And I went to see my amigo who was taking medicina again and he had no money to give me and didn't want to do anything but take more medicina and stood there waiting for me to leave so he could take it after saying he was not going to take any more so I said, "William no me hagas caso." And met a Cuban that night in The Mar Chica who told me I could work in his band—The next day I said good-bye to William and there was nobody there to listen and I could hear him reaching for his medicina and needles as I closed the door—When I saw the knife I knew Meester William was death disguised as any other person—Pues I saw El Hombre Invisible in a hotel room somewhere tried to reach him with the knife and he said: "If you kill me this crate will come apart at the seams like a rotten undervest"—And I saw a monster crab with hot claws at the window and Meester William took some white medicina and vomited into the toilet and we escaped to Greece with a boy about my age who kept calling Meester William "The Stupid American"—And Meester William looked like a hypnotist I saw once in Tétuan and said: "I have gimmick to beat The Crab but it is very technical"—And we couldn't read what he was writing on transparent sheets—In Paris he showed me The Man who paints on these sheets pictures in the air—And The Invisible Man said:

"These colorless sheets are what flesh is made from—
Becomes flesh when it has color and writing—That is
Word And Image write the message that is you on
colorless sheets determine all flesh."

And I said: "William, tu éres loco."

NO GOOD—NO BUENO

So many years—that image—got up and fixed in the
sick dawn—*No me hagas caso*—Again he touched like
that—smell of dust—The tears gathered—In Mexico
again he touched—Codeine pills powdered out into the
cold Spring air—Cigarette holes in the vast Thing
Police—Could give no information other than wind
identity fading out—dwindling—"Mr. Martin" couldn't
reach is all—Bread knife in the heart—Shadow turned
off the lights and water—We intersect on empty walls
—Look anywhere—No good—Falling in the dark mutinous door—Dead Hand stretching zero—Five times
of dust we made it all the living and the dead—Young
form went to Madrid—Demerol by candlelight—Wind
hand—The Last Electrician to tap on pane—Migrants
arrival—Poison of dead sun went away and sent papers
—Ferry boat cross flutes of Ramadan—Dead muttering in the dog's space—Cigarette hole in the dark—
give no information other than the cold Spring cemetery—The Sailor went wrong in corridors of that hospital—Thing Police keep all Board Room Reports is

all—Bread knife in the heart proffers the disaster accounts—He just sit down on "Mr. Martin"—Couldn't
reach flesh on Niño Perdido—A long time between
flutes of Ramadan—No me hagas caso sliding between
light and shadow—

"The American trailing cross the wounded galaxies
con su medicina, William."

Half your brain slowly fading—Turned off the lights
and water—Couldn't reach flesh—empty walls—Look
anywhere—Dead on tracks see Mr. Bradly Mr. Zero—
And being blind may not refuse the maps to my blood
whom I created—"Mr. Bradly Mr. Martin," couldn't
you write us any better than that?—Gone away—You
can look any place—No good—No bueno—

I spit blood under the sliding vulture shadows—At
The Mercado Mayorista saw a tourist—A Meester
Merican fruto drinking pisco—and fixed me with the
eyes so I sit down and drink and tell him how I live in
a shack under the hill with a tin roof held down by
rocks and hate my brothers because they eat—He says
something about "malo viento" and laughs and I went
with him to a hotel I know—In the morning he says I
am honest and will I come with him to Pucallpa he is
going into the jungle looking for snakes and spiders
to take pictures and bring them back to Washington
they always carry something away even if it is only a
spider monkey spitting blood the way most of us do
here in the winter when the mist comes down from the
mountains and never leaves your clothes and lungs and
everyone coughed and spit blood mist on the mud

floor where I sleep—We start out next day in a Mixto Bus by night we are in the mountains with snow and the Meester brings out a bottle of pisco and the driver gets drunk down into the Selva came to Pucallpa three days later—The Meester locates a brujo and pays him to prepare Ayuhuasca and I take some too and muy mareado—Then I was back in Lima and other places I didn't know and saw the Meester as child in a room with rose wallpaper looking at something I couldn't see—Tasting roast beef and turkey and ice cream in my throat knowing the thing I couldn't see was always out there in the hall—And the Meester was looking at me and I could see the street boy words there in his throat—Next day the police came looking for us at the hotel and the Meester showed letters to the Commandante so they shook hands and went off to lunch and I took a bus back to Lima with money he gave me to buy equipment—

SHIFT COORDINATE POINTS

K9 was in combat with the alien mind screen—Magnetic claws feeling for virus punch cards—pulling him into vertiginous spins—

"Back—Stay out of those claws—Shift coordinate points—" By Town Hall Square long stop for the red light—A boy stood in front of the hot dog stand and blew water from his face—Pieces of grey vapor drifted

back across wine gas and brown hair as hotel faded
photo showed a brass bed—Unknown mornings blew
rain in cobwebs—Summer evenings feel to a room
with rose wallpaper—Sick dawn whisper of clock
hands and brown hair—Morning blew rain on copper
roofs in a slow haze of apples—Summer light on rose
wallpaper—Iron mesas lit by a pink volcano—Snow
slopes under the Northern shirt—Unknown street·stir-
ring sick dawn whispers of junk—Flutes of Ramadan in
the distance—St. Louis lights wet cobblestones of
future life—Fell through the urinal and the bicycle
races—On the bar wall the clock hands—My death
across his face faded through the soccer scores—smell
of dust on the surplus army blankets—Stiff jeans
against one wall—And KiKi went away like a cat—
Some clean shirt and walked out—He is gone through
unknown morning blew—"No good—No bueno—
Hustling myself—" Such wisdom in gusts—

K9 moved back into the combat area—Standing now
in the Chinese youth sent the resistance message jolting
clicking tilting through the pinball machine—Enemy
plans exploded in a burst of rapid calculations—Clicking in punch cards of redirected orders—Crackling
shortwave static—Bleeeeeeeeeeeeeeep—Sound of thinking metal—

"Calling partisans of all nations—Word falling—
Photo falling—Break through in Grey Room—Pinball
led streets—Free doorways—Shift coordinate points—"

"The ticket that exploded posed little time so I'll say
'good night'—Pieces of grey Spanish Flu wouldn't

photo—Light the wind in green neon—You at the dog —The street blew rain—If you wanted a cup of tea with rose wallpaper—The dog turns—So many and sooo—"

"In progress I am mapping a photo—Light verse of wounded galaxies at the dog I did—The street blew rain—The dog turns—Warring head intersected Powers—Word falling—Photo falling—Break through in Grey Room—"

He is gone away through invisible mornings leaving a million tape recorders of his voice behind fading into the cold spring air pose a colorless question?

"The silence fell heavy and blue in mountain villages—Pulsing mineral silence as word dust falls from demagnetized patterns—Walked through an old blue calendar in Weimar youth—Faded photo on rose wallpaper under a copper roof—In the silent dawn little greỹ men played in his block house and went away through an invisible door—Click St. Louis under drifting soot of old newspapers—'Daddy Longlegs' looked like Uncle Sam on stilts and he ran this osteopath clinic outside East St. Louis and took in a few junky patients for two notes a week they could stay on the nod in green lawn chairs and look at the oaks and grass stretching down to a little lake in the sun and the nurse moved around the lawn with her silver trays feeding the junk in—We called her 'Mother'— Wouldn't you?—Doc Benway and me was holed up there after a rumble in Dallas involving this aphrodisiac ointment and Doc goofed on ether and mixed in too much Spanish Fly and burned the prick off the Police Commissioner straight away—So we come to 'Daddy Longlegs' to cool off and found him cool and casual in a dark room with potted rubber plants and a silver tray on the table where he liked to see a week in advance—The nurse showed us to a room with rose wallpaper and we had this bell any hour of the day or night ring and the nurse charged in with a loaded hypo—Well one day we were sitting out in the lawn chairs with lap robes it was a fall day trees turning and the sun cold on the lake—Doc picks up a piece of grass—

"Junk turns you on vegetable—It's green, see?—A green fix should last a long time."

We checked out of the clinic and rented a house and Doc starts cooking up this green junk and the basement was full of tanks smelled like a compost heap of junkies—So finally he draws off this heavy green fluid and loads it into a hypo big as a bicycle pump—

"Now we must find a worthy vessel," he said and we flush out this old goof ball artist and told him it was pure Chinese H from The Ling Dynasty and Doc shoots the whole pint of green right into the main line and the Yellow Jacket turns fibrous grey green and withered up like an old turnip and I said: "I'm getting out of here, me," and Doc said: "An unworthy vessel obviously—So I have now decided that junk is not green but blue."

So he buys a lot of tubes and globes and they are flickering in the basement this battery of tubes metal vapor and quicksilver and pulsing blue spheres and a smell of ozone and a little high-fi blue note fixed you right to metal this junk note tinkling through your crystals and a heavy blue silence fell *klunk*—and all the words turned to cold liquid metal and ran off you man just fixed there in a cool blue mist of vaporized bank notes—We found out later that the metal junkies were all radioactive and subject to explode if two of them came into contact—At this point in our researches we intersected The Nova Police—

Chinese Laundry

CHINESE LAUNDRY

WHEN YOUNG SUTHERLAND asked me to procure him a commission with the nova police, I jokingly answered: "Bring in Winkhorst, technician and chemist for The Lazarus Pharmaceutical Company, and we will discuss the matter."

"Is this Winkhorst a nova criminal?"

"No just a technical sergeant wanted for interrogation."

I was thinking of course that he knew nothing of the methods by which such people are brought in for interrogation—It is a precision operation—First we send out a series of agents—(usually in the guise of journalists)—to contact Winkhorst and expose him to a battery of stimulus units—The contact agents talk and record the response on all levels to the word units while a photographer takes pictures—This material is passed along to The Art Department—Writers write "Winkhorst," painters paint "Winkhorst," a method actor *becomes* "Winkhorst," and then "Winkhorst" will answer our questions—The processing of Winkhorst was already under way—

Some days later there was a knock at my door— Young Sutherland was standing there and next to him a man with coat collar turned up so only the eyes were visible spitting indignant protest—I noticed that the overcoat sleeves were empty.

"I have him in a strait jacket," said Sutherland propelling the man into my room—"This is Winkhorst."

I saw that the collar was turned up to conceal a gag —"But—You misunderstood me—Not on this level— I mean really—"

"You said bring in Winkhorst didn't you?"

I was thinking fast: "All right—Take off the gag and the strait jacket."

"But he'll scream the fuzz in—"

"No he won't."

As he removed the strait jacket I was reminded of an old dream picture—This process is known as retroactive dreaming—Performed with precision and authority becomes accomplished fact—If Winkhorst did start screaming no one would hear him—Far side of the world's mirror moving into my past—Wall of

glass you know—Winkhorst made no attempt to
scream—Iron cool he sat down—I asked Sutherland to
leave us promising to put his application through
channels—

"I have come to ask settlement for a laundry bill."
Winkhorst said.

"What laundry do you represent?"

"The Chinese laundry."

"The bill will be paid through channels—As you
know nothing is more complicated and time consuming
than processing requisition orders for so-called 'personal expenses'—And you know also that it is strictly
forbidden to offer currency in settlement."

"I was empowered to ask a settlement—Beyond that
I know nothing—And now may I ask why I have been
summoned?"

"Let's not say summoned—Let us just say invited—
It's more humane that way you see—Actually we are
taking an opinion poll in regard to someone with whom
I believe you have a long and close association, namely
Mr. Winkhorst of The Lazarus Pharmaceutical Company—We are interviewing friends, relatives, co-
workers to predict his chances for reelection as captain
of the chemical executive softball team—You must of
course realize the importance of this matter in view of
the company motto 'Always play *soft* ball' is it not?—
Now just to give the interview life let us pretend that
you are yourself Winkhorst and I will put the questions
directly ketch?—Very well Mr. Winkhorst, let's not
waste time—We know that you are the chemist re-

sponsible for synthesizing the new hallucinogen drugs many of which have not yet been released even for experimental purposes—We know also that you have effected certain molecular alterations in the known hallucinogens that are being freely distributed in many quarters—Precisely how are these alterations effected? —Please do not be deterred from making a complete statement by my obvious lack of technical knowledge —That is not my job—Your answers will be recorded and turned over to the Technical Department for processing."

"The process is known as stress deformation—It is done or was done with a cyclotron—For example the mescaline molecule is exposed to cyclotron stress so that the energy field is deformed and some molecules are activated on fissionable level—Mescaline so processed will be liable to produce, in the human subject— (known as 'canine preparations')—uh unpleasant and dangerous symptoms and in particular 'the heat syndrome' which is a reflection of nuclear fission—Subjects complain they are on fire, confined in a suffocating furnace, white hot bees swarming in the body—The hot bees are of course the deformed mescaline molecules—I am putting it simply of course—"

"There are other procedures?"

"Of course but always it is a question of deformation or association on a molecular level—Another procedure consists in exposing the mescaline molecule to certain virus cultures—The virus as you know is a very small particle and can be precisely associated on molecular chains—This association gives an additional tune-in with anybody who has suffered from a virus infection such as hepatitis for example—Much easier to produce the heat syndrome in such a preparation."

"Can this process be reversed? That is can you decontaminate a compound once the deformation has been effected?"

"Not so easy—It would be simpler to recall our stock from the distributors and replace it."

"And now I would like to ask you if there could be benign associations—Could you for example associate mescaline with apomorphine on a molecular level?"

"First we would have to synthesize the apomorphine formulae—As you know it is forbidden to do this."

"And for very good reason is it not, Winkhorst?"

"Yes—Apomorphine combats parasite invasion by stimulating the regulatory centers to normalize metabolism—A powerful variation of this drug could deactivate all verbal units and blanket the earth in silence, disconnecting the entire heat syndrome."

"You could do this, Mr. Winkhorst?"

"It would not be easy—certain technical details and so little time—" He held up his thumb and forefinger a quarter inch apart.

"Difficult but not impossible, Mr. Winkhorst?"

"Of course not—If I receive the order—This is unlikely in view of certain facts known to both of us."

"You refer to the scheduled nova date?"

"Of course."

"You are convinced that this is inevitable, Mr. Wink-horst?"

. "I have seen the formulae—I do not believe in miracles."

"Of what do these formulae consist, Mr. Winkhorst?"

"It is a question of disposal—What is known as Uranium and this applies to all such raw material is actually a form of excrement—The disposal problem of radioactive waste in any time universe is ultimately insoluble."

"But if we disintegrate verbal units, that is vaporize the containers, then the explosion could not take place in effect would never have existed—"

"Perhaps—I am a chemist not a prophet—It is considered axiomatic that the nova formulae can not be broken, that the process is irreversible once set in motion—All energy and appropriations is now being channeled into escape plans—If you are interested I am empowered to make an offer of evacuation—on a time level of course."

"And in return?"

"You will simply send back a report that there is no evidence of nova activity on planet earth."

"What you are offering me is a precarious aqualung existence in somebody else's stale movie—Such people made a wide U turn back to the '20s—Besides the whole thing is ridiculous—Like I send back word from Mercury: 'The climate is cool and bracing—The natives are soo friendly'—or 'On Uranus one is conscious of a lightness in the limbs and an exhilarating

sense of freedom'—So Doctor Benway snapped, 'You
will simply send back spitting notice on your dirty nova
activity—It is ridiculous like when the egg cracks the
climate is cool and bracing'—or 'Uranus is mushroom-
ing freedom'—This is the old splintered pink carnival
1917—Sad little irrigation ditch—Where else if they
have date twisting paralyzed in the blue movies?—
You are offering me aqualung scraps—precarious flesh
—soiled movie, rag on cock—Intestinal street boy
smells through the outhouse.' "

"I am empowered to make the offer not assess its
validity."

"The offer is declined—The so-called officers on this
planet have panicked and are rushing the first life boat
in drag—Such behavior is unbecoming an officer and
these people have been relieved of a command they
evidently experienced as an intolerable burden in any
case—In all my experience as a police officer I have
never seen such a downright stupid conspiracy—The
nova mob operating here are stumble bums who
couldn't even crash our police line-up anywhere else—"

This is the old needling technique to lure a criminal
out into the open—Three thousand years with the
force and it still works—Winkhorst was fading out in
hot spirals of the crab nebula—I experienced a moment
of panic—walked slowly to the tape recorder—

"Now if you would be so kind, Mr. Winkhorst, I
would like you to listen to this music and give me
your reaction—We are using it in a commercial on the
apomorphine program—Now if you would listen to

this music and give me advantage—We are thinking of sullen street boy for this spot—"

I put on some Gnaova drum music and turned around both guns blazing—Silver needles under tons focus come level on average had opened up still as good as he used to be pounding stabbing to the drum beats—The scorpion controller was on screen blue eyes white hot spitting from the molten core of a planet where lead melts at noon, his body half concealed by the portico of a Mayan temple—A stink of torture chambers and burning flesh filled the room— Prisoners staked out under the white hot skies of Minraud eaten alive by metal ants—I kept distance surrounding him with pounding stabbing light blasts seventy tons to the square inch—The orders loud and clear now: "Blast—Pound—Strafe—Stab—*Kill*"—The screen opened out—I could see Mayan codices and Egyptian hieroglyphs—Prisoners screaming in the ovens broken down to insect forms—Life-sized portrait of a pantless corpse hanged to a telegraph pole ejaculating under a white hot sky—Stink of torture when the egg cracks— always to insect forms—Staked out spines gathering mushroom ants—Eyes pop out naked hanged to a telegraph pole of adolescent image—

The music shifted to Pan Pipes and I moved away to remote mountain villages where blue mist swirled through the slate houses—Place of the vine people under eternal moonlight—Pressure removed—Seventy tons to the square inch suddenly moved out—From a calm grey distance I saw the scorpion controller explode in the low pressure area—Great winds whipping across a black plain scattered the codices and hieroglyphs to rubbish heaps of the earth—(A Mexican boy whistling Mambo, drops his pants by a mud wall and wipes his ass with a page from the Madrid codex) Place of the dust people who live in sand storms riding the wind—*Wind wind wind* through dusty offices and archives—Wind through the board rooms and torture banks of time—

("A great calm shrouds the green place of the vine people.")

INFLEXIBLE AUTHORITY

When I handed in my report to The District Supervisor he read it through with a narrow smile—"They have distracted you with a war film and given false information as usual—You are inexperienced of course—Totally green troops in the area—However your unauthorized action will enable us to cut some corners—Now come along and we will get the real facts—"

The police patrol pounded into the home office of Lazarus & Co—

"And now Mr. Winkhorst and you gentlemen of the board, let's have the real story and quickly or would you rather talk to the partisans?"

"You dumb hicks."

"The information and quickly—We have no time to waste with such as you."

The D.S. stood there translucent silver sending a solid blast of inflexible authority.

"All right—We'll talk—The cyclotron processes image—It's the microfilm principle—smaller and smaller, more and more images in less space pounded down under the cyclotron to crystal image meal—We can take the whole fucking planet out that way up our ass in a finger stall—Image of both of us good as he used to be—A *stall* you dig—Just old showmen packing our ermines you might say—"

"Enough of that show—Continue please with your statement."

"Sure, sure, but you see now why we had to laugh till we pissed watching those dumb rubes playing around with photomontage—Like charging a regiment of tanks with a defective slingshot."

"For the last time out of me—Continue with your statement."

"Sure, sure, but you see now why we had such lookout on these dumb rubes playing around with a splintered carnival—Charging a regiment of tanks with a defective sanitarium 1917—Never could keep his gas —Just an old trouper is all"—(He goes into a song and dance routine dancing off stage—An 1890 cop picks him up in the wings and brings back a ventriloquist dummy.)

"This, gentlemen, is a death dwarf—As you can see

manipulated by remote control—Compliments of Mr. & Mrs. D."

"Give me a shot," says the dwarf. "And I'll tell you something interesting."

Hydraulic metal hands proffer a tray of phosphorescent meal yellow brown in color like pulverized amber —The dwarf takes out a hypo from a silver case and shoots a pinch of the meal in the main line.

"Images—millions of images—That's what I eat— Cyclotron shit—Ever try kicking *that* habit with apomorphine?—Now I got all the images of sex acts and torture ever took place anywhere and I can just blast it out and control you gooks right down to the molecule—I got orgasms—I got screams—I got all the images any hick poet ever shit out—My Power's coming —My Power's coming—My Power's coming—" He goes into a faith healer routine rolling his eyes and frothing at the mouth—"And I got millions and millions and millions of images of Me, Me, Me, meee." (He nods out—He snaps back into focus screaming and spitting at Uranian Willy.) "You hick—You rat—Called the fuzz on me—All right—(Nods out)—I'm finished but you're still a lousy fink—"

"Address your remarks to me," said the D.S.

"All right you hick sheriffs—I'll cook you all down to decorticated canine preparations—You'll never get the apomorphine formulae in time—Never! Never! Never!" —(Caustic white hot saliva drips from his teeth—A smell of phosphorous fills the room)—"Human dogs"—

He collapses sobbing—"Don't mind if I take another shot do you?"

"Of course not—After giving information you will be disintoxicated."

"Disintoxicated he says—My God look at me."

"Good sir to the purpose."

"Shit—Uranian shit—That's what my human dogs eat—And I like to rub their nose in it—Beauty—Poetry —Space—What good is all that to me? If I don't get the image fix I'm in the ovens—You understand?—All the pain and hate images come loose—You understand *that* you dumb hick? I'm finished but your eyes still pop out—Naked candy of adolescent image Panama—*Who* look out different?—Cook you all down to decorticated mandrake—"

"Don't you think, Mr. D, it is in your interest to facilitate our work with the apomorphine formulae?"

"It wouldn't touch me—Not with the habit I got—"

"How do you know?—Have you tried?"

"Of course not—If I allowed anyone to develop the formulae he would be *out* you understand?—And it only takes one out to kick over my hypo tray."

"After all you don't have much choice Mr. D."

Again the image snapped back fading now and flickering like an old film—

"I still have the Board Room Reports—I can split the planet wide open tomorrow—And you, you little rat, you'll end up on ice in the ovens—Baked Alaska we call it—Nothing like a Baked Alaska to hold me vegetable—

Always plenty wise guys waiting on the Baked Alaska."
The dwarf's eyes sputtered blue sparks—A reek of
burning flesh billowed through the room—

"I still mushroom planet wide open for jolly—Any
hick poet shit out pleasures—Come closer and see my
pictures—Show you something interesting—Come
closer and watch them flop around in soiled linen—The
Garden Boys both of us good as we used to be—Sweet
pictures start coming in the hanged man knees up to
the chin—You know—Beauty bare and still as good—
Cock stand up spurting whitewash—Ever try his crotch
when the egg cracks?—Now I got all the images in
backward time—Rusty black pants—Delicate gooks in
the locker room rubbing each other—I got screams—I
watched—Burning heavens, idiot—Don't mind if I
take another shot—Jimmy Sheffield is still as good as
he used to be—Flesh the room in pink carnival—"

A young agent turned away vomiting; "Police work
is not pleasant on any level," said the D.S. He turned
to Winkhorst: "This special breed spitting notice on
your dirty pharmaceuticals—Level—"

"Well some of my information was advantage—It *is*
done with a cyclotron—But like this—Say I want to
heat up the mescaline formula what I do is put the
blazing photo from Hiroshima and Nagasaki under my
cyclotron and shade the heat meal in with mescaline
—Indetectible—It's all so simple and magnificent really
—Beauty bare and all that—Or say I want 'The
Drenched Lands' on the boy what I do is put the image

from his cock under the cyclotron spurting whitewash
in the white hot skies of Minraud."

The death dwarf opens one eye—"Hey, copper, come
here—Got something else to tell you—Might as well
rat—Everyone does it here the man says—You know
about niggers? Why darkies were born?—Travel flesh
we call it—Transports better—Tell you something
else—" He nods out.

"And the apomorphine formula, Mr. Winkhorst?"

"Apomorphine is no word and no image—It is of
course misleading to speak of a silence virus or an apomorphine virus since apomorphine is anti-virus—The
uh apomorphine preparations must be raised in a culture containing sublethal quantities of pain and pleasure cyclotron concentrates—Sub-virus stimulates anti-
virus special group—When immunity has been established in the surviving preparations—and many will
not survive—we have the formulae necessary to defeat
the virus powers—It is simply a question of putting
through an inoculation program in the very limited
time that remains—Word begets image and image *is*
virus—Our facilities are at your disposal gentlemen
and I am at your disposal—Technical sergeant I can
work for anybody—These officers don't even know
what button to push." He glares at the dwarf who is on
the nod, hands turning to vines—

"I'm not taking any rap for a decorticated turnip—
And you just let me tell you how much all the kids in
the office and the laboratory hate you stinking heavy
metal assed cunt sucking board bastards."

Technical Deposition of the Virus Power. "Gentlemen, it was first suggested that we take our own image and examine how it could be made more portable. We found that simple binary coding systems were enough to contain the entire image however they required a large amount of storage space until it was found that the binary information could be written at the molecular level, and our entire image could be contained within a grain of sand. However it was found that these information molecules were not dead matter but exhibited a capacity for life which is found elsewhere in the form of virus. Our virus infects the human and creates our image in him.

"We first took our image and put it into code. A technical code developed by the information theorists. This code was written at the molecular level to save space, when it was found that the image material was not dead matter, but exhibited the same life cycle as the virus. This virus released upon the world would infect the entire population and turn them into our replicas, it was not safe to release the virus until we could be sure that the last groups to go replica would not notice. To this end we invented variety in many forms, variety that is of information content in a molecule, which, *enfin,* is always a permutation of the existing material. Information speeded up, slowed down, permutated, changed at random by radiating the virus material with high energy rays from cyclotrons, in short we have created an infinity of variety at the information level, sufficient to keep so-called scientists busy for ever exploring the 'richness of nature.'

"It was important all this time that the possibility of a human ever conceiving of being without a body should not arise. Remember that the variety we invented was permutation of the electromagnetic structure of matter energy interactions which are not the raw material of nonbody experience."

Note From The Technical Department of Nova Police: Winkhorst's information on the so-called "apomorphine formulae" was incomplete—He did not mention alnorphine—This substance like apomorphine is made from morphine—Its action

is to block morphine out of the cells—An injection of alnorphine will bring on immediate withdrawal symptoms in an
addict—It is also a specific in acute morphine poisoning—
Doctor Isbell of Lexington states in an article recently published in *The British Journal of Addiction* that alnorphine is
not habit-forming but acts even more effectively as a pain
killer than morphine but can not be used because it produces
"mental disturbances"—What is pain?—Obviously damage to
the image—Junk is concentrated image and this accounts for
its pain killing action—Nor could there be pain if there was
no image—This may well account for the pain killing action
of alnorphine and also for the unspecified "mental disturbances"—So we began our experiments by administering alnorphine in combination with apomorphine.

COORDINATE POINTS

The case I have just related will show you something
of our methods and the people with whom we are
called upon to deal.

"I doubt if any of you on this copy planet have ever
seen a nova criminal—(they take considerable pains to
mask their operations) and I am sure none of you have
ever seen a nova police officer—When disorder on any
planet reaches a certain point the regulating instance
scans POLICE—Otherwise—SPUT—Another planet
bites the cosmic dust—I will now explain something of
the mechanisms and techniques of nova which are always deliberately manipulated—I am quite well aware
that no one on any planet likes to see a police officer so
let me emphasize in passing that the nova police have

no intention of remaining after their work is done—
That is, when the danger of nova is removed from this
planet we will move on to other assignments—We do
our work and go—The difference between this department and the parasitic excrescence that often travels
under the name 'Police' can be expressed in metabolic
terms: The distinction between morphine and apomorphine. 'Apomorphine is made by boiling morphine with
hydrochloric acid. This alters chemical formulae and
physiological effects. Apomorphine has no sedative
narcotic or addicting properties. It is a metabolic regulator that need not be continued when its work is done.
I quote from *Anxiety and Its Treatment* by Doctor John
Dent of London: 'Apomorphine acts on the back brain
stimulating the regulating centers in such a way as to
normalize the metabolism.' It has been used in the
treatment of alcoholics and drug addicts and normal-
izes metabolism in such a way as to remove the need
for any narcotic substance. Apomorphine cuts drug
lines from the brain. Poison of dead sun fading in
smoke—"

The Nova Police can be compared to apomorphine,
a regulating instance that need not continue and has
no intention of continuing after its work is done. Any
man who is doing a job is working to make himself obsolete and that goes double for police.

Now look at the parasitic police of morphine. First
they create a narcotic problem then they say that a
permanent narcotics police is now necessary to deal
with the problem of addiction. Addiction can be con-

trolled by apomorphine and reduced to a minor health problem. The narcotics police know this and that is why they do not want to see apomorphine used in the treatment of drug addicts:

PLAN DRUG ADDICTION

Now you are asking me whether I want to perpetuate a narcotics problem and I say: "Protect the disease. Must be made criminal protecting society from the disease."

The problem scheduled in the United States the use of jail, former narcotics plan, addiction and crime for many years—Broad front "Care" of welfare agencies—Narcotics which antedate the use of drugs—The fact is noteworthy—48 stages—prisoner was delayed—has been separated—was required—

Addiction in some form is the basis—must be wholly addicts—Any voluntary capacity subversion of The Will Capital And Treasury Bank—Infection dedicated to traffic in exchange narcotics demonstrated a Typhoid Mary who will spread narcotics problem to the United Kingdom—Finally in view of the cure—cure of the social problem and as such dangerous to society—

Maintaining addict cancers to our profit—pernicious personal contact—Market increase—Release The Prosecutor to try any holes—Cut Up Fighting Drug Addiction by Malcolm Monroe Former Prosecutor, in *Western World,* October 1959.

As we have seen image *is* junk—When a patient loses

a leg what has been damaged?—Obviously his image of himself—So he needs a shot of cooked down image —The hallucinogen drugs shift the scanning pattern of "reality" so that we see a different "reality"—There is no true or real "reality"—"Reality" is simply a more or less constant scanning pattern—The scanning pattern we accept as "reality" has been imposed by the controlling power on this planet, a power primarily oriented towards total control—In order to retain control they have moved to monopolize and deactivate the hallucinogen drugs by effecting noxious alterations on a molecular level—

The basic nova mechanism is very simple: Always create as many insoluble conflicts as possible and always aggravate existing conflicts—This is done by dumping life forms with incompatible conditions of existence on the same planet—There is of course nothing "wrong" about any given life form since "wrong" only has reference to conflicts with other life forms— The point is these forms should not be on the same planet—Their conditions of life are basically incompatible in present time form and it is precisely the work of the Nova Mob to see that they remain in present time form, to create and aggravate the conflicts that lead to the explosion of a planet that is to nova—At any given time recording devices fix the nature of absolute need and dictate the use of total weapons—Like this: Take two opposed pressure groups—Record the most violent and threatening statements of group one with regard to group two and play back to group two—Record the answer and take it back to group one—Back and forth between opposed pressure groups—This process is known as "feed back"—You can see it operating in any bar room quarrel—In any quarrel for that matter—Manipulated on a global scale feeds back nuclear war and nova—These conflicts are deliberately created and aggravated by nova criminals—The Nova Mob: "Sammy The Butcher," "Green Tony," "Iron Claws," "The Brown Artist," "Jacky Blue Note," "Limestone John," "Izzy The Push," "Hamburger Mary," "Paddy The Sting," "The Subliminal Kid," "The Blue Dinosaur," and "Mr. & Mrs. D," also known as "Mr. Bradly Mr. Martin" also known as "The Ugly Spirit" thought to be the leader of the mob—The Nova Mob— In all my experience as a police officer I have never seen such total fear and degradation on any planet— We intend to arrest these criminals and turn them over to the Biological Department for the indicated alterations—

Now you may well ask whether we can straighten out this mess to the satisfaction of any life forms involved and my answer is this—Your earth case must be processed by the Biologic Courts—admittedly in a deplorable condition at this time—No sooner set up than immediately corrupted so that they convene every day in a different location like floating dice games, constantly swept away by stampeding forms all idiotically glorifying their stupid ways of life—(most of them quite unworkable of course) attempting to seduce the judges into Venusian sex practices, drug the court offi-

cials, and intimidate the entire audience chambers with
the threat of nova—In all my experience as a police officer I have never seen such total fear of the indicated
alterations on any planet—A thankless job you see and
we only do it so it won't have to be done some place
else under even more difficult circumstances—

The success of the nova mob depended on a blockade of the planet that allowed them to operate with
impunity—This blockade was broken by partisan activity directed from the planet Saturn that cut the control lines of word and image laid down by the nova
mob—So we moved in our agents and started to work
keeping always in close touch with the partisans—The
selection of local personnel posed a most difficult problem—Frankly we found that most existing police agencies were hopelessly corrupt—the nova mob had seen
to that—Paradoxically some of our best agents were
recruited from the ranks of those who are called criminals on this planet—In many instances we had to use
agents inexperienced in police work—There were of
course casualties and fuck ups—You must understand
that an undercover agent witnesses the most execrable
cruelties while he waits helpless to intervene—sometimes for many years—before he can make a definitive
arrest—So it is no wonder that green officers occasionally slip control when they finally do move in for the
arrest—This condition, known as "arrest fever," can upset an entire operation—In one recent case, our man in
Tangier suffered an attack of "arrest fever" and de-
tained everyone on his view screen including some of

our own undercover men—He was transferred to paper work in another area—

Let me explain *how* we make an arrest—Nova criminals are not three-dimensional organisms—(though they are quite definite organisms as we shall see) but they need three-dimensional human agents to operate —The point at which the criminal controller intersects a three-dimensional human agent is known as "a coordinate point"—And if there is one thing that carries over from one human host to another and establishes identity of the controller it is *habit*: idiosyncrasies, vices, food preferences—(we were able to trace Hamburger Mary through her fondness for peanut butter) a gesture, a certain smile, a special look, that is to say the *style* of the controller—A chain smoker will always operate through chain smokers, an addict through addicts—Now a single controller can operate through thousands of human agents, but he must have a line of coordinate points—Some move on junk lines through addicts of the earth, others move on lines of certain sexual practices and so forth—It is only when we can block the controller out of all coordinate points available to him and flush him out from host cover that we can make a definitive arrest—Otherwise the criminal escapes to other coordinates—

We picked up our first coordinate points in London.

Fade out to a shabby hotel near Earl's Court in London. One of our agents is posing as a writer. He has written a so-called pornographic novel called Naked Lunch in which The Orgasm Death Gimmick is de-

scribed. That was the bait. And they walked write in.
A quick knock at the door and there It was. A green
boy/girl from the sewage deltas of Venus. The colorless vampire creatures from a land of grass without
mirrors. The agent shuddered in a light fever. "Arrest
Fever." The Green Boy mistook this emotion as a trib-
ute to his personal attractions preened himself and
strutted round the room. This organism is only dangerous when directed by The Insect Brain Of Minraud.
That night the agent sent in his report:

"Controller is woman—Probably Italian—Picked up
a villa outside Florence—And a Broker operating in
the same area—Concentrate patrols—Contact local partisans—Expect to encounter Venusian weapons—"

In the months that followed we turned up more and
more coordinate points. We put a round-the-clock
shadow on The Green Boy and traced all incoming and
outgoing calls. We picked up The Broker's Other Half
in Tangier.

A Broker is someone who arranges criminal jobs:

"Get that writer—that scientist—this artist—He is
too close—Bribe—Con—Intimidate—Take over his coordinate points—"

And the Broker finds someone to do the job like:
"Call 'Izzy The Push,' this is a defenestration bit—Call
'Green Tony,' he will fall for the sweet con—As a last
resort call 'Sammy The Butcher' and warm up The
Ovens—This is a special case—"

All Brokers have three-dimensional underworld contacts and rely on The Nova Guards to block shadows

and screen their operations. But when we located The Other Half in Tangier we were able to monitor the calls that went back and forth between them.

At this point we got a real break in the form of a defector from The Nova Mob: Uranian Willy The Heavy Metal Kid. Now known as "Willy The Fink" to his former associates. Willy had long been put on the "unreliable" list and marked for "Total Disposal In The Ovens." But he provided himself with a stash of apomorphine so escaped and contacted our Tangier agent. Fade out.

URANIAN WILLY

Uranian Willy The Heavy Metal Kid. Also known as Willy The Rat. He wised up the marks. His metal face moved in a slow smile as he heard the twittering supersonic threats through antennae embedded in his translucent skull.

"Death in The Ovens."

"Death in Centipede."

Trapped in this dead whistle stop, surrounded by The Nova Guard, he still gave himself better than even chance on a crash out. Electrician in gasoline crack of history. His brain seared by white hot blasts. One hope left in the universe; Plan D.

He was not out of The Security Compound by a long way but he had rubbed off the word shackles and sounded the alarm to shattered male forces of the earth:

THIS IS WAR TO EXTERMINATION. FIGHT CELL BY CELL THROUGH BODIES AND MIND SCREENS OF THE EARTH. SOULS ROTTEN FROM THE ORGASM DRUG, FLESH SHUDDERING FROM THE OVENS, PRISONERS OF THE EARTH COME OUT. STORM THE STUDIO—

Plan D called for Total Exposure. Wise up all the marks everywhere. Show them the rigged wheel of Life-Time-Fortune. Storm The Reality Studio. And retake the universe. The Plan shifted and reformed as reports came in from his electric patrols sniffing quivering down streets and mind screens of the earth.

"Area mined—Guards everywhere—Can't quite get through—"

"Order total weapons—Release Silence Virus—"

"Board Books taken—Heavy losses—"

"Photo falling—Word falling—Break Through in Grey Room—Use Partisans of all nations—*Towers, open fire*—"

The Reality Film giving and buckling like a bulkhead under pressure and the pressure gauge went up and up. The needle was edging to NOVA. Minutes to go. Burnt metal smell of interplanetary war in the raw noon streets swept by screaming glass blizzards of enemy flak. He dispersed on grey sliding between light and shadow down mirror streets and shadow pools. Yes he was wising up the marks. Willy The Fink they called him among other things, syndicates of the universe feeling for him with distant fingers of murder. He stopped in for a cup of "Real English Tea Made Here" and a thin grey man sat at his table with inflexible authority.

"Nova Police. Yes I think we can quash the old Nova Warrants. Work with us. We want names and co-ordinate points. Your application for Biologic Transfer will have to go through channels and is no concern of this department. Now we'll have a look at your room if you don't mind." They went through his photos and papers with fingers light and cold as spring wind. Grey Police of The Regulator, calm and grey with inflexible authority. Willy had worked with them before. He knew they were undercover agents working under conditions as dangerous as his own. They were dedicated men and would sacrifice him or any other agent to arrest The Nova Mob:

"Sammy The Butcher," "Green Tony," "Iron Claws," "The Brown Artist," "Jacky Blue Note," "Limestone John," "Izzy The Push," "Hamburger Mary," "The Subliminal Kid," "The Green Octopus," and "Willy The Rat," who wised up the marks on the last pitch. And they took Uranus apart in a fissure flash of metal rage.

As he walked past The Sargasso Café black insect flak of Minraud stabbed at his vitality centers. Two Lesbian Agents with glazed faces of grafted penis flesh sat sipping spinal fluid through alabaster straws. He threw up a Silence Screen and grey fog drifted through the café. The deadly Silence Virus. Coating word pat-

terns. Stopping abdominal breathing holes of The Insect People Of Minraud.

    The grey smoke drifted   the grey that stops
shift   cut   tangle   they   breathe   medium
    the   word   cut   shift   patterns   words
    cut   the insect   tangle   cut   shift
that coats   word   cut   breath   silence
shift   abdominal   cut   tangle   stop   word
    holes.

He did not stop or turn around. Never look back. He
had been a professional killer so long he did not remember anything else. Uranian born of Nova Conditions. You have to be free to remember and he was
under sentence of death in Maximum Security Birth
Death Universe. So he sounded the words that end
"Word"—
    Eye take back color from "word"—
Word dust everywhere now like soiled stucco on the
buildings. Word dust without color drifting smoke
streets. Explosive bio advance out of space to neon.

    At the bottom of the stairs Uranian Willy engaged
an Oven Guard. His flesh shrank feeling insect claws
under the terrible dry heat. Trapped, cut off in that
soulless place. Prisoner eaten alive by white hot ants.
With a split second to spare he threw his silver blast
and caught the nitrous fumes of burning film as he
walked through the door where the guard had stood.

    "Shift linguals—Free doorways—Cut word lines—
Photo falling—Word falling—Break Through in Grey

Room—Use partisans of all nations—*Towers, open fire—*"

WILL HOLLYWOOD NEVER LEARN?

"Word falling—Photo falling—Break through in Grey Room—"

Insane orders and counter orders issue from berserk Time Machine—

"Terminal electric voice of C—Shift word lines—Vibrate 'tourists.' "

"I said The Chief of Police skinned alive in Baghdad not Washington D.C."

"British Prime Minister assassinated in rightist coup."

"Switzerland freezes all foreign assets—"

"Mindless idiot you have liquidated the Commissar—"

"Cut word lines—Shift linguals—"

Electric storms of violence sweep the planet—Desperate position and advantage precariously held—Governments fall with a whole civilization and ruling class into streets of total fear—Leaders turn on image rays to flood the world with replicas—Swept out by counter image—

"Word falling—Photo falling—Pinball led streets."

Gongs of violence and how—Show you something—Berserk machine—"Mr. Bradly Mr. Martin" charges in with his army of short-time hype artists and takes over

The Reality Concession to set up Secretary Of State
For Ruined Toilet—Workers paid off in SOS—The
Greys came in on a London Particular—SOS Governments fade in worn metal dawn swept out through
other flesh—Counter orders issued to the sound of
gongs—Machine force of riot police at the outskirts
D.C.—Death Dwarfs talking in supersonic blasts of
Morse Code—Swept into orbit of the Saturn Galaxy
high on ammonia—Time and place shift in speed-up
movie—

"Attack position over instrument like pinball—Towers, open fire—"

Atmosphere and climate shifted daily from carbon
dioxide to ammonia to pure oxygen—from the dry heat
of Minraud to the blue cold of Uranus—One day the
natives forced into heavy reptile forms of overwhelming gravity—next floated in tenuous air of plaintive
lost planets—Subway broke out every language—D
took pictures of a million battle fields—"Will Hollywood never learn?—Unimaginable and downright
stupid disaster—"

Incredible forms of total survival emerged clashed
exploded in altered pressure—Desperate flesh from
short time artists—Transparent civilizations went out
talking—

"Death, Johnny, come and took over."

Bradly and I supported by unusual mucus—Stale
streets of yesterday precariously held—Paths of desperate position—Shifting reality—Total survival in altered pressure—Flesh sheets dissolving amid vast ruins

of berserk machine—"SOS ··· ——— ··· Coughing enemy faces—"

"Orbit Sammy and the boys in Silent Space—Carbon dioxide work this machine—Terminal electric voice of C—All Ling door out of agitated—"

What precariously held government came over the air—Total fear in Hicksville—Secretary Of State For Far Eastern Hotel Affairs assassinated at outskirts of the hotel—Death Diplomats of Morse code supported in a cocktail lounge—

"Oxygen Law no cure for widespread blue cold." The Soviet Union said: "The very people who condemn altered pressure remain silent—"

Displacement into orbit processes—The Children's Fund has tenuous thin air of lost places—Sweet Home Movement to flood it with replicas—

So sitting with my hat on said: "I'm not going to do anything like that—"

Disgusting death by unusual mucus swept into orbit of cosmic vomit—(Tenuous candlelight—Remember I was carbon dioxide)—Rousing rendition of shifting reality—John lost in about 5000 men and women—Everyone else is on The Grey Veil—Flesh frozen to particles called "Good Consciousness" irrevocably committed to the toilet—Colorless slides in Mexican people—Other feature of the code on Grey Veil—To be read so to speak naked—Have to do it in dirty pictures—Reverse instructions on car seat—

"Mindless idiot you have liquidated The Shadow Cabinet—"

Swept out tiny police in supersonic Morse code—
Emergency Meeting at entrance to the avenue—

"Calling partisans of all nations—Cut word lines—
Shift linguals—Vibrate tourists—Free doorways—Word
falling—Photo falling—Break through in Grey Room—

——— .— .——— ———— .——. —.. ..—. .— .—..

.—.. —. .——. .——. .... ———— — ——— ..—.

.— .—.. .—.. ..—. ———."

TOWERS OPEN FIRE

Concentrate Partisans—Take Towers in Spanish
Villa—Hill 32—The Green Airborne poured into the
garden—Lens googles stuttering light flak—Antennae
guns stabbing strafing The Vampire Guards—They
pushed the fading bodies aside and occupied The
Towers—The Technician twirled control knobs—He
drank a bicarbonate of soda and belched into his hand
—*Urp.*

"God damned captain's a brown artist—Uranus is
right—What the fuck kind of a set is this—?? Not
worth a fart—Where's the reverse switch?—Found it
—Come in please—*Urp Urp Urp.*"

"Target Orgasm Ray Installations—Gothenberg Freelandt—Coordinates 8 2 7 6—Take Studio—Take
Board Books—Take Death Dwarfs—"

Supersonic sex pictures flickered on the view screen
—The pilots poised quivering electric dogs—Antennae

light guns twisting searching feeling enemy nerve centers—

"Focus."

"Did it."

"Towers, open fire—"

Strafe—Pound—Blast—Tilt—Stab—*Kill*—Air Hammers on their Stone Books—Bleep Bleep Bleep—*Death to The Nova Guard—Death to The Vampire Guards—*

Pilot K9 blasted The Scorpion Guards and led Break Through in Grey Room—Place Of the Board Books And The Death Dwarfs—A vast grey warehouse of wire mesh cubicles—Tier on tier of larval dwarfs tube-fed in bottles—The Death Dwarfs Of Minraud—Operation Total Disposal—Foetal dwarfs stirred slowly in green fluid fed through a tube in the navel—Bodies compacted layer on layer of transparent sheets on which was written The Message Of Total Disposal when the host egg cracks—Death Dwarfs waiting transfer to The Human Host—Written on The Soft Typewriter from The Stone Tablets of Minraud—

"Break Through in Grey Room—Death Dwarfs taken—Board Books taken—"

"Proceed to Sex Device and Blue Movie Studio—Behind Book Shop—Canal Five at Spiegel Bridge—"

"Advancing on Studio—Electric storms—Can't quite get through—"

"Pilot K9, you are hit—back—down"

The medics turned drum music full blast through his head phones—"Apomorphine on the double"—Frequency scalpel sewing wounds with wire photo polka

dots from The Image Bank—In three minutes K9 was
back in combat driving pounding into a wall of black
insect flak—The Enemy Installation went up in searing
white blast—Area of combat extended through the
vast suburban concentration camps of England and
America—Screaming Vampire Guards caught in stabbing stuttering light blast—

"*Partisans of all nations, open fire—tilt—blast—
pound—stab—strafe—kill—*"

"*Pilot K9, you are cut off—back. Back. Back before
the whole fucking shit house goes up—Return to base
immediately—Ride music beam back to base—Stay out
of that time flak—All pilots ride Pan pipes back to
base—*"

The Technician mixed a bicarbonate of soda surveying the havoc on his view screen—It was impossible to
estimate the damage—Anything put out up till now is
like pulling a figure out of the air—Installations shattered—Personnel decimated—Board Books destroyed
—Electric waves of resistance sweeping through mind
screens of the earth—The message of Total Resistance
on short wave of the world—*This is war to extermination—Shift linguals—Cut word lines—Vibrate tourists
—Free doorways—Photo falling—Word falling—Break
through in grey room—Calling Partisans of all nations
—Towers, open fire—*"

Crab Nebula

THEY DO NOT HAVE what they call "emotion's oxygen"
in the atmosphere. The medium in which animal life
breathes is not in that soulless place—Yellow plains
under white hot blue sky—Metal cities controlled by
The Elders who are heads in bottles—Fastest brains
preserved forever—Only form of immortality open to
The Insect People of Minraud—An intricate bureaucracy wired to the control brains directs all movement
—Even so there is a devious underground operating
through telepathic misdirection and camouflage—The
partisans make recordings ahead in time and leave the
recordings to be picked up by control stations while
they are free for a few seconds to organize underground
activities—Largely the underground is made up of adventurers who intend to outthink and displace the
present heads—There has been one revolution in the

history of Minraud—Purges are constant—Fallen heads destroyed in The Ovens and replaced with others faster and sharper to evolve more total weapons—The principal weapon of Minraud is of course heat—In the center of all their cities stand The Ovens where those who disobey the control brains are brought for total disposal —A conical structure of iridescent metal shimmering heat from the molten core of a planet where lead melts at noon—The Brass And Copper Streets surround The Oven—Here the tinkers and smiths work pounding out metal rhythms as prisoners and criminals are led to Disposal—The Oven Guards are red crustacean men with eyes like the white hot sky—Through contact with oven pain and captured enemies they sometimes mutate to breathe in emotions—They often help prisoners to escape and a few have escaped with the prisoners—

(When K9 entered the apartment he felt the suffocation of Minraud crushing his chest stopping his thoughts—He turned on reserve ate dinner and carried conversation—When he left the host walked out with him down the streets of Minraud past the ovens empty and cold now—calm dry mind of the guide beside him came to the corner of 14th and Third—

"I must go back now," said the guide—"Otherwise it will be too far to go alone."

He smiled and held out his hand fading in the alien air—)

K9 was brought to the ovens by red guards in white and gold robe of office through the Brass and Copper

Street under pounding metal hammers—The oven heat drying up life source as white hot metal lattice closed around him—

"Second exposure—Time three point five," said the guard—

K9 walked out into The Brass And Copper Streets— A slum area of vending booths and smouldering slag heaps crossed by paths worn deep in phosphorescent metal—In a square littered with black bones he encountered a group of five scorpion men—Faces of transparent pink cartilage burning inside—stinger dripping the oven poison—Their eyes flared with electric hate and they slithered forward to surround him but drew back at sight of the guard—

They walked on into an area of tattoo booths and sex parlors—A music like wind through fine metal wires bringing a measure of relief from the terrible dry heat —Black beetle musicians saw this music out of the air swept by continual hot winds from plains that surround the city—The plains are dotted with villages of conical paper-thin metal houses where a patient gentle crab people live unmolested in the hottest regions of the planet—

Controller of The Crab Nebula on a slag heap of smouldering metal under the white hot sky channels all his pain into control thinking—He is protected by heat and crab guards and the brains armed now with The Blazing Photo from Hiroshima and Nagasaki—The brains under his control are encased in a vast structure of steel and crystal spinning thought patterns that control whole galaxies thousand years ahead on the chessboard of virus screens and juxtaposition formulae—

So The Insect People Of Minraud formed an alliance with the Virus Power Of The Vegetable People to occupy planet earth—The gimmick is reverse photosynthesis—The Vegetable People suck up oxygen and all equivalent sustenance of animal life—Always the colorless sheets between you and what you see taste touch smell eat—And these green vegetable junkies slowly using up your oxygen to stay on the nod in carbon dioxide—

When K9 entered the café he felt the colorless smell of the vegetable people closing round him taste and sharpness gone from the food people blurring in slow motion fade out—And there was a whole tank full of vegetable junkies breathing it all in—He clicked some reverse combos through the pinball machine and left the café—In the street citizens were yacking like supersonic dummies—The SOS addicts had sucked up all the silence in the area were now sitting around in blue blocks of heavy metal the earth's crust buckling ominously under their weight—He shrugged: "Who am I to be critical?"

He knew what it meant to kick an SOS habit: White hot agony of thawing metal—And the suffocating panic of carbon dioxide withdrawal—

Virus defined as the three-dimensional coordinate point of a controller—Transparent sheets with virus perforations like punch cards passed through the host on the soft machine feeling for a point of intersection—

The virus attack is primarily directed against affective animal life—Virus of rage hate fear ugliness swirling round you waiting for a point of intersection and once in immediately perpetrates in your name some ugly noxious or disgusting act sharply photographed and recorded becomes now part of the virus sheets constantly presented and represented before your mind screen to produce more virus word and image around and around it's all around you the invisible hail of bring down word and image—

What does virus do wherever it can dissolve a hole and find traction?—It starts eating—And what does it do with what it eats?—It makes exact copies of itself that start eating to make more copies that start eating to make more copies that start eating and so forth to the virus power the fear hate virus slowly replaces the host with virus copies—Program empty body—A vast tapeworm of bring down word and image moving through your mind screen always at the same speed on a slow hydraulic-spine axis like the cylinder gimmick in the adding machine—How do you make someone feel stupid?—You present to him all the times he talked and acted and felt stupid again and again any number of times fed into the combo of the soft calculating machine geared to find more and more punch cards and feed in more and more images of stupidity disgust propitiation grief apathy death—The recordings leave electromagnetic patterns—That is any situation that causes rage will magnetize rage patterns and draw around the rage word and image recordings—Or some disgusting sex practice once the connection is made in childhood whenever the patterns are magnetized by sex desire the same word and image will be presented—And so forth—The counter move is very simple—This is machine strategy and the machine can be redirected—Record for ten minutes on a tape recorder—Now run the tape back without playing and cut in other words at random—Where you have cut in and re-recorded words are wiped off the tape and new words in their place—You have turned time back ten minutes and wiped electromagnetic word patterns off the tape and substituted other patterns— You can do the same with mind tape after working with the tape recorder—(This takes some experimentation)—The old mind tapes can be wiped clean—Magnetic word dust falling from old patterns—Word falling—Photo falling —"Last week Robert Kraft of the Mount Wilson and Palomar Observatories reported some answers to the riddle of exploding stars—Invariably he found the exploding star was locked by gravity to a nearby star— The two stars are in a strange symbiotic relationship— One is a small hot blue star—(Mr. Bradly) Its companion is a larger red star—(Mr. Martin)—Because the stellar twins are so close together the blue star continually pulls fuel in the form of hydrogen gas from the red star—The motion of the system spins the hydrogen into an incandescent figure eight—One circle of the eight encloses one star—The other circle encloses the other—supplied with new fuel the blue star ignites."—Quote, *Newsweek*, Feb. 12, 1962—

The Crab Nebula observed by the Chinese in 1054 A.D. is the result of a supernova or exploding star— Situated approximately three thousand light years from the earth—(Like three thousand years in hot claws at the window—You got it?—)—Before they blow up a star they have a spot picked out as many light years away as possible—Then they start draining all the fuel and charge to the new pitch and siphon themselves there right after and on their way rejoicing—You notice we don't have as much time as people had say a hundred years ago?—Take your clothes to the laundry write a letter pick up your mail at American Express and the day is gone—They are short-timing us as many light years as they can take for the getaway—It seems that there were survivors on The Crab Pitch who are not in all respects reasonable men—And The Nova Law moving in fast—So they start the same old lark sucking all the charge and air and color to a new location and then?—*Sput*—You notice something is sucking all the flavor out of food the pleasure out of sex the color out of everything in sight?—Precisely creating the low pressure area that leads to nova—So they move cross the wounded galaxies always a few light years ahead of the Nova Heat—That is they did—The earth was our set—And they walked right into the antibiotic hand-cuffs—It will readily be seen that having created one nova they must make other or answer for the first—I mean three thousand years in hot claws at the window like a giant crab in slag heaps of smouldering metal— Also the more novas the less time between they are running out of pitches—So they bribe the natives with a promise of transportation and immortality—

"Yeah, man, flesh and junk and charge stacked up bank vaults full of it—Three thousand years of flesh—So we leave the bloody apes behind and on our way rejoicing right?—It's the only way to live—"

And the smart operators fall for it every fucking time —Talk about marks—One of our best undercover operators is known as The Rube—He perfected The Reverse Con—Comes on honest and straight and the smart operators all think they are conning him—How could they think otherwise until he slips on the antibiotic handcuffs—

"There's a wise guy born every minute," he says. "Closing time gentlemen—The stenographer will take your depositions—"

"So why did I try to blow up the planet?—Pea under the shell—Now you see it now you don't—Sky shift to cover the last pitch—Take it all out with us and hit the road—I am made of metal and that metal is radioactive—Radioactivity can be absorbed up to a point but radium clock hands tick away—Time to move on—Only one turnstile—Heavy planet—Travel with Minraud technicians to handle the switchboard and Venusians to make flesh and keep the show on the road—Then The Blazing Photo and we travel on—Word *is* flesh and word *is* two that is the human body is compacted of two organisms and where you have two you have word and word is flesh and when they started tampering with the word that was it and the blockade

was broken and The Nova Heat moved in—The Venusians sang first naturally they were in the most immediate danger—They live underwater in the body with an
air line—And that air line is the word—Then the technicians spilled and who can blame them after the conditions I assigned to keep them technicians—Like three
thousand years in hot claws—So I am alone as always
—You understand nova is where I am born in such pain
no one else survives in one piece—Born again and again
cross the wounded galaxies—I am alone but not what
you call 'lonely'—Loneliness is a product of dual mammalian structure—'Loneliness,' 'love,' 'friendship,' all the
rest of it—I am not two—I am *one*—But to maintain
my state of oneness I need twoness in other life forms—
Other must talk so that I can remain silent—If another
becomes one then I am two—That makes two ones
makes two and I am no longer one—Plenty of room in
space you say?—But I am not one in space I am one in
time—Metal time—Radioactive time—So of course I
tried to keep you all out of space—That is the end of
time—And those who were allowed out sometimes for
special services like creating a useful religious concept
went always with a Venusian guard—All the 'mystics'
and 'saints'—All except my old enemy Hassan i Sabbah
who wised up the marks to space and said they could
be one and need no guard no other half no word—

"And now I have something to say to all you angle
boys of the cosmos who thought you had an in with
The Big Operator—*'Suckers! Cunts! Marks!—I hate
you all—And I never intended to cut you in or pay you*

off with anything but horse shit—And you can thank The Rube if you don't go up with the apes—Is that clear enough or shall I make it even clearer? You are the suckers cunts marks I invented to explode this dead whistle stop and go up with it—' "

A BAD MOVE

Could give no other information than wind walking in a rubbish heap to the sky—Solid shadow turned off the white film of noon heat—Exploded deep in the alley tortured metal Oz—Look anywhere, Dead hand—Phosphorescent bones—Cold Spring afterbirth of that hospital—Twinges of amputation—Bread knife in the heart paid taxi boys—If I knew I'd be glad to look any-place—No good myself—Clom Fliday—Diseased wind identity fading out—Smoke is all—We intersect in the dark mutinous door—Hairless skull—Flesh smeared—Five times of dust we made it all—consumed by slow metal fires—Smell of gasoline envelops last electrician —I woke up with dark information from the dead—Board Room Reports waiting for Madrid—Arrested mo-tion con su medicina—Soft mendicant "William" in the dark street—He stood there 1910 straw words falling—Dead lights and water—Either way is a bad move—Better than that?—Gone away can tell you—No good No bueno—White flash mangled silver eyes—Flesh flakes in the sky—Explosive twinges of amputation—

Mendicant the crooked crosses and barren the dark street—No more—No más—Their last end—Wounded galaxies tap on the pane—Hustling myself—Clom Friday—And one fine tell you—No good—No bueno—

Be cheerful sir our revels touch the sky—The white film made of Mr. Martin—Rotting phosphorescent bones carried a gasoline dream—Hand falling—White flash mangled "Mr. Bradly Mr. Martin"—Thing Police, Board Room Death Smell, time has come for the dark street—No more—No más wounded galaxies—I told him you on aid—Died out down stale streets through convolutions of our ever living poet—On this green land the dollar twisted to light a last cigarette—Last words answer you—

Long time between suns behind—Empty hunger cross the wounded sky—Cold your brain slowly fading —I said by our ever living poet dead—Last words answer your summons—May not refuse vision in setting forth the diary—Mr. Martin Mr. Corso Mr. Beiles Mr. Burroughs now ended—These our actors, William —The razor inside, sir—Jerk the handle—That hospital melted into air—Advance and inherit the insubstantial dead—Flakes fall that were his shadow—

Metal chess determined gasoline fires and smoke in motionless air—Smudge two speeds—DSL walks "here" beside me on extension lead from hairless skull—Flesh-smeared recorder consumed by slow metal fires—Dog-proof room important for our "oxygen" lines—Group respective recorder layout—"Throw the gasoline on them" determined the life form we invaded: insect

screams—I woke up with "marked for invasion" recording set to run for as long as phantom "cruelties" are
playing back while waiting to pick up Eduardo's "corrupt" speed and volume variation Madrid—Tape recorder banks tumescent flesh—Our mikes planning
speaker stood there in 1910 straw word—Either way
is a bad move to The Biologic Stairway—The whole
thing tell you—No good—No bueno outright or partially—The next state walking in a rubbish heap to
Form A—Form A directs sound channels heat—White
flash mangled down to a form of music—Life Form A
as follows was alien focus—Broken pipes refuse "oxygen"—Form A parasitic wind identity fading out—
"Word falling—Photo falling" flesh-smeared counter
orders—determined by last Electrician—Alien mucus
cough language learned to keep all Board Room Reports
waiting sound formations—Alien mucus tumescent
code train on Madrid—Convert in "dirty pictures 8"—
simple repetition—Whole could be used as model for
a bad move—Better than shouts: "No good—No
bueno"—

"Recorders fix nature of absolute need: *occupy*—
"*Here*"—Any cruelties answer him—Either unchanged
or reverse—Clang—Sorry—Planet trailing somewhere
along here—Sequential choice—Flesh plots con su
medicina—The next state according to—Stop—Look
—Form A directs sound channels—Well what now?—
Final switch if you want to—Dead on Life Form B by
cutting off machine if you want to—Blood form determined by the switch—Same need—Same step—Not

survive in any "emotion"—Intervention?—It's no use I tell you—Familiar will be the end product?—Reciprocate complete wires? You fucking can't—Could we become part of the array?—In The American Cemetery —Hard to distinguish maps came in at the verbal level —This he went to Madrid?—And so si learn? The accused was beyond altered arrival—So?—So mucus machine runs by feeding in over The American—Hear it? —Paralleled the bell—Hours late—They all went away —You've thought it out?—A whole replaced history of life burial tapes being blank?—Could this 'you' 'them' 'whatever' learn? Accused was beyond altered formations—No good—Machine runs by feeding in 'useless' —Blood spilled over Grey Veil—Parallel spurt—How many looking at dirty pictures—? Before London Space Stage tenuous face maybe—Change—Definite—The disorder gets you model for behavior—Screams?— Laughter?"—Voice fading into advocate:

"Clearly the whole defense must be experiments with two tape recorder mutations."

Again at the window that never was mine—Reflected word scrawled by some boy—Greatest of all waiting lapses—Five years—The ticket exploded in the air— For I dont know—*I do not know* human dreams— Never was mine—Waiting lapse—Caught in the door —Explosive fragrance—Love between light and shadow—The few who lived cross the wounded galaxies—Love?—Five years I grew muttering in the ice— Dead sun reached flesh with its wandering dream—

Buried tracks, Mr. Bradly, so complete was the lie—
Course—Naturally—Circumstances now Spanish—
Hermetic you understand—Locked in her heart of ooze
—A great undersea blight—Atlantis along the wind in
green neon—The ooze is only colorless question drifted
down—Obvious one at that—Its goal?—That's more
difficult to tap on the pane—One aspect of virus—An
obvious one again—Muttering in the dogs for generali-
zations—The lice we intersect—Poison of dead sun
anywhere else—What was it the old crab man said
about the lice?—Parasites on "Mr. Martin"—My ice my
perfect ice that never circumstances—Now Spanish
cautiously my eyes—And I became the form of a young
man standing—My pulse in unison—Never did I know
resting place—Wind hand caught in the door—cling—
Chocada—to tap on the pane—

Chocada—Again—Muttering in the dogs—Five years
—Poison of dead sun with her—With whom?—I
dunno—See account on the crooked crosses—And your
name?—Berg?—Berg?—Bradly?—"Mr. Martin si" Disaster Snow—Crack—Sahhk—Numb—Just a fluke came
in with the tide and The Swedish River of Gothenberg—

THE DEATH DWARF IN THE STREET

Biologic Agent K9 called for his check and picked up
supersonic imitation blasts of The Death Dwarfs—
"L'addition—Ladittion—Laddittion—Garcon—Garcon

Garcon"—American tourist accent to the Nth power—
He ordered another coffee and monitored the café—A
whole table of them imitating word forms and spitting
back at supersonic speed—Several patrons rolled on the
floor in switch fits—These noxious dwarfs can spit out
a whole newspaper in ten seconds imitating your words
after you and sliding in suggestion insults—That is the
entry gimmick of The Death Dwarfs: supersonic imitation and playback so you think it is your own voice—
(do you own a voice?) they invade The Right Centers
which are The Speech Centers and they are in the right
—in the right—in thee write—"RIGHT"—"I'm in the
right—in the right—You know I'm in the right so long
as you hear me say inside your right centers 'I am in
the right' "—While Sex Dwarfs tenderize erogenous
holes—So The Venusian Gook Rot flashed round the
world—

Agent K9 was with The Biologic Police assigned to
bring the Dwarf Plague under control by disconnecting
the dwarfs from Central Control Station: The Insect
Brain of Minraud enclosed in a crystal cylinder from
which run the cold wires to an array of calculating
machines feeding instructions to The Death Dwarf In
The Street—The brain is surrounded by Crab Guards
charged from The Thermodynamic Pain And Energy
Bank—Crab Guards can not be attacked directly since
they are directly charged by attack—K9 had been in
combat with The Crab Guards and he knew what can
happen if they get their claws on your nerve centers—

K9 left the café and surveying the street scene he

could not but feel that someone had goofed—The Death
Dwarfs had in many cases been separated from the
human host but they were still charged from Central
Control and yacked through the streets imitating words
and gestures of everyone in sight—While Sex Dwarfs
squirmed out of any cover with a perfunctory, "Hello
there," in anyone who stood still for it, dissolved erogenous holes immediately attacked by The Talk Dwarfs
so that in a few seconds the unfortunate traveler was
torn to pieces which the dwarfs snatch from each
other's mouth with shrill silver screams—In fact the
noxious behavior of this life form harried the citizens
beyond endurance and everyone carried elaborate
home-made contrivances for screening out the Talk
Dwarfs and a special plastic cover to resist erogenous
acids of the Sex Dwarfs—

Without hesitation K9 gave the order: "Release Silence Virus—Blanket area"—So The Silence Sickness
flashed round the world at speed of light—As a result
many citizens who had been composed entirely of word
went ape straight away and screamed through the
streets attacking the passers-by who in many cases
went ape in turn as The Silence Sickness hit—To combat these conditions, described as "intolerable," politi-
cal leaders projected stern noble image from control
towers and some could occupy and hold up the ape
forms for a few days or weeks—Invariably the leader
was drained by the gravity of unregenerate apes, torn
in pieces by his relapsing constituents, or went ape
himself on TV—So the Survivors as they call themselves

lived in continual dread of resistant dwarfs always
more frantic from host hunger—Knowing that at any
minute the man next to you in the street might go
Mandril and leap your your throat with virginal canines
—K9 shrugged and put in a call for Technicians—"The
error in enemy strategy is now obvious—It is machine
strategy and the machine can be redirected—Have
written connection in The Soft Typewriter the machine
can only repeat your instructions since it can not create
anything—The operation is very technical—Look at a
photomontage—It makes a statement in flexible picture
language—Let us call the statement made by a given
photomontage X—We can use X words X colors X odors
X images and so forth to define the various aspects of
X—Now we feed X into the calculating machine and X
scans out related colors, juxtapositions, affect-charged
images and so forth we can attenuate or concentrate X
by taking out or adding elements and feeding back into
the machine factors we wish to concentrate—A Technician learns to think and write in association blocks
which can then be manipulated according to the laws
of association and juxtaposition—The basic law of association and conditioning is known to college students
even in America: Any object, feeling, odor, word, image
in juxtaposition with any other object feeling, odor,
word or image will be associated with it—Our technicians learn to read newspapers and magazines for juxtaposition statements rather than alleged content—We
express these statements in Juxtaposition Formulae—
The Formulae of course control populations of the

world—Yes it is fairly easy to predict what people will
think see feel and hear a thousand years from now if
you write the Juxtaposition Formulae to be used in that
period—But the technical details you understand and
the machines—all of which contain basic flaws and
must be continually overhauled, checked, altered whole
blocks of computing machines purged and disconnected
from one minute to the next—fast our mind waves and
long counts—And let me take this opportunity of re-
plying to the criticisms of my creeping opponents—It
is not true that I took part in or instigated experiments
defining pain and pleasure thresholds—I used abstract
reports of the experiments to evolve the formulae of
pain and pleasure association that control this planet—
I assume no more responsibility than a physicist working from material presented to an immobilized brain—
I have constructed *a* physics of the human nervous system or more accurately the human nervous system de-
fines the physics I have constructed—Of course I can
construct another system working on quite different
principals—Pain is a quantitative factor—So is pleasure
—I had material from purge trials and concentration
camps and reports from Nagasaki and Hiroshima defining the limits of courage—Our most precise data
came from Lexington Ky. where the drug addicts of
America are processed—The pain of heroin withdrawal
in the addict lends itself perfectly to testing under control conditions—Pain is quantitative to degree of addiction and stage of withdrawal and is quantitatively relieved by cell-blanketing agents—With pain and pleas-

ure limits defined and the juxtaposition formulae set up
it is fairly easy to predict what people will think in a
thousand years or as long as the formulae remain in
operation—I can substitute other formulae if I am permitted to do so—No one has given much thought to
building a qualitative mathematics—My formulae saw
to that—Now here is a calculating machine—Of course
it can process qualitative data—Color for example—I
feed into the machine a blue photo passes to the Blue
Section and a hundred or a thousand blue photos rustle
out while the machine plays blues in a blue smell of
ozone blue words of all the poets flow out on ticker
tape—Or feed in a thousand novels and scan out the
last pages—That is quality is it not? Endingness?"

"Green Tony squealed and I'm off for Galaxy X—"

"The whole mob squealed—Now we can move in for
some definitive arrests—Set arrest machinery in operation—Cover all agents and associations with juxtaposition formulae—Put out scanning patterns through coordinate points of the earth for Mr. & Mrs. D—Top
Nova Criminals—Through mind screens of the earth
covering coordinate points blocking D out of a hand a
mouth a cold sore—Silver antibiotic handcuffs fitting D
virus filters and—Lock—Click—We have made the arrest—You will understand why all concepts of revenge
or moral indignation must be excised from a biologic
police agent—We are not here to keep this tired old
injustice show on the road but to stop it short of
Nova—"

"Nova—Nova—Nova—" shriek the Death Dwarfs—

"Arrest good kind Mr. D?—Why he paid for my hernia operation—"

"That did it—Release Silence Virus—Blanket Area—"

"Thinking in association blocks instead of words enables the operator to process data with the speed of light on the association line—Certain alterations are of course essential—"

EXTREMELY SMALL PARTICLES

Dec. 17, 1961—Past Time—The error in enemy strategy is now to be gathered I was not at all close and the machine can be redirected—These youths of image and association now at entrance to the avenue carrying banners of inter language—

Time: The night before adventurers who hope to form another blazing photo—Injury Headquarters Concentration with reports from Hiroshima—Some of the new hallucinogens and Nagasaki—Slight overdose of dimethyltryptamine—Your cities are ovens where South American narcotic plants brought total disposal—Brain screams of millions who have controller lives in that place screamed back from white hot blue sky—Can always pull the nova equipped now with tower blasts from Hiroshima and Nagasaki—In such pain he has only one turnstile—

Bureaucracy tuned in on all—Incredibly devious conditions hatch cosmologies of telepathic misdirection

—Mind screen movies overlapping make recordings ahead and leave before thinking was recorded—Our most precise data came from U.N. (United Narcotics) —His plan was drug addicts of America slip through the cordon—Pain of heroin failure often the cause of windows to pursue ends not compatible cell-blanketing agent—Our most precise data with The Silent People— Plan was almost superhuman drug burned through his juxtapositions—He was naked now to Nagasaki defining the limits against him—The projector can shift its succinct army before flesh dissolving—

Integrity and bravery are difficulties in the laboratory—Experiments to evolve ill took control this planet —Through the streets Nagasaki defining the limits of bravery—We find nationalisms and clashings to degree of addiction—It is fairly easy to predict inter police taking arms to protect their own forgeries from the taken over—Might reach 500 Ideology Headquarters armed with Board Officers produced synthetically— The hallucinogen drugs bottle three-dimensional coordinate points—New hallucinogens directed against affective animal life—Slight overdose of ugliness fear and hate—The ovens were image dust swirling round you total disposal—Some ugly noxious disgusting act sharply recorded becomes now part of "Photo falling—Word Falling"—Presented and represented before towers open fire—Alien virus can dissolve millions—It starts eating—Screamed back white hot copies of itself—So the Fear Species can replace the host armed now with tapeworm of bring down word and image plus Nagasaki—Injury Headquarters—Dual mammalian structure

—Hiroshima People—Or some disgusting officers produced the rest of it—

Attorney General For Fear announced yesterday the discovery that cries of nepotism might "form a new mineral damaging to the President"—Insidious form of high density silica as extremely small particles got into politics with Lyndon B. Johnson, wife of two Negro secret service men—Another Mineral American formed by meteorite impact—"And it would make a splendid good talker," he said—

At these tables there is virtually jostling diplomats—Some displacements of a sedate and celebrated rose garden but ideal for the processes of a quiet riverview restaurant—Police juice and the law are no cure for widespread public petting in chow lines the Soviet Union said yesterday—Anti-American promptly denounced Kennedy's moribund position of insistence:

"Washington know-how to deal with this sort demonstration in Venezuela of irresponsible propaganda—Outside Caracas I am deeply distressed at the Soviet Union's attempt to drag us back just when we was stoned in violation of the administration's twenty billion dollar solemn word—"

He begged as a personal thing scattered uprisings—

Error in enemy strategy is switchboard redirected—Word is TWO that is the noxious human inter language recorded—And where you have TWO you have odor's and nationalism's word—They started tampering with net—Injury Headquarters blockade was broken—"Calling partisans of all nations—Crab word falling—Virus photo falling—Break through in Grey Room—"

From A Land of Grass
Without Mirrors

THE CADET stepped out of a jungle of rancid swamp pools covered with spider webs through a slat fence in a place of wooden runways and barriers—walked through a forbidden door and someone said:

"What do you want?"

The cadet looked at the ground and said: "I didn't mean anything."

He walked down a wooden ramp to a school desk of shellacked brown maple where a woman sat.

"Where have you been?"

"I have been to The Far Assembly Meeting—I am on my way back to school—"

"What Assembly Meeting? Where?"

"The Far Assembly Meeting—Over there—"

"That's a lie. The Far Assembly Meeting is in *that* direction."

He composed his face for Basic Pain as he had been taught to compose his face to show nothing.

"I have been to a meeting," he said.

"You have six hours forced work—Guard—"

And the club crushed into his ribs and kidneys and the sides of his neck jabbed his testicles and stomach no matter how he did or did not do the work assigned and loss of composure was punishable by death. Then taken back to World Trade School K9 and whether he walked fast or slow or between slow and fast more bone-crushing shocks fell through him—So the cadets learn The Basic Formulae of Pain and Fear—Rules and staff change at arbitrary intervals—Cadets encouraged or forced into behavior subject to heaviest sanctions of deprivation, prolonged discomfort, noise, boredom all compensation removed from the offending cadets who were always being shifted from one school to another and never knew if they were succeeding brilliantly or washed out report to disposal—

Lee woke with his spine vibrating and the smell of other cigarette smoke in his room—He walked streets swept by color storms slow motion in spinal fluid came to the fish city of marble streets and copper domes —Along canals of terminal sewage—the green boy-girls tend gardens of pink flesh—Amphibious vampire creatures who breathe in other flesh—double sex sad as the drenched lands of swamp delta to a sky that does not change—Where flesh circulates stale and rotten as the

green water—by purple fungoid gills—They breathe in
flesh—settling slow in caustic green enzymes dissolving
body—eating gills adjusted to the host's breathing
rhythm—eat and excrete through purple gills and move
in a slow settling cloud of sewage—They are in pairs
known as The Other Half—the invisible Siamese twin
moving in and out of one body—talk in slow flesh grafts
and virus patterns exchanging genital sewage breathe in
and out of each other on slow purple gills of half sleep
with cruel idiot smiles eating Terminal Addicts of The
Orgasm Drug under a sign cut in black stone:

> The Nature of Begging
> Need?—Lack.
> Want?—Need.
> Life?—Death.

"It is a warning," said The Prince with a slow bronze
smile—"We can do no more—Here where flesh circulates like clothes on stale trade flesh of Spain and
Forty-Second Street—scanning pattern of legs—pant
smell of The Vagrant Ball Players—"

Lee woke with the green breathing rhythm—Gills
slow stirring other cigarette smoke in other gills adjusted to the host by color storms—It is in pairs known
as The Other Half sweet and rotten they move in and
out and talk in spinal fluid exchanging genital sewage
on slow purple gills of half sleep—Addicts of The Orgasm Drug—Flesh juice in festering spines of terminal
sewage—Run down of Spain and 42nd St. to the fish
city of marble flesh grafts—Diseased beggars with cruel
idiot smiles eating erogenous holes inject The Green

Drug—Sting insect spasms—It is a warning—We can do not—Doesn't change—Even the sky stale and rotten dissolving—

Lee woke in other flesh the lookout different—His body was covered by transparent sheets dissolving in a green mist—

"Lie still—Wait—Flesh frozen still—Deep freeze—Don't move until you can feel arms and legs—Remember in that hospital after spinal anesthesia and tried to get out of bed to my heroin stash and fell-slid all over the floor with legs like blocks of wood."

He moved his head slightly to one side—Rows and tiers of bunks—A dank packing-house smell—Stinging sex nettles lashed his crotch and hot shit exploded down his thigh to the knee—

"Lie still—Wait—"

The sweet rotten smell of diarrhea swept through the air in waves—The Others were moving now—Larval flesh hanging in rags—Faces purple tumescent bursting insect lust rolled in shit and piss and sperm—

"Watch what everyone else is doing and don't do it (—General Orders for Emergency Conditions—)"

He could move his arm now—He reached for his stash of apomorphine and slipped a handful of tablets under his tongue—His body twisted forward and emptied and he jetted free and drifted to the ceiling—Looked down on quivering bodies—crab and centipede forms flashed here and there—Then red swirls of violence—The caustic green mist settled—In a few minutes there was no movement—

Lee was not surprised to see other people he knew—
"I brought them with me"—He decided—"We will
send out patrols—There must be other survivors"—

He moved cautiously forward the others fanned out
on both sides—He found that he could move on his projected image from point to point—He was already
accustomed to life without a body—

"Not much different—We are still quite definite and
vulnerable organisms"—Certainly being without a body
conveyed no release from fear—He looked down—The
green mist had formed a carpet of lichen over the bunks
and floor of what looked like a vast warehouse—He
could see surviving life forms with body—Green creatures with purple fungoid gills—"The atmosphere must
be largely carbon dioxide," he decided—He passed a
screen through and wiped out all thought and word
from the past—He was conversing with his survivors in
color flashes and projected concepts—He could feel
danger—All around him the familiar fear urgent and
quivering—

The two agents sat in basement room 1920 Spanish
villa—Rotten spermy insect smell of The Green People
swirling in bare corners quivering through boneless
substance in color blats—He felt out through the open
door on thin music down dark streets swept by enemy
patrols and the paralyzing white flak—He moved like
an electric dog sniffing pointing enemy personnel and
installations through bodies and mind screens of the
silent fish city his burning metal eyes Uranian born in
the face of Nova Conditions— his brain seared by flash
blasts of image war—

In this area of Total Conditions on The Nova Express the agents of shadow empires move on hideous electric needs—Faces of scarred metal back from The Ovens of Minraud—Orgasm Drug addicts back from The Venusian Front—And the cool blue heavy metal addicts of Uranus—

In this area the only reason any agent contacts any other agent is for purpose of assassination—So one assumes that any one close to him or her is there precisely to kill—What else? We never knew anything else here —None the less we are reasonably gregarious since nothing is more dangerous than withdrawing from contact into a dead whistle stop—So every encounter quivers with electric suspicion— ozone smell of invisible flash bulbs—

Agents are always exchanging identities as articles of clothing circulate in strata of hustlers—These exchanges marked by last-minute attempts to switch the package and leave you standing with some old goofball bum in 1910 Panama—Lee had such a deal on with the other agent and of course both were falsifying and concealing defects in the merchandise—Of course no agent will allow a trial run since the borrower would be subject to take off with the package and fuck everybody they'll do it every time—So all the deals are sight unseen both parties gathering what information he can delving into the other identity for hidden miles and engineering flaws that could leave him with faulty equipment in a desperate position—His patrols were checking the other agent—Sending in reports—Conveying instructions—intercepting messages—

"Present Controller is The American Woman—Tracer on all connections—Taping all lines in and out—Santa Monica California—She is coming in loud and clear now—"

The young man dropped Time on the bed—His face was forming a smooth brown substance like the side of an electric eel—His left hand dissolved in a crystal bulb where a stinger of yellow light quivered sharp as a hypo needle—Orgasm Sting Ray—Venusian weapon—A full dose can tear the body to insect pieces in electric orgasms—Smaller doses bring paralysis and withered limbs of blighted fiber flesh—Lee hummed a little tune and cut the image lines with his grey screen—The Orgasm Sting dissolved in smoke—Lee picked the boy up by one elbow rigid as a clothing dummy and weightless now Lee guided him down the street steering the body with slight movements of the arm—The screen was empty—The boy sat on Lee's bed his face blank as a plate—The Nova police moved in calm and grey with inflexible authority—

" 'Paddy The Sting' arrested—Host empty—Heavy scar tissue—Surgery indicated—Transfer impractical —"

TOO FAR DOWN THE ROAD

—The Boy, driven too far down the road by some hideous electric hand—I don't know—Perhaps the boy never existed—All thought and word from the past—

It was in the war—I am not sure—You can not know the appalling Venusian Front—Obscure hand taping all messages in and out—Last human contacts—suddenly withdrawn—The Boy had never existed at all—A mouth against the pane—muttering—Dim jerky far away voice: "Know who I am? You come to 'indicated accident' long ago . . . old junky selling Christmas seals on North Clark St. . . . 'The Priest' they called him . . . used to be me, Mister" shabby quarters of a forgotten city . . . tin can flash flare . . . smell of ashes . . . wind stirs a lock of hair . . . "Know who I am? hock shop kid like mother used to make . . . Wind and Dust is my name . . . Good Bye Mister is my name . . . quiet now . . . I go . . ." (flickering silver smile).

NO GOOD AT THIS RATE

Smell of other cigarette smoke on child track—Proceed to the outer—All marble streets and copper domes inside air—Signature in scar tissue stale and rotten as the green water—Moldy pawn ticket by purple fungoid gills—The invisible Siamese twin moving in through flesh grafts and virus patterns—Exchanging weight on slow purple gills—Addicts of the purpose—Flesh juice vampires is no good—All sewage—Idiot smiles eating erogenous deal—Sweet rotten smell of ice—Insect smell of the green car wreck—The young agent to borrow your body for a special half made no face to conceal the ice—He dies many years ago—He said: "Yes you want to—Right back to a size like that—Said on child track—Screaming on the deal?"

She didn't get it—All possessed by overwhelming inside air—Shoeshine boy, collapse it—Could make or break any place by his male image back in—The shoeshine boy didn't get jump—Wait till the signs are right —And shit sure know to very—Wait a bit—No good —Fast their mind waves and long counts—No use— Don't know the answer—Arsenic two years—Go on treating it—In the blood arsenic and bleeding gums— Now I had my light weight 38 like for protection—

He dies many years ago—"Sunshine of your smile," he said and stomped your ambassador to the mud flats where all died addicted in convulsions of insect—They were addicted to this round of whatever visits of a special kind—

"Grow to a size like that," said Nimum—"So where is my ten percent on the deal?"

The shoeshine boy collapsed and they revived him with secret techniques—The money pinned to an old man's underwear is like that is the best—

So I said: "We can do it here—They won't see us— When I walk with Dib they can't see me—"

Careful—Watch the exits—Don't go to Paris—Wait till the signs are right—Write to everyone—Wait a bit —No good at this rate—Watch the waves and long counts—No use moving out—Try one if you want to— Right back to the track, Jack—Vampires is no good all possessed by overwhelming Minraud girl—All dies in convulsions—Don't go to Paris—Venusian front—On child track screaming without a body—Still quite definite and vulnerable organisms—Nova signature in scar tissue—Purpose of "assassination" back to a size like that—Her is there precisely to kill—Fast their mind waves and attempts to switch the package—Know the answer?: Arsenic two years: Goofball bum in 1910 Panama—They'll do it every time—The young man dropped Time on us with all the Gods of Life—Giggles canal talk from the sewage drifting round the gallows turning cartwheels—Groveled in visits of a special kind —Know the answer?: Arsenic two years: Operation completed—WE are blood arsenic and bleeding gums—

"Are you sure they are not for protection or perhaps too quick?"

"Quite sure—Nothing here but to borrow your body for a special purpose":: ("Excellent—Proceed to the ice")

He dies many years ago—Screen went dead—The smell of gasoline filled straw hat and silk scarf—Won't be much left—Have to move fast—Wouldn't know his name—No use of them better than they are—You want to?—Right back to the track, Jack—The Controller at the exits—

WIND HAND TO THE HILT

White sat quietly beaming "humanity's condition"— Wise Radio Doctor started putting welfare officers in his portable—The Effects Boys to see if they can do

any locks over the Chinese—Told me to sit down—
Gave me Panorama Comfortable and then said:

"Well? Anything to go by? What are we going to
do?"

What weighted the program down was refusal to
leave—

"Well what are you going to do? Perhaps alone?"

"You'd like to do half of it for me would you?"

He slung me out and Worth and Vicky talked usefully about that was that—Maybe I've met Two Of A
Kind—They both started share of these people—Vicky
especially sounded him—It wasn't what he had—You
know is why?—What they are meant to do is all?—
Going to get out of it?—An interview with Modigliani
obvious usually sooner than later—I've seen a lot of
these old men you visit on a P&O—You know sixty
seventy years east voyage—Do you see yourself ending
up in Cathay?—Trying to pinch suitcase like that you'll
end up buying the deluxe straight—The job will be
there—No cleaner—

If you or any of your pals foretold you were all spirits
curtains for them—And trouble for me—Globe is self
you understand until I die—Why do they make soldiers
out of "Mr. Martin?"—Wind hand to the hilt as it is—
work we have to do and the way the flakes fall—Be
trouble in store for me every time—For him always
been and always will be wounded galaxies—We intersect in a strange and crazy bio advance—On the night
shift working with blind—End getting to know whose

reports are now ended—These our rotten guts and aching spine accounts—

One more chance he said touching circumstance—Have you still—Come back to the Spanish bait its curtains under his blotter—The square fact is many spirits it's curtains for them—Fed up you understand until I die—No wish to see The Home Secretary "Mr. Martin—"

Wind hand to the hilt—work we have to do and way got the job—Jobbies would like to strike on night shift working the end of hanging—All good thing come to answer Mr. Of The Account screaming for a respectable price—What might be called in air lying about wholesale—*Belt Her*—Find a time buyer before ports are now ended—These are rotten if they start job for instance—Didn't last—Have you still—Come back work was steady at the gate under his blotter—Cover what's left of the window—Do they make soldiers out of present food in The Homicide Act as it is?—Blind bargain in return for accepting "one more chance"—Generous?—Nothing—That far to the bait and it's curtains—End getting to know whose price—Punishment and reward business the bait—No wish to see The Home Secretary "humanity's condition"—Wise radio doctor reprieving officers in his portable got the job—So think before they can do any locks over the Chinese that abolition is war of the past—Jobbies would like to strike a bargain instead of bringing you up fair—The end of hanging generous?—Just the same position—Changed places of years in the end is just the same—

What might be called the program was refusal lying about wholesale—Going to do?—Perhaps alone would you?—All good things come to about that was that—Screaming for respectable share of these people—Vicky especially—*Belt her*—Know what they meant if they start job for instance? An interview with further scream along the line—

White sat quietly beaming "human people" out of hospital and others started putting their time on casual —Effects Boys anyway after that—Chinese accusation of a bargain—What are we going to do level on average?—I was on the roof so I had to do Two Of A Kind—They both started before doing sessions—There's no choice—Sounded him—Have to let it go cheap and start do is all—A *journey*, man—The job will be there —No punishment and reward business—

A DISTANT THANK YOU

"I am having in Bill&Iam," she said—

"But they don't exist—tout ça—my dear have you any idea what—certain basic flaws in the—"

"You can afford it—You told me hole is always there to absorb yesterday—and whatever—"

"The Market you understand—Bill tossed a rock and a very dear friend of mine struck limestone with dried excrement purposes. And what purpose more has arisen —quite unlooked for—"

"All the more reason to redecorate Silent Workers—"
They had arrived where speech is impossible.

"Iam is very technical," said Bill as he walked around smoking smoke patterns in the room—"Have flash language of The Silent Ones—Out all this crap—Tonight, Madame—Age to grim Gothic Foreman—"

The Studio had set up a desert reek Mayan back to peasant hut—In a few minutes there mountain slope of the Andes—House had stood in the air—

"Limestone country," said Bill—"We might start with a photo-collage of The House—yes?—of course and the statues in clear air fell away to a Mayan Ball Court with eternal gondolas—a terminal life form of bookies and bettors changing black berries in little jade pipes—slow ebb of limestone luck and gills—Controllers of The Ugly Spirit Spinal Fluid—hydraulic vegetable centuries—"

"But what about The House Itself?"

"Lost their enemy—ah yes Madame, The House—You are Lady—Can't we contact them?—I mean well taken care of I hope—"

"I think, Bill, they exist at different pressure—"

"Ah yes The House—Hummm—Permutate at different pressure and sometimes a room is lost in—"

"Bill, they exist at different pressure—"

"In the shuffle?—The Bensons?—But they don't exist—Tout ca c'est de l'invention—There are of course certain basic flaws in the hydraulic machinery but the marl hole is always there to absorb the uh errors—"

At the bottom of the crater was a hole—Bill tossed a

rock and the echo fainter and fainter as the rock struck limestone on down—Silence—

"Bottomless you see for practical purposes—and what purpose more practical than disposal??"

Slow The House merged created in silent concentration of the workers from The Land Of Silence where speech is impossible—

"Lucky bastards," Bill always said as he walked around smoking Havanas and directing the work in color flash language of The Silent Ones—showing his plans in photo-collage to grim Gothic foreman—

And The House moved slowly from Inca to Mayan back to peasant hut in blighted maize fields or windy mountain slopes of The Andes—Gothic cathedrals soared and dissolved in air—The walls were made of blocks that shifted and permutated—cave paintings— Mayan relief—Attic frieze—panels—screens—photo-collage of The House in all periods and stages—Greek temples rose in clear air and fell to limestone huts by a black lagoon dotted with gondolas—a terminal life form of languid beautiful people smoking black berries in little jade pipes*—And The Fish People with purple fungoid gills—And The Controllers drifting in translucent envelopes of spinal fluid with slow hydraulic gestures of pressure authority—These people are without weapons—so old they have lost their enemy—

* Reference to the Pakistan Berries, a small black fruit of narcotic properties sometimes brought to southern Morocco by caravan—when smoked conjures the area of black lagoons sketched in these pages—

"But they are exquisite," said The Lady. "Can't we contact them?—I mean for dinner or cocktails?—"

"It is not possible, Madame—They exist at different pressure—"

"I am having in Bill&Iam"—she said during breakfast—

Her husband went pale—"My dear, have you any idea what their fee is?—"

"You can afford it—You told me only yesterday—"

"That was yesterday and whatever I may have told you in times long past—The Market you understand—Something is happening to money itself—A very dear friend of mine found his *special* deposit box in Switzerland filled with uh dried excrement—In short an emergency a shocking emergency has arisen—quite unlooked-for—"

"All the more reason to redecorate—There they are now—"

They had arrived—Bill in "banker drag he calls it now isn't that cute?"

"Iam is very technical"—said Bill puffing slowly on his Havana and watching smoke patterns—"Have to get some bulldozers in here—clean out all this crap—Tonight, Madame, you sleep in a tent like the Bedouin—"

The Studio had set up a desert on the lawn and The Family was moved out—In a few hours there was only a vast excavation where The House had stood—

"Limestone country," said Bill touching outcrops on walls of the crater—

"We might start with a Mayan temple—or The Greeks—"

"Yes of course and the statuary—City Of Marble Flesh Grafts—I envisage a Mayan Ball Court with eternal youths—and over here the limestone bookmakers and bettors changing position and pedestal—slow ebb of limestone luck—and just here the chess players—one beautiful the other ugly as The Ugly Spirit—playing for beauty—slow game of vegetable centuries—"

"But what about The House itself?"—said The Lady—

"Ah yes, Madame, The House—You are comfortable in your present quarters and well taken care of I hope—I think your son is very talented by the way—Hummm—perhaps—ah yes The House—Gothic Inca Greek Mayan Egyptian—and also something of the archaic limestone hut you understand the rooms and walls permutate on hydraulic hinges and jacks—and sometimes a room is lost in—"

"In the shuffle—The Bensons—during breakfast—" Her husband went pale—"C'est l'invention—Fee is?"

"Fee is hydraulic machinery marl yesterday errors told you in times long past—at the bottom of the crater was happening to money itself—echo fainter and fainter special deposit box in Switzerland—"

"A shocking emergency—"

"Bottomless you see for practical pee—practical disposal—There they are now—"

Slow the House merged—created in drag he calls it.

"Isn't that cute?—Workers from The Land Of Silence whiffing slowly on his Havana and watching—"

" 'Lucky Bill' always said: 'Get some bulldozers in here.' "

The Family was moved and The House moved slowly —only a vast excavation in blighted maize fields and wind—Gothic cathedrals soared on walls of the crater —Blocks shifted relief and panel screens of marble flesh grafts—

"I envisage stages—Gothic Cathedral soured—And over here the limestone huts by a black lagoon dotted position and pedestal—smoke chess players—and Fish People playing for beauty—slow games in their translucent envelopes—"

"Gestures of Pressure Author—" said The Lady—

"You understand so old they are comfortable in present quarters—"

"But they are exquisite"—said Tower Son—(very talented by the way for dinner or cocktails Gothic Inca Mayan Greek Egyptian—and also—)

"You understand the rooms and walls—and sometimes a room is lost—"

"They exist at different pressure playing their slow games by The Black Lagoon—You understand the mind works with une rapidité incroyable but the movements are very slow—So a player may see on the board great joy or a terrible fate see also the move to take or avoid see also that he can not make the move in time— This gives rise of course to great pain which they must always conceal in a round of exquisite festivals—"

The lagoon now was lighted with flicker lanterns in color—floating temples pagodas pyramids—

"The festivals rotate from human sacrifice to dawn innocence when the envelope dissolves—This happens very rarely—They cultivate The Fish People like orchids or pearls—always more exquisite strains blending beauty and vileness—strains of idiot cruelty are specially prized—" He pointed to a green newt creature with purple fungoid gills that stirred in a clear pool of water under limestone outcroppings and ferns—

"This amphibious-hermaphrodite strain is motivated by torture films—So their attractions are difficult to resist—"

The green boy-girl climbed out on a ledge—A heavy narcotic effluvia drifted from his half open mouth— Her squirmed towards the controller with little chirps and giggles—The controller reached down a translucent hand felt absently into the boneless jelly caressing glands and nerve centers—The green boy-girl twisted in spasms of ingratiation—

"They are very subservient as you can see in the right hands—But we must make an excursion to the place of The Lemur People who die in captivity—They are protected—We are all protected here—Nothing really happens you understand and the human sacrifice takes a bow from the flower floats—It is all exquisite and yet would you believe me we are all intriguing to unload this gold brick on some rube for an exit visa —Oh there's my travel agent the controller engaged—"

Playing their slow games by man in the black suit with long mind—works with une rapidité—

"He has been cheating me for months—slow so that a player may see believe the ridiculous travel arrange great joy and see also the move to fastest brain—"

"Yes we have all—Can not make the move in time—This other here—Roles must conceal in anything to go."

"If we could only just flush our flower floats on child track without a body from human sacrifice—"

"Rather bad taste, Old-Thing-Whose-Envelope-Has-Dissolved—The Flayed Man Stand—"

"They Cultivate The Fish People—"

"Oh yes whose doing it?"

"*Not* for more exquisite strains—??"

"I tell you nobody can scream—Over there is The Land of The Lemur People—"

"He dissolved after the performance—Beautiful strain of idiot cruelty—"

"So he got his exit visa?—and green newt creature with purple fungoid now?"

"Pool of water under limestone—He has contacted someone—Know is motivated by torture films—"

"Willy The Rube?—I knew him to resist—The green boy climbed hook and he fades out with Effluvia—drifted from his half open mouth all our exquisite food and smoke bones—He fade out in word giggles—He beat Green Tony into The Green Boy-Girl's Boneless Dream Concession—He defend nerve centers—The Green Boy twisted in Sammy The Butcher—"

"Still he may fall for The Hero—They are very sub-servient—"

"We are an old people you are sus—Make an excursion to the land of persona and statuary—They are protected of course—Here is he now—Really happens you understand—"

"I understand you people need the flower floats—It is all Mongolian Archers—They are—we are all scheming to unload an exit visa—" (The controller engaged short furtive conversation—man in a black suit with one long fingernail and gold teeth—)

"He has been cheating me for months of course they all do—You wouldn't believe the ridiculous travel arrangements they unload on our fastest brains—Yes we have all been laughing stock at one time or another—Here where roles and flesh circulate—There is no place for anything to go—"

"If we could only just flush ourselves down the drain," she said seeing her life time fortunes fade on The Invisible Board—

"Rather bad taste, old thing—Embalm yourself—Tonight is The Festival Of The Flayed Man—"

"Oh yes and whose doing it?—Juanito again?—"

"He dissolved after the last performance—"

"Oh yes he went away—And what is The Travel Agent selling you now?"

"He has contacted someone known as Willy the Rube —perhaps—"

"Willy The Rube??—I know him from Uranus— Think you have him on the hook and he fades out with a train whistle—He beat Green Tony in a game of limestone stud and walked out with The Dream Concession—He defenestrated Izzy the Push and cowboyed Sammy The Butcher."

"Still he may fall for The Hero: Protect us—We are an old people—Protect our exquisite poisonous life and our *statuary*—Well?"

"Here is he now."

"I understand you people need protection—I am moving in a contingent of Mongolian Archers—They are expensive of course but well worth it—"

The Mongolian Archers with black metal flesh moved in grill arrangements of a ritual dance flexing their bows —silver antennae arrows sniffing dowsing quivering for The Enemy—

"My dear, they make me terribly nervous—Suppose there is no enemy??"

"That would be unfortunate, Madame—My archers must get relief—You did ask for protection and now— Where are the Lemur People?"

The Lemur People live on islands of swamp cypress peering from the branches and it took many hours to coax them down—Iridescent brown copper color— liquid black eye screens swept by virginal emotions—

"They are all affect you understand—That is why they die in captivity—" A Lemur touched The Rube's face with delicate tentative gestures and skittered again into the branches—

"No one has ever been able to hold a lemur for more than a few minutes in my memory—And it is a thou-

sand years since anyone had intercourse with a lemur—
The issue was lost—They are of such a delicacy you
understand the least attempt-thought of holding or
possessing and they are back in the branches where
they wait the master who knew not hold and possess—
They have waited a long time—Five hundred thousand
years more or less I think—The scientists can never
make up their mind about anything—"

The lemur dropped down on Lee's shoulder and play-
fully nipped his ear—Other lemurs raised sails on a
fragile bamboo craft and sailed away over the lagoon
under the red satellite that does not change position—

"There are other islands out there where no one has
ever been—The lemurs of such delicacy that they die
if one sets foot on the island—They exist at different
prenatal flesh in black lagoons—"

"You understand silver arrows sniffing pointing incroyable but the movements on The Board a terrible
doom: ('Suppose there is no enemy?') Take or avoid
but see also that gives rise to great pain—You did a
round of exquisite festivals—"

"Me see your lemur people with flicker lights in
swamp cypress?"

"Hours to coax them down—Finally the dawn innocence of control sent liquid flickering screens like pearl
—All affect, you understand, that is blending beauty
and flesh—"

A Lemur touched Lee's face with delicate people
who die in captivity—skittering again into the specially prized—this stressing they are back in who will

not hold and possess—out on a ledge—a heavy narcotic indeed—thousand years more or less—

The Mongolian Archers with short black conversation of ritual dancing flexed there—dowzing feeling for The Enemy like of course they all do—

"You wouldn't—"

"My dear, they make me. terrible arrangements that have been sold to our—"

"That would be unfortunate, Madame—Been laughing stock at one time or ask for protection—and now—"

"Tonight is the festival of Nice Young Emotions—Why they die in captivity—Juanito again?—Where is he now?—"

"Branches no one has ever been—He far now is—"

"They are of such a hat—Is your travel agent selling you attempt or thought of holding the branches where they wait?"

"Perhaps—They have waited a long time—Five Uranus—"

"The Pakistan Berries lay all our dust of a distant thank you on Lee's shoulder—"

REMEMBER I WAS CARBON DIOXIDE

Nothing here now but the recordings—in another country.

"Going to give some riot noises in the old names?"

"Mr. Martin I have survived" (smiles).

"All right young countryman so we took Time . . .
Human voices take over my job now . . . Show you
around alien darkroom . . . their Gods fading . . . departed file . . . Mrs. Murphy's rooming house left no
address. . . . You remember the 'third stair' it was
called? You wrote last flight . . . seals on North Beach
. . . the lights flashing . . . Clark St. . . . The Priest
against a black sky . . . rocks gathered just *here* on this
beach . . . Ali *there*, hand lifted . . . dim jerky far away
street . . . ash on the water . . . last hands . . . last human
voices . . . last rites for Sky Pilot Hector Clark . . . He
carries the man who never was back . . . Shall these
ticker bones live?? My host had been a long time in
inquisition. . . ."

Through all the streets no relief—I will show you
fear on walls and windows people and sky—Wo weilest
du?—Hurry up please its accounts—Empty is the third
who walks beside you—Thin mountain air here and
there and out the window—Put on a clean shirt and
dusk through narrow streets—Whiffs of my Spain from
vacant lots—Brandy neat—April wind revolving lips
and pants—After dinner sleep dreaming on rain—The
soldier gives no shelter—War of dead sun is a handful
of dust—Thin and tenuous in gray shivering mist of
old Western movies said: "Fill your hand, Martin."

"I can't, son—Many years ago that image—Remember I was carbon dioxide—Voices wake us and we
drown—Air holes in the faded film—End of smoky
shuttered rooms—No walls—Look anywhere—No good
—Stretching zero the living and the dead—Five for

rain—Young hair too—Hurry up please its William—I
will show you fear in the cold spring cemetery—Kind,
wo weilest du?"

"Here," said she, "is your card: Bread knife in the
heart—"

"What thinking, William?—Were his eyes—Hurry
up please its half your brain slowly fading—Make yourself a bit smart—It's them couldn't reach flesh—Empty
walls—Good night, sweet ladies—Hurry up please it's
time—Look any place—Faces in the violet light—
Damp gusts bringing rain—"

Got up and fixed in the sick dusk—Again he touched
like that—Smell of human love—The tears gathered—
In Mexico committed fornication but—Cold spring—
besides you can say—could give no information—vast
Thing Police—

"What have I my friend to give you?—Identity
fading out—dwindling—Female smells—knife in the
heart—boy of dust gives no shelter—left no address"

"I'd ask alterations but really known them all—
Closed if you wanted a Greek—I do not find The
Hanged Man in the newspapers—blind eyes—see—
Who walks beside you?" "Will you let me tell you lost
sight a long time ago . . . Smell taste dust on the window
. . . touch . . . touch?? How should I from remote landing dim jerky far away."

At dawn—Put on a clean shirt in another country—
Soccer scores and KiKi give you?—Empty to the barrier
—Shuttered dawn is far away—Bicycle races here in
this boy were no relief—Long empty noon—Dead re-

cordings—Moments I could describe that were his eyes in countries of the world—Left you these sick dawn bodies—Fading smiles—in other flesh—Far now—Such gives no shelter—Shifted the visiting address—The wind at noon—walks beside you?" Piece of a toy revolver there in nettles of the alley . . . over the empty broken streets a red white and blue kite.

Gave Proof Through the Night

(This section, first written in 1938 in collaboration with Kells Elvins who died in 1961, New York, was later cut back in with the "first cut-ups" of Brion Gysin as published in Minutes to Go.*)*

CAPTAIN BAIRNS was arrested today in the murder at sea of Chicago—He was The Last Great American to see things from the front and kept laughing during the dark—Fade out

S.S. America—Sea smooth as green glass—off Jersey Coast—An air-conditioned voice floats from microphones and ventilators—:

"Keep your seats everyone—There is no cause for alarm—There has been a little accident in the boiler room but everything is now/"

BLOOOMMM

Explosion splits the boat—The razor inside, sir—He jerked the handle—

A paretic named Perkins screams from his shattered wheelchair:

"You pithyathed thon of a bidth."

Second Class Passenger Barbara Cannon lay naked in First Class State Room—Stewart Hudson stepped to a porthole:

"Put on your clothes, honey," he said. "There's been an accident."

Doctor Benway, Ship's Doctor, drunkenly added two inches to a four-inch incision with one stroke of his scalpel—·

"Perhaps the appendix is already out, doctor," the nurse said peering over his shoulder—"I saw a little scar—"

"The appendix *OUT! I'M* taking the appendix out— What do you think I'm doing here?"

"Perhaps the appendix is on the left side, doctor— That happens sometimes you know—"

"Stop breathing down my neck—I'm coming to that —Don't you think I know where an appendix is?—I studied appendectomy in 1910 at Harvard—" He lifted the abdominal wall and searched along the incision dropping ashes from his cigarette—

"And fetch me a new scalpel—This one has no edge to it"—

BLOOOMM

"Sew her up," he ordered—"I can't be expected to work under such conditions"—He swept instruments cocaine and morphine into his satchel and tilted out of The Operating Room—

Mrs. J. L. Bradshinkel, thrown out of bed by the explosion, sat up screaming: "I'm going right back to

The Sheraton Carlton Hotel and call the Milwaukee Braves"—

Two Philippine maids hoisted her up—"Fetch my wig, Zalameda," she ordered. "I'm going straight to the captain—"

Mike B. Dweyer, Politician from Clayton Missouri, charged the First Class Lounge where the orchestra, high on nutmeg, weltered in their instruments—

"Play The Star Spangled Banner," he bellowed.

"You trying to corn somebody, Jack?—We got a union—"

Mike crossed to the jukebox, selected The Star Spangled Banner With Fats Terminal at The Electric Organ, and shoved home a handful of quarters—

Oh say can you seeeeeeeeee

The Captain sitting opposite Lucy Bradshinkel—He is shifty redhead with a face like blotched bone—

"I own this ship," The Lady said—

The deck tilted and her wig slipped over one ear— The Captain stood up with a revolver in his left hand —He snatched the wig and put it on—

"Give me that kimona," he ordered—

She ran to the porthole screaming for help like everyone else on the boat—Her head was outlined in the porthole—He fired—

"And now you God damned old fool, *give me that kimona*—"

I mean by the dawn's early light

Doctor Benway pushed through a crowd at the rail and boarded The First Life Boat—

"Are you all right?" he said seating himself among the women—"I'm the doctor."

The Captain stepped lightly down red carpeted stairs—In The Purser's Office a narrow-shouldered man was energetically shoving currency and jewels into a black suitcase—The Captain's revolver swung free of his brassiere and he fired twice—

By the rocket's red glare

Radio Operator Finch mixed a bicarbonate of soda and belched into his hand—"SOS—URP—SOS—God damned captain's a brown artist—SOS—Off Jersey Coast—SOS—Might smell us—SOS—Son of a bitching crew—SOS—URP—*Comrade* Finch—SOS—Comrade in a pig's ass—SOS—SOS—SOS—URP—URP—URP—"

The Captain stepped lightly into The Radio Room— Witnesses from a distance observed a roaring blast and a brilliant flash as The Operator was arrested—The Captain shoved the body aside and smashed the apparatus with a chair—

Our flag was still there

The Captain stiff-armed an old lady and filled The First Life Boat—The boat was lowered jerkily by male passengers—Doctor Benway cast off—The crew pulled on the oars—The Captain patted his bulging suitcase absently and looked back at the ship—

Oh say do that star spangled banner yet wave

Time hiccoughs—Passengers fighting around Life
Boat K9—It is the last boat that can be launched—Joe
Sargant, Third Year Divinity student and MRA, slipped
through the crowd and established Perkins in a seat
at the bow—Perkins sits there chin drawn back eyes
shining clutching a heavy butcher knife in his right
hand

By the twilight's last gleamings

Hysterical waves from Second Class flood the deck—
"Ladies first," screamed a big faced shoe clerk with
long teeth—He grabbed a St. Louis matron and shoved
her ahead of him—A wedge of shoe clerks formed behind—A shot rang and the matron fell—The wedge
scattered—A man with nautical uniform buttoned in
the wrong holes carrying a World War I 45 stepped
into the last boat and covered the men at the launching
ropes—

"Let this thing down," he ordered—The boat hit the
water—A cry went up from the reeling deck—Bodies
hurtled around the boat—Heads bobbed in the green
water—A hand reached out of the water and closed on
the boat side—Spring-like Perkins brought down his
knife—The hand slipped away—Finger stubs fell into
the boat—Perkins worked feverishly cutting on all
sides:

"Bathdarths—Thons of bidth—Bathdarth—thon
bidth—Methodith Epithcopal God damn ith—"

O'er the land of the freeee

Barbara Cannon showed your reporter her souvenirs of the disaster: A life belt autographed by the crew and a severed human finger—

And the home of the brave

"I don't know," she said. "I feel sorta bad about this old finger."

Gave proof through the night that our flag was still there

SOS

The cold heavy fluid settled in a mountain village of slate houses where time stops—Blue twilight—Place Of The Silence Addicts—They move in and corner SOS and take it away in lead bottles and sit there on the nod in slate houses—On The Cool Blue or The Cold Grey—leave a wake of yapping ventriloquist dummies —They just sit there in cool blocks of blue silence and the earth's crust undulates under their weight of Heavy Time and Heavy Money—The Blue Heavy Metal People Of Uranus—Heavy con men selling issues of fraudulent universe stock—It all goes back into SOS—[Solid Blue Silence.]

"Nobody can kick an SOS habit, kid—All the screams from The Pain Bank—from The Beginning you understand exploded deep in the tortured metal."

Junk poured through my screaming flesh—I got up
and danced The Junky Jig—I had my spoons—That's
all I need—Into his spine falling some really great shit
lately ("Shoot your way to peat bog") The cold heavy
fluid settled—hydraulic beginning you understand—
Exploded time stops in blue metal—Surburban galaxies
on the nod— blue silence in the turnstile—village of
slate houses—This foreign sun in bottles—

Martin came to Blue Junction in a heavy blue twilight where time stops—Slow hydraulic driver got out
and moved away—Place of The Silent People—The
Foreman showed him to The Bunk House—The men
sat in blocks of cool blue silence at a long table and
laid out photos in silent language of juxtaposition
projecting the work—playing poker for position and
advantage—

The work was hard and silent—There were irrigation canals and fish ponds with elaborate hydraulic
locks and motors—The windmills and weather maps—
(The Proprietor took photos of sky clouds and mountains every day moving arranging his weather maps in
a vast flicker cylinder that turned with the wind on
roof of The Main Building—Picture panels on walls of
The Bunk House and Day Room changed with weather
sky and mountain shadows in a silent blue twilight—
The men took photos of each other and mixed picture
composites shifting combos to wind and water sounds
and frogs from the fish pools—(green pastures crisscrossed with black water and springs overhung with
grass where Martin fished in the evening with Bradly
who slept in the bunk next to his or in his bunk back

and forth changing bodies in the blue silence—Tasks shifted with poker play and flesh trade—)

Blue—Flicker along the fish ponds—Blue shadows twilight—street—frogs and crickets—(crisscrossed my face)

The knife fell—The Clerk in the bunk next to his bled blue silence—Put on a clean shirt and Martin's pants—telling stories and exchanging smiles—dusty motors—The crop and fish talk muttering American dawn words—Sad rooming house—Picture wan light on suburban ponds and brown hair—Grey photo pools and springs over brass bed—Stale morning streets— sifting clouds and sky on my face—crisscrossed with city houses—

"Empty picture of a haunted ruin?" He lifted his hands sadly turned them out . . . "Some boy just wrote last good-bye across the sky . . . All the dream people of past time are saying good-bye forever, Mister" Late afternoon shadows against his back magic of all movies in remembered kid standing there face luminous by the attic window in a lost street of brick chimneys exploded star between us . . . You can look back along the slate shore to a white shirt flapping gunsmoke.

SHORT COUNT

The Heavy Metal Kid returned from a short blue holiday on Uranus and brought suit against practically everybody in The Biologic Courts—

"They are giving me a short count," he said in an
interview with your reporter—"And I won't stand still
for it—" Fade out

Corridors and patios and porticos of The Biologic
Courts—Swarming with terminal life forms desperately
seeking extension of canceled permissos and residence
certificates—Brokers, fixers, runners, debarred lawyers,
all claiming family connection with court officials—
Professional half-brothers and second cousins twice removed—Petitioners and plaintiffs screaming through
the halls—Holding up insect claws, animal and bird
parts, all manner of diseases and deformities received
"In the service" of distant fingers—Shrieking for compensations and attempting to corrupt or influence the
judges in a thousand languages living and dead, in
color flash and nerve talk, catatonic dances and pan-
tomimes illustrating their horrible conditions which
many have tattooed on their flesh to the bone and
silently picket the audience chamber—Others carry
photo-collage banners and TV screens flickering their
claims—Willy's attorneys served the necessary low
pressure processes and The Controllers were sucked
into the audience chamber for the The First Hearing—
Green People in limestone calm—Remote green contempt for all feelings and proclivities of the animal
host they had invaded with inexorable moves of Time
-Virus-Birth-Death—With their diseases and orgasm
drugs and their sexless parasite life forms—Heavy
Metal People of Uranus wrapped in cool blue mist of
vaporized bank notes—And The Insect People of Minraud with metal music—Cold insect brains and their

agents like white hot buzz saws sharpened in the Ovens—The judge, many light years away from possibility of corruption, grey and calm with inflexible authority reads the brief—He appears sometimes as a slim young man in short sleeves then middle-aged and redfaced sometimes very old like yellow ivory "My God what a mess"—he said at last—"Quiet all of you—You all understand I hope what is meant by biologic mediation—This means that the mediating life forms must simultaneously lay aside all defenses and all weapons—it comes to the same thing—and all connection with retrospective controllers under space conditions merge into a single being which may or may not be successful—" He glanced at the brief—"It would seem that The Uranians represented by the plaintiff Uranian Willy and The Green People represented by Ali Juan Chapultepec are prepared to mediate—Will these two uh personalities please stand forward—Bueno—I expect that both of you would hesitate if you could see—Fortunately you have not been uh overbriefed—You must of course surrender all your weapons and we will proceed with whatever remains—Guards—Take them to the disinfection chambers and then to The Biologic Laboratories"—He turned to The Controllers—"I hope they have been well prepared—I don't need to tell you that—Of course this is only The First Hearing—The results of mediation will be reviewed by a higher court—"

Their horrible condition from a short blue holiday

on Uranus—Post everybody in The Biologic Courts:
Willy's attorney served "Count."—He said in an interview pushing through and still for it—Fade out—
Chambers—Green People—remote green contempt
forms fixers and runners all claiming the animal hosts
they had—(The Court Of Professional Brothers and
Moves Of Vegetable Centuries)—The petitioners and
plaintiffs their green sexless life screaming through the
halls remote mineral calm received—in slate blue houses
and catatonic dances illustrating The Heavy Metal Kid
returned—Many have tattooed in diseases and brought
suit against The Audience Chambers—

"They are giving me a short necessary process"—
Screaming crowds entered the corridors the audience
and the patios—The feeling and proclivities of connection with officials invaded with inexorable limestone
and cousins twice removed—Virus and drugs plaintiff
and defendant—Heavy Metal People Of Uranus in a
thousand languages live robes that grow on them blue
and hideous diseases—The little high-fi junk note
shrieking for compensation—Spine frozen on the nod
color flashes the heavy blue mist of bank notes—The
petitioners and plaintiffs screaming through the halls
wrapped in: "My God what a mess"—Holding up insect claws remote with all understand I hope what
service—He appeared sometimes as whatever remains
—All understand I hope what proclivities of the animal
means that the mediating lie inexorable moves of
Time—

TWILIGHT'S LAST GLEAMING

The Gods of Time-Money-Junk gather in a heavy blue twilight drifting over bank floors to buy con force an extension of their canceled permits—They stand before The Man at The Typewriter—Calm and grey with inflexible authority he presents The Writ:

"Say only this should have been obvious from Her Fourth Grade Junk Class—Say only The Angel Profound Lord Of Death—Say I have canceled your permissos through Time-Money-Junk of the earth—Not knowing what is and is not knowing I knew *not*. All your junk out in apomorphine—All your time and money out in word dust drifting smoke streets—Dream street of body dissolves in light . . ."

The Sick Junk God snatches The Writ: "Put him in The Ovens—Burn his writing"—He runs down a hospital corridor for The Control Switch—"He won't get far." A million police and partisans stand quivering electric dogs—antennae light guns drawn—

"You called The Fuzz—You lousy fink—"

"They are your police speaking your language—If you must speak you must answer in your language—"

"*Stop—Alto—Halt—*" Flashed through all I said a million silver bullets—The Junk God falls—Grey dust of broom swept out by an old junky in backward countries—

A heavy blue twilight drifting forward snatches The Writ—Time-Money-Junk gather to buy: "Put him in The Ovens—Burn his writing—"

"Say only The Angel Profound Lord of D—Runs
down a hospital corridor—Your bodies I have written—
Your death called the police—The Junk God sick from
"*Stop—Alto—Halt—*" The Junk God falls in a heavy
blue twilight drifting over the ready with drawn guns—
Time-Money-Junk on all your languages—Yours—Must
answer them—Your bodies—I have written your death
hail of silver bullets—So we are now able to say *not*.
Premature?? I think the auditor's mouth is stopped with
his own—With her grey glance faded silver understanding out of date—Well I'd ask alterations but there
really isn't time is there left by the ticket that exploded
—Any case I have to move along—Little time so I'll say
good night under the uh *circumstances*—Now the
Spanish Flu would not be again at the window touching the wind in green neon—You understanding the
room and she said: "Dear me what a long way down"
—Meet Café is closed—if you wanted a cup of tea—
burst of young you understand—so many and soo—
The important thing is always courage to let go—in the
dark—Once again he touched the window with his cool
silver glance out into the cold spring air a colorless
question drifted down corridors of that hospital—

"Thing Police keep all Board Room Reports"—And
we are not allowed to proffer The Disaster Accounts—
Wind hand caught in the door—Explosive Bio-Advance
Men out of space to employ Electrician—In gasoline
crack of history—Last of the gallant heroes—"I'm you
on tracks Mr. Bradly Mr. Martin"—Couldn't reach flesh
in his switch—And zero time to the sick tracks—A long

time between suns I held the stale overcoat—Sliding between light and shadow—Muttering in the dogs of unfamiliar score—Cross the wounded galaxies we intersect—Poison of dead sun in your brain slowly fading—Migrants of ape in gasoline crack of history—Explosive bio advance out of space to neon—"I'm you, Wind Hand caught in the door—" Couldn't reach flesh—In sun I held the stale overcoat—Dead Hand stretching the throat—Last to proffer the disaster account on tracks—See Mr. Bradly Mr.—

And being blind may not refuse to hear: "Mr. Bradly Mr. Martin, disaster to my blood whom I created"—(The shallow water came in with the tide and the Swedish River of Gothenberg.)

This Horrible Case

ANGLE BOYS of the cosmos solicit from lavatories and broom closets of the Biologic Court Buildings charge out high on ammonia peddling fixes on any case from The Ovens Rap to a summons for biologic negligence —After buying a few short fixes in rigged courts, the pleaders defendants court officials and guilty bystanders learn to use a filter screen that scans out whole wave-lengths of ill-intentioned lunacy—This apparatus, sold in corridors and patios of the court buildings, enables any life form in need of legal advice to contact an accredited biologic counselor trained in the intricacies and apparent contradictions of biologic law—The classic case presented to first year students is The Oxygen Impasses: Life Form A arrives on alien planet from a crippled space craft—Life Form A breathes "oxygen" —There is no "oxygen" in the atmosphere of alien planet

but by invading and occupying Life Form B native
to alien planet they can convert the "oxygen" they
need from the blood stream of Life Form B—The Occupying Life Form A directs all the behavior and
energies of Host Life Form B into channels calculated
to elicit the highest yield of oxygen—Health and
interest of the host is disregarded—Development of
the host to space stage is arrested since such development would deprive the invaders by necessity of
their "oxygen" supply—For many years Life Form A
remains invisible to Life Form B by a simple operation
scanning out areas of perception where another life
form can be seen—However an emergency a shocking
emergency quite unlooked-for has arisen—Life Form B
sees Life Form A—(Watching you have they thought
debarred) and brings action in The Biologic Courts
alleging unspeakable indignities, metal and physical
cruelty, deterioration of mind body and soul over thousands of years, demanding summary removal of the
alien parasite—To which Form B replies at The First
Hearing: "It was a question of food supply—of absolute
need—Everything followed from that: Iron claws of
pain and pleasure squeezing a planet to keep the host
in body prison working our 'oxygen' plants—Knowing
that if he ever saw even for an instant who we are and
what we are doing—(Switched our way is doomed in
a few seconds)—And now he sees us planning to use
the host as a diving suit back to our medium where of
course Life Form B would be destroyed by alien condi-

tions—Alternative posed by the aroused partisans
fumbling closer and closer to the switch that could lock
us out of Form B and cut our 'oxygen' lines—So what
else could we do under the circumstances? The life form
we invaded was totally alien and detestable to us
—We do not have what they call 'emotions'—soft
spots in the host marked for invasion and manipulation—"

The Oxygen Impasse is a basic statement in the al-
gebra of absolute need—"Oxygen" interchangeable factor representing primary biologic need of a given life
form—From this statement the students prepare briefs
—sift cut and rearrange so they can view the case from
varied angles and mediums:

The trial of The Nova Mob brought in emergency
quite unlooked-for: Broom arisen—sweeps Life Form
B—*Sees* fixes in The Biologic Courts—Deterioration of
mind body and soul buying a few short fixes in rigged
Any Place—Learns the years—the long—the many—
such a place—scans out whole lengths of alien parasite
—and brings action from unspeakable indignities and
negligence demanding summary biologic lawyers who
never hustle a form—The best criminal counselor was
Uranian U—His clients from heavy metal—Impression
Thing followed from that Iron Claws Brief—From one
interview he got Sammy squeezing a planet in The
Switch—The Green Octopus working Vegetable Sentence—And now they have seen there is no "oxygen" in
the diving suit—Local life would be destroyed by the
"oxygen" they breathe—

"This pressure—Health cut our 'oxygen' lines—so disregarded—"

"So *that* the circumstances?"

"Life of the host beyond 'THE' detestable to us— Would deprive the invaders by soft spots in the host—"

With the material you have nature of absolute need and The First Hearing in Biologic Court—

"Alleging you understand I must fight indignities and cruelties and the natives are all mind body and soul demanding and I can't account for poison—(to which of course I have never lost a client)—Specific facts and cases a question of food supply not adequate—Owed from that the two claws intimidate and corrupt—"

"Enables an arrested criminal of pleasure and pain to squeeze counselor trained in the body-prison contradictions of biologic law—Diving suit of thousand years back to our medium instead of The Reverse Switch— Alternative Word Island—"

So where to first year students of Biologic Law Circumstances?—Life Form A was totally alien crippled space craft—Do not have what they call "emotion's oxygen" in the atmosphere—

A student who represents Life Form A must anticipate questions of the Biologic Prosecutor:—

"How did the space craft 'happen' to be crippled in such convenient proximity?—Was not the purpose of the expedition to find 'oxygen' and extract it by any means?—During many years of occupancy was any effort towards biologic reconversion made by Life Form A prior to intervention of The Biologic Police?—Was not Life Form A conspiring to cut off the 'oxygen' of Life Form B as soon as their 'travel arrangements' were completed? Did they not in fact plan to liquidate Life Form B by cutting off 'emotion's oxygen' the charge on which human and other mammalian life forms run?— (Doctor W. Reich has suggested that human life is activated by units he calls 'orgones' which form a belt around the planet)—Life Form A obviously conspired to blockade the orgone belt and leave Form B to suffocate in a soulless vacuum at the high surface temperatures that obtain on Life Form A's planet of origin: 600 Degrees Fahrenheit—"

In short the plea of need offered by Life Form A is inadequate—To prepare a case would be necessary to investigate the original conditions and biologic history of Life Form A on location—A Biologic Counselor must know his client and be "trained in the body-prison contradictions of biologic law"—It will not be easy for Life Form A to find a counselor willing to handle "this horrible case—"

BRIEF FOR THE FIRST HEARING

Biologic Counselors must be writers that is only writers can qualify since the function of a counselor is to *create* facts that will tend to open biologic potentials for his client—One of the great early counselors was Franz Kafka and his briefs are still standard—The student first writes his own brief then folds his pages down the middle and lays it on pages of Kafka relevant to the case in hand—(It is not always easy to say what is and is not relevant)—To indicate the method here is a tentative brief for The First Hearing in Biologic Court:—A preparation derived from one page of Kafka passed through the student's brief and the original statement back and forth until a statement of biologic position emerges—From this original statement the student must now expand his case—

QUOTE FROM *The Trial*—FRANZ KAFKA

"I fancy," said the man who was stylishly dressed, "that the gentleman's faintness is due to the atmosphere here—You see it's only here that this gentleman feels upset, not in other places—" Accustomed as they were to the office air felt ill in the relatively fresh air that came up from the stairway—They could scarcely answer him and the girl might have fallen if K had not shut the door with the utmost haste—He had already, so he would relate, won many similar cases either outright or partially—That was very important for the first impression made by the defense frequently determined the whole course of subsequent proceedings—Especially when a case they had conducted was suddenly taken out of their hands—That was beyond all doubt the worst thing that could happen to an advocate— Not that a client ever dismissed an advocate from the case—For how could he keep going by himself once he

had pulled in someone to help him?—But it did sometimes happen that a case took a turn where the advocate
could no longer follow it—The case and the accused
and everything was simply withdrawn from the advocate—Then even the best connection with officials
could no longer achieve any result—For even they
knew nothing—The case had simply reached the stage
where further assistance was ruled out—It had vanished
into remote inaccessible courts where even the accused
was beyond the reach of an advocate—The advocate's
room was in the very top attic so that if you stumbled
through the hole your leg hung down into the lower
attic in the very corridor where the clients had to
wait—

BRIEF FOR FIRST HEARING//
CASE OF LIFE FORM A

They sometimes mutate to breathe *"here"*—The gentleman *is* Biologic Court Building *"here"*—You see it's
only *"here"* fixes any case from The Ovens—Not in
other places—after buying the relatively fresh air—
Life Form A arrives on worst thing that could happen
to a space craft—Life Form A breathes from the atmosphere of alien planet—Form A directs all behavior
withdrawn from the advocate into channels calculated
to no longer achieve health and interest of the host—
The case had simply reached to space stage—Assistance

was ruled out—Even the accused was beyond years—
Life Form A's room was in the very top—

"I fancy," said the man who was on alien planet, "that
crippled faintness is due to the 'oxygen'—There is no
'oxygen' this gentleman feels but by invading and occupying 'the office air' they can convert the 'oxygen' up
from the stairway of Life Form B."

The first impression made determines whole course
of subsequent "oxygen" supply—A shocking emergency
case—For how could he keep Form A??—Sees someone to help him but it debarred action in turn—Could
scarcely answer the people of Minraud—Brain directs
all movement—Use a filter screen that scans the door
with intentioned lunacy—Won many similar cases operating through telepathic misdirection—There has been
dismissed an advocate from Minraud—Pulled in and
replaced—Worst thing that could happen to present
heads—Sometimes happened that a case took total
weapons—The principal no longer follow it—The case
had simply reached molten core of a planet where assistance was ruled out—

"I fancy," said the man, "that this gentleman feels
white hot blue skies—Haste he had already so?"

Even so there is a devious underground either outright or partial misdirection—The office air are heads
in bottles—Beyond all doubt intend to outthink and
replace the advocate—A client revolution—For how
could he keep fallen heads to help him?—Metal shimmering heat from the stage where further assistance
melts at noon into remote inaccessible courts—

"Word falling—Photo falling stylishly dressed—The

gentleman's insane orders and counter orders *'here'*—
You see it's only *'here'*—Accustomed D.C. felt ill in the
relatively fresh air, what?—British could scarcely answer him—Shut the door with the utmost haste—"

"Mindless idiot you have won many similar cases—"
Electric defense frequently determined the whole
civilization and proceedings—Especially when a case
fear desperate position and advantage suddenly taken
out of their hands—The case had simply reached incredible life forms—Even the accused was beyond altered pressure—The very top operation—The client of
mucus and urine said the man was an alien—Unusual
mucus coughing enemy "oxygen" up from the stairway—Speed up movie made such forms by overwhelming gravity supply—Flesh frozen to supply a shocking
emergency case—Amino acid directs all movement—
won code on Grey Veil—To be read telepathic misdirection—"Office air" they can convert in dirty pictures of Life Form B—liquidate enemy on London
Space Stage—Tenuous air debarred action of yesterday
—Coughing enemy pulled in and replaced—

"The gentleman in body prison working our *'here'*—
You see it's only *'here'* he ever saw even for an instant
—Not in other places—Switched our way is doomed in
the relatively fresh air—That's us—Planning to use the
host could scarcely answer him—Of course Life Form
B with the utmost haste would shut the door that was
very important for our *'oxygen'* lines—So what else?—
Defense frequently determined the life form we invaded—"

Especially when a case marked for invasion and

manipulation suddenly taken out of their hands—Dismissed an advocate from Biologic Need once he had you pulled in to prepare briefs—The trial of The Nova Mob withdrawn from the advocate—The case had simply reached rigged any place—Pain and pleasure to squeeze the "office air" felt contradictions of biologic stairway—Crippled in such convenient advocate—For how could he keep means during many years of someone to help him?—

"I fancy faintness is due to the atmosphere offered by Life Form A is inadequate—That this gentleman feels necessary to investigate the original 'office air' story of Life Form A on location—A came up from the stairway —He had already counselor willing to handle 'this horrible case' either outright or partially—You see it's only *'here'* fixes nature of absolute need—A question of food supply not alien planet—Form A direct claws intimidate and corrupt advocate into channels calculated to squeeze host—Assistance back to our medium—"

Life Form A's room was on Ward Island—Crippled in such convenient Life Form B—Minraud an intricate door to cut off "oxygen" of life—Similar case operating through arrangements that could liquidate Life Form B by cutting off advocate from Minraud—

"Life Form A was totally alien," said the man who was an alien—

"Have what they call 'emotion' due to the 'oxygen.'"

"Was not the purpose supply Life Form A prior to intervention directing all movement?"

"Pleader a diving suit back to our medium—Scarcely

answer him—Be destroyed by alien conditions—Ally
detestable to us—For how could he keep Form A seen
parasite?"

The best criminal counselor was similar case operating through metal—Impression followed to present interview—He got Sammy advocate from Minraud—
Pulled in and replaced history of Life Form A on location—

Clearly this is a difficult case to defend particularly
considering avowed intention of the accused to use the
counselor as a diving suit back to their medium where
counselor would be destroyed by alien conditions—
There is however one phrase in the brief on which a
defense can be constructed—"They sometimes mutate
to breathe here"—That is if a successful mutation of
Life Form A can be called in as witness—Clearly the
whole defense must be based on possibility of mutation
and the less said about "absolute biologic need" to
maintain a detrimental parasitic existence at the total
expense of Form B the better chance of a compromise
verdict suspended pending mutation proceedings—

TWO TAPE RECORDER MUTATIONS

"I fancy," said the man, "this gentleman feels totally
stupid and greedy Venus Power—Tentacles write out
message from stairway of slime—"

"That's us—Strictly from 'Sogginess Is Good For You'

—Planning no bones but an elementary nervous system
—Scarcely answer him—"

"The case simply at terminal bring down point—Desperate servants suddenly taken out of their hands—Insane orders and counter orders on the horizon—And I playing psychic chess determined the whole civilization and personal habits—"

"Iron claws of pain and pleasure with two speeds—with each recorder in body prison working our 'here' on extension leads—Even for an instant not in operation the host recorder saw the loudspeakers—Way is doomed in relatively soundproof 'room'—Would shift door led to the array—Many recorders important for our oxygen lines—Each to use host connected to its respective recorder layout—For example with nine recorders determined the life form we invaded by three square—Each recorder marked for invasion recording —You see it's only 'here' fixes nature of need set to run for as long as required—'Indignities' and 'cruelties' are playing back while other record—'Intimidate' and 'corrupt' speed and volume variation—Squeeze host back into system—Any number of tape recorders banked together for ease of operation switch in other places— Our mikes are laid out preferably in 'fresh air'—That's us—Planning speaker and mike connected to host— Scarcely answer him—Of course static and moving are possible—Very simplest array would be three lines— Two speeds can be playing especially when a 'case' has four possible states—Fast manipulation suddenly taken

out of slow playback—The actual advocate from biologic need in many ways—

"a-Simple hand switching advocate

"b-Random choice fixed interval biologic stairway—
The whole thing is switched on either outright or partially—at any given time recorders fix nature of absolute need—Thus sound played back by any 'cruelties'
answer him either unchanged or subject to alien
planet—

"c-Sequential choice i.e. flesh frozen to amino acid determines the next state according to" —That is a
"book"—

Form A directs sound channels—Continuous operation in such convenient Life Form B—Final switching
off of tape cuts "oxygen" Life Form B by cutting off
machine will produce cut-up of human form determined by the switching chosen—Totally alien "music"
need not survive in any "emotion" due to the "oxygen"
rendered down to a form of music—Intervention directing all movement what will be the end product?—Re-
ciprocation detestable to us for how could we become
part of the array?—Could this metal impression follow
to present language learning?—Talking and listening
machine led in and replaced—

Life Form A as follows was an alien—The operator
selects the most "oxygen" appropriate material continuous diving suit back to our medium—Ally information
at the verbal level—Could he keep Form A seen parasitic?—Or could end be achieved by present interview?
—Array treated as a whole replaced history of life?

Word falling photo falling tapes being blank—Insane orders and counter orders of machine "music"—The Police Machine will produce a cut-up of it determined by the switching chosen—Could this alien mucus cough language learn? Accused was beyond altered sound formations—Alien Mucus Machine runs by feeding in overwhelming gravity—Code on Grey Veil parallel the spread of "dirty pictures"—Reverse instruction raises question how many convert in "dirty pictures" before London Space Stage—Tenuous simple repetition to one machine only—Coughing enemy pulled in whole could be used as a model for behavior —Screams laughter shouts raw material—Voice fading into advocate:

"Clearly the whole defense must be experiments with two tape recorder mutations."

Pay Color

"THE SUBLIMINAL KID" moved in and took over bars cafés and juke boxes of the world cities and installed radio transmitters and microphones in each bar so that the music and talk of any bar could be heard in all his bars and he had tape recorders in each bar that played and recorded at arbitrary intervals and his agents moved back and forth with portable tape recorders and brought back street sound and talk and music and poured it into his recorder array so he set waves and eddies and tornadoes of sound down all your streets and by the river of all language—Word dust drifted streets of broken music car horns and air hammers— The Word broken pounded twisted exploded in smoke—

Word Falling ///

He set up screens on the walls of his bars opposite mirrors and took and projected at arbitrary intervals shifted from one bar to the other mixing Western Gangsters films of all time and places with word and image of the people in his cafés and on the streets his agents with movie camera and telescope lens poured images of the city back into his projector and camera array and nobody knew whether he was in a Western movie in Hongkong or The Aztec Empire in Ancient Rome or Suburban America whether he was a bandit a commuter or a chariot driver whether he was firing a "real" gun or watching a gangster movie and the city moved in swirls and eddies and tornadoes of image explosive bio-advance out of space to neon—

Photo Falling ///

"The Subliminal Kid" moved in seas of disembodied sound—He then spaced here and there and instaff opposite mirrors and took movies each bar so that the music and talk is at arbitrary intervals and shifted bars —And he also had recorder in tracks and moving film mixing arbitrary intervals and agents moving with the word and image of tape recorders—So he set up waves and his agents with movie swirled through all the streets of image and brought back street in music from the city and poured Aztec Empire and Ancient Rome— Commuter or Chariot Driver could not control their word dust drifted from outer space—Air hammers word

and image explosive bio-advance—A million drifting
screens on the walls of his city projected mixing sound
of any bar could be heard in all Westerns and film of
all times played and recorded at the people back and
forth with portable cameras and telescope lenses
poured eddies and tornadoes of sound and camera array until soon city where he moved everywhere a Western movie in Hongkong or the Aztec sound talk suburban America and all accents and language mixed and
fused and people shifted language and accent in mid-
sentence Aztec priest and spilled it man woman or
beast in all language—So that People-City moved in
swirls and no one knew what he was going out of space
to neon streets—

*"Nothing Is True—Everything Is Permitted—" Last
Words Hassan I Sabbah*

The Kid stirred in sex films and The People-City
pulsed in a vast orgasm and no one knew what was
film and what was not and performed all kinda sex acts
on every street corner—

He took film of sunsets and cloud and sky water and
tree film and projected color in vast reflector screens
concentrating blue sky red sun green grass and the city
dissolved in light and people walked through each
other—There was only color and music and silence
where the words of Hassan i Sabbah had passed—

"Boards Syndicates Governments of the earth *Pay*
—Pay back the *Color* you stole—

"Pay Red—Pay back the red you stole for your ly-

ing flags and your Coca-Cola signs—Pay that red back
to penis and blood and sun—

"*Pay Blue*—Pay back the blue you stole and bot-
tled and doled out in eye droppers of junk—Pay back
the blue you stole for your police uniforms—Pay that
blue back to sea and sky and eyes of the earth—

"*Pay Green*—Pay back the green you stole for
your money—And you, Dead Hand Stretching The
Vegetable People, pay back the green you stole for your
Green Deal to sell out peoples of the earth and board
the first life boat in drag—Pay that green back to flowers and jungle river and sky—

"Boards Syndicates Governments of the earth pay
back your stolen colors—*Pay Color* back to Hassan
i Sabbah—"

PAY OFF THE MARKS?

Amusement park to the sky—The concessioners gathered in a low pressure camouflage pocket—

"I tell you Doc the marks are out there pawing the
ground,

" 'What's this Green Deal?'

" 'What's this Sky Switch?'

" 'What's this Reality Con?'

" 'Man, we been short-timed?'

" 'Are you a Good Gook?'

    " 'A good Nigger?'

      " 'A Good Human Animal?'

"They'll take the place apart—I've seen it before—like a silver flash—And The Law is moving in—Not locals—This is Nova Heat—I tell we got to give and fast—Flicker, The Movies, Biologic Merging Tanks, The lot—Well, Doc?"

"It goes against my deepest instincts to pay off the marks—But under the uh circumstances—caught as we are between an aroused and not in all respects reasonable citizenry and the antibiotic handcuffs—"

The Amusement Gardens cover a continent—There are areas of canals and lagoons where giant gold fish and salamanders with purple fungoid gills stir in clear black water and gondolas piloted by translucent green fish boys—Under vast revolving flicker lamps along the canals spill The Biologic Merging Tanks sense withdrawal capsules light and soundproof water at blood temperature pulsing in and out where two life forms slip in and merge to a composite being often with deplorable results slated for Biologic Skid Row on the outskirts: (Sewage delta and rubbish heaps—terminal addicts of SOS muttering down to water worms and floating vegetables—Paralyzed Orgasm Addicts eaten alive by crab men with white hot eyes or languidly tortured in charades by The Green Boys of young crystal cruelty)

Vast communal immersion tanks melt whole peoples into one concentrate—It's more democratic that way you see?—Biologic Representation—Cast your vote into the tanks—Here where flesh circulates in a neon haze and identity tags are guarded by electric dogs sniffing quivering excuse for being—The assassins wait

broken into scanning patterns of legs smile and drink
—Unaware of The Vagrant Ball Player pant smell running in liquid typewriter—

Streets of mirror and glass and metal under flickering
cylinders of colored neon—Projector towers sweep the
city with color writing of The Painter—Cool blue
streets between walls of iron polka-dotted with lenses
projecting The Blue Tattoo open into a sea of Blue
Concentrate lit by pulsing flickering blue globes—
Mountain villages under the blue twilight—Drifting
cool blue music of all time and place to the brass
drums—

Street of The Light Dancers who dance with color
writing projected on their bodies in spotlight layers
peel off red yellow blue in dazzling strip acts, translucent tentative beings flashing through neon hula hoops
—stand naked and explode in white fade out in grey—
vaporize in blue twilight—

Who did not know the name of his vast continent?—
There were areas left at his electric dogs—Purple fungoid gills stirred in being—His notebooks running
flicker screens along the canals—

"Who him?—Listen don't let him out here."

Two life forms entered the cracked earth to escape
terrible dry heat of The Insect People—The assassins
wait legs by water cruel idiot smiles play a funeral
symphony—For being he was caught in the zoo—Cages
snarling and coming on already—The Vagrant passed
down dusty Arab street muttering: "Where is he now?"
—Listening sifting towers swept the city—American
dawn words falling on my face—Cool Sick room with

rose wallpaper—"Mr. Bradly Mr. Martin" put on a
clean shirt and walked out—stars and pool halls and
stale rooming house—this foreign sun in your brain—
visit of memories and wan light—silent suburban poker
—worn pants—scratching shower room and brown
hair—grey photo—on a brass bed—stale flesh exploded
film in basement toilets—boys jack off from—this
drifting cobweb of memories—in the wind of morning
—furtive and sad felt the lock click—

He walked through—Summer dust—stirring St.
Louis schoolrooms—a brass bed—Cigarette smoke—
urine as in the sun—Soccer scores and KiKi when I
woke up—Such wisdom in gusts—empty spaces—
Fjords and Chimborazi—Brief moments I could describe to the barrier—Pursuits of future life where boy's
dawn question is far away—What's St. Louis or any
conveyor distance? St. Louis on this brass bed? Comte
Wladmir Sollohub Rashid Ali Khan B Bremond d'Ars
Marquis de Migre Principe di Castelcicale Gentilhomo
di Palazzo you're a long way from St. Louis . . . Let
me tell you about a score of years' dust on the window
that afternoon I watched the torn sky bend with the
wind . . . *white white white as far as the eye can see
ahead a blinding flash of white* . . . (The cabin reeks
of exploded star). . . . Broken sky through my nostrils—
Dead bare knee against the greasy dust—Faded photo
drifting down across pubic hair, thighs, rose wallpaper
into the streets of Pasto—The urinals and the bicycle
races here in this boy were gone when I woke up—
Whiffs of my Spain down the long empty noon—Brief
moments I could describe—The great wind revolving

lips and pants in countries of the world—Last soldier's
fading—Violence is shut off Mr. Bradly Mr.—I am
dying in a room far away—last—Sad look—Mr. Of
The Account, I am dying—In other flesh now Such
dying—Remember hints as we shifted windows the
visiting moon air like death in your throat?—The great
wind revolving lip smoke, fading photo and distance
—Whispers of junk, flute walks, shirt flapping—Bicycle
races here at noon—boy thighs—Sad—Lost dog—He
had come a long way for something not exchanged . . .
sad shrinking face . . . He died during the night. . . .

SMORBROT

Operation Sense Withdrawal* is carried out in silent
lightless immersion tanks filled with a medium of salt
bouillon at temperature and density of the human body

* The most successful method of sense withdrawal is the
immersion tank where the subject floats in water at blood
temperature sound and light withdrawn—loss of body outline, awareness and location of the limbs occurs quickly, giving rise to panic in many American subjects—Subjects frequently report feeling that another body is floating half in
and half out of the body in the first part—Experiments in
sense withdrawal using the immersion tanks have been performed by Doctor Lilly in Florida—There is another experimental station in Oklahoma—So after fifteen minutes in the
tank these marines scream they are losing outlines and have
to be removed—I say put two marines in the tank and see
who comes out—Science—Pure science—So put a marine
and his girl friend in the tank and see who or what emerges—

—Cadets enter the tank naked and free floating a few inches apart—permutate on slow currents—soon lose the outlines of body in shifting contact with phantom limbs—Loss of outline associated with pleasant sensations—frequently orgasms occur—

K9 took off his clothes in a metal-lined cubicle with a Chinese youth—Naked he felt vertigo and a tightening of stomach muscles as they let themselves down into the tank and floated now a few inches apart warm liquid swirling through legs and genitals touching—His hands and feed lost outline—There was sudden sharp spasm in his throat and a taste of blood—The words dissolved—His body twisted in liquid fish spasms and emptied through his spurting penis—feeling other spasms shiver through the tank—He got out and dresses with a boy from The Alameda—Back in flesh —street boy words in his throat—Kerosene light on a Mexican about twenty felt his pants slide down his stomach his crotch unbuttoned sighed and moved his ass off—He was naked now in lamp—Mexican rolled marijuana cigarette—naked body of the other next to his turning him over on his stomach—his crotch unbuttoned wind and water sounds—sighed and moved his ass in shadow pools on rose wallpaper—brass bed stale against him—Felt naked body of the other explode in his spine—Room changed with flesh—Felt his pants slide—The cadet's ass was naked now—A few inches apart in the tank the Mexican—His lips felt propositions—A few inches apart K9 moved his ass in scratching shower—Wave of pleasure through his stomach—

He was floating moving in food—City of Chili Houses exploded in muscles and the words went in—There in his throat—Kerosene light on with street boy— Outskirts of The City—First spurts of his crotch— The naked cadets entered a warehouse of metal-lined cubicles—stood a few inches apart laughing and talking on many levels—Blue light played over their bodies*—Projectors flashed the color writing of Hassan i Sabbah on bodies and metal walls—Opened into amusement gardens—Sex Equilibrists perform on tight-ropes and balancing chairs—Trapeze acts ejaculate in

* Reference to the orgone accumulators of Doctor Wilhelm Reich—Doctor Reich claims that the basic charge of life is this blue orgone-like electrical charge—Orgones form a sphere around the earth and charge the human machine—He discovered that orgones pass readily through iron but are stopped and absorbed by organic matter—So he constructed metal-lined cubicles with layers of organic material behind the metal—Subjects sit in the cubicles lined with iron and accumulate orgones according to the law of increased returns on which life functions—The orgones produce a prickling sensation frequently associated with erotic stimulation and spontaneous orgasm—Reich insists that orgasm is an electrical discharge—He has attached electrodes to the appropriate connections and charted the orgasm—In consequence of these experiments he was of course expelled from various countries before he took refuge in America and died in a federal penitentiary for suggesting the orgone accumulator in treating cancer—It has occurred to this investigator that orgone energy can be concentrated to disperse the miasma of idiotic prurience and anxiety that blocks any scientific investigation of sexual phenomenon—Preliminary experiments indicate that certain painting—like Brion Gysin's—when projected on a subject produced some of the effects observed in orgone accumulators—

the air—The Sodomite Tumblers doing cartwheels and whirling dances stuck together like dogs—Boys masturbate from scenic railways—Flower floats in the lagoons and canals—Sex cubicles where the acts performed to music project on the tent ceiling a sky of rhythmic copulation—Vast flicker cylinders and projectors sweep the gardens writing explosive bio-advance to neon—Areas of sandwich booths blue movie parlors and transient hotels under ferris wheels and scenic railways—soft water sounds and frogs from the canals —K9 stood opposite a boy from Norway felt the prickling blue light on his genitals filling with blood touched the other tip and a warm shock went down his spine and he came in spasms of light—Silver writing burst in his brain and went out with a smell of burning metal in empty intersections where boys on roller skates turn slow circles and weeds grow through cracked pavement—

Mexican rolled cigarette the soft blue light deep in his lungs—Mexican hands touching felt his pants slide down in soundless explosion of the throat and a taste of blood—His body twisted—Sleeps naked now—wind and water sounds—Outskirts of the city—shadow areas of sandwich booths and transient hotels under scenic railways—

We drank the beer and ate the smorbrot—I dropped half a sandwich in my lap and she wiped the butter off with a napkin laughing as the cloth bulged under her fingers my back against a tree the sun on my crotch tingling filling with blood she opened my belt and:

"Raise up, darling," pulled my pants down to the knee—

We ate the smorbrot with hot chocolate from the thermos bottle and I spilled a cup of chocolate in my lap and jumped up and she wiped the chocolate off with a paper napkin and I dodged away laughing as the cloth bulged under her fingers and she followed me with the napkin and opened my belt—I felt my pants slide down and the sun on my naked crotch tingling and filling with blood—We did it half undressed—When I came there was silver light popped in my eyes like a flash bulb and looking over her shoulder I saw little green men in the trees swinging from branch to branch turning cartwheels in the air—And sex acts by naked acrobats on tightropes and balancing poles—Jissom drifting cobwebs through clear green light—Washed in the stream and pulled up my pants— We rode back to Copenhagen on my motor scooter—I left her in front of her flat block and arranged a meeting for Sunday—As she walked away I could see the grass stains on the back of her dress—That night I was blank and went back to a bar in Neuerhaven where I can usually find a tourist to buy drinks—and sat down at a table with a boy about my age—I noticed he had a very small narrow head tapering from his neck which was thick and smooth and something strange about his eyes—The iris was shiny black like broken coal with pinpoint green pupils—He turned and looks straight at me and I got a feeling like scenic railways in the stomach—Then he ordered two beers—"I see that you are blank," he said—The beers came—"I work with the circus," he said—balancing his chair—"Like this on wires—never with net—In South America I did it over a gorge of a thousand meters in depth."

Balancing he drank the Tuborg—"There are not many who can see us—Come and I will show you our real acts."

We took a cab to the outskirts of the city—There was a warm electric wind blowing through the car that seemed to leave the ground—We came to what looked like a ruined carnival by a lake—In a tent lit by flickering blue globes I met more boys with the same narrow head and reversed eyes—They passed around a little pipe and I smoked and felt green tingling in my crotch and lips—A Negro drummer began pounding his drum with sticks—The boys got up laughing and passing the pipe and talking in a language like bird calls and took off their clothes—They climbed a ladder to the high wire and walked back and forth like cats—A magic lantern projected color writing on their bodies that looked like Japanese tattooing—They all got erections and arching past each other on the wire genitals touched in a shower of blue sparks—One boy balanced a steel chair on the wire and ejaculated in a crescendo of drum beats and flickering rainbow colors—jissom turning slow cartwheels dissolved in yellow light—Another boy with earphones crackling radio static and blue sparks playing around his yellow hair did a Messerschmidt number—the chair rocking in space—tracer bullets of jissom streaking cross interstellar void—

(Naked boys on roller skates turn slow circles at the intersection of ruined suburbs—falling through a maze
of penny arcades—spattered the cracked concrete
weeds and dog excrement—) The boys came down
from the wire and one of them flicked my jacket—I
took off my clothes and practiced balancing naked in a
chair—The balance point was an electrical field holding
him out of gravity—The charge built up in his genitals
and he came in a wet dream the chair fluid and part of
his body—That night made sex with the boy I met in
Neuerhaven for the first time with each other in space
—Sure calm of wire acts balanced on ozone—blue
electric spasms—Smell of burning metal in the penny
arcade I got a hard on looking at the peep show and
Hans laughed pointing to my fly: "Let's make the roller
coaster," he said—The cashier took our money with
calm neutral glance—A young Italian clicked us out—
We were the only riders and as soon as the car started
we slipped off our shorts—We came together in the first
dip as the car started up the other side throwing blood
into our genitals tight and precise as motor parts—open
shirts flapping over the midway—Silver light popped
in my head and went out in blue silence—Smell of
ozone—You see sex is an electrical charge that can be
turned on and off if you know the electromagnetic
switchboard—Sex is an electrical flesh trade—It is
usually turned on by water sounds—Now take your
sex words on rose wallpaper brass bed—Explode in red
brown green from colors to the act on the association
line—Naked charge can explode sex words to color's

rectal brown green ass language—The sex charge is usually controlled by sex words forming an electromagnetic pattern—This pattern can be shifted by substituting other factors for words—Take a simple sex word like "masturbate"—"jack off"—Substitute color for the words like: "jack"—red "off"—white—red—white—Flash from words to color on the association screen—Associate silently from colors to the act—Substitute other factors for the words—Arab drum music—Musty smell of erections in outhouses—Feel of orgasm —Color-music-smell-feel to the million sex acts all time place—Boys red-white from ferris wheel, scenic railways, bridges, whistling bicycles, tree houses careening freight cars train whistles drifting jissom in winds of Panhandle—shivering through young bodies under boarding house covers rubbly outskirts of South American city ragged pants dropped to cracked bleeding feet black dust blowing through legs and genitals—Pensive lemur smell of erection—cool basement toilets in St. Louis—Summer afternoon on car seats to the thin brown knee—Bleak public school flesh naked for the physical the boy with epilepsy felt The Dream in his head struggling for control locker room smells on his stomach—He was in The Room with many suitcases all open and drawers full of things that had to be packed and only a few minutes to catch the boat whistling in the harbor and more and more drawers and the suitcases won't close arithmetical disorder and the wet dream tension in his crotch—The other boys laughing and pointing in the distance now as he got out of con-

trol silver light popped in his eyes and he fell with a
sharp metal cry—through legs and genitals felt his
pants slide—shivering outskirts of the city—wind of
morning in a place full of dust—Naked for a physical
orgasms occur—tightening stomach muscles—scenic
railways exploded in his crotch—Legs and genitals lost
outline careening through dream flesh—smell of the
mud flats—warm spurts to sluggish stream water
from the tree house—a few inches apart laughing in
the sunlight jissom cartwheels in the clear air of masturbating afternoons—pulled up my pants—Explosion
of the throat from color to the act jumped up laughing
in the transient hotels—careening area of sandwich
booths—Silver writing burst in moonlight through a
Mexican about twenty shifting his crotch sighed and
moved naked now a few inches in his hand—pleasure
tingling through cracked bleeding feet—With phantom
limbs his cock got hard sensations on roller skates—
slow intersection of weeds and concrete—Penny arcades spattered light on a Mexican about twenty—Wet
dreams of flight sighed in lamp—Flash from word to
color sex acts all time place exploded in muscles drifting sheets of male flesh—Boys on wind of morning—
first spurts unbuttoned my pants—Area of sandwich
booths and intolerable scenic railways he came wet
dream way—(In the tree house black ants got into our
clothes pulling off shirts and pants and brushing the
ants off each other he kept brushing my crotch—
"there's an ant there" and jacked me off into the stream
of masturbating afternoons)—Hans laughed pointing

to my shorts—Pants to the ankle we were the only
riders—Wheee came together in the first dip open
shorts flapping genitals—Wind of morning through
flesh—Outskirts of the city—

ITS ACCOUNTS

Now hazard flakes fall—A huge wave rolled treatment "pay back the red you stole"—Farewell for Alexander—Fading out in Ewyork, Onolulu, Aris, Ome,
Oston—Sub editor melted into air—I Sekuin hardly
breathe—Dreams are made of might be just what I
am look: Prerecorded warning in a woman's voice—
Scio is pulling a figure out of logos—A huge wave
bowled a married couple off what you could have—
Would you permit that person in Ewyork, Onolulu,
Aris, Ome, Oston?—One assumes a "beingness" where
past crimes highlighted the direction of a "havingness"
—He boasted of a long string of other identities—She
gave no indication of fundamental agreement—We returned to war—Process pre-clear in absurd position for
conditions—Scio is like pulling a figure out of The
Homicide Act—Logos got Sheraton Call and spent the
weekend with a bargain—Venus Vigar choked to pas-
sionate weakness—The great wind identity failed—So
did art loving Miss West—Every part of your dust yesterday along the High Street Air—The flakes fall that
were his cruelest lawyer: show you fear on walls and

windows treatment—Farewell trouble for Alexander—
Pay back the red you stole living or dead from the sky
—Hurry up please its accounts—Empty thing police
they fading out—Dusk through narrow streets, toilet
paper, and there is no light in the window—April wind
revolving illness of dead sun—Woman with red hair is
a handful of dust—Departed have left used avenue—
Many years ago that youngster—It was agony to
breathe in number two intake—Dreams of the dead—
Prerecorded warning—Remember I was carbon dioxide
—It is impossible to estimate the years in novitiate
postulating Sheraton Carlton Call—Loose an arrow—
Thud—Thing Police fading out in Ewyork, Onolulu,
Aris, Ome, Oston—See where he struck—Oh no dis-
counts and compensations—Stop tinkering with what
you could have—Must go in time—Stop tinkering with
recompense—You'll know me in dark mutinous mirrors
of the world—Yesterday along high street massive
treatment: "Pay back the red you stole"—A shame to
part with it?? Try various farewell trouble?? Near
curtains for them and trouble shuffled out of the die—
Along high street account reaching to my chest—Pay
back the red you stole happened—Effects Boys said
farewell to Alexander Bargain—"What are we going
to do? Thing police they fading out—Sub editor melted
into air—So I had to do Two Of A Kind on toilet paper
—Obvious sooner that air strip."

"It was agony to breathe—What might be called the
worried in number two intake—Barry going to do?—
Partisans of all nations learn all about it—Red Hair we

were getting to use on anyone—Pit too—Going to get out of it?"

A colorless question drifted down corridors of that hospital—"I Sekuin—Tell me what you would permit to remain?"

SIMPLE AS A HICCUP

Mr. Martin, hear us through something as simple as a hiccup tinkering with the disaster accounts—All Board Room Reports are classified as narcotic drugs— Morphine is actually "Mr. Martin," his air line the addict—I have said the basic techniques: every reason to believe the officers dictate in detail with a precise repetition of stimuli place of years—Techniques of nova reports are stimuli between enemies—Dimethyl- tryptamine pain bank from "disagreeable symptoms"— Overdose by precise repetition can be nightmare ex- perience owing to pain headphones send nova spirit from Hiroshima and Nagasaki—"Mr. Martin," hear us through mushroom clouds—Start tinkering with disas- ter brains and twisting all board room reports—Their pain line is the addict—Pain bank from the torture chambers—Every reason to believe the officers torn into insect fragments by precise repetition of years— Tortured metal pain spirit Uranian born of nova con- ditions send those blasts—Great wind revolving the nova spirit in image flakes—Every part of your trans-

lucent burning fire head shut off, Mr. Bradly, in the
blue sky writing of Hassan i Sabbah—That hospital
melted in Grey Room—Writing of Hassan i Sabbah
postulating you were all smoke drifting from something
as simple as a hiccup—I have said the basic techniques
of the world and mutilated officers dictate in detail
with iron claws of the chessmen place of years—Hassan i Sabbah through all disaster accounts—Last door
of nova and all the torture expanding drugs—Pressure
groups teach mechanisms involved—Disaster of nova
pulsed need dictates use of throat bones—I Sabbah
walk in the recordings write dripping faucet and five
flashes per second—The rhythmic turrets destroy
enemy installations—Cortex winds overflowing into
mutinous areas hearing color seeing "Mr. Bradly Mr.
Martin"—Just time—Just time—I quote from Anxiety
And Its Treatment in Grey Room—Apomorphine as a
hiccup—Hassan i Sabbah through apomorphine acts
on the hypothalamus and regulates blood serum of the
world and mutilated officers—Melted a categorical "no
mercy for this enemy" as dust and smoke—

THERE'S A LOT ENDED

New York, Saturday March 17, Present Time—For
many he accidentally blew open present food in The
Homicide Act—Anyway after that all the top England
spent the weekend with a bargain—Intend to settle

price—I had work in Melbourne before doing sessions
—Australia in the gates—Dogs must be carried—Re-
luctant to put up any more Amplex—Go man go—
There's a lot ended—Flashes The Maharani of Check
Moth—The clean queen walks serenely down dollars—
Don't listen to Hassan i Sabbah—We want Watney's
Woodbines and all pleasures of the body—Stand clear
of The Garden Of Delights—And love slop is a Bristol
—Bring together state of news—Inquire on hospital—
At the Ovens Great Gold Cup—Revived peat victory
hopes of Fortria—Premature Golden sands in Sheila's
cottage?—You want the name of Hassan i Sabbah so
own the unborn?—Cool and casual through the hole in
thin air closed at hotel room in London—Death reduces the college—Seriously considered so they are
likely to face lung cancer disciplinary action—

Venus Vigar choked to death with part-time television—Ward boy kept his diary thoughts and they
went back meticulously to the corridor—He pointed
out that the whole world had already watched Iden-
tikit—"Why, we all take satisfaction—Rode a dancing
horse on sugar avenue—Prettiest little thought you
ever saw"—

The capsule was warm in Soho—An operation has
failed to save American type jeans—Further talks today with practical cooperation—There are many sim-
ilarities—Solicitor has ally at Portman Clinic—The
Vital Clue that links the murders is JRR 284—Finished
off in a special way just want to die—When his body
was found three young men are still dancing the twist

in The Swede's Dunedin muck spreading The New
Zealand after 48 hours in his bed sitter—Stephen film
was in the hospital—Definition of reasonable boy body
between his denials—Identity popped in flash bulb
breakfast—Yards and yards of entrails hung around the
husband irrevocably committed to the toilet—The Observer left his friend in Cocktail Probation—Vanished
with confessed folk singer—Studio dresser John Vigar
found dead on the old evacuation plan—The body,
used in 1939, year of Vigar's birth, was naked—Both
men had been neatly folded—As the series is soon
ending are these experiments really necessary? Uncontrolled flash bulbs popped in rumors—Said one: "All
this is typical Dolce just before Christ Vita—"—Quiet
man in 624A said the tiny bedroom as doctor actor
would never do—Police examined the body counter
outside little groups of denials—Miss Taylor people
hung around the husband—He plays Mark even An-
thony with Liz—There was great bustle through the
red hair—Born in Berlin and made his first threat to
peace at the age of 17—Hanratty was then brought up
as a Jew—Over 100 police in unfashionably dressed
women search for boy who had protested definition of
"reasonable friend" and "circumstantial police"—Prime
haggling going on—Sir, I am delighted to see that/
writes about/ I am quite prepared to/ Last attention
is being paid to routine foundations on the Square
Generation/ The light woman is at the clear out/ if
they wish to live their moment without answering to
me/ this of course they will not do

James swaggering about in arson to be considered—
Murder in the operating theater at Nottingham—
Stephen said to be voting through yards and yards of
entrails irrrevocably committed to the toilet—

ONE MORE CHANCE?

Scientology means the study of "humanity's condition"—Wise radio doctor—Logos Officers in his portable—The Effects Boy's "scientology release" is locks
over the Chinese—Told me to sit by Hubbard guide—
"What are you going to do?—That person going to
get out of 'havingness??' "
Will cover the obvious usually sooner than later—
Globe is self you understand until assumed unwittingly
"reality" is made out of "Mr. Martin"—To agree to be
Real is "real" and the way the flakes fall—Game conditions and no game every time—For him always been a
game consists of "freed galaxies"—End getting an effect
on the other team now ended—Look around here it's
curtains for them—Be able to not know his past circumstances—Scio is knowing and wind hand to the
hilt—Work we have logos you got it? Dia through
noose—Jobbies would like to strike—Release certificate
is issued for a respectable price—Find a process known
as "overwhelming," what?—Come back work was what
you could have—What would you permit that person—?? Food in The Homicide Act??—Look around

and accept "one more chance??" "Havingness" bait
and it's curtains—End anatomy of games—The fundamental reward business the bait—The cycle of "Humanity's condition"—Apparent because we believe it—
One assumes a "beingness" over the Chinese—Like to
strike a bargain: Other identities—Is false identity—
In the end is just the same—Fundamentally agreement
—All games for respectable share of these "barriers"
and "purposes"—Know what they mean if they start
"no-effect??"

Cool and casual the anatomy of games closed at
hotel room in London—

The District Supervisor looked up with a narrow
smile. "Sit down young man and smoke . . . occupational
vice what? . . . only vice left us . . . You have studied
Scientology of course?"

"Oh yes sir . . . It was part of our *basic* training sir
. . . an unforgettable experience if you'll pardon the
expression sir . . ."

"Repeat what you know about Scientology."

"The Scientologists believe sir that words recorded
during a period of unconsciousness . . . (anesthesia,
drunkenness, sleep, childhood amnesia for trauma) . . .
store pain and that this pain store can be plugged in
with key words represented as alternative mathematical
formulae indicating number of exposures to the key
words and reaction index, the whole battery feeding
back from electronic computers . . . They call these
words recorded during unconsciousness *engrams* sir . . .

If I may say so sir the childhood amnesia for trauma is
of special interest sir . . . The child *forgets* sir but since
the controllers have the engram tapes sir any childhood
trauma can be plugged in at any time . . . The pain that
overwhelms that person is known as *basic basic* sir and
when *basic basic* is wiped off the tape . . . Oh sir *then*
that person becomes what they call a *clear* sir . . . Since
Lord Lister sir . . . since the introduction of *anesthesia*
sir . . ." (Amnesia smiled) "Oh let me yes sir tell you
about a score of years' dust on the expression sir . . . If
you'll pardon the expression sir are known as engrams
sir."

"You have occupational experience?"

"Oh yes sir . . . It was part of our Basic Scientology
Police Course sir"

"You have studied the risks of 'dancing'?"

"Sir the Scientologists believe this pain can be
plugged in from Oaxaca photo copies and middle ages
jacking off in deprostrated comrades"

(The living dead give a few cool hints . . . artificial
arms and legs . . . soulless winded words)

"With the advent of *General Anesthesia* sir words recorded during *operations* became . . . (The nurse leans
over the doctor's shoulder dropping cigarette ashes
along the incision—'What are you looking for?' snarls
the doctor . . . 'I know what I'm doing right enough . . .
appendectomy at least . . . But why stop there?? Enemy
anesthetized we advance . . . Fetch me another scalpel
. . . This one's filthy . . .' Chorus of street boys outside:
'Fingaro?? one cigarette?? please thanks you very much

. . . You like beeg one? . . . son bitch bastard . . .' 'Go
away you villainous young toads' snarls the doctor pelt-
ing them with tonsils . . . 'Wish I had an uterine tumor
. . . like a bag of cement . . . get one of them with any
luck . . . You nurse . . . Put out that cigarette . . . *You
wanta cook my patient's lungs out??"*

Shrill screams from maternity blast through the
loudspeaker . . . The Technician mixes a bicarbonate of
soda and belches into his hand . . . 'Urp urp urp . . .
Fucking set picks up every fart and passes it along' A
hideous sqwawk of death rattles smudges the instrument panel out of focus . . . White no smell of death
from a cell of sick junkies in the prison ward swirls
through the operating room . . . The doctor sags ominously severing the patient's femoral artery . . . 'I die
. . . I faint . . . I fail . . . Fucking sick Coolies knock all
the junk right out of a man . . .' He staggers towards the
narco cabinet trailing his patient's blood . . . 'GOM for
the love of God') It's a little skit I wrote for the *Post
Gazette* sir . . . Anesthesia on stage sir words recorded
during operations became the most reliable engrams . . .
Operation Pain they called it sir . . . I can feel it now
sir . . . in my tonsils sir . . . ether vertigo sir . . . (*The
patient is hemorrhaging . . . nurse . . . the clamps . . .
quick before I lose my patient*) . . . Another instrument
of these pain tourists is the *signal switch* sir . . . what
they call the 'yes no' sir . . . 'I love you I hate you' at
supersonic alternating speed . . . Take orgasm noises
sir and cut them in with torture and accident groans

and screams sir and operating-room jokes sir and flicker
sex and torture film right with it sir" . . .

"And what is your counter?"

"Just do it sir . . . in front of everybody sir . . . It
would have a comic effect sir . . . We flash a sex pic
with torture in the background sir then snap that torture pic right in your bloody face sir . . . if you'll pardon
the expression sir . . . we do the same with the sound
track sir . . . *varying distances* sir . . . It has a third
effect sir . . . right down the old middle line sir . . . if
you'll pardon the expression sir . . . the razor inside
sir . . .

"Jerk the handle . . . It sounds like this sir: 'Oh my
God I can't stand it . . . That hurts that hurts that hurts
so gooood . . . Oooooohhhh fuck me to death . . . Blow
his fucking guts out . . . You're burning up baby . . .
whole sky burning . . . I'll talk . . . Do it again . . . Come
in . . . Get out . . . Slip your pants down . . . What's
that?? *nurse* . . . the clamps . . . Cut it off . . .' with the
pics sir . . . popping like fireworks sir . . . sex and pain
words sir . . . vary the tape sir . . . switch the tape sir . . .

Now all together *laugh laugh laugh* . . . Oh sir we
laugh it right off the tape sir . . . We *forget* it right off
the tape sir . . . You see sir we can *not know it* if we
have the engram tapes sir . . . simple as a hiccup sir . . .
melted a categorical no mercy for this enemy as dust
and smoke sir . . . The man who never was reporting
for no duty sir . . . A young cop drew the curtains sir
. . . Room for one more operating-room joke inside sir"

You can still see the old operating room kinda run

down now . . . Do you begin to see there is no patient there on the table?

ARE THESE EXPERIMENTS NECESSARY?

Saturday March 17, 1962, Present Time Of Knowledge—Scio is knowing and open food in The Homicide Act—Logos you got it?—Dia through noose—England spent the weekend with a bargain before release certificate is issued—Dogs must be carried reluctant to the center—It's a grand feeling—There's a lot ended—This condition is best expressed queen walks serenely down dollar process known as overwhelming—What we want is Watney's Woodbines and the Garden Of Delights— And what could you have?—What would you? State of news?—Inquire on hospital? what?—Would you permit that person revived peat victory hopes of Fortria? Pre-clear to look around and discover Sheila's Cottage? —Death reduces the cycle of action—Venus Vigar choked to death in the direction of "havingness"—His diary thoughts they went back other identities—The whole world had valence is false identity—Further talks today with "barriers" and "purposes"—Vital clue that links the murders is: game one special way just want to die—Spreading the New Zealand after film was in the hospital—Yards of entrails hung about the toilet—The observer left his scio and vanished with confessed folk singer logos—Dia through noose found dead on the old evacuation—Release certificate of Vigar's birth is issued naked—This condition is best expressed uncontrolled flash bulbs popped process known as "overwhelming"—

"Sir I am quite prepared—other identities—Woman is at the clear out if is fundamentally agreement"—

"Look around here and tell me are these experiments really necessary?"—All this to "overwhelm"—? Apparency bustle through the red hair—I have said Scio Officers at any given time dictate place of years—Dead absolute need condition expressed process known as "overwhelming"—Silence—Don't answer—What could that person "overwhelm?"—Air?—The great wind revolving what you could have—What would you?—Sound and image flakes fall—It will be seen that "havingness" no more—

Paralyzed on this green land the "cycle of action"—The cycle of last door—Shut off "Mr. Bradly Mr. Apparent Because We Believe It"—Into air—You are yourself "Mr. Bradly Mr. Other Identities"—Action is an apparency creating and aggravating conflict—Total war of the past—I have said the "basic pre-clear identities" are now ended—Wind spirits melted "reality need" dictates use of throat bones—"Real is real" do get your heavy summons and are melted—Through all the streets time for him be able to not know his past walls and windows people and sky—Complete intentions falling—Look around here—No more flesh scripts dispense Mr.—Heard your summons—Melted "Mr. Bradly Mr. Martin"

MELTED INTO AIR

Fade out muttering: "There's a lover on every corner cross the wounded galaxies"—

Distant fingers get hung up on one—"Oh, what'll we do?"

Slowly fading—I told him you on tracks—All over for sure—I'm absolutely prophesized in a dream grabbing Yuri by the shirt and throwing last words answer his Yugoslavian knife—I pick up Shannon Yves Martin may not refuse vision—Everybody's watching—But I continue the diary—"Mr. Bradly Mr. Martin?"—You are his eyes—I see suddenly Mr. Beiles Mr. Corso Mr. Burroughs presence on earth is all a joke—And I think: "Funny—melted into air"—Lost flakes fall that were his shadow: This book—No good junky identity fading out—

"Smoke is all, boy—Dont intersect—I think now I go home and it's five times—Had enough slow metal fires—Form has been inconstant—Last electrician to tap on the bloody dream"—

"I see dark information from him on the floor—He pull out—Keep all Board Room Reports—Waiting chair to bash everybody—Couldn't reach tumescent daydream in Madrid—Flash a jester angel who stood there in 1910 straw words—Realize that this too is bad move—No good—No bueno—Young angel elevated among the subterraneans—Yes, he heard your summons—Nodded absently—"

"And I go home having lost—Yes, blind may not refuse vision to this book—"

CLOM FLIDAY

I have said the basic techniques of nova are very simple consist in creating and aggravating conflicts— "No riots like injustice directed between enemies"—At any given time recorders fix nature of absolute need and dictate the use of total weapons—Like this: Collect and record violent Anti-Semitic statements—Now play back to Jews who are after Belsen—Record what they say and play it back to the Anti-Semites—Clip clap—You got it?—Want more?—Record white supremacy statements—Play to Negroes—Play back answer—Now The Women and The Men—No riots like injustice directed between "enemies"—At any given time position of recorders fixes nature of absolute need —And dictates the use of total weapons—So leave the recorders running and get your heavy metal ass in a space ship—Did it—Nothing here now but the recordings—Shut the whole thing right off—*Silence*—When you answer the machine you provide it with more recordings to be played back to your "enemies" keep the whole nova machine running—The Chinese character for "enemy" means to be similar to or to answer—Don't answer the machine—Shut it off—

"The Subliminal Kid" took over streets of the world —Cruise cars with revolving turrets telescope movie lenses and recorders sweeping up sound and image of the city around and around faster and faster cars racing through all the streets of image record, take, play back, project on walls and windows people and sky—And slow moving turrets on slow cars and wagons slower and slower record take, play back, project slow motion street scene—Now fast—Now slow—slower—*Stop*— Shut off—No More—My writing arm is paralyzed—No more junk scripts, no more word scripts, no more flesh scripts—He all went away—No good—No bueno— Couldn't reach flesh—No glot—Clom Fliday—Through invisible door—Adios Meester William, Mr. Bradly, Mr. Martin—

I have said the basic techniques creating and aggravating conflict officers—At any given time dictate total war of the past—Changed place of years in the end is just the same—I have said the basic techniques of Nova reports are now ended—Wind spirits melted between "enemies"—Dead absolute need dictates use of throat bones—On this green land recorders get your heavy summons and are melted—Nothing here now but the recordings may not refuse vision in setting forth—*Silence*—Don't answer—That hospital melted into air— The great wind revolving turrets towers palaces—Insubstantial sound and image flakes fall—Through all the streets time for him to forbear—Blest be he on walls and windows people and sky—On every part of your dust falling softly—falling in the dark mutinous "No more"—My writing arm is paralyzed on this green land—Dead Hand, no more flesh scripts—Last door—Shut off Mr. Bradly Mr.—He heard your summons—Melted into air—You are yourself "Mr. Bradly Mr. Martin—" all the living and the dead—You are yourself —There be—

Well that's about the closest way I know to tell you and papers rustling across city desks . . . fresh southerly winds a long time ago.

September 17, 1899 over New York

July 21, 1964
Tangier, Morocco

William Burroughs

The Wild Boys

A BOOK OF THE DEAD

CONTENTS

Tío
Mate
Smiles

The camera is the eye of a cruising vulture flying over an area of scrub, rubble and unfinished buildings on the outskirts of Mexico City.

Five-story building no walls no stairs . . . squatters have set up makeshift houses . . . floors are connected by ladders . . . dogs bark, chickens cackle, a boy on the roof makes a jack-off gesture as the camera sails past.

Close to the ground we see the shadow of our wings, dry cellars choked with thistles, rusty iron rods sprouting like metal plants from cracked concrete, a broken bottle in the sun, shit-stained color comics, an Indian boy against a wall with his knees up eating an orange sprinkled with red pepper.

The camera zooms up past a red-brick tenement

studded with balconies where bright pimp shirts flutter purple, yellow, pink, like the banners of a medieval fortress. On these balconies we glimpse flowers, dogs, cats, chickens, a tethered goat, a monkey, an iguana. The *vecinos* lean over the balconies to exchange gossip, cooking oil, kerosene and sugar. It is an old folklore set played out year after year by substitute extras.

Camera sweeps to the top of the building where two balconies are outlined against the sky. The balconies are not exactly one over the other since the top balcony recedes a little. Here the camera stops . . . ON SET.

It is a bright windy morning China-blue half-moon in the sky. Joselito, the *maricón* son of Tía Dolores, has propped up a mirror by the rain barrel and is shaving the long silky black hairs from his chest in the morning wind while he sings

"NO PEGAN A MIO." ("DON'T HIT ME.")

It is an intolerable sound that sets spoons tinkling in saucers and windowpanes vibrating. The *vecinos* mutter sullenly.

"Es el puto que canta." ("It is the queer who sings.")
"The son of Dolores." She crosses herself.

A young man rolls off his wife despondently.
"No puedo con eso puto cantando." ("I can't do it with that queer singing.")
"The son of Dolores. She has the evil eye."

In each room the face of Joselito singing *"NO PEGAN A MIO"* is projected onto the wall.

Shot shows an old paralyzed man and Joselito's face inches from his screaming *"NO PEGAN A MIO."*
"Remember that he is the son of Dolores."
"And one of Lola's 'Little Kittens.'"

Tía Dolores is an old woman who runs a newspaper-and-tobacco kiosk. Clearly Joselito is her professional son.

On the top balcony is Esperanza just down from the mountains since her husband and all her brothers are in prison for growing opium poppies. She is a massive woman with arms like a wrestler and a permanent bucktoothed snarl. She leans over the balcony wall.

"Puto grosero, tus chingoa de pelos nos soplan en la cocina."

("Vulgar queer, your fucking hairs are blowing into our food.")

Shot shows hairs sprinkling soup and dusting an omelet like fine herbs.

The epithet *"grosero"* is too much for Joselito. He whirls cutting his chest. He clutches the wound with an expression of pathic dismay like a dying saint in an El Greco painting. He gasps *"MAMACITA"* and folds to the red tiles of the balcony dripping blood.

This brings Tía Dolores from her lair under the stairs, a rat's nest of old newspapers and magazines. Her evil eyes rotate in a complex calendar, and these calculations occupy her for many hours each night settled in her nest she puffs and chirps and twitters and writes in notebooks that are stacked around her bed with magazines on astrology . . . "Tomorrow my noon eye . will be at its full." . . . This table of her power is so precise that she has to know the day hour minute and second to be sure of an ascendant eye and to this end she carries about with her an assortment of clocks, watches and sundials on thongs and chains. She can make her two eyes do different things, one spinning clockwise the other counterclockwise or she can pop one eye out onto her cheek laced with angry red veins while the other sinks back into an enigmatic grey slit. Latterly she has set up a schedule of *"ojos dulces"* ("sweet eyes") and gained some renown as a healer though Tío Mate says he would rather have ten of her evils than one of her sweets. But he is a bitter old man who lives in the past.

Dolores is a formidable war machine rather like a gun turret, dependent on split-second timing and the reflector disk of her kiosk, she is not well designed for surprise encounters.

Enter the American tourist. He thinks of himself as a good guy but when he looks in the mirror to shave this good guy he has to admit that "well, other people are different from me and I don't really like them." This makes him feel guilty toward other people. Tía Dolores hunches her cloak of malice closer and regards him with stony disapproval.

"Buenas días señorita."

"Desea algo?"

"Sí . . . Tribune . . Tribune Americano . . ."

Silently pursing her lips she folds the *Herald Tribune* and hands it to him. Trying not to watch what the woman is doing with her eyes, he fumbles for change. Suddenly his hand jumps out of the pocket scattering coins on the pavement. He stoops to pick them up.

A child hands him a coin.

"Gracias . . . Gracias."

The child looks at him with cold hatred. He stands there with the coins in his hand.

"Es cuanto?"

"Setenta centavos."

He hands her a peso. She drops it into a drawer and
pushes the change at him.
"*Gracias . . . Gracias . . .*"
She stares at him icily. He stumbles away. Halfway
down the block he screams out
"I'LL KILL THE OLD BITCH."
He begins to shadowbox and point pistols. People stop
and stare.
Children scream after him.
"Son bitch Merican crazy man."
A policeman aproaches jerkily.
"*Señor oiga . . .*"
"OLD BITCH . . . OLD BITCH."
He lashes out wildly in a red haze blood cold on his
shirt.

Enter a pregnant woman. She orders the Spanish edition of *Life*. Looking straight at the woman's stomach,
Dolores' eyes glaze over and roll back in her head.
"*Nacido muerto*" ("Born dead") whispers Tío Pepe who
has sidled up beside the woman.

On "sweet eye" days she changes her kiosk to a flower
stall and sits there beaming the sweetest old flower lady
of them all.
Enter the American tourist his face bandaged his arm
in a sling.

"Ah! the American caballero wishes the *Tribune*. Today
I sell flowers but this paper I have kept for you."
Her eyes crease in a smile that suffuses her face with
gentle light.
"*Aquí señor, muchas gracias.*"
The paper smells faintly of roses. The coins leap into his
hand.

Giving him the change she presses a coin into his palm and folds his fingers over it.

"This will bring you luck señor."

He walks down the street smiling at children who smile back . . . "I guess that's what we come here for . . . these children . . . that old flower lady back there . . ."

Enter the woman whose male child was born dead. She has come to buy a flower for his grave. Tía Dolores shakes her head sadly.

"*Pobrecito.*" ("Poor little one.")

The woman proffers a coin. Tía Dolores holds up her hands.

"*No señora . . . Es de mío . . .*"

However, her timing schedule necessitates a constant shift of props and character . . . "My sweet eye wanes with the moon" . . . That day the tourist reached his hotel in a state of collapse for a terrible street boy followed him from the kiosk screaming

"Son bitch puto queer, I catching one clap from fucky you asshole."

Sometimes half her booth is a kiosk and the other half a flower stall and she sits in the middle, her sweet eye on one side and her kiosk eye on the other. She can alternate sweet and evil twenty-four times a second her eyes jumping from one socket to the other.

Confident from her past victories, Tía Dolores waddles out onto the balcony like a fat old bird.

"*Pobrecito*" . . . She strokes Joselito's head gathering her powers.

"Tell your *maricón* son to shave in the house."

With a hasty glance at three watches, Dolores turns to

face this uncouth peasant woman who dares to challenge her dreaded eye.

"*Vieja loca, que haces con tu ojos?*" sneers Esperanza. "*Tu te pondrás ciego como eso.*" ("Old crazy one, what are you doing with your eyes? You will blind yourself doing that."

Dolores gasps out "TÍO PEPE" and sinks to the deck by her stricken son.

And Tío Pepe pops out tying his pants in front with a soggy length of grey rope. Under a travesty of good nature his soul is swept by raw winds of hate and mischance. He reads the newspapers carefully gloating over accidents, disasters and crime he thinks he is causing by his "*sugestiónes.*" His magic consists in whispering potent phrases from newspapers ". . . there are no survivors . . . condemned to death . . . fire of unknown origins . . . charred bodies . . ." This he does in crowds where people are distracted or better, much better right into the ear of someone who is sleeping or unconscious from drink. If no one is around and he is sure of his flop he reinforces his "*sugestiónes*" by thumping him in the testicles, grinding a knuckle into his eye or clapping cupped hands over his ears.

Here is a man asleep on a park bench. Tío Pepe approaches. He sits down by the man and opens a paper. He leans over reading into the man's ear, a thick slimy whisper.

"*No hay supervivientes.*" The man stirs uneasily. "*Muerto en el acto.*" The man shakes his head and opens his eyes. He looks suspiciously at Tío Pepe who has both hands on the paper. He stands up and taps his pockets. He walks away.

And there is a youth sleeping in a little park. Tío Pepe drops a coin by the boy's head. Bending down to pick up the coin he whispers . . . *"un joven muerto."* ("a dead youth.")

Several times the *vecinos* shoo him away from a sleeper and he hops away like an old vulture showing his yellow teeth in a desperate grin. Now he has picked up the spoor of drunken vomit and there is the doll sprawled against a wall, his pants streaked with urine. Bending down as if to help the man up, Tío Pepe whispers in both ears again and again . . . *"accidente horrible"* . . . He stands up and shrieks in a high falsetto voice . . . *"EMASCULADO EMASCULADO EMASCULADO"* and kicks the man three times gently in the groin.

He finds an old drunken woman sleeping in a pile of rags and claps a hand over her mouth and nose whispering . . . *"vieja borracha asfixiado."* ("old drunken woman asphyxiated.")

Another drunk is sleeping in dangerous proximity to a brush fire.

Tío Pepe drops a burning cigarette butt into the man's outstretched hand squatting down on his haunches he whispers slimily . . . *"cuerpo carbonizado . . . cuerpo carbonizado . . . cuerpo carbonizado. . . ."* He throws back his head and sings to the dry brush, the thistles the wind . . . *"cuerpo carbonizado . . . cuerpo carbonizado . . . cuerpo carbonizado . . ."*

He looks up at Esperanza with a horrible smile.

"Ah! the country cousin rises early." While he croons a little tune.

"Resbalando sobre un pedazo de jabón   Slipping on a piece of soap *se precipito de un balcón."*   fell over a balcony.

Esperanza swings her great arm in a contemptuous arc and wraps a wet towel around the balcony wall spattering Tío Pepe, Dolores and Joselito with dirty water. Sneering over her shoulder she turns to go inside.

The beaten team on the lower balcony lick their wounds and plot revenge.

"If I can but get her in front of my kiosk at 9:23 next Thursday . . ."

"If I could find her *borracho* . . ."

"And I will have her gunned down by *pistoleros* . . ."

This boast of Joselito is predicated on his peculiar relationship with Lola La Chata. Lola La Chata is a solid 300 pounds cut from the same mountain rock as Esperanza. She sells heroin to pimps and thieves and whores and keeps the papers between her massive dugs.

Joselito had a junky boy friend who took him to meet Lola.

Joselito danced flamenco screeching like a peacock. Lola laughed and adopted him as one of her "Little Kittens." In a solemn ceremony he had suckled at her great purple dug bitter with heroin. It was not uncommon for Lola to service customers with two "Little Kittens" sucking at her breasts.

As Esperanza turns to go inside six pimpish young men burst through the door in a reek of brilliantine and lean over the balcony screaming insults at Joselito.

This brings reinforcements to the faltering lower balcony. Tío Mate stalks out followed by his adolescent Ka El Mono.

Tío Mate is an old assassin with twelve deer on his gun. A thin ghostly old man with eyes the color of a faded grey flannel shirt. He wears a black suit and a black Stetson. Under the coat a single action Smith & Wesson tip up forty-four with a seven-inch barrel is strapped to his lean flank. Tío Mate wants to put another deer on his gun before he dies.

The expression a "deer" (*un "venado"*) derives from the mountainous districts of northern Mexico where the body is usually brought into the police post draped over a horse like a deer.

A young district attorney just up from the capital. Tío Mate has dropped by to give him a lesson in folklore.

Tío Mate (rolling a cigarette): "I'm going to send you a deer, *señor abogado.*"

The D.A. (he thinks "well now that's nice of him"): "Well thank you very much, if it isn't too much trouble . . ."

Tío Mate (lighting the cigarette and blowing out smoke): "No trouble at all *señor abogado.* It is my pleasure."

Tío Mate blows smoke from the muzzle of his forty-four and smiles.

Man is brought in draped over a saddle. The horse is led by a woodenfaced Indian cop. The D.A. comes out. The cop jerks his head back . . . "*un venado.*"

Tío Mate had been the family *pistolero* of rich landowners in northern Mexico. The family was ruined by expropriations when they backed the wrong presidential candidate and Tío Mate came to live with relatives in the capital. His room is a bare, white cell, a cot, a trunk, a little wooden case in which he keeps his charts, sextant and compass. Every night he cleans and oils his forty-four. It is a beautiful custom-made gun given to him by the *patrón* for killing "my unfortunate brother the General." It is nickel-plated and there are hunting scenes engraved on the cylinder and barrel. The handles are of white porcelain with two blue deer heads. There is nothing for Tío Mate to do except oil his gun and wait. The gun glints in his eyes a remote mineral calm. He sits for hours on the balcony with his charts and instruments spread out on a green felt card table. Only his eyes move as he traces vultures in the sky. Occasionally he draws a line on the chart or writes down numbers in a logbook. Every Independence Day the *vecinos* assemble to watch Tío Mate blast a vulture from the sky with his forty-four. Tío Mate consults his charts and picks a vulture. His head moves very slightly from side to side eyes on the distant target he draws aims and fires: a vulture trailing black feathers down the sky. So precise are Tío Mate's calculations that one feather drifts down on to the balcony. This feather is brought to Tío Mate by El Mono his Feather Bearer. Tío Mate puts the feather in his hat band. There are fifteen black years in his band.

El Mono has been Tío Mate's Feather Bearer for five years. He sits for hours on the balcony until their faces fuse. He has his own little charts and compass. He is learning to shoot a vulture from the sky. A thin agile boy of thirteen he climbs all over the building spying on the *vecinos*. He wears a little blue skullcap and when he takes it off the *vecinos* hurry to drop a coin in it. Otherwise he will act out a recent impotence, a difficult bowel movement, a cunt-licking with such precise mimicry that anyone can identify the party involved.

El Mono picks out a pimp with his eyes. He makes a motion of greasing a candle. The pimp licks his lips speechless with horror his eyes wild. Now El Mono is shoving the candle in and out his ass teeth bare eyes rolling he gasps out: *"Sangre de Cristo . . ."* The pimp impaled there for all to see. Joselito leaps up and stomps out a triumphant fandango. Awed by Tío Mate and fearful of a recent impotence, a difficult bowel movement, a cunt-licking, the pimps fall back in confusion.

Tío Paco now mans the upper balcony with his comrade in arms Fernández the drug clerk. Tío Paco has been a waiter for forty years. Very poor, very proud, contemptuous of tips, he cares only for the game. He brings the wrong order and blames the client, he flicks the nastiest towel, he shoves a tip back saying "The house pays us." He screams after a client *"Le service n'est-ce pas compris."* He has studied with Pullman George and learned the art of jiggling arms across the room:

hot coffee in a quiet American crotch.

And woe to a waiter who crosses him:

tray flies into the air. Rich well-dressed clients dodge cups and glasses, bottle of Fundador broken on the floor.

Fernández hates adolescents, pop stars, beatniks, tourists, queers, criminals, tramps, whores and drug addicts. Tío Paco hates their type too.

Fernández likes policemen, priests, army officers, rich people of good repute. Tío Paco likes them too. He serves them quickly and well. But their lives must be above reproach.

A newspaper scandal can mean long waits for service.

The client becomes impatient. He makes an angry gesture. A soda siphon crashes to the floor.

What they both love most of all is to inflict humiliation on a member of the hated classes, and to give information to the police.

Fernández throws a morphine script back across the counter.

"*No prestamos servicio a los viciosos.*" ("We do not serve dope fiends.")

Tío Paco ignores a pop star and his common-law wife until the cold sour message seeps into their souls:

"We don't want your type in here."

Fernández holds a prescription in his hand. He is a plump man in his late thirties. Behind dark glasses his eyes are yellow and liverish. His low urgent voice on the phone.

"*Receta narcótica falsificado.*" ("A narcotic prescription forged.")

"Your prescription will be ready in a minute *señor.*"

Tío Paco stops to wipe a table and whispers . . . "Marijuana in a suitcase . . . table by the door" . . . The cop pats his hand.

Neither Tío Paco nor Fernández will accept any reward for services rendered to their good friends the police.

When they first came to live on the top floor five years ago Tío Mate saw them once in the hall.

"Copper-loving bastards," he said in his calm final voice.

He did not have occasion to look at them again. Anyone Tío Mate doesn't like soon learns to stay out of Tío Mate's space.

Fernández steps to the wall and his wife appears at his side. Her eyes are yellow her teeth are gold. Now his daughter appears. She has a mustache and hairy legs. Fernández looks down from a family portrait.

"*Criminales. Maricónes. Vagabundos.* I will denounce you to the police."

Tío Paco gathers all the bitter old men in a blast of sour joyless hate. Joselito stops dancing and droops like a wilted flower. Tío Pepe and Dolores are lesser demons. They shrink back furtive and timorous as dawn rats. Tío Mate looks at a distant point beyond the old waiter tracing vultures in the sky. El Mono stands blank and cold. He will not imitate Fernández and Tío Paco.

And now Tía María, retired fat lady from a traveling carnival, comes out onto the lower balcony supporting her vast weight on two canes. Tía María eats candy and reads love stories all day and gives card readings the cards sticky and smudged with chocolate. She secretes a heavy sweetness. Sad and implacable it flows out of her like a foam runway. The *vecinos* fear her sweetness which they regard fatalistically as a natural hazard like earthquakes and volcanoes. "The Sugar of Mary" they call it. It could get loose one day and turn the city into a cake.

She looks up at Fernández and her sad brown eyes pelt him with chocolates. Tío Paco tries desperately to out-flank her but she sprays him with maraschino cherries from her dugs and coats him in pink icing. Tío Paco is the little man on a wedding cake all made out of candy. She will eat him later.

Now Tío Gordo, the blind lottery-ticket seller, rolls his immense bulk out onto the upper balcony, his wheel chair a chariot, his snarling black dog at his side. The dog smells all the money Tío Gordo takes. A torn note brings an ominous growl, a counterfeit and it will break the man's arm in its powerful jaws, brace its legs and hold him for the police. The dog leaps to the balcony wall and hooks its paws over barking, snarling, bristling, eyes phosphorescent. Tía María gasps and the sugar runs out of her. She is terrified of "rage dogs" as she calls them. The dog seems ready to leap down onto the lower balcony. Tío Mate plots the trajectory its body would take. He will kill it in the air.

Tío Pepe throws back his head and howls:

"*Perro attropellado para un camión.*" ("Dog run over by a truck.")

The dog drags its broken hindquarters in a dusty noon street.

The dog slinks whimpering to Tío Gordo.

González the Agente wakes up muttering "*Chingoa*" the fumes of Mescal burning in his brain. Buttoning on his police tunic and forty-five he pushes roughly to the wall of the upper balcony.

González is a broken dishonored man. All the *vecinos* know he has much fear of Tío Mate and crosses the street to avoid him. El Mono has acted out both parts.

González looks down and there is Tío Mate waiting. The hairs stand up straight on González's head.

"CHINGOA."

He snatches out his forty-five and fires twice. The bullets whistle past Tío Mate's head. Tío Mate smiles. In one smooth movement he draws aims and fires. The heavy slug catches González in his open mouth ranging up through the roof blows a large tuft of erect hairs out the back of González's head. González folds across the balcony wall. The hairs go limp and hang down from his head. The balcony wall begins to sway like a horse. His forty-five drops to the lower balcony and goes off.

Shot breaks the camera. A frozen still of the two balconies tilted down at a forty-five-degree angle. González still draped over the wall sliding forward, the wheel chair halfway down the upper balcony, the dog slipping down on braced legs, the *vecinos* trying to climb up and slipping down.

"GIVE ME THE SIXTEEN."

The cameraman shoots wildly . . . pimps scream by teeth bare eyes rolling, Esperanza sneers down at the Mexican earth, the fat lady drops straight down her pink skirts billowing up around her, Tía Dolores sails down her eyes winking sweet and evil like a doll, dog falls across a gleaming empty sky.

The camera dips and whirls and glides tracing vultures higher and higher spiraling up.

Last take: Against the icy blackness of space ghost faces of Tío Mate and El Mono. Dim jerky faraway stars splash the cheek bones with silver ash. *Tío Mate smiles.*

The
Chief
Smiles

Marrakech 1976 . . . Arab house in the Medina charm-
ing old pot-smoking Fatima drinking tea with the trade
in the kitchen. Here in the middle of a film to find myself one of the actors. The Chief has asked me to his
house for dinner.

"Around Eight Rogers."

He received me in his patio mixing a green salad thick
steaks laid out by the barbecue pit.

"Help yourself to a drink Rogers." He gestures to the
drink wagon.

"There's kif of course if you want it."

I mixed myself a short drink and declined the kif.

"It gives me a headache."

I'd seen the Chief smoking with his Arab contacts but

that didn't give me a license to smoke. Besides it does give me a headache.

The Chief's cover story is an eccentric old French *comte* who is translating the Koran into Provencal and sometimes he will pull cover and bore his guests catatonic. You see, he really knows Provençal and Arabic. You have to study for years on a real undercover job like this. The Chief wasn't pulling cover tonight. He was expansive and "watch your step, Rogers" I told myself, sipping a weak Scotch.

" 'I think you are the man for a highly important and I may add highly dangerous assignment, Rogers.' You fell for that crap?"

"Well sir he is impressive," I said cautiously.

"He's a cheap old ham," said the Chief. He sat down and filled his kif pipe with one hand. He smoked and blew the ash out absently caressing a gazelle that nuzzled his knee.

" 'Gotta stay ahead of the Commies or everybody's kids will be learning Chinese.' What a windbag."

I endeavored to look noncommittal.

"Have you any idea what we're doing here, Rogers?"

"Well, no sir."

"I thought not. Never tell them what you want until you've got them where you want them. I'm going to show you a documentary film."

Two Arab servants carry out a six-foot screen and set it up ten feet in front of our chairs. The Chief gets up turning switches adjusting dials.

A jungle seen through a faceted eye that looks simultaneously in any direction up or down . . . close-up of a green snake with golden eyes . . . telescopic lens picks out a monkey caught by an eagle between two vast

trees. The monkey is borne away screaming. I can feel
a probing insect intelligence behind the camera, pyramids ahead fields and huts. In the fields workers are
planting maize seeds under the direction of an overseer
with staff and headdress. Close-up of a worker's face.
Whatever it is that makes a man a man, all feeling and
all soul has gone out in that face. Nothing is left but
body needs and body pleasures. I have seen faces like
that in the back wards of state hospitals for the insane.
Faces that live to eat, shit and masturbate. Satisfied
with the inspection the camera moves back to observe
group patterns of the workers. They are moving
through a three-dimensional film of the operation that
covers them with a grey sheen. Occasionally the overseer adjusts a slow worker with his eyes.

Next take shows a room in the temple suffused with
underwater light. An old priest naked to his pendulous
dugs and atrophied testicles sits cross-legged on a toilet
seat set in the floor. The seat is cushioned with human
skin on which are tattooed pictures of a man turning
into a giant centipede. The centipede is eating him
from inside legs and claws grow through screaming
flesh. Now the centipede is eating his screaming mouth.

"Criminals and captives sentenced to death in centipede are tattooed with those pictures on every inch of
their bodies. They are left for three days to fester. Then
they are brought out given a powerful aphrodisiac,
skinned alive in orgasm and strapped into a segmented
copper centipede. The centipede is placed with obscene
endearments in a bed of white-hot coals. The priests
gather in crab suits and eat the meat out of the shell
with gold claws."
The old priest looks like a living part in an exotic com-

puter. From festering sockets in his spine fine copper wires trail in a delicate fan. The camera follows the wires. Here in a little copper cage a scorpion is eating her mate. Here the head of a captive protrudes through the floor. Red ants have made a hill in his head. They crawl in and out of empty eye sockets. They have eaten his lips away from a gag. A muffled scream without a tongue torn through his perforated palate showers the floor with bloody ants. In jade aquariums human rectums and genitals grafted onto other flesh . . . a prostate gland quivers rainbow colors through a pink mollusk . . . two translucent white salamanders squirm in slow sodomy golden eyes glinting enigmatic lust . . . Lesbian electric eels squirm on a mud flat crackling their vaginas together . . . erect nipples sprout from a bulbous plant.

"They know an aphrodisiac so potent that it shatters the body to quivering pieces. The Sweet Death is reserved for comely youths and maidens. This wonderful old people had a rich folklore. Well I happened onto this good thing through a Mexican shoe-shine boy . . . Yoo-hoo Kiki. . . Come out and show Mr. Rogers how pretty you are . . ."

Kiki stands in a doorway smiling like a shy young animal.
"Now that lad . . . he's a doll isn't he? . . . is one of the best deep trance mediums I have ever handled. Through him I was able to teleport myself to a Mayan set and bring back the pictures. The whole thing was so frantic I cooled it all the way in my reports. All I said was it looks like a lovely WUP. That's code for Weapon of Unlimited Potential . . . He's hotting up now."

The old priest rocks back and forth. The wires stand up on his spine and his eyes light up inside. His lips part and a dry insect music buzzes out.

"It's known as singing the pictures. The principle is alternating current. That old fuck can alternate pain and pleasure on a subvocal perhaps even a molecular level twenty-four times a second goading the natives around on stock probes in out up down here there into the prearranged molds laid down in the sacred books. A few singers can deliver direct current and they are only called in an emergency. The control system you have just seen broke down. This happened quite suddenly a whole generation was born that felt neither pain nor pleasure. There were no soldiers to bring captives from other tribes since soldiers would have endangered the control machine. They relied entirely on local criminals for the pain and pleasure pictures. As a last resort they called in the Incomparable Yellow Serpent."

The Serpent is carried in on his amber throne blue snake eyes skin like yellow parchment two long serpent fangs grafted into the upper jaw. As the current pulses through him he begins to rock back and forth. He shifts from A.C. to D.C. A thin siren wail breaks from his lips now open to the yellow fangs.
DEATH DEATH DEATH
The pictures crash and leap from his eyes blasting worker and priest alike to smoldering fragments.
DEATH DEATH DEATH
A thin siren wail rises and falls over empty cities.

"This secret of the ancient Mayans which few are competent to practice.
When comes such another singer as the Old Yellow Serpent?"

"Now the Technical Department think we are all as crazy as our way of life is reprehensible.

" 'Bring us the ones that work' they say 'facts, figures, personnel.

" 'Put that joker DEATH on the line. Take care of Mao and his gang of cutthroats.'

"I was privileged to assist in a manner of speaking at the Yellow Serpent's last broadcast in Washington D.C."

Room in the Pentagon. Generals, CIA, State Department fidget about with that top secret hottest thing ever look open line to the President Strategic and NATO standing by. The Old Yellow Serpent is carried in by four marine guards. He begins to rock back and forth. He breathes in baby coos and breathes out death rattles. He sucks in wheat fields and spits out dust bowls.

"He's just warming up," says the CIA man to a five-star general.

The Old Serpent shifts to D.C. blazing like a comet.

DEATH DEATH DEATH

The pictures lash and crackle from his eyes.

DEATH DEATH DEATH

A wall blows out and spills screaming brass eighteen floors to the street.

DEATH DEATH DEATH

And now the Serpent swings his whip in the sky.

Here lived stupid vulgar sons of bitches who thought they could hire DEATH as a company cop . . . empty streets, old newspapers in the wind, a rustle of darkness and wires.

In the night sky over St Louis the Mayan Death God does a Cossack dance shooting stars from his eyes. *The Chief smiles.*

Old
Sarge
Smiles

The Green Nun has stopped the unfortunate traveler in front of her red-brick priory set among oak trees, green lawns and flower beds.

"Oh do come in and see my mental ward and the wonderful things we are doing for the patients."

She walks with him up the gravel drive to the priory door pointing to her flowers.

"Aren't my primroses doing nicely."

She opens the door of the priory with a heavy brass key at her belt. Down a long hall and flight of stairs she opens another door with her keys. She shows Audrey into a bare cold ward room crayon drawings on the wall. A nun walks up and down with a ruler. The patients are busy with plasticene and crayons. It looks like a kindergarten but some of the children are middle-aged. The door clicks shut and her voice changes.

"You'll find plasticene and crayons over there. You must have permission to leave the room for any purpose."

"Now see here . . ."

A paunchy guard with a tin helmet and wide leather belt stands beside her. The guard looks at him with cold ugly hate and says:

"He wants Bob and his lawyers."

At six o'clock there is a tasteless dinner of cold macaroni that Audrey does not touch. After dinner the night sister comes on.

Cots are set up by the patients and the ward room is converted into a dormitory.

"Anyone want potty before lights out?"

She jangles the keys. The lavatory cubicles stand at one end of the dormitory. The sister on duty unlocks the doors and stands in the open door watching coldly.

"Now don't try and play with your dirty thing again Coldcliff or you'll have six hours in the kitchen."

A dim religious light burns all night in the dormitory. The patients sleep on their backs under a thin blanket. Erections are sanctioned with a sharp ruler tap from the night sister.

And so the years passed. Sometimes as a special treat there were nature walks in the garden, Bob there with three snarling Alsatians on a lead. The patients could watch a praying mantis eat her mate.

Daily confessions were heard by the Green Nun on a lie detector that could also give a very nasty shock in the nasty places while the Green Nun intoned slowly "Thou shalt not bear false witness."

These confessions she wrote out in green ink keeping a separate ledger book for each patient. Once after a particularly degraded confession she levitated to the ceiling in the presence of an awed young nun. Every night she put on Christ drag with a shimmering halo and visited some young nun in her cell. She liked to think of herself as the nun in a poem by Sara Teasdale.

"Infinite tenderness infinite irony is hidden forever in her closed eyes.

Who must have learned too well in her long loneliness how empty wisdom is even to the wise."

She was an inveterate hypochondriac and dosed herself liberally with laudanum. As a result she suffered from constipation which could put a comely young nun on high colonic duty. This honor was invariably followed by a nocturnal visit from Christ with a strap-on. In her youth the Green Nun had toyed with the idea of ordering Bob to raid a sperm bank. Then she could claim the Christ child. She put aside these ambitious thoughts. Her work in the kindergarten was more important than worldly glamor, her picture on the cover of *Life*.

You learn not to have a thought you will be ashamed to tell the Green Nun and never to do anything you would be ashamed to do in front of her. And sooner or later you join the Quarter G Club. Converted patients are allowed a quarter grain of morphine every night before lights out, a privilege which is withdrawn for any trespass.

"Now you know that dream about flying is WRONG don't you? For that you go to bed without your medicine."

Shivering with junk sickness in the icy ward room all next day he has to look bright and happy as he busies himself with crayons and plasticene. He has learned to draw pictures of the Virgin Mary and Saint Teresa with an unmistakable resemblance to the Green Nun. Crosses are always safe in plasticene. Soon after his commitment he made the error of molding a naked Greek statue. That day sister's ruler slashed down on his thin blue wrist and he was forced to write out *i am a filthy little beast* ten thousand times in many places.

Dizzy dance of rooms and faces, murmur of many voices smell of human nights . . . St. Louis backdrop of red-brick houses, slate roofs, back yards and ash pits . . . As a child he had an English governess with references so impeccable that Audrey later suspected they had been forged by a Fleet Street hack in a shabby pub near Earl's Court.

"You can't put in too many Lords and Lydies I always sy."

Listening back with a writer's crystal set he picked up mutters of the servant underworld . . . the pimping blackmailing chauffeur . . . "You don't get rid of me that easy Lord Brambletie."

Overdose of morphine in a Kensington nursing home . . . "She said that Mrs. Charrington was sleeping and could not be disturbed."

The governess left quite suddenly after receiving a letter from England.

Then there was an old Irish crone who taught him to call the toads. She could go out into the back yard and croon a toad out from under a stone and Audrey learned

to do it too. He had his familiar toad that lived under
a rock by the goldfish pool and came when he called it.
And she taught him a curse to bring "the blinding
worm" from rotten bread.

Audrey went to a progressive grade school where the
children were encouraged to express themselves, model
in clay, beat out copper ash trays and make stone axes.
A sensitive inspirational teacher is writing the school
play out on the blackboard as the class makes sugges-
tions:

ACT 1

SCENE ONE: *Two women at the water hole.*

Woman 1: "I hear the tiger ate Bast's baby last night."

Woman 2: "Yes. All they found was the child's toy
   soldier."

Woman 1: "One doesn't feel safe with that tiger
   about." (*She looks around nervously.*) "It's getting
   dark Sextet and I'm going home."

One of the truly great bores of St Louis was Colonel
Greenfield. He had dinner jokes that took half an hour
to tell during which no one was expected to eat. Audrey
sits there watching his turkey go cold with half a mind
to put the "blinding worm" on him. It seems this old
black Jew has crashed the Palace Hotel in Palm Beach.
At that very moment the night clerk, a new man just
in from a Texas hotel school, withers in Major Brady's
cold glare.

"Did you check in Mr. Rogers nee Kike?"
"Why, yes sir, I did. He had a reservation."
"No, he didn't. There was a mistake you dumb hick.
Don't you know a black Jew when you see one?"

Meanwhile the old black Jew has called room service
. . . "Will you please send up a little pepper."
"I'm sorry sir the kitchen is closed. Why it's three in
the morning."
"I don't care is the kitchen closed. I don't care is it three
in the morning. I want a little pepper."
"I'm sorry sir."
"I vant to talk with the manager plis" . . . (The dialect
gets heavier as the Colonel warms up.)
Call from the night manager to Major Brady's office . . .
"That old black Jew in 23 wants pepper of all things at
this hour."
"All right. We run a first-class hotel here. Open the
kitchen and give him anything he wants . . . Brought
his own carp most likely."
So the night manager calls the old black Jew. "All right
sir what kind of pepper do you want? Red pepper?
White pepper? Black pepper?"
"I don't vant red pepper. I don't vant white pepper. I
don't vant black pepper. All I vant is a little toilet
pepper."

eye in needle needle in eye

The Colonel burned down St Louis. One day when
Audrey reluctantly visited Colonel Greenfield's house
to deliver a message he found the Colonel telling his
interminable anecdotes to the Negro butler.
"Now on the old Greenfield plantation we had house
niggers and field niggers and the field niggers never
came into the house."
"No sir the field niggers never came into the house."
"The house niggers saw to that didn't they George?"
"Yes sir. The house niggers saw to that sir."
"Now wherever I go I always get out the telephone

book and look up anybody who bears the name of Greenfield. There are so few of them and they are all so distinguished. Well some years ago in Buffalo New York I had written down the address of Abraham L. Greenfield and showed it to a nigra cab driver."

"I think you got the wrong number boss."

"The address is correct driver."

"I still think you got the wrong number boss."

"Shut your black face and take me where I want to go."

"Yahsuh boss. Here you are boss. Niggertown boss."

"And that's where we were right in Niggertown."

"Yes sir. Right in Niggertown sir."

"So I get out and knock on the door and an old coon comes to the door with his hat in his hands."

"With his hat in his hands sir."

"Good evening Massa and God bless you" he says.

"Is your name Greenfield?" I ask him.

"Yahsuh boss. Abraham Lincoln Greenfield."

"Well it turns out he was one of our old house niggers."

"One of your old house niggers sir."

"He invited me in and served me a cup of coffee with homemade caramel cake. He wouldn't sit down just stood there nodding and smiling . . . The right kind of darky."

"The right kind of darky sir."

And Bury
the Bread
Deep
in a Sty

Audrey was a thin pale boy his face scarred by festering spiritual wounds. "He looks like a sheep-killing dog," said a St Louis aristocrat. There was something rotten and unclean about Audrey, an odor of the walking dead. Doormen stopped him when he visited his rich friends. Shopkeepers pushed his change back without a thank you. He spent sleepless nights weeping into his pillow from impotent rage. He read adventure stories and saw himself as a gentleman adventurer like the "Major" . . . sun helmet, khakis, Webley at the belt a faithful Zulu servant at his side. A dim sad child breathing old pulp magazines. At sixteen he attended an exclusive high school known as The Poindexter Academy where he felt rather like a precarious house nigger.

Still he was invited to most of the parties and Mrs Kindheart made a point of being nice to him.

At the opening of the academy in September a new boy appeared. Aloof and mysterious where he came from nobody knew. There were rumors of Paris, London, a school in Switzerland. His name was John Hamlin and he stayed with relatives in Portland Place. He drove a magnificent Dusenberg. Audrey, who drove a battered Moon, studied this vast artifact with openmouthed awe, the luxurious leather upholstery, the brass fittings, the wickerwork doors, the huge spotlight with a pistol-grip handle. Audrey wrote: "Clearly he has come a long way travel stained and even the stains unfamiliar, cuff links of a dull metal that seems to absorb light, his red hair touched with gold, large green eyes well apart."

The new boy took a liking to Audrey while he turned aside with polished deftness invitations from sons of the rich. This did not endear Audrey to important boys and he found his stories coldly rejected by the school magazine.

"Morbid" the editor told him. "We want stories that make you go to bed feeling good."

It was Friday October 23, 1929 a bright blue day leaves falling, half-moon in the sky. Audrey Carsons walked up Pershing Avenue . . . "*Simon, aime tu le bruit des pas sur les feuilles mortes?*" . . . He had read that on one of E. Holdeman Julius's little Blue Books and meant to use it in the story he was writing. Of course his hero spoke French. At the corner of Pershing and Walton he stopped to watch a squirrel. A dead leaf caught for a moment in Audrey's ruffled brown hair.

"Hello Audrey. Like to go for a ride?"

It was John Hamlin at the wheel of his Dusenberg. He opened the door without waiting for an answer. Hamlin made a wide U-turn and headed West . . . left on Euclid right on Lindell . . . Skinker Boulevard City Limits . . . Clayton . . . Hamlin looked at his wrist watch.

"We could make St Joseph for lunch . . . nice riverside restaurant there serves wine."

Audrey is thrilled of course. The autumn countryside flashes by . . . long straight stretch of road ahead.

"Now I'll show you what this job can do."

Hamlin presses the accelerator slowly to the floor . . . 60 . . . 70 . . . 80 . . . 85 . . . 90 . . . Audrey leans forward lips parted eyes shining.

At Tent City a top-level conference is in progress involving top level executives in the CONTROL GAME. The Conference has been called by a Texas billionaire who contributes heavily to MRA and maintains a stable of evangelists. This conference is taking place outside St Louis Missouri because the Green Nun flatly refuses to leave her kindergarten. The high teacup queens thought it would be fun to do a tent city like a 1917 Army camp. The conferents are discussing Operation W.O.G. (Wrath of God).

At the top level people get cynical after a few drinks. The young man from the news magazine has discovered a good-looking Fulbright scholar and they are witty in a corner over Martinis. A drunken American Sergeant reels to his feet. He has the close-cropped iron-grey hair and ruddy complexion of the Regular Army man.

"To put it country simple for a lay audience . . . you don't even know what buttons to push . . . we take a bunch of longhair boys fucking each other while they puff reefers, spit cocaine on the Bible, and wipe their asses with Old Glory. We show this film to decent, church-going, Bible Belt do-rights. We take the reaction. One religious sheriff with seven nigger notches on his gun melted the camera lens. He turned out to be quite an old character and the boys from *Life* did a spread on him—seems it had always been in the family, a power put there by God to smite the unrighteous: his grandmother struck a whore dead in the street with it. When we showed the picture to a fat Southern senator his eyes popped out throwing fluid all over your photographer. Well I've been asparagrassed in Paris, kneed in the groin by the Sea Org in Tunis, maced in Chicago and pelted with scorpions in Marrakech so a face full of frog eggs is all in the day's work. What the Narco boys call 'society's disapproval' reflected and concentrated twenty million I HATE YOU pictures in one blast. When you want the job done come to the UNITED STATES OF AMERICA. AND WE CAN TURN IT IN ANY DIRECTION. You Limey leftovers . . ." He points to a battery of old grey men in club chairs frozen in stony disapproval of this vulgar drunken American. When will the club steward arrive to eject the bounder so a gentleman can read his *Times?*

"YOU'RE NOTHING BUT A BANANA REPUBLIC. AND REMEMBER WE'VE GOT YOUR PICTURES."

"And we've got yours too Yank," they clip icily.

"MINE ARE UGLIER THAN YOURS."

The English cough and look away fading into their spectral clubs, yellowing tusks of the beast killed by the improbable hyphenated name, OLD SARGE screams after them . . . "WHAT DO YOU THINK THIS IS A BEAUTY CONTEST? You Fabian Socialist vegetable

peoples go back to your garden in Hampstead and re-
lease a hot-air balloon in defiance of a local ordinance
delightful encounter with the bobby in the morning.
Mums wrote it all up in her diary and read it to us at
tea. WE GOT ALL YOUR PANSY PICTURES AT
ETON. YOU WANTA JACK OFF IN FRONT OF
THE QUEEN WITH A CANDLE UP YOUR ASS?"
"You can't talk like that in front of decent women,"
drawled the Texas billionaire flanked by his rangers.
"You decorticated cactus. I suppose you think this con-
ference was your idea? Compliments of SID in the
Sudden Inspiration Department . . . And you lousy
yacking fink queens my photographers wouldn't take
your pictures. You are nothing but tape recorders. With
just a flick of my finger frozen forever over that Martini.
All right get snide and snippy about that HUH? . . .
And you" . . . He points to the Green Nun . . . "Write
out ten thousand times under water in indelible ink
OLD SARGE HAS MY CHRIST PICTURES. SHALL
I SHOW THEM TO THE POPE?

"And now in the name of all good tech sergeants everywhere . . ."

A gawky young sergeant is reading *Amazing Stories*.
He flicks a switch . . . Audrey and Hamlin on screen.
Wind ruffles Audrey's hair as the Dusenberg gathers
speed.
"Light Years calling Bicarbonate . . . Operation Little
Audrey on target . . . eight seconds to count down . . .
tracking . . ."

A thin dyspeptic technician mixes a bicarbonate of
soda.
"URP calling Fox Trot . . . six seconds to count
down . . ."

English computer programer is rolling a joint.

"Spot Light calling Accent . . . four seconds to count down . . ."

Computers hum, lights flash, lines converge.

Red-haired boy chews gum and looks at a muscle magazine.

"Red Dot calling Pin Point . . . two seconds to count down . . ."

The Dusenberg zooms over a rise and leaves the ground. Just ahead is a wooden barrier, steamroller, piles of gravel, phantom tents. DETOUR sign points sharp left to a red clay road where pieces of flint glitter in the sunlight.

"OLD SARGE IS TAKING OVER."

He looks around and the crockery flies off every table spattering the conferents with Martinis, bourbon, whipped cream, maraschino cherries, gravy and vichyssoisse frozen forever in a 1920 slapstick.

"COUNT DOWN."

End over end a flaming pin wheel of jagged metal slices through the conferents. The Green Nun is decapitated by a twisted fender. The Texas billionaire is sloshed with gasoline like a burning nigger. The broken spotlight trailing white-hot wires like a jellyfish hits the British delegate in the face. The Dusenberg explodes throwing white-hot chunks of jagged metal, boiling acid, burning gasoline in all directions.

Wearing the uniforms of World War I Audrey and Old Sarge lean out of a battered Moon in the morning sky and smile. Old Sarge is at the wheel.

The
Penny Arcade
Peep Show

Unexpected rising of the curtain can begin with a Dusenberg moving slowly along a 1920 detour. Just ahead Audrey sees booths and fountains and ferris wheels against a yellow sky. A boy steps in front of the car and holds up his hand. He is naked except for a rainbow colored jock strap and sandals. Under one arm he carries a Mauser pistol clipped onto a rifle stock. He steps to the side of the car. Audrey has never seen anyone so cool and disengaged. He looks at Audrey and he looks at John. He nods.

"We leave the car here," John says. Audrey gets out. Six boys now stand there watching him serenely. They carry long knives sheathed at their belts which are studded with amethyst crystals. They all wear rainbow-colored jock straps like souvenir post cards of Niagara

Falls. Audrey follows John through a square where acts
are in progress surrounded by circles of adolescent onlookers eating colored ices and chewing gum. Most of
the boys wear the rainbow jock straps and a few of them
seem to be completely naked. Audrey can't be sure
trying to keep up with John. The fair reminds Audrey
of 1890 prints. Sepia ferris wheels turn in yellow light.
Gliders launched from a wooden ramp soar over the fair
ground legs of the pilots dangling in air. A colored
hot-air balloon is released to applause of the onlookers.
Around the fair ground are boardwalks, lodging houses,
restaurants and baths. Boys lounge in doorways. Audrey
glimpses scenes that quicken his breath and send the
blood pounding to his groin. He catches sight of John
far ahead outlined in the dying sunlight. Audrey calls
after him but his voice is blurred and muffled. Then
darkness falls as if someone has turned out the sky.
Some distance ahead and to the left he sees PENNY
ARCADE spelled out in light globes. Perhaps John has
gone in there. Audrey pushes aside a red curtain and
enters the arcade. Chandeliers, gilt walls, red curtains,
mirrors, windows stretch away into the distance. He
cannot see the end of it in either direction from the
entrance. It is a long narrow building like a ship cabin
or a train. Boys are standing in front of peep shows
some wearing the rainbow jock straps others in prep
school clothes loincloths and jellabas. He notices shows
with seats in front of them and some in curtained
booths. As he passes a booth he glimpses through parted
curtains two boys sitting on a silk sofa both of them
naked. Shifting his eyes he sees a boy slip his jock strap
down and step out of it without taking his eyes from
the peep show. Moving with a precision and ease he
sometimes knew in flying dreams Audrey slides onto a

steel chair that reminds him of Doctor Moor's Surgery in the Lister Building afternoon light through green blinds. In front of him is a luminous screen. Smell of old pain, ether, bandages, sick fear in the waiting room, yes this is Doctor Moor's Surgery in the Lister Building.

The doctor was a Southern gentleman of the old school. Rather like John Barrymore in appearance and manner he fancied himself as a witty raconteur which at times he was. The doctor had charm which Audrey so sadly lacked. No doorman would ever stop him no shopkeeper forget his thank you under eyes that could suddenly go cold as ice. It was impossible for the doctor to like Audrey. "He looks like a homosexual sheep-killing dog" he thought but he did not say this. He looked up from his paper in his dim gloomy drawing room and pontificated "the child is not wholesome."

His wife went further: "It is a walking corpse," she said. Audrey was inclined to agree with her but he didn't know whose corpse he was. And he was painfully aware of being unwholesome.

There is a screen directly in front of him, a screen to his left, a screen to his right, and a screen in back of his head. He can see all four screens from a point above his head.

Later Audrey wrote these notes: "The scenes presented and the manner of presentation varies according to an underlying pattern.

"1. Objects and scenes move away and come in with a slow hydraulic movement always at the same speed. The screens are three-dimensional visual sections punctuated by flashing lights. I once saw the Great Thurston who could make an elephant disappear do an act with a screen on stage. He shoots a man in the film. The actor clutches his ketchup to his tuxedo shirt and falls then Thurston steps into the screen as a detective to investigate the murder, steps back outside to commit more murders, busts in as a brash young tabloid reporter, moves out to make a phone call that will collapse the market, back in as ruined broker. I am pulled into the film in a stream of yellow light and I can pull people out of the film withdrawal shots pulling the flesh off naked boys. Sequences are linked by the presence of some arbitrary object a pin wheel, a Christmas-tree ornament, a pyramid, an Easter egg, a copper coil going away and coming in always in the same numerical order. Movement in and out of the screen can be very painful like acid in the face and electric sex tingles.

"2. Scenes that have the same enigmatic structure presented on one screen where the perspective remains constant. In a corner of the frames there are punctuation symbols. This material is being processed on a computer. I am in the presence of an unknown language spelling out the same message again and again in cryptic charades where I participate as an actor. There are also words on screen familiar words maybe we read them somewhere a long time ago written in sepia and silver letters that fade into pictures.

"3. Fragmentary glimpses linked by immediate visual impact. There is a sensation of speed as if the pictures were seen from a train window.

"4. Narrative sections in which the screens disappear. I experience a series of quite understandable and coherent events as one of the actors. The narrative sequences are preceded by the title on screen then I am in the film. The transition is painless like stepping into a dream. The structuralized peep show may intersperse the narrative and then I am back in front of the screen and moving in and out of it."

Audrey looked at the screen in front of him. His lips parted and the thoughts stopped in his mind. It was all there on screen sight sound touch at once immediate and spectrally remote in past time.

THE PENNY ARCADE PEEP SHOW

1. On screen 1 a burning red pin wheel distant amusement park. The pin wheel is going away taking the lights the voices the roller coaster the smell of peanuts and gunpowder further and further away.

2. On screens 2 and 3 a white pin wheel and a blue pin wheel going away. Audrey catches a distant glimpse of two boys in the penny arcade. One laughs and points to the other's pants sticking out straight at the crotch.

3. On screens 1 2 3 three pin wheels spinning away red white and blue. Young soldier at the rifle range beads of sweat in the down on his lip. Distant firecrackers burst on hot city pavements . . . night sky parks and ponds . . . blue sound in vacant lots.

4. On screens 1 2 3 4 four pin wheels spinning away, red, white, blue and red. A low-pressure area draws Audrey into the park. July 4, 1926 falls into a silent roller.

1. On screen 1 a red pin wheel coming in . . . smoky moon over the midway. A young red-haired sailor bites into an apple.

2. On screens 2 and 3 two pin wheels coming in white and blue light flickers an adolescent face. The pitch-

man stirs uneasily. "Take over will you kid. Gotta see a man about a monkey."

3. On screens 1 2 3 three pin wheels coming in red white and blue. A luminous post card sky opens into a vast lagoon of summer evenings. A young soldier steps from the lake from the hill from the sky.

4. On screens 1 2 3 4 four pin wheels spinning in red white blue red. The night sky is full of bursting rockets lighting parks and ponds and the upturned faces.

"The rocket's red glare the bombs bursting in air
Gave proof through the night that our flag was still there."

A light in his eyes. Must be Doctor Moor's mirror with a hole in it.

1. A flattened pyramid going away into distant bird-calls and dawn mist . . . Audrey glimpses bulbous misshapen trees . . . Indian boy standing there with a machete . . . The scene is a sketch from an explorer's notebook . . . dim in on a stained yellow page . . . "No one was ever meant to know the unspeakable evil of this place and live to tell of it . . ."

2. Two pyramids going away . . . "The last of my Indian boys left before dawn. I am down with a bad attack of fever . . . and the sores . . . I can't keep myself from scratching. I have even tried tying my hands at night when the dreams come, dreams so indescribably loathsome that I cannot bring myself to write down their content. I untie the knots in my sleep and wake up scratching . . ."

3. Three pyramids going away . . . "The sores have

eaten through my flesh to the bone and still this hideous craving to scratch. Suicide is the only way out. I can only pray that the horrible secrets I have uncovered die with me forever . . ."

4. Four pyramids going away . . . Audrey experienced a feeling of vertigo like the sudden stopping of an elevator . . . skeleton clutches a rusty revolver in one fleshless hand . . .

1. A pyramid coming in . . . Audrey can see stonework like broken lace on top of the pyramid. Damp heat closes round his body a musty odor of vegetable ferment and animal decay. Figure in a white loin-cloth swims out of the dawn mist. An Indian boy with rose-colored flesh and delicate features stands in front of Audrey. Two muscular Indians with long arms carry jars and tools. "You crazy or something walk around alone? This bad place. This place of flesh plants."

2. Two pyramids coming in . . . "You not careful you grow here. Look at that." He points to a limp pink tube about two feet long growing from two purple mounds covered with fine red tendrils. As the boy points to the tube it turns toward him. The boy steps forward and rubs the tube which slowly stiffens into a phallus six feet high growing from two testicles . . . "Now I make him spurt. Jissom worth much *dinero*. Jissom make flesh" . . . He strips off his loincloth and steps onto the vegetable scrotum embracing the shaft. The red hairs twist around his legs reaching up to his groin and buttocks . . .

3. Three pyramids coming in . . . The mist is lifting. In the milky dawn light Audrey sees a blush spread through the boy's body turning the skin to a swollen

red wheal. Pearly lubricant pours from the head of
the giant phallus and runs down the sides. The boy
squirms against the shaft caressing the great pulsing
head with both hands. There is a soft muffled sound,
a groan of vegetable lust straining up from tumescent
roots as the plant spurts ten feet in the air. The
bearers run around catching the gobs in stone jars.

4. Four pyramids coming in . . . The flesh garden is
located in a round crater four pyramids spaced
around it on higher ground North South East and
West. Slowly the tendrils fall away the Phallus goes
limp and the boy steps free . . . "Over there ass
tree" . . . He points to a tree of smooth red buttocks
twisted together between each buttock a quivering
rectum. Opposite the orifices phallic orchids red,
purple, orange sprout from the tree's shaft . . . "Make
him spurt too" . . . The boy turns to one of the bearers and says something in a language unknown to
Audrey. The boy grins and slips off his loincloth . . .
The other bearer followed his movements . . . "He
fuck tree. Other fuck him" . . . The two men dip
lubricant from a jar and rub it on their stiffening
phalluses. Now the first bearer steps forward and
penetrates the tree wrapping his legs around the
shaft. The second bearer pries his buttocks open with
his thumbs and squirms slowly forward men and
plant moving together in a slow hydraulic peristalsis
. . . The orchids pulse erect dripping colored drops
of lubricant . . . "We catch spurts" . . . The boy hands
Audrey a stone jar. The two boys seem to writhe into
the tree their faces swollen with blood. A choking
sound bursts from tumescent lips as the orchids spurt
like rain. "This one very dangerous" . . . The boy

points to a human body with vines growing through the flesh like veins. The body of a green pink color excretes a milky substance . . . The boy draws on parchment gloves . . . "You touch him you get sores itch you scratch spread sores feel good scratch more scratch self away" . . . Slowly the lids open on green pupils surrounded by black flower flesh. He is seeing them now you can tell. His body quivers with horrible eagerness . . . "He there long time. Need somebody pop him." . . . The boy reaches up takes the head in both hands and twists it sharply to one side. There is a sound like a stick breaking in wet towels as the spine snaps. The feet flutter and rainbow colors spiral from the eyes. The penis spurts again and again as the body twists in wrenching spasms. Finally the body hangs limp . . . "He dead now" . . . The bearers dig a hole. The boy cuts the body down and it plops into the grave . . . "Soon grow another" . . . said the boy matter of factly . . . "over there shit tree" . . . He points to a black bush in the shape of a man squatting. The bush is a maze of tentacles and caught in these tendrils Audrey sees animal skeletons . . . "Now I make him asshole" . . . The boy dipped sperm from a jar and rubbed it between the parted buttocks. Nitrous fumes rise the plant writhes in peristalsis and empties itself . . . "Very good for garden. Make flesh trees grow. Now I show you good place" . . . He leads the way up a steep path to an open place by one of the pyramids . . . In niches carved from rock Audrey sees vines growing in human forms. The figures give off a remote vegetable calm . . . "This place of vine people very calm very quiet. Live here long long time. Roots reach down to garden."

The rising sun hits Audrey in the face

⊚ Dawn light on a naked *youth* poised to dive into a pond. ————

⊚ A thousand Japanese *youths* leap from a balcony into a round swimming tank.

⊚ *Audrey* taking a shower. Water runs down his lean stomach. He is getting stiff.

⊚ Locker room toilet on five levels seen from ferris wheel . . . flash of white legs, shiny pubic hairs, lean brown arms . . . *boys* masturbating under a rusty shower.

⊚ Naked *boy* on yellow toilet seat sunlight in pubic hairs a twitching foot.

⊚ *Boys* masturbating in bleak public school toilets, outhouses, locker rooms . . . a blur of flesh.

⊚ *Farja* sighs deeply and rocks back hugging his knees against his chest. Nitrous fumes twist from pink rectal flesh in whorls of orange, sepia, rose.

⊚ Red fumes envelop the *two bodies*. A scream of roses bursts from tumescent lips roses growing through flesh tearing thorns of delight intertwined the quivering bodies crushed them together writhing gasping in an agony of roses.

⊚ What happens between my legs is like a cold drink to me it is just a feeling . . . cool round stones against my back sunshine and shadow of Mexico. It is just a feeling between the legs a sort of tingle. It is a feeling by which *I am* here at all.

⊚ We squat there our knees touching. Kiki looks down between his legs watching himself get stiff. I feel the tingle between my legs and I am getting stiff too.

⊚ cadavers. Electron microscope shows cells, nerves, bone.

⊚ Telescope shows stars and planets and space. Click microscope. Click telescope.

⊚ *He* wasn't there really. Pale the picture was pale. I could see through him. In life used address I give you for that belated morning.

⊚ Young *ghosts* blurred faces boys and workshops the old February 5, 1914.

⊚ *I am* not a person and I am not an animal. There is something I am here for something I have to do before I can go.

⊚ *The dead* around like birdcalls rain in my face.

⊚ Flight of geese across a gleaming empty sky . . . Peter John S . . . 1882–1904 . . . the death of a child long ago . . . cool remote spirit to his world of shades . . . I was waiting there pale character in someone else's writing breathing old pulp magazines. Turn your face a little to eyes like forget-me-nots . . . flickering silver smile melted into air . . . The boy did not speak again.

⊚ Cold stars splash the empty house faraway toys. Sad whispering *spirits* melt into coachmen and animals of dreams, mist from the lake, faded family photos.

⊚ Museum bas-relief of the *God* Amen with erection. A thin boy in prep school clothes stands in the presence of the God. The boy in museum toilet takes down his pants phallic shadow on a distant wall.

⊚ All the *Gods* of Egypt

⊚ The *God* Amen the boy teeth bare gasping

⊚ Clear light touching marble porticos and fountains
. . . the *Gods* of Greece . . . Mercury, Apollo, Pan

Light drains into the red walls of Marrakech

Le
Gran
Luxe

April 3, 1989 Marrakech . . . Unlighted streets carriages with carbide lamps. It looks like an 1890 print from some explorer's travel book. Wild boys in the streets whole packs of them vicious as famished dogs. There is almost no police force in operation and everyone who can afford it has private guards. My Marrakech contact has kindly lent me two good Nubians and found me suitable quarters.

Waves of decoration and architecture have left a series of strata-like exposed geologic formations. There isn't a place in the world you can't find a piece of it in Marrakech, a St Louis street, a Mexican cantina, that house straight from England, Alpine huts in the mountains, a vast film set where the props are continually shifting. The city has spread in all directions up into the Atlas

mountains to the east, south to the Sahara, westward
to the coastal cities, up into the industrial reservations
of the north. There are fantastic parties, vast estates and
luxury such as we read about in the annals of the
Roman Empire.

The chic thing is to dress in expensive tailor-made rags
and all the queens are camping about in wild-boy drag.
There are Bowery suits that appear to be stained with
urine and vomit which on closer inspection turn out to
be intricate embroideries of fine gold thread. There are
clochard suits of the finest linen, shabby-gentility suits,
Graham Greene outfits for seedy agents who are bad
Catholics on a mission they don't really believe in, felt
hats seasoned by old junkies, dungarees faded on farm
boys, coolie clothes of yellow pongee silk, loud cheap
pimp suits that turn out to be not so cheap the loudness
is a subtle harmony of colors only the very best Poor
Boy Shops can turn out tailored to your way of walking
sitting down bending over the color of your hair and
eyes your house and backdrop. It is the double take
and many carry it much further to as many as six takes.
Looks like an expensive suit trying rather crudely to
look cheap humm the cheapness is rather carefully
planned on closer inspection suits that shift changing
color and texture before your eyes he is standing in
what looks like a rented dress suit now the Billy Graham look no it is 120 dollar knocked down to 69.23
FBI agent suit or it could be a smooth Mexican 'pocho'
beyond the Glen Plaid stage on the other hand something of an uncomfortable young cop first day in plain
clothes the collar too tight the sleeves too short. All
these suits were full of gimmicks, retractable sleeves,
invisible pockets and not a few of the looners keep

some concealed pet about their person a rat, a mongoose, a cobra, a nest of scorpions that can be suddenly released to enliven a social gathering. He appears say in a raccoon-skin coat from which leaps a live raccoon to kill Bubbles de Cocuera's six prize Chihuahuas. And Reggie in a blue mutation mongoose cape killed every cobra in the Djemalfna. Funny at first but they run it into the ground. "My God here comes Reggie in a tiger suit! Run for your lives chaps!" They will put on armor or protect themselves some way and dump almost anything into your lap. You learn to stay away from fat citizens in python suits, any swelling or protuberance is something to avoid and pregnant women have the street to themselves. Everyone has reversible linings and concealed pockets and a way to pass a pet from one pocket to the other thus foiling the searches which are now routine at the door of any gathering. The next step is skin suits and men are hunted like animals for their pelts. Then synthetics hit the market. Think of it termite-proof moth-proof age-proof in sixteen tasteful shades furniture and walls to match. People start buying anything they want a red-haired ass a Mexican crotch a Chinese stomach folks is going piebald thin black arms cracker farm boy smile then horns and goat hooves wolf boys lizard boys some frantic character got arms smooth and red as terra cotta ending in lobster claws.

There is almost no petroleum left and gasoline engines are a rarity. Steam cars and electrics are coming back. The silent electric dirigibles of the rich sail majestically across the evening sky the cabin an open-air restaurant wafting a scent of wet lawns and golf courses calm happy voices 1920 music. Le gran luxe flourishes as never before in history on the vast estates of the rich. The foremost advocate and practitioner of luxury is A.J. who owns a private steam railroad which he stocks with 1890 drummers and bankers, 1920 prep school boys on vacation, 1918 card sharps and con men according to his whim, anyone wishing to travel A.J. is required to report to casting.

"I maintain my railroads for the train whistles at lonely sidings, the smell of worn leather, steam, soot, hot iron and good cigar smoke, for the glass-covered stations and the red-brick station hotels."

He contributes lavishly to the guerrilla units, maintains a vast training center and hires fugitive scientists to develop new weapons in his laboratories and factories. He thinks nothing of spending millions of dollars to put a single dish on his table. His annual party collapses currencies and bankrupts nations.

"I want a dinner of fresh hog's liver, fried squirrel, wild asparagrass, turnip greens, hominy grits, corn on the cob and blackberries. The hog must be an Ozark razorback fed on acorns, peanuts, mulberries and Missouri apples. My hog must be kept under discreet observation round the clock to insure that it does not eat anything unclean like bullshit, baby rabbits or dead frogs the surveillance being unobtrusive so as not to render the animal self-conscious."

"When you want this by, boss? A year from now?"

"Next Sunday at the latest."

"But boss how in the hell . . . ?"

"Go to Hell if need be but find me such a hog."

"Yes boss."

"Once found he must be brought here. As you know hog's liver that has been on ice for even a few hours is quite unfit to eat. The hog must be butchered in my kitchens and the twitching liver conveyed immediately to the skillet to be cooked in the bacon grease of another such hog."

"Well sure boss . . . We could crate the hog up and jet it out here."

"Are you mad? My hog would be terrorized and this would surely have an adverse effect on its liver."

"Well boss we could take over an ocean liner fix it up like an Ozark range and . . ."

"Are you trying to poison me? The hog would become seasick and I would lose my dinner. Obviously the hog must be gently wafted here on a raft slung between two giant zeppelins, a raft lifted bodily from the Ozark Mountains. My squirrels, blackberries and wild asparagrass will of course accompany the hog and send a farm boy with it a thin boy with freckles. He will tend my hog during the trip. He will shoot and dress my squirrels. Then he will make himself useful in other ways."

"Boss the hog is here."

A.J. steps onto his balcony and there in the sky suspended between two vast blue zeppelins is a piece of Missouri trailing the smoke of hardwood forests . . .

"I want a dinner of walleyed pike, yellow perch and channel catfish from clear cold spring-fed rivers."

"Right boss I'll have a jet plane lined with aluminum and filled with water."

"Did you say *a* jet plane?"

"Sure boss."

"Mindless idiot the pike would eat the perch and the catfish would eat everything. When the plane landed there would be nothing but one gorged sluggish catfish

quite unfit for my inhuman consumption. Three planes
must be outfitted."

"Sorry boss but the catfish crashed. All that water slopping around and the boulders come loose."

"Praise be to Allah it was not the pike that crashed."

As a piquant offset to all this luxury there is hunger and
fear and danger in the street. A man's best friends are his
Colt and his Nubs experts with their staves jabbing with
both ends blocking out teeth with a straight-thrust stave
held level.

It is a day like any other. Breakfast in the patio served
by my Malay boy. The patio is a miniature oasis with a
pool, palms, a cobra, a sand fox, and some big orange
lizards mean and snappy which eat melon rinds. So after
breakfast I set out for the Djemalfna to meet Reggie. We
are going to plan our route to A.J.'s annual party which is
tomorrow it will be the do of the season. We call ourselves the "Invited" and we all have punch card invitations around our necks like dog tags that will punch us
through A.J.'s electric gates. So I am cutting through the
noon market sun helmet Colt cartridge belt the lot
flanked by my magnificent Nubs when we run into a pack
of twenty wild boys. At sight of us their eyes light up
inside like a cat's will and the hair stands up straight on
their heads spitting snarling they are all around us slashing at my Nubs. The leader has a patch over one eye and a
hog castrator screwed into a wood and leather stump
where his right hand used to be. Quick as a weasel he
darts under the Nub's staff his hand flashes in and up you
can feel cold steel cut intestines like spaghetti. Now it is
very unchic to lose your head and use the gun for trouble
the Nubs should handle like say a pack of diseased beggars. You have to decide and decide quick is this or isn't it

a Colt case. I decide it is definitely a Colt case get my
eyes converged on the leader's skinny stomach and fire.
The heavy forty-four slug knocks him ten feet. I shift and
fire shift and fire gun empty reach for my snub-nosed
thirty-eight in a special leather-lined inside breast pocket
when they scatter and fade out like ghosts. Taking inventory I count seven wild boys dead or dying. The priest
darts out of a potato bin and starts giving unction. I saw
two wild boys spit at him with their last spark of life. The
Nub's eyes are glazing over, intestines steam in the noon
sun drawing flies. A policeman approaches reluctantly
and I give him some orders in crisp Arabic. I find Reggie
on the square sipping a pink gin shaded by a screen of
beggars. An old spastic woman twitches and spatters
Reggie's delicate skin with sunlight. "Uncontrolled slut!"
he screams. He turns to his henchman. "Give this worthless hag a crust of stale bread and find me a sturdy shade
beggar."

I sit down and order a Stinger. "Rumble in a square. I
lost a Nub."

"Saw it all from here. I think Donald knows about a
good Nub."

"I am burying my Nub in the American cemetery. We
can meet there and plan our route to the party. Might
have a spot of bother on the way you know."

"More than likely. A.J. has been criticized for his lavish-
ness by a few ridiculous malcontents the eternal bane
of the very rich."

Next day after the Nub is laid away with taps and all
the trimmings thirty of us join forces and set off for
A.J.'s compound which is outside the walls. Rather con-
spicuous we are too with our Nubs clad in aluminum
jockstraps and sandals carrying wire shields to screen us

from stones and at their belts for emergency use the razor-sharp machetes. So we walk along between our Nubs very *dégagé* as if we aren't actually there.

"The old man will break a stack of bricks with his karate of course it's a bore but there's no stopping him. Any case it's free meals and drinks for a month. I will say for him when he does a do it's a do."

The streets are worse than I ever see them the walking dead catatonic from hunger jammed in like so many sacks of concrete the Nubs shove with the stave the bodies bend and come right back up again they are all shuffling slowly forward and all headed for A.J.'s. From between the legs of this river of flesh the wild boys dart like vicious little cats slashing with razor blades and pieces of glass, slash and then dart back into their burrows of walking flesh. A young agent just down from West Point where they call him the Ferret he can snake through a football line like a ferret down a rat hole follows a wild boy in there and what we found after some fast machete work you don't tell the next of kin.

There it is just ahead now the electric gates thirty feet high set in a wall of black granite. Stumbling over legs we make the gate and click in while the crowd sticks its hands through the bars and shoves fingers in their mouths drooling like cows with the aftosa.

A.J. resplendent in white robes greets us from a dais over the outer courtyard. He smiles and waves to the slobbering crowd.

"They know the score right enough. The better I eat the better they eat. Le gran luxe makes tasty leavings."

The outer courtyard is a small arena with balconies around the sides. We get up in the balconies and A.J. walks down into the middle of the arena.

"Release the bull."

There is a blast of music and the bull rushes out a chute sees the old man and heads straight for him. He stands there fist drawn back and there is a light seismic tremor as he plants himself for the kill. Then his fist flashes forward and I see the brains go. The bull stumbles by him and falls on its side one leg in the air kicking spasmodically. Within seconds the carcass is butchered and the raw bleeding meat heaved to the crowd.

We go through the inner gates into the compound. There are open air restaurants serving smörgåsbord, beer, chilled aquavit and the hot fish soups of Peru, quiet riverside restaurants in blue evening shadow, red-brick houses with slate roofs whole blocks serving home-cooked American food the way they used to serve it turkey, fried chicken, iced tea, hot biscuits and corn bread, steak, roast beef, homemade strawberry ice cream, duck, wild rice, hominy grits, creamed chestnuts. There are pools and canals, floating restaurants covered with flowers, old riverboats with a menu of passenger pigeon, lark, woodcocks, wild turkey and venison, zeppelins and dining cars, chateaus of haute cuisine ruled by eccentric tyrants, Russian country sideboards with sturgeon, caviar, smoked eel, vodka, champagne and hock, farm restaurants and all varieties of plain peasant cooking, inaccessible cliff restaurants famous for a pigeon with white meat. And every famous restaurant in the world has been duplicated to the last detail, the 1001 from Tangier, the old Lucullus restaurant from Marseilles, Maxim's, the Tour D'argent, Tony Faustus from St Louis.

I notice that if anything is left on a plate or in a glass it is scraped or poured by the waiters into hampers one

for liquids the other for solids. After we have circulated
and put away what we could we are summoned to a
balcony overlooking the main gate where the poor of
Marrakech mill around waiting. A.J. harangues us
briefly on the importance of maintaining a strong be-
nevolent image in the native mind and at this point a
panel slides back in the wall on one side of the gate
and a huge phallus slides out pissing Martinis, soup,
wine, Coca-Cola, grenadine, vodka, bourbon, beer, hot
buttered rum, pink gin, Alexanders, glog, corn whisky
into a trough forty feet long labeled DRINKS. From a
panel on the other side of the gate a rubber asshole
protrudes spurting out Baked Alaska, salted herring,
duck gravy, chili con carne, peach melba, syrups,
sauces, jam, fat bone and gristle into another trough
labeled EATS. Screaming clawing drooling the crowd
throws itself at the troughs scooping up food and drinks
with both hands. The odor of vomit rises in clouds. A.J.
presses a button that seals the balcony over. Ventilators
whir and a smell of cool summer pools and mossy
stones envelops the guests. We all stay a month which
isn't hard to do considering what is inside and what is
outside.

In addition to the restaurants of the compound culinary
expeditions on location to all parts of the globe are or-
ganized for the more vigorous guests. The guests are up
at six for a breakfast of fruit juice, fried eggs perfectly
cooked so that the yolk runs slowly when you cut it,
bacon that bends slightly over the fork neither too
crisp nor too limp, homemade bread, tea and coffee a
cigarette and a rest and they start out through the flaming autumn hills. It is a bright blue October day. They
walk ten miles to a river where the flatboats are waiting.

The river is cold and clear and deep. They float downstream fishing along the way in pools and bays and inlets. Tying up the boats for lunch the guests arm themselves with springy clubs and walk along the bank killing frogs and skinning the legs which they fry in bacon grease and eat crisp with cold beer. By late afternoon when they arrive at the farm ferry they have an ample string of jack salmon (also known as walleyed pike), black bass, perch and channel cat. Red-brick house on the hill bourbon and marijuana grown in Missouri summer heat on poor hill soil has a special tang, purple weed they call it. A twilight like blue dust sifting into the river valley as they sit down to a meal of jack salmon steaks, fried perch and bass cooked in bacon grease with a faint smoky tang cider and apples from the farm orchard. They hunt through the autumn woods and return to a dinner of quail, wild turkey and squirrel with chestnuts, spring onions and sweet potatoes. Other locations feature skiing in preparation for smörgåsbord with chilled aquavit, hot chili dishes after a ride through the mountains of northern Mexico, lobsters and clams on the beach, iced tea and fried chicken at The Green Inn.

Food is only one attraction. Every pleasure, sport, diversion, interest, hobby, pursuit or instruction is provided for. To list some of the facilities: computerized libraries with complete references on any subject, expert instructors on any subject, sport or skill. There are gliders, balloons, parachutes, aqualungs and deep-sea diving from the coastal estates. There are sense-withdrawal chambers, immersion tanks, no-gravity capsules simulating space conditions. There are ranges where you can practice with every weapon from a laser gun to a boomerang. There are blue movies of incomparable artistry. Every period of history and every place or country is represented in A.J.'s International Pavilion. You can enjoy a trip to the 1920's, Renaissance Italy, Mandarin China, ancient Greece or Rome. Every sexual taste is provided for in any setting you want. Jack off in the 1920's? Fuck temple virgin? You make Gemini with nice astronaut? Greek youths clad only in beauty and sunlight? Forecastle on whaling ship? Afternoon in the Roman baths? See me fuck Cleopatra? Kinky Chimu kicks? Sex in a 1910 outhouse? Rumble seat? Bomb shelter in the blitz? Bedroll for two in the Yukon? The old swimming hole? Viking ship? Bedouin tent? Public school toilet? Anything that you like.

This morning after a breakfast of fruit, yogurt and pheasant eggs I walk over to the glider hangar. A.J. has several hundred gliders derived from the early models you launch by running and land on your feet sometimes. There are gliders that can be launched from skis, roller skates and bicycles. In all cases the gliders have been designed to most closely approximate the dream of wings and flight. If you have your own ideas for a new model the designers will make it up for you in a few days. The gliders are of many materials and colors to match different landscapes and sky conditions and many of them are painted with landscapes. There are red models for sunset gliding, transparent plastic for ski gliding, blue wings for the mountains. I select a mountain model that shades from lightest egg blue to blue black. The wings are of ramie fabric. A small electric dirigible takes us to the launching station up in the

Atlas mountains. From the station a steep concrete runway slopes down. I put on roller skates and pick up the
glider, the wings on each side my hands braced on two
struts. The ship is piloted by shifting weight with the
hands the pilot being suspended between two struts at
the center. When your arms get tired there is a sling
seat. I start down the launching run faster faster knees
bent I zoom right off across the valley legs dangling
over two thousand feet of space. This is really flying like
you do in a dream, piloting the glider with both hands
feeling it vibrate through me I am out there now in the
wings, my wings sailing across the valley. I sit down on
the sling seat and see the city spread out between my
legs. I bring it down on a cracked weed-grown subdivision street and skate back to the compound for an
afternoon in the blue movies.

Some years ago the actors went on strike protesting
conditions prejudicial to their dignity.
"Your flesh diseased dirty pictures how long you want
us to fuck very nice Meester Slastobitch? We is fucking
tired of fuck very nice." Accordingly the great Slasto-
bitch introduced a series of reforms. Considering the
demands of the workers he decided that the blue movies must have story, character development and background in which sex scenes are incidental. For example
a story of a whaling voyage 1859 two hours in length
contains only eighteen minutes of sex scenes scattered
through the film.
"The blue movies as a separate genre have ceased to
exist. We show sex as it occurs in the story as a part of
life not a mutilated fragment."
I go to the old Palace Theatre on Market Street. The

first number is an educational short showing how le gran luxe can be achieved on a modest income.

"Now here is my immersion trough in the blue room just a trough full of glycerine sheet aluminum I got it all through the PX for almost nothing my dear now if you'll just slip into this plastic cover Yage and Majoun for this trip Majoun is good on a bluie your first solo my dear and you are well prepared you see it's all so simple home is where your ass is and if you want to move you move your ass the first step is learning to change homes with someone else and have someone else's ass. I remember a science-fiction thing about an institute called Fishook given over to paranormal psychic things they have a box they get in and their minds travel to other planets. Well one of these planets is so 'evil' it drives an astronaut back to the Bible Belt where he preaches up a holy war against the 'Parries' they are called and by now everyone outside Fishook hates the 'Parries' and there are signs up 'Parry, Don't Let The Sun Set On You Here.' And Fishook has closed the doors whole villages of nice old 'Parries' and the teenage 'Parries' all bucking for Fishook will be slaughtered."

But there is another astronaut on the lam from Fishook security who knows about a nice quiet planet and he wants to rescue all good "Parries" everywhere but how to transport the paranormal assholes? In a flash the know-how comes to him from that "evil" planet and when he tells the villagers what to do they say
"But that's dirty."
"Not dirty just alien" he says. "Besides you don't have much choice." He points to a long row of headlights approaching the paranormal village. "The vigilantes

are on the way. So you see it's time to move on. And
what you find outside is only what you put there in the
first place. Time to move into first place."

He was lying on a bed in his shorts split bamboo walls
top floor of the hotel. A knock at the door. The Indian
boy stood there a quart beer bottle in one hand.

"*Aquí Yage Ayahuasca . . . muy bueno . . . muy fuerte . . .*"
The boy came in closing the door and put the bottle on
a table. The American boy who was thin and blond got
two tin cups from his rucksack. The Indian boy poured
out the mixture from the beer bottle filling each cup
two-thirds full. He passed his hands back and forth
over the cups humming a little tune. He stopped humming looked at the American and smiled.

"This very good for fuck Johnny." He made a tight
brown fist and shoved a finger in and out. "We take
Yage then fuck." He unbuttoned his shirt. "*Ambos nudo
Johnny* . . . both naked." He dropped his shirt on a
chair, kicked off his sandals, shoved his pants and
shorts down. He waited until the American was stripped.
"Now take Yage . . . act very fast." The American drank
and shuddered. "*Muy amargo sí Johnny.*"

Almost at once the American boy felt a blue tide cool
evening air on his naked rectum his legs . . . "*Tomamos
eso . . . ambos nudo*" . . . shadows fading hand on a tin
cup eyes smiling and knowing the bare rectum the other
was looking pressure the groin facing each other . . .
"*Vuelvete*" . . . getting hard in the blue light . . . "Bend
over Johnny" . . . The boy picked up a tin of Vaseline
and slowly with a calm intent expression rubbed it on
his cock . . . "Bend over Johnny and spread ass" . . .
feeling the eyes and fingers on his rectum ass hairs
spread the slow penetration . . . "Hand on knees
Johnny" . . . He twisted his body in a slow circle hands

braced on knees stirring whirlpools of blue tighter
tighter tighter spurting blue Chinese characters in the
purple dusk of Lima gasps *"muy bueno"* hands on knees
Carl's eyes sputtering blue his face blurred out bone-
wrenching spasms popped egg-blue worlds in air a wake
of jissom across the sky.

"Now I've been thinking of a communal immersion
tank in the swimming pool but I may make a fish pond
instead. Really it should be filled with raw oysters and
. . ." A trough cut in pink coral dome-shaped room
lined with sea shells the boy spread his legs and squirms
down into the oysters the tight conch of his nuts spurting pearly gobs sea wind through a porthole. "Yes of
course they are soundproof rooms in various degrees
but we do have sound tracks and odors now in the blue
room ozone and burning leaves and in the red room
roses and carbolic soap Lifebuoy isn't making it any
more but you can still get it down here and I've laid in
several cases now here is the rainbow room for Dim-N
and Psylocybin rather tacky isn't it smell of orange
crush plastics and carnivals you come the world's fair
my dear and of course I need a yellow room but there
are so few Chinese boys in Casa I haven't gotten to it
but you can see the daffodils and crocuses whiffs of
straw and urine and saffron and ambergris the yellow
tower of amber chamois pallet the boy yellow hair
brown eyes teeth bared coming inside out and of course
you mix your skin colors say black and red brown and
yellow red and white rather limited here but we don't
do too badly and the sound tracks distant train whistles
and fog horns for the blue room sea sounds in the pink
room and music special for the two parties and sometimes more than two of course. Is your Majoun working? I need a laboratory to work out all the drug prob-

lems synthesis, blending new formulae now if you are taking Majoun which works so much slower than Yage or Dim-N you have to wait two hours on the Majoun. Oh! here's Ali . . . Now if you'll put on these headphones Genua music in the blue room of course you'll find the Yage already measured out."

When the music started in his head the lower half of his body came loose in fluid gyrations come yell cracked his head rainbow room stars on the table knees of amber brown teeth bared.

"And the image track of course we take movies and mix the movies all up with color shots blue mist and attic rooms under slate roofs sunsets autumn leaves apples red moon in the smoky sky all mixed with sex pictures we take five or six cameras one on the face one on the genitals twitching feet coming eyes and usually we project these in the white room which has plain white walls for screens a rainbow cocktail of LSD Majoun Yage very little LSD it isn't good for you really and the natural plants are better."

Red-haired boy on his side chewing his knuckles as the Arab boy browns him pictures on the walls and ceilings five projectors a kaleidoscope of legs, spurting cocks, tight nuts, eyes, faces, a twitching foot, sunsets and blue mist, urine in straw, yellow sky, quivering buttocks, sperm spurting vapor trails, snow-capped mountains, rainbows, Niagara Falls, souvenir post cards, Northern lights as the boy turns him with his knees up he is on top looking at the ceiling pictures now on hands and knees both facing the wall come seeing themselves in television mixed in with all the others "right on location but rather over our budget I'm afraid so lucky to find all these dome-shaped rooms rather like the inside of a huge phallus aren't they now here is the rose room."

Red bed cover sprinkled with rose petals feeling the red egg in his groin spurting sunsets, freckles, red hair, autumn leaves, knees up he was coming in the autumn sky.

The Penny Arcade Peep Show

1. A round red Christmas tree ornament going away
   . . . Indian boy with bright red gums spits blood
   under the purple dusk of Lima.
   "Fight tuberculosis folks."
   Christmas Eve . . . An old junky selling Christmas
   seals on North Clark Street. The "Priest" they called
   him.
   "Fight tuberculosis folks."

2. Two round ornaments going away one blue one
   green . . . fading train whistles blue arc lights flickering empty streets half buried in sand . . . jelly in green
   brown rectal flesh twisting finger turns to vine tendril
   ass hairs spread over the tide flats . . . sea weed . . .
   green pullman curtains . . . blue prep school clothes.

3. Three ornaments going away red, blue, green . . .
Holly wreaths, red ribbons, children bobbing for
apples . . . It was getting late and no money to score
he turned into a side street and the lake wind hit him
like a knife . . . a lost street of brick chimneys and
slate roofs . . . heavy blue silence . . . lawn sprinklers
summer golf course . . . *The Green Hat* folded on her
knee.

4. Four ornaments going away red, blue, green, gold
. . . freckles, autumn leaves, smoky red moon over the
river
"When the autumn weather turns the leaves to flame
And I haven't got time for a waiting game."

Cab stopped just ahead under a street light and a boy
got out with a suitcase thin kid in blue prep school
clothes familiar face the "Priest" told himself watching
from a doorway reminds me of something a long time
ago the boy there with his overcoat unbuttoned reaching into his pants pockets for the cab fare . . . blue
magic of all movies in remembered kid standing at the
attic window waving to a train . . . a sighing sound the
empty room . . . distant smell of weeds in vacant lots
little green snakes under rusty iron . . . pirate chests
pieces of eight on golden sands . . . urine in straw . . .
the Traveller walks on and on through the plain of
yellow grass. He stops by a deep black pool. A yellow
fish side turns in the dark water.

1. Red ornament coming in . . . red leg hairs rubbing
rose wall paper . . . Irish terrier under the Christmas
tree . . . light years away the pale skies fall apart.
T.B. waiting at the next stop. Spit blood at dawn.
I was waiting there.
"Doctor Harrison. They called me."

Led the way up . . . stairs worn red carpeting . . .
smell of sickness is in the room.

2. Two ornaments coming in one blue one green . . .
blue evening shadows a cool remote Sunday . . . dead
stars drifting . . . twisting coming in green brown
rectal flesh grass stains on brown knees.

3. Three ornaments coming in red, blue, green . . .
smell of roses, carbolic soap . . . there was nothing
for me to do. Spit blood at dawn. Agony to remember
the words . . . "Too late" . . . German living room outside the China blue northern sky and drifting clouds
. . . bad seascapes of the dying medical student.
"A schnapps I think Frau Underschnitt."
Room over the florist shop flower smell green curtains
. . . He was a caddy it seems. His smile across the
golf course.

4. Four ornaments coming in red, blue, green, gold . . .
heart pulses in the rising sun . . . smell of raw meat
. . . the heretic spits boiling blood . . . 18th Century
room . . . snow at the latticed window . . . fire in the
hearth . . . An old gentleman wrapped in red shawls
is measuring laudanum into a medicine glass . . .
Have you seen Patapon Rose? . . . blue shadows in the
attic room . . . the boy's picture is framed in forget-
me-nots . . . dust on the broken greenhouse . . . in the
ruined garden a pool is covered with green slime . . .
thin blond boy . . . sunlight in pubic hairs . . . I remember daffodils and yellow wallpaper . . . a gold
watch that played "Silver Threads Among the Gold"
. . . an old book with gilt edges . . . in golden letters
. . . The Street of Chance.

Dim far away the Star of Bethlehem from the school
play.

The
Miracle
of
the Rose

June 23, 1988. Today we got safely through the barrier
and entered the Blue Desert of Silence. The silence is
devastating at first you drown in it our voices are muted
as if we were speaking through felt. I have two guides
with me Ali a Berber lad with bright blue eyes and
yellow hair a wolfish Pan face unreadable as the sky.
The other Farja of a dusky rose complexion with long
lashes straight black hair gums a bright red color. We
are wearing standard costumes for the area: blue silk
knee-length shorts, blue silk shirts, Mercury sandals and
helmets. The Mercury sandals and helmets once fitted
are never removed. We are carrying nothing but light
mattresses, mess kits, rations of dried fish, rice, peppers,
dates, brown sugar and tea. It is a beautiful country
and the predominant color is blue. Like many so-called

deserts it is far from being a desert. There are wooded areas and we glimpse bodies of water from time to time. In the late afternoon we came to a vast deserted city streets cracked and broken weeds growing through houses and villas all empty overgrown with vines the scent of flowers always heavier in the air like a funeral parlor and no sign of life in the ruined court-yards empty hotels and cafés. As the sun was setting we took a road leading out of the city. None of us wanted to camp for the night in that necropolis of silent flowers. On a hill over the city we came to a ruined villa covered with rose vines. The building was in ruins little more than the walls remaining and it was not a place I would have chosen to camp. But Ali stopped and pointed. He said something in a low voice to Farja who looked down sulkily and bit his lip. Ali took a flute from his belt. Playing a little piper tune he stepped forward and we followed. Exploring the ruin we found a room with rose wallpaper. Two walls remained the support posts and bare beams of the ceiling covered with rose vines formed an arbor. Rose petals had fallen on the faded pink coverlet of a brass bed. As soon as we found this room Ali seemed pos-sessed by a curious excitement. He prowled about like a cat playing his flute. He turned to Farja and said one word I did not catch. Farja stood there his eyes down-cast blushing and trembling. He looked at the bed the walls and the rose vines. He nodded silently and the blood rushed to his face. The two boys stripped to their sandals and helmets. Farja's whole body was blushing to his sandals. His skin is a dusky rose color the genitals perfectly formed neither small nor large black shiny pubic hairs precise as wires. He poised and cleared the bed stand in a leap that carried him to the center of the bed on hands and knees. Then he rolled over and lay on his back with the knees up. Ali stood at the foot of the bed. Like all so-called the boy lay down with his knees up gasping late afternoons deserted streets slow pressure of semen rectal smell of flowers two naked bodies bathed in smoky rose of the dying sun phantom bed from an old movie set long since abandoned to weeds and vines. Their eyes locked and they breathed together. I could see Farja's heart pulsing under the dusky flesh and Ali's heart beating with his. Both phalluses stiffened to the blood drums and throbbed erect. On the tip of each phallus a pearl of lubricant squeezed out. Farja sighed deeply and rocked back holding his knees. Nitrous fumes twisted from the pink rectal flesh in whorls of orange and sepia. A musty odor filled the air that sent blood pounding and singing in my ears. The sepia fumes cleared and Farja's rectum was a quivering breathing rose of flesh. With a quick movement Ali stepped over the bed stand and kneeled in front of the rose breathing deeply his lips swollen with blood. The rose pulled his loins forward and breathed his phallus in. Red fumes enveloped the two bodies. A scream of roses burst from tumescent lips roses growing in flesh tearing thorns of delight intertwined their quivering bodies crushed them together writhing gasping choking in an agony of roses sharp reek of sperm.

Sepia picture in an old book with gilt edges. THE MIRACLE OF THE ROSE written in gold letters. I turn the page. A red color that hurts transparent roses growing through flesh the other leans forward drinking roses from his mouth their hearts translucent roses squirming in naked agony blushing gasping the air of empty hotels mouth speaking of a brass bed luminous excitement on his back with the knees up red fumes that burn erogenous holes in writhing flesh naked choking in that phantom bed when I came to the room was abandoned to weeds and vines star dust on a bench silent empty room kid of darkness fading over the florist shop flickering look an old wash stand musty house slow smile you there dim jerky bedroom 18 on the top floor : : : my flesh : : : I could : : : the film breaks : : : jerky silent film : : : look at the fading body : : : I looked about nineteen. "But not that one word?" It is getting dark : : : boy : : : remember so intense it hurts : : : sadness in his eyes 1920 movie : : : peanuts : : : "Thank you" : : : the film breaks : : : naked boy on yellow toilet fingers from a long time ago the boy solid quick and silent coming so intense it hurts teeth bared see solid now I could touch my flesh pants down evening sky : : : naked boy fading erased out : : : "Thank you" : : : the film breaks : : : pose is a long time ago memory noises frayed magazine over there room grainy like an old movie dim silver sky : : : the other leans forward laughing comparing : : : pieces of the blurred 1920 afternoon : : : jerky bed twisted feet buttocks quivering phantom boy nods the other straddles rectum exposed squeezed out musty odor luminous bodies quiver together deserted city dying sun old movie set. I turn the page. Sepia of each phallus a drop of the red color that hurts blood pounding singing naked rectum breathing rose flesh mouth speaking prickles of delight. I turn the page each picture framed in roses.

The Proposition. a ruined wall with rose paper the bed. Ali points to the bed. Farja stands there sullen eyes downcast long lashes.

The Agreement. Farja looks at the bed blushing to his bare feet.

The Consummation. Roses and thorns through translucent flesh squirming a slow scream of roses. I turn the page.

The Elixir of the Rose. Farja knees up rectum rose pulsing. The monk drains off a red fluid that flows from his translucent phallus.

The Tree of Flesh. A musty odor rises from the pages. A Mayan priest is drawing the flesh sap from a bulbous phallic tree. He has inserted an obsidian tube into the soft flesh of the tree and is draining the sap into a stone jar.

Discovery of the Jars. A Mayan pyramid. The monks have broken a door and found the jars.

The Flesh Sheets. The monk has rolled sheets of the flesh sap out on a table. The flesh sap is of a pearly grey color.

The Writing. The monk is writing on the sheets the pictures from an old book.

The Body Builder. The monk is wrapping flesh sheets around the two skeletons. Two youths have been formed. Mouth rectum and penis sealed.

The Creation. The monk has arranged the youth on a canopy knees up. He picks up a crystal phallic jar of the elixir. He lets a drop fall between the parted buttocks a drop on the end of the penis. With a crystal rod he rubs a drop on the lips. Where the fluid touches nitrous fumes arise sepia orange dusky rose. The lips part rectum quivers phallus spurts. The youth is breathing. I turn the page.

The Academy. red-brick building over a river autumn leaves the rising sun.

Morning Sleep. Naked boy with a hard-on sleeping lips parted. Roommate stands at the foot of the bed with sheet he has just pulled off the other.

The Awakening. The boy's eyes looking down at his erection blushing to his bare feet as he sees other standing there.

The Recognition. The other has dropped the sheet from his naked body laughing comparing sepia gobs in air.

The Proposition. Two boys in the room. "That's kid stuff. I wanta." One boy with eyes downcast sullen.

The Agreement. Rose of flesh on all fours quivering in a red haze. He pulls Jerry over on top of him Jerry knees up feet in the air kicking like a frog. John reaches down rubs lubricant around the tip of Jerry's cock pumping his slow deep ecstasy as they squirm together knees up kicking out the spurts. Ali plays the flute. Two boys by a pool on all fours faces turned to the full moon light June knees. Ali points to the silent YES.

At dawn the two boys got up and walked out naked into the ruined garden. Coming to a thick tangle of rosebushes Farja leaped through and emerged untouched by the thorns on the other side and then I jumped a sweet tearing pain landed on hands and knees fell forward on my elbows gasping feeling the rose in my trembling buttocks a red steam along the backs of my thighs as Farja kneeled behind me. Ali sat on the edge of a pool playing his flute dangling his feet in the black water. The boy stands holding a sheet in front of his body turned to the full moon. He drops the sheet. Boys laughing comparing sepia pictures. I turn the page. The Proposi-

tion. Ali points to the rectum. Frayed magazine one
with eyes down on the pages and pictures quivering
mouth turned to the full moon boy just pulled off the
other getting browned there coming gobs in the air
sulky youth a silent YES blushing buttocks. Ali points
to the rectum. Downcast eyes to his bare feet blushing
erogenous roses the agony of that color so intense it
hurts quivering prickles of delight deserted city rose
vines empty hotels boys laughing comparing sepia
knees. "Kid stuff. I wanta." The Agreement on all fours
parted buttocks bare feet in an old book dusk by a pool
the youth breathing deeply sullen eyes downcast and
the slow YES sweet pain blushing red steam along his
thighs spasms of delight thorns through the buttocks.
I turn the page feeling the rose twist alive in my flesh.
Dawn eyes tight knees the youth breathing from his
mouth the slow YES erogenous agony the body writes
out musty odors squeezed to the full moon. A sighing
sound back. The film breaks. An old book with gilt
stars silver paper fingers from another memory naked
shorts and shirt there a fourteen-year-old boy flesh
steaming.

Look at that compass of age and wind. Mister about?
Dim jerky bed is there. I am the empty room pieces
of the dim picture a rustle of darkness fading. Now
I remember so intense it hurts. Mrs Murphy's rooming house. They got up remembered "Thank you."
Room eighteen on the top floor background grainy
like an old movie. The film breaks. Kid standing there
talking to another. There are two. They got up naked
shorts and shirts there room eighteen on the top floor
my flesh steaming.

We tried various ways of slipping the tight blue shorts

down over the Mercury sandals but any way you slip the feathers are being rubbed the wrong way. It is not hot. It is not cold. There are no noxious animals or insects. A fresh wind sprang up and wafted my blue shorts away. So we wave good-by to shirt and shorts. Ali is fucking Farja on all fours. His wolfish eyes light up inside and the hair stands up on his head. Then they did a hot Mercury crackling all over with blue fire and a classic Mercury with porticos and glades and pools. We lie there on the magic carpet of shared bodies the old fear of the border cities still heard still felt. Farja shudders in his sleep.

We are in an area of electric sex currents. Suddenly we get prickles in the crotch and then pictures start of what we are going to do like you are watching a picture of yourself doing it and you plop right into the screen with a delicious squeeze, Ali and Farja chasing and wrestling each other in and out of the film. We camped in a ruined signal tower on a promontory of land jutting out over the desert. We reached it at twilight a blue mist settling on the narrow flagstone path, a rusty gate a sign overgrown with vines: U.S. Army Reservation. Authorized Personnel Only. The old M.P. box still there. The boys give it a push and it crashes into the valley. Here is the old tower. We climb up to the control room great laser guns broken the top of the tower blasted away. We camp there and after the evening meal Ali brings out his flute and we follow the music further and further out into the silence.

The following day we find ourselves walking down a country road red clay pieces of flint here and there. Farja finds an arrowhead. We came to a deserted village of red-brick houses with slate roofs by a stream.

1. An Easter egg with a peephole going away . . . bits of vivid and vanishing detail . . . rainbow a post card road . . . boy there by the creek bare feet twisted on a fence.

2. Two Easter eggs going away . . . ghostly flower smell by the stagnant creek the boy still there waiting.

3. Three Easter eggs going away . . . click of distant heels . . . footsteps on a windy street . . . sad open hand.

4. Four Easter eggs going away . . . empty streets half-buried in sand . . . a house . . . a weed-grown golf course . . . blue prep school clothes further and further away.

1. An egg coming in . . . Road corner stone bridge rainbow over a stream green fields . . . Boy there naked. He is lying on his stomach eating an apple legs curled over his thighs. He claps his feet together. A book is open in front of him on the grass.

2. Two eggs coming in . . . sad old human papers I carry . . . two adolescents by the garage faraway toy cars.

3. Three eggs coming in . . . Smell of carbolic soap . . . Three boys in shower. A boy turns mocking him off.

4. Four eggs coming in. Audrey squeezes through the peephole wet dream tension tingling in his crotch. He is in the shower with John on a Saturday afternoon. They are facing each other Audrey uneasy feeling John's eyes on his body . . . "Wanta feel something nice Audrey?" . . . John reaches forward with soapy fingers feeling Audrey's crotch . . . sudden raw hard-on.

Dim dead boy so I haunted your old flower smell of young nights on musty curtains empty prep school clothes further and further away. Come closer. Listen across empty back yards and ash pits.

He is bending over in the shower while John washes his back glancing down along his stomach to the crotch biting his lip hoping that John will finish before he gets out of control. John is rubbing soap just above the buttocks. He leans forward and says in Audrey's ear ... "Wanta feel something nice Audrey?" ... John slides a finger up his ass and jiggles it to a car horn outside. Audrey drops his head gasping as his body contracts squeezing out the hot spurts.

American house ... rain outside ... boy standing by the ghost car ... sunset ... blue clothes ... the phone rings ... child voice across a distant sky ... "Long long expected call from you" ... fingers from the phone like wood. Audrey drying himself carefully trying to keep it down. He turned away holding a towel in front of him. John reached out and pulled the towel away looking at Audrey's half-erection ... "You ever been goosed Audrey?" ... Audrey shook his head blushing ... "Lean over and brace your hands on your knees" ... He heard John unscrew a jar then felt the greased finger slide up him. He gasped and threw his head back ... "You ever been rosed Audrey?" ... Thumbs prying his buttocks apart as John squirmed forward. Pink eggs popped in his crotch.

Souvenir post cards a violet evening sky rising from the boy's groin ... sad 1920 scraps ... dim jerky faraway stars splash the stagnant creek ... "I was wait-

ing there" . . . held a little-boy photo in his withered
hand . . . The boy was footsteps down the windy
street a long time ago.

Silver light popped in his eyes.

A
Silver
Smile

Tonight Reggie and I had dinner with the Great Slasto-bitch and he expounded the new look in blue movies. "The movies must first be written if we are to have living characters. A writer may find it difficult to make the reader see a scene clearly and it would seem easier to show pictures. No. The scene must be written before it is filmed.

"The new look in blue movies stresses story and character. This is the space age and sex movies must express the longing to escape from flesh through sex. The way out is the way through." He switches on a projector. "The scene where Johnny has crabs and Mark makes him undress . . .

"Who are these boys? Where will they go? They will become astronauts playing the part of American married idiots until the moment when they take off on a Gemini expedition bound for Mars, disconnect and leave the earth behind forever" . . . (It happened a few minutes after take-off. The screen went dead. The radio went dead. The astronauts had disconnected. There was a talk of space madness.)

Mark's wife told reporters: "He frightened me at times. There was something in him I could never quite reach." John's wife said: "He was a dutiful husband but I never got any warmth out of him." (The FBI did not publicize the fact that they had found in a locked drawer of John's desk a number of muscle magazines.)

The sex scenes of their adolescence are seen as image dust in space through which they pass to other planets. The set is the 1920's. Sex scenes are intercut with lawn sprinklers, country clubs, summer golf courses, classrooms, silver stars, morning sleep of detour, frogs in 1920 roads, cocktail shakers, black Cadillacs, cool basement toilets, a boy's twitching foot, the Charleston, iced tea and fried chicken at The Green Inn, 1920 ponds, naked boy hugging his knees sunlight in pubic hairs.

A suburban room afternoon light bleakly clear. Mark is eighteen. He is stripped to his shorts reading a copy of *Amazing Stories* one leg thrown over the arm of a chair. He is smoking a cigarette. The other boy John is fifteen, thin, pale, his face spattered with adolescent pimples. He is barefoot dressed in khaki pants and a white shirt. Without looking up from his magazine Mark says: "I heard you got laid the other night."

"Oh! uh! yes . . . down on Westminster Place."

"Like it?"

"Well uh! I guess it was all right," says the boy dubiously.

"Maybe it isn't what you want."

The boy John is standing by the window looking out. He scratches his crotch.

"I itch something awful."

Lazily Mark drops his magazine on the floor. He looks at Johnny through cigarette smoke. "You itch Johnny? Where?"

John turns from the window. "Right here" he says scratching his crotch.

"Come over here Johnny."

Johnny walks over in front of the chair. Mark spreads his legs. Right here." Johnny stands in front of him between his knees.

"Drop your pants Johnny."

"Huh? Why?"

"Just drop your pants like I tell you. I wanta see something."

Johnny fumbles awkwardly with his belt.

"I'll do it." Mark unbuckles Johnny's belt. With gentle precise fingers he unbuttons pants and shorts and shoves them down. They fall to Johnny's ankles. Johnny stands there his cock half-up from the scratching mouth dry heart pounding. Mark reaches forward and takes Johnny's cock by the tip with two fingers moving it to one side and with the other hand parts pubic hairs. He points to red mark . . . "Look there Johnny" . . . Oh! Christ! it is happening he can't stop it. Mark looks up at him and Johnny blushes bright red biting his lip. Mark smiles slow and brings his finger up in three jerks as Johnny's cock stands out all the way up and throbs to his pounding heart.

Sunlight in pubic hairs sad muscle magazines over the florist shop pants down green snakes under rusty iron

in the vacant lot the old family soap opera lock of
yellow hair stirs in September wind shirt open on the
golf course grass squeezed under quivering hard-ons
wet grass between his legs pale buttocks sex sweat dim
jerky faraway toilet pants down looking down now
twisted slow smile . . . "Relax Johnny. It happens" . . .
The old film stops . . . naked boy on yellow toilet seat
buttocks quivering smell of rectal mucous windy
oranges I remember a dim building overgrown with
disuse and later in Mexico City I see myself looking at
him as if trying to focus to remember who the stranger
was standing under a dusty tree lean and ragged ruffled
brown hair blue eyes vacant blank I remember London
stairs worn red carpeting and I could see his pants were
sticking up between his legs colored photo had something written on it . . . "*Vuelvete y aganchete*" . . . I let
myself go limp inside blank factual he slid it in out
through the little dusty window afternoon hills the old
broken point of origin St Louis Missouri emaciated
body head on the grimy pillow my face . . . The film
stops in his eyes . . . blue morning naked boy on yellow
toilet seat a quivering foot in front of the wash stand
soapy hands turned to me and finished machine gun
noises as he came street shadows his distant hand there
it is just to my shoulder smell of sickness in the room a
shooting star silence floats down on falling leaves and
blood spit the smell of decay shredded to dust and
memories pieces of legs and cocks and assholes drifting
fragments in sunlight ass hairs spread on the bed dust
of young hand fading flickering thighs and buttocks
smell of young nights.

One day we come home very tired and fall asleep naked
in the bed. We wake up and the room is full of moon

light. Kiki is lying there on his face and says he is very
stiff and sore from carrying clubs all day will I rub his
back. I start at the shoulder and work down to his ass
and run my hands along the back of his thighs and he says
. . . "*Más Johnny . . . Más*" . . . So I shove his ass apart
with both hands and jiggle it and he keeps saying . . .
"*Más . . . Más*" . . . I dip my finger in Vaseline not letting him see what I am doing and rub my finger around
his ass outside at first and he says . . . "*Más . . . Más*"
. . . So I twist my finger around until it sinks all the
way in up to his pearl and he sighs and says . . . "*Más
. . . Más*" . . . And I say . . . "*Qué más Kiki?*" . . . He
doesn't want to say it but I keep twisting my finger and
he is squirming and finally he says . . . "Fucking me
Johnny" . . . "*Apartate las piernas*" . . . .He spreads his
legs and I slide it in slow feeling the ring squeeze me
and I can tell when he spurts. Afterward he doesn't
want to turn over and show me but I turn him over and
his juice is silver in the moonlight.

Next day he says it didn't happen and slaps me when I
try to do it but a few nights later he gets out of bed
to put out a cigarette leaning forward on the table and
I stand up behind him spit on my finger and slide it up
his ass all the way and he just sighs and falls forward
with his elbows on the table and looks at me over his
shoulder and says . . . "*Qué me haces Johnny?*" . . . I
get the Vaseline and rub it in standing behind him
hitch my arms around his hips and shove it in we are
standing in front of the mirror I can see my white rump
pumping and he had his head down on his hands biting
his knuckles and whimpering. I reach around and play
with his eggs and pull his foreskin back gently he gasps
and I am feeling the scratchy pressure all the way up
pumping him inside we are both coming. I can feel

goose pimples on my back and then suddenly an electric shiver and my hair stands up straight and I can see my eyes light up inside like a cat.

Johnny stands in front of Mark tight pants slow finger reaches up and unbuttons his fly parting pubic hairs points to a red mark . . . "You got crabs Johnny. Come in the bathroom" . . . Mark locks the door . . . "All right Johnny. Strip down" . . . Awkwardly Johnny takes off his shirt and hangs it on the bathroom door. Mark spreads a yellow towel on the toilet seat . . . "Take off your pants and shorts and sit there" . . . Johnny swallows feeling cold in the stomach . . . "All right" . . . Mouth dry heart pounding he sits down naked on the toilet seat. Mark selects a bottle of Campho-Phenique from the medicine cabinet. He squats in front of Johnny. Their knees touch . . . "Spread your legs apart so I can see what I'm doing" . . . He opens the bottle and tips it against his finger. He lifts Johnny's penis by the tip moving it around as he rubs the camphorated oil in pubic hairs at the root. The oil leaves a cold burn. Johnny licks his lips and blushes . . . "Christ Mark" . . . Mark rests his hands on Johnny's and looks up at Johnny who blushes to his bare feet as his cock floats up throbbing . . . "Relax Johnny. It happens" . . . He rubs the oil around Johnny's tight nuts. Johnny's embarrassment changes to excitement. He squirms and a drop of lubricant squeezes slowly out the end of his phallus and glitters in the afternoon sun . . . "You take off *your* shorts" . . . "Sure Johnny" . . . Mark squirms his shorts off . . . "Like I say it happens" . . . The two boys look at each other. "You probably got them in your ass too. Come over here" . . . He points to the bath mat . . . "Lie down on your back" . . . He shoves Johnny's knees up . . . "Hold them there against your chest" . . . He squats with the bottle of Campho-Phenique . . . "Spread your legs apart so I can see what I'm doing . . . That's right" . . . He rubs the oil in Johnny's ass hairs and lightly around the rectum. Johnny sighs feeling the cold burn and looks down at his throbbing cock . . . "Like that Johnny?" . . . Mark takes a jar of mentholated Vaseline from the medicine cabinet. He rubs the Vaseline around Johnny's ass parting the soft pink flesh and shoves the middle finger all the way up vibrating the finger. Burning inside Johnny squirms and whimpers. His body pulls up his ass contracts spasmodically hot white spurts cover his thin stomach.

Feet twitching in the air shred to dust and memories pieces of legs and cocks and assholes drifting fragments falling softly through penny arcades and basement toilets playground finger stained with grass points to a red mark . . . "And there's another. Spread your legs" . . . Oh! Christ! it is happening a little whimper brings his finger up in three jerks blushes to his pounding heart looks down pointing naked boy on yellow toilet seat and later in Mexico City trying to remember who the stranger was in front of him ruffled brown hair blue eyes pants open far pale sun colored photo unbuttoned his shirt.

He looked at his young cousin just in from the country wondering if the boy would let him. They shared a room on the roof. They went to a movie that night and afterward in the roof room he got his cousin to smoke marijuana for the first time the boy laughing and rolling on the floor until he pissed in his pants sharp smell of urine in the Mexican night . . . *"Desnudate chico"* . . . The boy peeled off his wet pants and shorts and stood there naked and suddenly embarrassed under Kiki's knowing eyes. Then Kiki pulled him down on the bed tickling him in the ribs the boy laughing out of control . . . *"Por favor Kiki . . . Por favor"* . . . Trying to hide his hard-on turned over on his stomach Kiki straddled him and spread his ass cheeks and felt the body go limp under him and the boy said . . . *"Bueno, Kiki, haz' lo"* . . . Kiki put a pillow under the boy's crotch to get his ass up and spread the legs and greased the boy's ass panting and squirming as Kiki slid it in ten strokes and they came together in a red pull teeth bared cocks crowing in the summer night musky smell of the boy's greased ass.

Unexpected rising of the curtain can begin with the apartment building lonely young face in the hall standing under a dusty name . . . "Abrupt question brought me Mister" . . . Princes Arcade closing the lost past hung in his eyes boys and workshops pointing down the pale skies . . . "Through the dead I trust you" . . . The stairs stretched out a shadow. It was 6:40 P.M. Young face looking for a name hand holding the door open memory noises dim sky the lonely 1920 afternoon jerky bed twisted I remember the other straddles rectum palpable odor fills the room the past hangs in the air rubbish and weeds drift of time a child laughing blurred faces the dying sun through a bathroom window.

"Come over here Johnny. Down on your hands and knees. That's right. Spread your legs apart" . . . Cold burn on his rectum nuts aching Johnny sighs and looks down at his throbbing cock . . . "Like that Johnny?" . . . Mark gets a jar of mentholated Vaseline from the medicine cabinet rubbing it around pulling Johnny's ass open two greased fingers all the way up twisting burning Johnny spurts across the bath mat.

Buttocks dim trying to focus Johnny's ass the cold burn blankness a hotel on the outskirts of East St Louis. Johnny has just taken a shower. Flesh steaming he walks across the room to his suitcase. He takes out a package of Band-Aids and bends down to put one on a blister. Bending down like that it begins to get stiff between his legs. Mark is in an adjoining room and Johnny hopes he won't come in now but suddenly he knows that Mark is standing in the doorway and then he hears Mark's voice right behind him . . . "You look like a statue of Mercury Johnny. Why don't you stand up?" . . . Johnny blushes it is all the way up between his legs. Now Mark is in front of him. Johnny closes his knees looking up at Mark helplessly. Mark shoves him and he falls on his back legs in the air. Laughing Mark pries his legs apart naked boy hugging his knees sunlight in pubic hairs the two boys have been swimming they were standing naked arms around each other's shoulders looking at a redheaded woodpecker drumming on a persimmon tree sixty feet up in the summer sky. Suddenly Johnny began to feel uncomfortable with the other's arm around his shoulder. He shifted and glanced down Oh! Christ! it was happening he blushed bright red and the other boy smiled . . . "Your pecker's getting hard" . . . the woodpecker drumming frogs croaking the two boys were cousins but they had just met they were riding donkeys across the plateau and came to a stream under the bridge of an abandoned railroad the politicos stole all the money and then the railroad was built somewhere else rusty tracks overgrown with weeds and vines the older boy slid off his

donkey . . . *"Nadamos"* . . . The younger boy had a
hard-on from riding the donkey. Very slowly he took off
his shirt and shoved his pants down it was still half-up
he turned away to hide it. The older boy was already
naked . . . *"Qué te pasa chico?"* . . . The older boy
turned him around and laughed . . . *"Tú te empalmas"*
. . . In water up to the knees the older boy was washing his back slid the bar of soap down across his ass
something melted in his stomach and the other boy was
inside him. The sky dimmed out of focus as he came
hearing an ass bray from a great distance music across
the golf course the boy had been swimming in the pond
he sat on the concrete dam dangling his feet in the
water he got up dried himself and caught a gleam of
white in the summer twilight a golf ball he picked it
up and soon found another bending over to pick up the
ball he felt someone behind him he turned and an older
boy was standing there he recognized one of the town-
ies who hung out in front of Jake's Pool Hall the
boy smiled and walked toward him he stood there
feeling his nakedness under the knowing eyes the boy
stopped just in front of him . . . "What's your name?"
. . . "John" . . . the boy reached forward and cupped
his crotch . . . "Hello! Johnny" . . . the boy took
a deep breath and let's see you're sure the townie
stripped slowly turned him around with a quick knee
dropped him forward on hands and knees in the wet
grass finger rubbing something on his ass rectum spread
frogs croaking he was coming in a red pull through a
labyrinth of pink eggs sobbing gasps frogs in his head
the two bodies stuck together twitching feeling the soft
night air on his naked body two white balls in wet grass
I remember a thin pale boy last sad smile dust of dead
hope in his hands the proposition bleakly clear pointed

to the bed I remember hope of strange flesh the mouth dim room pants rip quick and silent coming another scene in the shed rubbish and weeds the drift of time a child's room pieces of a blurred face the dark city dying sun naked boy hugging his knees sunlight in pubic hairs sad muscle magazines over the florist shop corduroy pants down green snakes under rusty iron in the vacant lot the old family soap opera phosphorescent clock hands tick away to basement walls back yards and ash pits a silver crescent moon cuts the film sky machine-gun noises as he came one of the boys looks up hands mocking me off an old book with gilt edges the drawer stuck his distant hand there it is just to my shoulder twilight boy with violet eyes shredded to dust and memories paper fingers peanuts 1920 movie the old film stops A SILVER SMILE.

The Frisco Kid

Front Street Nome Alaska 1898. Across the street is
RESTAURANT. I walk through a path in waist-high
drifts past a dog team dog's breath in the air and open
the door of the restaurant smell of chop suey and chili
wood tables Chinese waiter. Order a bowl of chili and
coffee. There are several miners at the tables. I am
eating my chili when the door opens behind me and
icy air touches the back of my neck. Some one comes in
and sits down at my table. It is a young man about
twenty-three with very pale eyes. He says "Howdy"
and orders chop suey. There is talk from the other
tables of dogs and strikes and custom duties. I have
finished the chili. I am drinking coffee from a heavy
white mug with a chipped handle. The curtain between
the kitchen and the restaurant stirs as the waiter walks

back and forth. I get a whiff of opium. The Chinese
railroad workers are smoking in a room behind the
kitchen. The young man opposite me eats his chop suey.
He leans back in his chair and looks at me.

"Didn't I see you someplace?"

"Maybe. Where you from?"

"Frisco."

"I've been there once."

I offered him a cigarette. He took it fished a match out
of his pocket and lit it with a dirty fingernail. We both
inhaled deeply. The waiter set his coffee on the table.
The party of miners paid and left. We were alone in the
restaurant. I jerked a thumb toward the kitchen.

"Smoking. It keeps out the cold."

He just nodded looking at my face the eyes very pale
like I could see through them and out the back of his
head.

"They call me the Frisco Kid" he said.

"I'm Fred Flash from St Louis. Photographer."

"You got a place to stay?"

"No just got here."

"You can bunk with me then."

"All right."

He lived in a boarding house on a side street run by
Mrs Murphy.

"That will be two dollars extra per week" she said
when the Frisco Kid told her I would be sharing the
room. Room 18 on the third floor. He lit a kerosene
lamp. The room was lined with green-painted metal in
patterns of scrolls and flowers. There was a copper-
luster wash basin, a tarnished mirror, a double brass
bed, two chairs, a sea chest by the bed. The window
was narrow the cracks stuffed with quilting and cov-

ered by a frayed red curtain. We sat down on the bed
and lit cigarettes.

I get a whiff of me then I see room 18 wardrobe a
tarnished mirror the window him a cigarette quilting red curtains his fingernail the bed my face drifts
out of the back of his head he nodded coffee eating
my chili there was a door we went through and
some one comes in and sits down pale eyes chop
suey Mrs Murphy the room kerosene light his smile
through cigarette smoke. It was the first time I had seen
him smile. I lay back on the bed blowing smoke toward
the ceiling looking at the scrolls. Here and there a white
crust had formed streaked with rust. I yawned.

"I'd like to turn in if it's all right with you."

"Sure" he said. "Why waste money on some sucker
trap."

He stood up unbuttoning his shirt. He pulled off his
trousers. He turned back the bed and whiff of stale
flesh came off the blankets. We got in and lay there side
by side. He leaned over and blew out the lamp and the
smell of the wick hung in damp cold air of the room.
Outside angry voices from some saloon a distant pistol
shot. Then I was looking up at the ceiling and the room
was full of grey light, my breath hanging in the air. I
looked around at the lamp on the table the curtains the
window. It was very quiet outside muffled by snow. I
took in the clothes on pegs the wash stand the mirror. I
was lying on my back the Frisco Kid close beside me
one leg sprawled across my crotch. Under the leg my
cock was stiff and standing out of my shorts. I turned
and looked at him. His eyes were open in the grey milky
light and I felt a shiver down the spine. He wasn't there
really. Pale the picture was pale. I could see through

him. He smiled slow and rubbed his leg back and forth.
I sighed and moved with it. He brought his hands up
under the covers where I could see and made a fist and
shoved a finger in and out. I nodded. He put his hands
down and shoved his shorts off. I did the same. We lay
there side by side our breath hanging in the air. He
hitched an arm under my shoulders. With the other
hand he turned me on my side. He spit into his hand
and rubbed it on himself. Slow pressure I took a deep
breath and it slid all the way in. Ten strokes and we
came together shuddering gasps his breath on my back.
Where from? Frisco. A kid he never returns. In life used
young pale eyes. Lungs out and finished. Tarnished air
sunlight through the curtains red curtains his fingernail
smiled then and rubbed his leg.
"You someplace?"
"They call me the Frisco Kid. I'm out Front Street
Nome Alaska 1898."
"To stay?"
"No. Just got here. Want to."
I give you for that belated morning man about twenty-
three kerosene lamp on a sea chest. Smile through
me then I looked at room 18 been there might have
seen peeling my breath in the tarnished mirror someone
comes in and sits down my crotch feeling the ache in
my crotch stiff pulsing against his leg. Shoved his finger in and out I saw the fingernail shiny with dirt under
it. Shoved his shorts down we lay there side by side
naked he reached over and slid his hand down my
stomach and felt it tight and aching when I touched
him electric shiver same size same feel feeling myself.
Nodded "Sure"
He said "Why waste money on a whore?"
Turned back the bed and spit into his hand pressure I

breathe cold air the snow was drifting here and there a white crust had formed on the window the wash stand the mirror.

"Like to turn in if it's all right with you." Shoved his shorts off stood there with nothing on stale flesh off the blankets and felt it slide in silver flash behind the eyes bright cold sunlight in the room every object sharp and clear. I took in the clothes streaked with rust the ache in my groin feeling a leg warm against it his pale smile spit on my ass on my side facing the wall sliding in tarnished sunlight I sighed and moved with it stiff he opened his eyes and looked where I could see he wasn't there really pale eyes looking down his leg.

"Call me the Frisco Kid. I'm out. Just got here. Want to." Whiff of breath belated morning the Frisco Kid's legs used out and finished pale. I could see through him my cock was up under the covers he smiled finger in and out going to turn me too smell peeling old places tarnished mirror shiver down my spine and through the crotch a white crust had formed on his leg.

"If it's all right with you" and stood there with nothing on the room was warm and I saw a wood stove. He walked over and threw in a log and put a kettle on the stove. He hung his coat on a wooden peg and I did the same. He sat down on the bed and pulled his boots off and I did the same. He took off his shirt and hung it up pulled down his trousers. He took the kettle off the stove and poured hot water in the copper-luster wash basin. He rubbed soap over his face and neck and dried himself standing in front of the mirror. He peeled off his socks and there was a smell of feet and soap in the room. He put the basin on the floor and washed his feet.

"Wash?"

"Sure."

He tossed me the towel and I dried myself.

"Warm in here" he said. He took off his long grey underwear matter of factly and hung it over his shirt. "If it's all right with you." He turned to me naked. He stood there and scratched his ass looking at me pale eyes touching me down my chest and stomach to the crotch and looking at him I could see his genitals were the same size and shape as mine he was seeing the same thing. We were standing a few feet apart looking at each other and I felt the blood rush to my crotch it was getting stiff I couldn't stop it his pale smile we stood there now both stiff looking at identical erections. We sat down on the edge of the bed. He made a fist and shoved his finger in and out. "That all right with you?" I nodded. He stood up and went to the wardrobe and came back with a tin of grease. He got on the bed and kneeled and made a motion with his hands pulling them in. I turned toward him on all fours he rubbed the grease in slow pressure and we were twisting he was pulling me up on my knees and shoving me down his hand on my eggs when I came there was a silver flash behind the eyes and I blacked out sort of there was a tarnished mirror over it stiff I looked at him his shorts stood out and I felt it naked.

"You figure to do?"

"I'm not here long."

Felt it tight and aching shiver down the spine.

"Why waste money on a whore?"

Shuddering gasps my groin shot pictures lawn streets sunlight faces a pale leg.

"Want to?"

Slow touching me down my chest genital smell peeling with nothing on the room was warm we stood there both stiff as wood.

In front of the basin and rubbed soap he turned to me and finished.

Rubbed his leg across my stomach to the crotch smiled finger in and out.

"All right with you?"

Getting stiff I couldn't stop it he peeled the bed "With you?" I nodded. "Just got here. Want to. Warm in here with you."

Shuddering off flash behind the eyes sunlight faces that's us all right in the mirror stiff standing by the wash basin wasn't there really. The Frisco Kid he never returns. In life used address I give you for that belated morning.

The
Penny Arcade
Peep Show

+ *" "* Billy the Kid said: *"Quién es?"* Pat Garrett killed him. Jesse James said: "That picture's awful dusty." He got on a chair to dust off the death of Stonewall Jackson. Bob Ford killed him. Dutch Schultz said: "I want to pay. Let them leave me alone." He died two hours later without saying anything else.

+ *" "* Sardine can cut open with scissors shoehorn has been used as spoon . . . dirty sock in a plate of moldy beans . . . toothpaste smear on wash stand glass . . . cigarette butt ground out in cold scrambled eggs . . .

+ *" "* The old broken point of origin St Louis Missouri . . . lawn sprinklers summer golf course . . . iced tea and fried chicken at The Green Inn . . . classrooms silver stars . . . dust of young hand fading flickering

thighs and buttocks made machine-gun noises as he
came . . . "Look the Milky Way" . . . "But that was
long ago and now my inspiration is in the stardust
of the sky" . . . dim jerky faraway stars the drawer
stuck his distant hand there it is just to my shoulder.

+ " " Wife waves as her husband takes off in an autogiro. The sky is full of them. She gives orders to a
robot that does the housework. In shattered cities
muttering cripples pick through garbage.
"We set out Friday, April 23, 1976."
"June 25, 1988 Casablanca 4 P.M. A rundown suburban street."
"April 3, 1989 Marrakech . . . unlighted streets carriages with carbide lamps. It looks like an 1890 print
from some explorer's travel book."

+ " " Clocks strike the hour. Seasons change. New Year
revelers sing "Auld Lang Syne." Bell rings. Fighters
go to their corners. Referee with stop watch ends
soccer game.

+ " " Tissue, minerals, wood seen through electron
microscope.

+ " " Stars and space seen through telescope.

+ " " Distant 1920 wind and dust.

The
Dead
Child

There is something special for me about golf courses something that is supposed to happen there. I remember the golf course in Tangier but it didn't happen there. I remember a room where the lights wouldn't turn on and later in Mexico City I see myself standing on a street under dusty trees, and through the trees and some telephone wires the Mexican sky so blue it hurts to look. I see myself streaking across the sky like a star to leave the earth forever. What holds me back? It is the bargain by which I am here at all. The bargain is this body that holds me here. I am fourteen years old a thin blond boy with pale blue eyes. My mind moves from one object to another in a series of blank factual stops. I am standing now in front of the country club. There is a doorman. I stand there until he no longer pays me any attention. If I stand somewhere long enough people stop looking at me and I can walk by them. People stop looking at me and then I can. The women in the market call me *"El Niño Muerto"* *"The Dead Child"* and cross themselves when I pass. I do not like the women young or old. I do not even like female animals and bitch dogs growl and whine at sight of me. I stand there under a dusty tree and wait. The members are walking in and out. Inside the gates is a building and beyond that the golf course. I want to get into the golf course but there is no hurry. A man sees me as he passes. He is looking not at me but around the edges drawing me out of the air. He stops and asks me if I want a sandwich. I tell him yes and he takes me inside where I sit at a table under vine trellises and he orders a sandwich and an orange drink.

(I buy the dead child a sandwich. An American boy here alone. Listen I made a wrong move finding that golf course to say sir and pretend to be the dead child. Way was blocked of course.)

The drink is very cold in my throat. I sit there and say nothing. There are several other men at the table. I can see the fuzzy word bits they call their "problems." I have no problems. I am supposed to reach the golf course to get into the golf course and through the trees. I remember a room beyond that golf course I want. A little shiny ball drifts out of my head and nudges the underside of the vine trellis like a balloon trying to fly up into the sky but a thin thread always holds it back. I am outside now. It is hot. The stranger has given me some money. There is a soda kiosk outside the gates

where I buy another orange drink. Other orange drink.
I am sleepy. I look around for a place to sleep. I find
a corner where there are little round stones against the
walls. Round stones are good to sleep on almost like
sand. I make myself a place and leaning my knees
against the wall fall asleep. When I wake up the stones
are cool under my shirt. A man is standing over me. He
is pink-faced and peevish. He asks me if I am a caddy.
His caddy isn't here and he wants to know what kind
of a club this is where he comes from clubs are run
right. Yes I tell him I am a caddy. "Well then come
along" he says. The doorman stops us. I am not a caddy
of the club. The man argues. The doorman says we will
have to clear it with the steward. Then we pass. The
steward doesn't care. He gives me an armband with a
little brass disk and number. I am 18. The man is not
able to knock the ball far and can't see where it has
gone. I find his balls for him right away. And he says I
am the best caddy he ever had and what is an American
boy doing here alone? I tell him I am an orphan which
is a lie and he gives me twenty pesos. After the man has
gone into the clubhouse I find my way blocked by several Mexican caddies.
"*Bueno, gringo . . . La plata.*"
Before my father started using morphine again he sent
me to a Japanese person to learn something called
Karate. I learn these things fast because I am blank
inside, and I have no special way of moving or doing
things so one way is the same to me as another. The
Japanese man said I was the best student he ever had.
He had a shower in his studio and in the shower he
rubbed soap between my legs to look at what happens
between my legs when a white juice spurts out. If I
promised not to tell anyone he would teach me all the

secrets he never showed other students. What happens between my legs is like a cold drink to me, it is just a feeling cold round stones against my back sunshine and shadow of Mexico. I know that other people think of it as something special to do with how they feel about someone else and there is a word love that means nothing to me at all. It is just a feeling between the legs, a sort of tingle.

The boy is there in front of me making a scene he saw in some movie. He is talking out of the corner of his mouth. He spits. I flip the back of my fist to his nose and blood spurts out. He covers his face and I punch him in the stomach. He falls down and lies there trying to get the air back. It is a long time coming and he is blue in the face before he can breathe again. When I come back next day a boy seventeen years old and nice to look at with white teeth and very red gums says that I am his pal and nobody will bother his pal. I am glad of that because what I am here for has nothing to do with that kind of fighting that dogs do and there is not much difference between people and dogs. I am not a person and I am not an animal. There is something I am here for something that I have to do before I can go. That day I caddy for an American colonel who tells me about keeping my eyes on the ball in life and on the golf course and life is a game and you have to keep your eyes on the ball and keeps telling me the ball is over here and when I find it over there he doesn't like it as if the ball should be where he thinks it is when the ball is someplace else. I am careful to say sir to him and pretend to listen, but I made a wrong move finding the balls too quick and he gives me a very small tip. After that I learn not to find the ball too quick and let the player think he has found it himself. And I get bigger tips and save the money. I don't like to go home. My father is taking morphine and always tying up his arm and talking to this old junky who has a government scrip and mother drinks tequila all day and there are kerosene heaters that smoke and the smell of kerosene in the cold blue morning. I rent a room near the club and stop going home at all. Now that I have more time to myself I can see what holds me back. It is not a thread like I thought a thin thread that holds a toy balloon a thread that might break and let me blow away across the sky. It is a net that is sometimes close around me and sometimes in the sky stretched between trees and telephone poles and buildings but always around me and I am always under it.

(Way is blocked beyond that golf course. Hands tingle. Morning legs in Mexico cool under my shirt. Standing there under a dusty tree hot white juice spurts out on the golf course. It is a feeling by which I am here at all.)

One afternoon I am in the shed where we change and take showers. The boy who said I was his pal is there. The others have gone because it is a fiesta. The boy has his shirt off and his skin is smooth like polished brown wood. He peels an orange and the smell of orange fills the shed. He breaks the orange in two and gives me half and pulls me down to sit beside him on the bench. He finishes the orange and licks his fingers. Then he puts his arms around my shoulders and I can see his pants are sticking up between his legs.

"*Yo muy caliente, Johnny.* Very hot." He rubs his face against mine. "*Quiero follarte.*"

His body is warm like an animal and I feel a soft tingle in my stomach and I say "*Muy bueno.*" We take off our

clothes. The boy has two blue roses tattooed on each
side of his rump. There is a musk smell from his tight
brown nuts. He brings out a little tin of Vaseline he
carries in his hip pocket because sometimes he would
fuck a tourist for money he has always carried it. I take
the tin and rub Vaseline on his cock feeling it jump in
my hand like a frog he is standing there teeth bared
gasping . . . *"Vuelvete y aganchete Johnny"* . . . I turn
around and bend over hands braced on knees and let
myself go limp inside as he slides it in I could see out
through a little dusty window the golf course and the
sun on the lake like bits of silver paper, and when I
spurt the golf course seems to stretch out and then snap
back pulling my eggs together and I am spurting out
the trees and the grass and the lake. Silver spots boil in
front of my eyes and the window blacks out.

I am sitting on the bench my head against the wall and
he is rubbing a towel on my face. "You black out Johnny."
He touched my cheek and looked at me showing the red
gums and belched a smell of oranges. "You very good
for fuck."

I don't remember. Maybe it didn't happen like that. One
time we are swimming naked in the pond and afterward
sitting on the dam. Behind the dam is a hollow place
shaded by trees where the balls get lost and I lean back
and see one down there through the leaves. I show him
and we climb down. He gets there first and picks up the
ball. *"Veya otra pelota."* He had found another. Squatting there he turned to me smiling holding a golf ball
in each hand. Finding the balls has excited him and his
eyes shine like an animal. We are completely hidden in
a bowl of leaves. There is a smell of mud and moss and
stagnant water. We squat there in the soft mud our

knees touching. He looks down between his legs watching himself get stiff. He looks up smiling. *"Buen lugar para follar, Johnny."* I feel the tingle between my legs and I am getting stiff too. *"Esperate un momento."* He climbs up through the leaves and comes back with our clothes. He reaches in his pants pocket and brings out a little tin of Vaseline. He opens it and rubs it on himself kneeling. He motions with his hands pulling them in toward his crotch. *"Así Johnny."* I get down on my hands and knees feeling his finger inside me and my ass opens up and he is all the way in his hot quick breath on my back we shiver together and both finish in a few seconds. We sit there naked with our knees together and pass a cigarette back and forth. Then he opens his knees and shows me he is stiff again and says *"Otra vez Johnny."* This time he pulls me back between his legs and lies on his back with me on top of him kicking like a frog kicking the spurts out.

The sky stretched between my legs go limp as he slid it in afternoon I was in the shed boy had his shirt off legs together sitting on the bench he was rubbing he touched my cheek and looked and belched a smell of oranges sticking up between his legs rubbed his face against mine in the pond swimming naked treading water he puts his arm around me and pulled me against him *"Bailar Johnny?"* and I can feel him getting stiff against me. Then he floated on his back and it was sticking up in the sunlight we floated there side by side his arm around my shoulders. We swim over to the shallow water and he reaches up and gets his pants and takes the tin of Vaseline out of his pocket. The water is about three feet deep here and we are covered by the branches of a willow tree he kneels in the green light the water reaches to his tight nuts. He dries his prong with a handkerchief and rubs Vaseline on it. "Stick your ass up Johnny." I raise myself out of the water and he dries me with the handkerchief and rubs the Vaseline inside. Then he hitches his hands under my hips and pulls me up and my belly goes loose under the water and it is inside me I am spurting off into the cool water feeling his hot gobs inside. Afterward we stayed like that stuck together and inched into a foot of water and I let myself sink down until my belly was on the sand hollow place with bushes and weeds where we took off our clothes squatting there I could feel my nuts aching a little dusty window bits of silver paper trees and grass the lake smell of oranges pushed me down on my face he finished the orange and licked his red shoulder *muy caliente* very hot Johnny a boy animal knees touching stiff between his legs sitting on the bench Johnny he touched in his pants pocket and rubbed it his face against mine feeling his finger feeling him get stiff he opened it sticking up in the sunlight finished in a few seconds kicking *para follar* my legs open *vuelvete y aganchete* Johnny I turned stretched sky between my legs limp inside as he slid it in legs go limp sun on the lake the golf course I spurted off hot white juice silver spots in my eyes I remember a room there naked musty smell of his tight nuts. I don't know. Japanese person sometime. This me as another rubbed soap between my legs he would show me what happens.

My room is on a roof. I can see blue mountains across the valley. Every day after work Kiki comes to my room and brings a packet of *griefa*. "*Muy bueno para follar Johnny.*" We are sitting on the edge of the roof our legs dangling in the air. I point to the sky above the blue mountains and tell him "Some day I will go away in that direction."

He looks at me and wrinkles his forehead like a dog and says I shouldn't think such things is *muy malo.* I can see he is sad feeling the sky between us.

Not long after that he was caddy for a rich Englishman and stopped coming to the club. I only saw him once after that. He drove to the club in a Jaguar car with new clothes and a big wrist watch. The clothes didn't look right on him. He was smiling but there was sadness and fear behind the eyes. He told me the man was taking him back to England. We shook hands and he drove away. At the end of the drive he turned and waved.

Stick your ass up Johnny few seconds kicking like a frog hands under my hips and pulled me up all the way in his face water and it was inside me stretched sky between my legs limp in the cool water we stayed like that stuck together I remember a little dusty room sometimes bits of silver paper child steps out of a shower feeling his tight nuts boy animal smiling he dried me hitched my legs open his hot gobs inside came there knees touching wrinkled his forehead like a dog sadness in his eyes waved good-by from his Jaguar.

What is it that makes a man a man and a cat a cat? It was broken there. It stretched and stretched and finally broke. Look at these broken fragments: centipede man, Jaguar man, limestone plant bursting out between his legs even the pain is no longer pain of man. This had started before I came there. I found the temple in ruins the stellae broken and no one knew any more how to use the calendar. Still the dead priests and their dead gods held us in a magic net and every day the overseer

came from the ruined temple and told us what to do
and for a while longer we did it in our minds and hands
still heard still felt we could not do anything else. I was
different from the others. I watched and waited. One
day when the overseer came with his magic staff I
raised my eyes and looked at him. I saw that his eyes
were dead and there was no more power left in them.
I knocked the staff out of his hands with my stone adze.
He couldn't believe what had happened and stood
there spitting pain pictures torture of the poison fish
that turns the blood to screaming fire. I swung the adze
up between his legs. He screamed and fell down thrash-
ing around in the weeds and vines of the clearing. My
friend Xolotl watched him and smiled. He stepped over
and put a foot on the overseer's throat. Xolotl was holding a sharp planting stick. He folded one hand around
it and with the other hand pumped it up and down between his legs like rubbing himself off making fire we
call it and put out the overseer's eyes. Then he raised
the stick and brought it down leaning his weight on it.
The stick went right through the overseer's belly and
pinned him to the ground. The others had gathered and
stood in a circle watching. Xolotl got a burning stick
from the fire and built a fire between the overseer's legs.
After that we went to the temple. In a back room we
found the old priestess like a paralyzed slug. We
couldn't touch her because of the smell and a green
slime over her body so we hooked vines around her and
dragged her out into the clearing. She died before we
could torture her. We burned the body. There were
about thirty of us left five women and some babies that
would not live long. Most of them had the terrible sickness from the old priestess that rots the bones inside.
The legs go first they can't walk and crawl around like

slugs then the spine and arms. Last of all the skull. Xolotl and I gathered our gourds and stone axes and knives and went into the jungle. We knew that if we stayed there we would catch the sickness. And I didn't want to stay where the women were. Xolotl and I went into the jungle where we lived by killing animals and catching fish. I can see the fish traps and the snares for delicate little jungle deer and animals that had a shell we could catch them with our hands and kill by bashing their heads against a tree. One time I smashed one of these gourd rats and the blood spurted out all over me. I threw him on the ground and he twisted around the sharp little black point between his legs was stiff. Xolotl laughed pointing to it then we were pointing to each other and laughing and I lay down pretending I was the gourd rat throwing myself around and Xolotl shoved my legs up and we made fire I was kicking like a frog. We lay there a long time until night came and it was cold on our bodies. Then we cooked the gourd rat in its shell scooping out the soft white meat. Next morning I looked around and decided this was a good place. There was a clear blue stream with deep pools and plenty of fish and a sand bank by the stream. So we made a clearing by burning the trees and built a hut there lashed to four great posts high above the ground. The biting flies do not come into a clear space. Fish were easy to catch with our traps and lines. And we snared deer and pigs and big rats and killed monkeys and animals that go upside down in trees with our bows and throwing sticks. But we did not kill the gourd rats after that. I knew it would be unlucky to do this. We ate and swam in the river and lay on the sand bank in the sun and made fire when we wanted. A lot of our time we spent making better bows and spears and

knives. I found some very hard wood and made myself
a long knife for cutting brush. It took me a long time to
smooth the wood down with sand and when it was
finished I could cut brush out of my way with it and
once I killed a big snake with one blow. So I always
carried this knife with me. We took animal skins and
smoked them and rubbed the brains into the skins to
make covers because it was cold at night and we used
the brains to make fire together. One night I had a
dream. A blue spirit came to me and showed me the
vine where it lived and showed me how to cook the
vine with other plants and make a medicine. The next
day I found the vine and made the medicine like the
spirit showed me. When it was dark I drank a little
gourd of the medicine and gave a gourd to Xolotl. I
felt the spirit come into me like soft blue fire and everything was blue. We got down on the ground growling and
whining like animals. I climbed a tree and hung upside
down from a branch. Xolotl was a jaguar, he pulled me
down onto the sand I could hear myself whimpering my
head bursting and flying away like stars that fall in the
sky stretched the soft magic net when I spurted my insides out on the sand the blue spirit filled me Xolotl and
I were part of the spirit and the vine where it lived
growling and whining in my throat. We lay there on the
sand bar and I saw places like the clearing where the
temples were with many temples and huts and people
green fields and lakes and little white balls flying
through the air. When the medicine wore off we were
very thirsty and went to the river and drank. Then we
heard a jaguar in the jungle close by and went to the
hut and covered ourselves with skins, we were shivering. The jaguar was always around after that we stayed
in the hut at nights. We set snares and dug pits with

spikes but we could never catch him, he was always out there grunting and snarling we could see his eyes shining in the dark. Xolotl had great fear of the jaguar. He would crawl whimpering into my arms like a child when he heard it outside sniffing around our hut. We took the vines but not often because it leaves a headache. I see the pot full of medicine on a slab of stone in the middle of the hut. Xolotl and I kneel naked in front of the pot. We dip out little gourds of the medicine and both drink it down. The medicine acts very fast. We are both stiff between the legs waiting for the spirit to come. Xolotl rubs animal brains on his fish. I lay down with my legs up and just as the spirit comes he slides the fish inside me, a blue fish swimming in my body swimming away into the sky where my head bursts spilling stars. I do it to him sometimes he is braced in the door of the hut head back whining in his throat as I swim into him I can feel my face in his and finally I feel my fish touch the tip of his and glow there with soft blue fire he is spurting into the night and the river the trees and birdcalls.

There was a full moon that night. I went to set out the fish traps and left Xolotl in the hut and told him not to go out. I have my wood knife with me if the jaguar jumps on me I will shove it right into his mouth. I find a deep silver pool and drop the trap into it. Then I hear the jaguar and screams from Xolotl. I run back to the clearing and there in front of the hut I see Xolotl on all fours. He tried to say something and a growl came instead his head twisted back by something is inside pulled his mouth open and teeth tore out dripping looking at me begging for help as the yellow light came from inside and put out his eyes and they shone green in the moonlight and the jaguar was there twisting and throwing himself about growling whining spitting something out his mouth a terrible black smell. My knife had fallen and I was spitting up against a tree. For a long time I was there against the tree the sharp smell of what I had spit up in my mouth. Finally I pushed myself away and got my knife. The jaguar had gone. Next day I left the hut. I couldn't stay there. I walked in the jungle and caught a few fish. Soon I was sick with fever. The clay that holds a body together was broken. Sometimes I was a tree or a rock and I would sit in one place for light and dark hungry and thirsty. Sometimes I took the vine and saw Xolotl solid I could touch almost and spoke to him but when he wasn't there I didn't speak. After a while I couldn't eat and stopped trying to catch anything. I left the river and walked a few steps at a time came to a clearing and caught my foot in some vines and fell down. I couldn't get up the leg was broken there and I saw it was the clearing where the temple was. I crawled to the edge of the clearing under a tree. I crawled past the bones of the overseer vines growing between his legs. The others must all be dead. Soon I will be dead too. I lay there under the tree and waited pictures in my head that move and shift and go out and come back mixed with smells and feeling and the taste of white meat and the bitter vine and what I spit up from my stomach and I was Xolotl. I saw that his eyes were dead jungle deer and animals. I knock the staff out of the overseer's hand with our hands. I throw the adze up between his legs. He screams the sharp little black point stiff in weeds and vines of the clearing laughed pointing pumped it up fire we call it and put out our bodies. For a while longer we did it in our jungle. I didn't want to stay

where the women watched and waited. I raised my eyes
and looked at fish traps and snares. There was no more
power left in them a shell my stone adze he couldn't
there head against a tree spitting pain pictures to
screaming fire. Xolotl throwing myself around and I
was kicking rubbing off until night came and it was cold
on our eyes. Making bets in the hut at night hard he
was smooth I could see his eyes shining finished. A slab
of brain to make fire together I kneel naked in front of
the legs waiting for Xolotl rubs animal brains in my
body on our hands and knees eggs bursting spilling
stars animals growling and whining in the door of the
hut between the legs I was stiff and I swim into him
like a jaguar the head bursting glows in the sky soft
spurts inside out on the sand he was spurting frogs and
birdcalls there with my head against a tree it was night
now and rain fell on my face and I held out my hands
and caught enough to drink fish were easy to catch sand
bar and I saw deer and little pigs kicking and squealing
in the snares many temples and huts and people that
go upside down in trees. I see the pot full of nights in
the hut.

I lay down with my legs up to Xolotl. He slides the fish
inside me and everything was blue swimming away into
the sky and I did it to him sometimes he is Xolotl
grabbed from behind head back whining in his throat
could hear myself whimpering face in his out into the
night stars glow there with soft blue fire when I squirted
my river of running water and vines. Light and biting
flies on my leg I couldn't feel them leg like wood except
when I moved he screamed sharp fire it was broken
limestone pain in animal's leg the dead around like
birdcalls rain in my face I didn't want to stay I see the

pot and twisted hut. Xolotl, I had a dream my friend
Xolotl laughed on the overseer's throat Xolotl my legs
up to Xolotl kicking off into the sky. For a while longer
my head against a tree. I held out my hands no more
power left in them head against a tree it was cold on
my eyes moon that night solid I could touch almost
couldn't get the leg was broken and teeth tore past the
bones at me begging for help pictures all cut up knife
had fallen I lay there my pieces moved and shifted
against a tree I spit up from my stomach green when
day came and mist steamed up to the top of the high
tree just under the leaves at the top and looking down
I could see my body lying there the leg all twisted and
the face caved in lips drawn back showing teeth I could
see and hear but I couldn't talk without a throat without a tongue sun moon and stars on the face down
there worms in the leg weeds growing through the
bones. I stayed in the treetops. When I tried to get
above the trees something held me back I couldn't move
from the clearing to go above it or out to the sides.
Without words there is no time. I don't know how long
it was. Once some Indians came and built a big hut and
planted manioc and fished in the river. I came down to
watch them at night when the men did it with the
women in the hammocks I would get between their legs
feeling a soft net pulling me closer and closer. I knew
that if I got in the man's eggs and spurted into a
woman I would be helpless in the net. So I stayed away
up in the treetops. Or I tried to get close to the boys
and young men when they were away from the women.
Once by the river two boys were stiff laughing and
pointing to each other they made a line in the sand and
stood side by side and started rubbing themselves I got
close between their legs and one of them saw me and

screamed and the two boys ran back to the hut. An old man took the vine and said an evil spirit lived in the clearing. They went away and the hut fell in. After that I came down and lived in the cool stones and the vines rain sunshine a long time I was there I didn't go into the treetops any more because I knew I could not get above them and I didn't try to leave the clearing any more I stayed in stones and vines and tree trunks near the ground couldn't get any further feeling the net pulling me and teeth tearing through his gums I know that if I fear begging for help the women I will be helpless in the yellow light running into them the dead around like birdcalls helpless in the net rubbing himself and I got hands pumped it for a while my head saw me and screamed the bones at me begging for help under the stones and vines I could see my body lying there empty I couldn't talk without a throat the face down there worms in the leg twisted back

two boys

laughing off into the sky. I held out my hands. "NO." Ran back to the hut. Begging for something held me long long how long it was. Dust of the dead gods like cobwebs in the air.

Then pictures come that leave footprints. They come in boats with motors behind them. A man a woman a thin pale boy and six Indians with them. They have boxes and tools and hammocks and tents and set up their tents on the sand bar. The Indians clear away the trees in the old clearing and the man finds the ruined temple. They begin digging and bring out pots and flints and statues. The boy sleeps in a tent by himself. I was careful not to show myself at first. He fishes in the river and I follow him. Sometimes he turns around quick and looks behind him he can feel me there and I dodge into a tree. He goes and looks at the tree and walks around it and touches it. A full moon that night. I went to the boy's tent. Inside he was lying naked on his cot it was stiff between his legs he was rubbing himself. I was very close now between his legs he looked down and saw me there. He opened his mouth and I thought he might scream but he smiled and wriggled and went on rubbing himself wanting me to watch him do it. I got into his eggs squeezing through the soft tubes tighter tighter spurting gasping looking down at the hot white juice on my stomach seeing it through his eyes. I am the boy as a child lying naked on his underwear rubbing himself dust of the dead in his eyes. The pale skies fell apart. Suburban streets afternoon light bleakly clear rusting key. I left by the back door with the dust of a thousand years. I buy the dead child a sandwich. An American boy here alone. Listen I made a wrong move finding that golf course to say "sir" and pretend to be the dead child. Way was blocked of course.

Pilot lands there was his shadow . . . He was a caddy it seems . . . his smile across the golf course . . . sepia hair stirs in September wind . . . urine in narrow streets . . . slow finger . . . magazines . . . arched in gold letters solid boy out of the page . . . dim jerky his penis ejaculates . . . dawn smell of strange boy . . . naked thighs and buttocks . . . forgotten ribs rising on the bed . . . sepia picture boy getting browned on hands and knees in the wet grass knees stained distant lips parted.

Late visitor peculiar smile adroit gaze from object to object usually there was no difficulty. Does he know? "Dim in here" said the doctor . . . morning smell of the golf course . . . a ruin . . . pilot lands there was nuts . . .

dim shadow . . . vacant eyes . . . he was a caddy it seemed
stained with grass . . . water on the boy's legs . . . lean
boy by the pool . . . quivering legs in the blue morning
. . . feeling the sky rock . . . flickering dawn film stops
. . . transparent hands fading leaned down pointing
. . . "It's off." You see this? Couldn't find the micro-
waves . . . golf course . . . a ruin . . . Pilot lands there
in September wind . . . slow fingers touched his thighs
and buttocks . . . magazines . . . stained page . . . gasping feeling the cock up . . . transparent hand . . . laughing comparing movements . . . "Does he?" . . . morning
smell . . . sepia nuts . . . dawn wind between his legs
. . . dim shadow vacant eyes arched in gold letters . . .
distant lips twisted slow smile . . . the florist shop . . .
knees flickering . . . leaned down pointing . . . you know
this pain shifting outlines? You see this boy? Forgotten
ribs gasping . . . teeth bared . . . agony in his eyes . . .
pictures of war . . .

"Just
Call
Me
Joe"

The American Crusade of 1976 . . . Chorus of youthful
laughter and machine-gun noises . . . A medley of 1920
tunes . . . Boyish voices sing: "Meet me in St Louie
Louie" . . . Flickering silver titles on screen . . . General
Lewis Greenfield played by himself . . . Major William
Bradshinkle played by Ishmael Cohen . . . The Mayor
played by Green Tony . . . The CIA man played by
Charles Ahearn . . . His two assistants played by Henry
Coyne and Joe Rogers . . . The young lieutenant played
by Jerry Wentworth . . . Wild boys played by native
boys on locations . . .

A grimy red-brick building. National Guard Post 23
St Louis Missouri. Through a dusty barred window the
gymnasium where businessmen in their middle and
late thirties are learning Karate judo and commando

tactics. The officers puff and lunge and throw each other awkwardly. Clearly some of them will require the services of a skilled osteopath in the foreseeable future. Vista of sagging bellies and fat buttocks in the locker room as the officers in various states of undress practice the holds . . . "No it works like this." Country club party table loaded with food and drinks. A guard officer has had one too many. He approaches a portly guest . . . "Bovard, I could kill you in twenty seconds . . . ten as a matter of fact . . . like this . . . I put my elbow against your Adam's apple throw a knee into your left kidney and bring the heel of my hand up sharp under your chin."

"Hey, what do you think you're doing?" The two men reel, lose balance and fall overturning the table of food. They roll around flailing at each other in a welter of lobster Newburgh, chicken salad, punch and baked Alaska.

"In the inland cities of America, men who are entering on middle age dream of a great task a great mission. They find a leader and a spokesman in General Lewis Greenfield."

General Greenfield on a white horse speaks from the top of Art Hill. He is a pompous red-faced man of fifty with a clipped white mustache.
Click of cameras.
"Over there." He points eastward with a statuesque arm. "Across the Atlantic is a sink of iniquity . . . A latter-day Sodom and Gomorrah. The reports compiled by our intelligence operators are difficult for decent people to believe" . . . Camera shows the CIA man, a tape recorder slung around his neck rests on his paunch. Naked youths flash on screen smoking hashish . . . "You

may say that what happens in a foreign land is no concern of ours. But the vile tentacles of that evil are reaching into decent American homes" . . . Suburban couple
in the boy's room school banners on the wall. They are
reading a note

Dear Mom and Dad:
I am going to join the wild boys. When you read this I
will be far away.

Johnny

"All over America kids like Johnny are deserting this
country and their great American heritage suborned by
the false promises of Moscow into a life of drugs and
vice. I say to you all that wherever anarchy, vice and
foul corruption rears the swollen hood of a cobra to
strike at everything we hold sacred, the very heart of
America is threatened. Can we stand idly by while our
youth, the very lifeblood of this great nation, drains
away into foreign sewers? Can we stand idly by while
the stench of corruption draws ever closer to our own
borders?" . . . Members of the audience cough and
cover their faces with handkerchiefs . . . "This plague
is spreading in every direction as deadly in its workings
as anything in the world. I am personally subscribing
ten million dollars for an expedition to crush the obscene thing once and for all."

"The press takes it up of course. National guard units
of every state in the union send officers and men.
Thousands of volunteers have to be turned away. Who
are these volunteers? Well I guess you could call them
plain ordinary American folk, decent tax-paying citizens
fed up with Godless anarchy and vice. You all know
the Wallace folks cop on the corner guy next door."

Scenes from World War I as the soldiers take leave of their loved ones.

  "Over there over there over there
  The Yanks are coming the Yanks are coming
  And we won't come back till it's over over there"

Crap games on the troopship. The boys are glad to be away from their wives in an atmosphere of rough male camaraderie. Touch down at Casa red carpets, brass band, the Mayor there with keys of the city. Dinner for the officers in the Mayor's house. The Mayor speaks through an interpreter. "He say very glad Americans here. He say wild boys very bad cause much trouble. Police here not able do anything." As the interpreter talks plates are heaped with steak, catfish, turkey, mashed potatoes, ham and eggs, hominy grits, fried chicken, hush puppies, hog jowl and turnip greens all stacked on top of each other. The camera picks out a young captain.

"The young captain is thinking 'why these are good people like people in America are good. I guess good people are the same the world over, it's just as simple as that!' "

"He say after dinner when ladies go he tell you things what wild boy do. He say time for big cleanup. He say Americans like vacuum cleaner."

The interpreter bellows in imitation of a Hoover. The officers chuckle politely all except the CIA man and his two assistants who look sour and suspicious.

The ladies have left. "He say" . . . sound track cuts to silent film.

Music from "The Afternoon of a Faun." Nude youths smoking hashish. A runaway American boy is led in. He looks around and blushes bright red. A bare arm passes him a hashish pipe. He smokes, coughs, then begins to laugh. Crazed by hashish he peels off his shirt. He unbuckles his belt. "That's enough" says General Greenfield gruffly pulling at his mustache. The officers look at each other then look away in embarrassment clearing their throats. They gulp brandy with one accord. Servants rush forward to fill the glasses which are emptied again and again.

"Well I guess we know now what we're up against" says the General huskily. "Jesus think of decent American kids . . . Why it could happen to your kid or mine . . ."

Deeply moved the young captain excuses himself and steps into the garden.

"He is proud of being an American. Proud of the decent American thing he is doing. Why when he thinks of those queers and dope freaks . . ."

A naked youth from the film appears in front of him. He swings wildly at a privet hedge and cuts his hand to the bone. He looks at his bloody hand.

"As we advance toward Marrakech cheering crowds strew flowers in our path."

Cheering faces turn cold and blank behind American backs. Cheering boys in this scene later appear in wild-boy roles. Two English officers watch the parade. One states flatly "They are the poorest excuse for soldiers I have ever seen."

"Arriving in Marrakech we are met by the Mayor, a fat smiling Italian."

"JUST CALL ME JOE" he says.

"He has put the officers' corps up in his villa. It makes me uneasy the guards everywhere with tommy guns looking us over."

The guards appear in shots from 1920 gangster films, black Cadillacs careening down city streets.

"And I can't tell him enough about my Eyetie buddies in the service, the one who got it in Vietnam I act it all out and die on the floor in my own arms taking both parts even the Eyeties were embarrassed but respectful too I'd outgroveled them one. Then we sit down to a good spaghetti dinner and I am telling the Mayor about Joe Garavelli's in St Louis spaghetti and roast-beef sandwiches after the skating rink."

The old broken point of origin St Louis Missouri. Mark and John, the Dib, Jimmy the Shrew, wild boys skating to old tunes and waltzes. The Blue Danube, Over the Waves, My Blue Heaven, Those Little White Lies, Stardust, What'll I Do with Just A Photograph To Remind Me of You, Tonight You Belong To Me, Meet Me In St Louie, Louie spinning lawn sprinklers, country clubs, summer golf courses, frogs in 1920 roads, cool basement toilets, a boy's twitching foot, the Varsity Drag, iced tea and fried chicken at The Green Inn, classrooms, silver stars, the old family soap opera . . . "When evening is nigh" . . . the dark city dying sun naked boy hugging his knees . . . "I hurry to my" . . . music across the golf course a crescent moon cuts the film sky . . . "blue heaven" . . . "The night that you told me" . . . decent people know they are right . . . "those little white lies" . . . White white white as far as the eye can see ahead a blinding flash of white fed up with Godless anarchy and corruption the cabin reeks of exploded stars. Made machine-gun noises as he came "Look the Milky Way" . . . "But that was long ago and now my inspiration is in the stardust of the sky" . . . dim jerky faraway stars the drawer stuck his distant hand there it is just to my shoulder . . . "What'll I do when you are far away" . . . far pale sun colored photo unbuttoned his shirt . . . "and I am blue" . . . colored photo has something written on it . . . "What'll I do with just a photograph" . . . *"Vuelvete y aganchete"* . . . "to remind me of you" . . . trying to focus to remember face on the grimy pillow . . . "If I had a talking picture of you" . . . "Abrupt question brought me Mister" . . . "I would play it every time I felt blue" . . . street shadows in his eyes . . . "I would give ten shows a day" . . . Mark squirms his shorts off . . . "and a midnight matinee" . . . standing in the dark room the boy said "I've come a long way" . . . "Oh! with the dawn I know you'll be gone" . . . dust of young hand fading flickering thighs and buttocks . . . "But tonight you belong to me" . . . dawn shirt on the bed smell of young nights urine in the gutter click of distant heels . . . "Meet me in St Louie Louie" . . . The broken point of origin St Louis Missouri muscle magazines over the florist shop pants down sad old soap opera. Johnny steps into the shower. Two boys turn with knowing smiles. What he sees turns Johnny's face bright red feeling the red pull in his groin sunsets freckles autumn leaves sun cold on a thin boy with freckles silver paper in the wind frayed sounds of a distant city. The boys are taking off their skates. They go across the Street to Joe Garavelli's. Faraway spaghetti roast-beef sandwiches the camera stops Joe's silver smile.

"You would have liked Joe" I am telling the Mayor.

Joe Garavelli and the Mayor sit at a kitchen table. Joe's fat smiling wife brings up a bottle of red wine from the cellar.

"Those tommy guns in the corridor aren't the only thing

makes me uneasy. It's Joe himself. I've seen him before."

Rome, Berlin, Naples, Saigon, Benghazi . . . "Here come
the Germans the Americans the English. Change the
welcome signs." Willkommen Deutschen is hastily taken
down and Hello! Johnny put up. "Sell your sister your
daughter your grandmother." Cigarettes chocolate and
K rations change hands.

"I have the uneasy feeling of being in someone else's
old film set. Yes I've seen Joe before. The smiling mouth
the cold treacherous eyes."
"We're going to win this war" I said quietly to a French
comte . . . (But loud enough so the CIA man can hear
me.) . . . *Le Comte* lifted his glass.
"I drink to the glorious victory of our brave American
allies over little boys armed with slingshots and scout
knives."
"I thought this was pretty nasty and told him America
was just doing a job we all knew had to be done and
we knew we were right and we knew we were going
to win, it was just as simple as that. *Le Comte* emitted
a sharp cold bray of laughter. Information as to the
number and disposition of enemy forces is vague and
contradictory."

The officers walk around passing out chocolate and
cigarettes. Boys point in various directions. These boys
appear later in wild-boy parts.

"They are somewhere to the south. All agree we have
only to show ourselves and the boys will surrender in
cheering crowds to escape their Russian and Chinese
slave drivers. This seems logical enough. None the less
we make careful plans for a military operation."

General Greenfield studying maps and pointing. "Just here is an old Foreign Legion fort. That should do for a base camp. Three days march from here."

"We set out Friday, April 23, 1976 the soldiers marching along singing 'Hinky Dinky Parlez Vous' and 'The Caissons Go Rolling Along.' The singing gets less and less lusty and finally stops altogether. It is evident the men are badly out of condition. It takes us six days to reach the fort. Three hundred yards from the fort the general holds up his hand and stops the column. All the officers whip out field glasses. The door is open three sand foxes sniffing around in the courtyard. They look up and see us and scamper off over a sand dune."

Fort from *Beau Geste*. Dry well thistles in the courtyard. The officers walk through empty rooms their footsteps muted by sand. The walls give off a spectral smell of stale sweat. "This will do for the wardroom."

KILROY JACKED OFF HERE   B. J. MARTIN   D & D

        BUEN LUGAR PARA FOLLAR   QUIÉN ES?   A.D. KID

Phallic drawings . . . (Two Arab boys. One shoves a finger in and out his fist. The other nods. They pull off their jellabas.) Three American boy scouts look at the drawings . . . "Let's play, huh?"

"How you mean play?" says the third who is younger.

"We'll show you." Younger boy blushes and wets his lips as he sees what they are doing. Phallic shadows on a distant wall. Camera shifts hastily like embarrassed eyes. General Greenfield clears his throat and pulls at his mustache. "Sergeant!"

"Yes sir"

"Get a detail to clean this place out . . . and uh whitewash these walls."

"Yes sir."

"It is the General's plan to leave half our force in the fort select the youngest and fittest, proceed south and engage the enemy. He has named the fort Portland Place after a block in St Louis."

Two hours out of base camp several hundred boys waving white flags burst over a sand dune and rush toward us screaming.

"Hello! Johnny."

"You very good man."

"Thank you very much one cigarette."

"Chocolate."

"Corned bif."

"Americans very good peoples."

"Russians Chinese very bad." They snarl and spit.

"We show you where water is where make camp."

"Kif anything what you like."

"My sister she live near here."

Things seem to be working out. The boys will lead us to the Communist guerrillas who organize them and that will be that. The boys are vague as to the location of the guerrillas. "That way." They point south.

They find no water but demand extra rations for looking. Camping places they pick always seem to feature some particular inconvenience a nest of scorpions a cave full of snakes.

The boys rush around with sticks beating at the snakes knocking down tents upsetting pots of food stampeding the mules.

"The boys are under foot day and night and more of them keep surrendering. Must be a thousand of them now. Rations are becoming a problem. There is something about these boys that doesn't add up. I have a feeling that they are not young at all."

General Greenfield, the CIA man and Major Brad-shinkle walk through the camp. Boys jump up in front of them. "Hello! Johnny." The boys point and make machine-gun noises. The CIA man looks at them with cold disfavor. "Little bastards" he mutters.
"Just kids" says the General.
The CIA man grunts. "Something wrong here General. They're not all that young."
As the officers turn away young eyes go cool and alert looking after them with alien calculation.

"As a professional soldier I have the gravest reserva-tions about the entire expedition. I keep these thoughts to myself. A blacklisting from that CIA bastard could mean the loss of my job. I think too much. Always have. The security checks at West Point used to give me headaches and I got the habit of taking codeine pills. I have a good supply of pills I bought in Casa for the chronic headache of this expedition. Not the first time a bad habit saved a man's life."

A lunar photograph of shallow craters. "This Place of Sand Fox. Good place to camp."
The CIA man looks around sourly. "I don't see any sand foxes."
"Sand fox very shy. When you see sand fox nobody live near."
As soon as camp is made the officers are summoned to the General's tent.
Something has to be done about the boys.
The CIA man says they are obvious saboteurs smartest thing would be to machine-gun the lot of them.
The Press Officer objects that such precipitate action would jeopardize our public image.
"What public image? While you jokers were lapping up

booze and feeding your face Joe and Henry and me
had a look around. They don't any of them like us one
bit. That Mayor in Marrakech would cut your throat
if you were down quick as he'd sell you his mother if
you were on top. I tell you those brats are leading us
straight into an ambush."

The General raises his hand for silence. "We will send
the main body of boys back to base camp under guard
retaining a few as guides. At the first hint of treachery
we will radio base camp and the prisoners will be shot.
This condition of course to be clearly impressed on the
guides."

The CIA man grunted. "Well the sooner we get them
under guard the better."

As we left the tent after receiving the General's decision
about fifty boys came to meet us. "We got very important informations where base camp. *Muchos Chinos*
there." The boys pull their eyes up at the corners yacking in false Chinese. The effect was irresistibly comic.
Then the boys laughed. They laughed and laughed
laughing *inside* us all the officers were laughing doubled
over holding their guts in. The boys sneezed and
coughed. They posted themselves in front of the CIA
man and began to hiccup. He glared at them then hiccuped loudly again and again. It was happening all over
the camp, a chorus of hiccups laughing, sneezing,
coughing. The CIA man grabbed a megaphone and hiccuped out like a great frog: "Machine/hick/gun/hick/the
little/hick/bastards!" And he reached for his forty-five.
The boys dodged away. Wracked by hiccups his shots
went wild killing two of our own men. The General
grabbed the megaphone: "Men . . . ACHOO, ACHOO,
ACHOO . . ."

"God bless you General ha! ha! ha!" said Rover Jones one of his old yard nigras. Soldiers were rolling on the ground pissing in their pants and then the boys were on them with sticks knees feet and elbows. They snatched up guns dodged behind some well-spaced rocks and opened up at point-blank range. It was a shambles. In a few seconds hundreds lay dead under a withering fire from the boys. And the contagion was spreading rapidly. One look at someone taken with the fits and you have it. And the sneezes blow down wind like tear gas. It is not just a ventriloquist act. It is a trained killer virus. At least half the men were already affected and those who weren't have been goofing off somewhere survivors are all the goldbricks in this stumblebum outfit. The CIA man caught a splash of forty-five slugs right across his fat gut. He hiccuped a rope of blood and went down like a sack of concrete. The General was still on his feet trying to massa the sneezes when a rifle bullet drilled him between the eyes. He flopped on his face and bounced. In the immortal words of Hemingway "the hole in the back of his head where the bullet came out was big enough to put your fist in if it was a small fist and you wanted to put it there." I am in command. I begin to breathe "heavy duty vast army ripped to shreds." I grab the megaphone: "Keep your heads men. All who can walk move out. Move out and take cover. If your buddies have the laugh sneeze cough fits don't look at them, don't go near them. Move out and take cover." The wild boys stay hidden and pour it on. I lose a lot of men before we get clear of the camp and take cover. Suddenly the boys stop shooting. I figure they are in the camp grabbing all the guns and ammo they can carry. After that they will move back and arm their con-

federates. Knowing how fast they can move over these
rocks no use following with N.G. soldiers still blazing
away at nothing. I give a cease fire. I doubt if the kids
have lost a boy. Laughing, coughing, sneezing in the
distance sounds like a congress of hyenas. Fifteen
minutes and everything is quiet. The hiccups were the
last to go. When we get back to camp not a man is left
alive. Those who hadn't been shot had died from the
fits, died spitting blood. It is a murderous biological
weapon and I owe my immunity to God's Own Medicine. I turn the General over on his back and I will
say one last thing for him he makes a fine-looking
corpse. Burial is out of the question, too many stiffs. So
I read the burial of the dead for morale and the bugler
plays taps. We make camp a mile away. I am on the
radio to base camp for reinforcements and medical
supplies and *water* . . . "Art Hill calling Portland Place
. . . Art Hill calling Portland Place . . . Come in please
. . . Come in please . . ." I try for half an hour. Radio
silence on Portland Place. From that point on I was
looking out for Billy B., St Louis Encephalitis by birth
and nickname.
"Save the water for those with a chance of making it."
The young lieutenant gulps "Yes sir."
Quicker we get these stretcher cases off our back the
better. They don't live long without water. Then we
are hit by an epidemic of hepatitis the yellow sickness
lives in straw the Arabs say and I remember the boys
were always bringing us straw to sleep on. Hepatitis
cases need bed rest and fruit juice. We are not in a
condition to supply either one. When they got too weak
to follow we left them there. It was the only thing to
do worthless bastards and I hoped to make full colonel
out of these slobs. The boys escort us with sniper fire

deadly accurate keeping about three hundred yards behind us well spaced out. So we are pretty well thinned out by the time we sight base camp. There it is in the distance an old film set. We advance cautiously. Three hundred yards. I scan the fort through my field glasses. Nobody in sight. No flag. The door is open and I see three sand foxes sniffing around in the courtyard. We move slowly forward ready to take cover. Two hundred yards. One hundred yards. Fifty yards. We are standing in front of the fort now. It looks exactly as it looked when we arrived from Marrakech. Guns at the ready we move into the courtyard. Thistles the dry well. Nothing nobody. I take the young lieutenant and start a tour of the rooms. Sand on the floor silence, emptiness. It occurs to me I don't want a witness when I reach the wardroom in case any legal tender is lying about unliberated among other considerations. I turn to the lieutenant: "I'm going on alone, lieutenant. You go back and stay with the men. In case anything happens to me there must be a surviving officer."
He looks at me with deep admiration and says "Yes sir." God is he dumb.
The wardroom is empty.

KILROY JACKED OFF HERE   B. J. MARTIN   D & D
   BUEN LUGAR PARA FOLLAR   QUIÉN ES?   A.D. KID

I remember the man left in charge of the fort one Colonel Macintosh a druggist in civilian life. He was a huge heavy-boned man of a sluggish malignant disposition. And the horrible religious constipated captain who had been a prison psychologist in Texas. Captain Knowland if my memory serves.

KILROY JACKED OFF HERE   B. J. MARTIN   D & D
   BUEN LUGAR PARA FOLLAR   QUIÉN ES?   A.D. KID

No colonel no captain no desk no maps . . . nothing.
Empty room justlikethat. I feel a shiver in the back
of my neck as if a small animal with a cold nose has
just nuzzled me there. Even my memory picture of
those two jokers is dimming out. I can hardly see their
faces. Two people I disliked very much a long time ago,
so long I forget what they looked like. The colonel is
dissolving in front of my eyes to dust and shredded
memories where the old Macintosh Drug Store used to
be. What force could have moved that heavy-boned
lump of congealed hate? Perhaps something as simple
as a hiccup of time. Empty room justlikethat. Now I
know what the crusades are about. The young are an
alien species. They won't replace us by revolution. They
will forget and ignore us out of existence. Place of the
Sand Foxes was simply a casual entertainment with
just the right shade of show you. Leave us alone.
Leaning on the wall I scrawled a note. "Have been
ordered back to the flagship"

Colonel Macintosh

I walk back to the courtyard and show it to the lieutenant thanking God for his dumbness. He says "Well
at least they might have left us some water and pro-
visions." "Are you questioning the actions of a superior
officer lieutenant?" His Adam's apple bobs up and down
"Uh! no sir." "Good. Get the men on their feet. We're
moving out."

Dimming out I can hardly see one hundred yards. Field
glasses *mucho* long time ago. Thistles dry well another
species

Kilroy ordered back to flagship

Colonel Phallic Drawings

A sand fox sniffing the back of my neck. "Let's play,

Macintosh" . . . laughing hiccup of time. God is dumb. Long long radio silence on Portland Place.

"No water. More jaundice. Second day we sight a village, palm trees, a pool. I shout a warning over the megaphone but those I.Q. 80s rush straight into a fire hose of rifle- and machine-gun fire from the village. I pull back what's left. No use trying to take the village with the boys under cover. We skirt the village and go on. Of the 20,000 soldiers who set out under General Greenfield's command 1500 ragged yellow delirious survivors stagger into the American compound in Casa. (*Le Comte* emitted a sharp cold bray of laughter.) I am not with them. I know they will want someone to take the rap for this disaster and it isn't going to be me. And I know some nosy FBI bastard will want to know what happened to the payroll. I have a new name now and a nice business in Casa."

Joe Garavelli's restaurant in the suburbs of Casablanca. Wild Boys Welcome.

"JUST CALL ME JOE."

"Mother and I Would Like to Know"

The uneasy spring of 1988. Under the pretext of drug control suppressive police states have been set up throughout the Western world. The precise programing of thought feeling and apparent sensory impressions by the technology outlined in bulletin 2332 enables the police states to maintain a democratic façade from behind which they loudly denounce as criminals, perverts and drug addicts anyone who opposes the control machine. Underground armies operate in the large cities enturbulating the police with false information through anonymous phone calls and letters. Police with drawn guns irrupt at the Senator's dinner party a very special dinner party too that would tie up a sweet thing in surplus planes.

"We been tipped off a nude reefer party is going on

here. Take the place apart boys and you folks keep your clothes on or I'll blow your filthy guts out."

We put out false alarms on the police short wave directing patrol cars to nonexistent crimes and riots which enables us to strike somewhere else. Squads of false police search and beat the citizenry. False construction workers tear up streets, rupture water mains, cut power connections. Infra-sound installations set off every burglar alarm in the city. Our aim is total chaos.

Loft room map of the city on the wall. Fifty boys with portable tape recorders record riots from TV. They are dressed in identical grey flannel suits. They strap on the recorders under gabardine topcoats and dust their clothes lightly with tear gas. They hit the rush hour in a flying wedge riot recordings on full blast police whistles, screams, breaking glass crunch of nightsticks tear gas flapping from their clothes. They scatter put on press cards and come back to cover the action. Bearded Yippies rush down a street with hammers breaking every window on both sides leave a wake of screaming burglar alarms strip off the beards, reverse collars and they are fifty clean priests throwing petrol bombs under every car WHOOSH a block goes up behind them. Some in fireman uniforms arrive with axes and hoses to finish the good work.

In Mexico, South and Central America guerrilla units are forming an army of liberation to free the United States. In North Africa from Tangier to Timbuctu corresponding units prepare to liberate Western Europe and the United Kingdom. Despite disparate aims and personnel of its constituent members the underground is agreed on basic objectives. We intend to march on the police machine everywhere. We intend to destroy the police machine and all its records. We intend to destroy all dogmatic verbal systems. The family unit and its cancerous expansion into tribes, countries, nations we will eradicate at its vegetable roots. We don't want to hear any more family talk, mother talk, father talk, cop talk, priest talk, country talk *or* party talk. To put it country simple we have heard enough bullshit.

I am on my way from London to Tangier. In North Africa I will contact the wild-boy packs that range from the outskirts of Tangier to Timbuctu. Rotation and exchange is a keystone of the underground. I am bringing them modern weapons: laser guns, infra-sound installations, Deadly Orgone Radiation. I will learn their specialized skills and transfer wild-boy units to the Western cities. We know that the West will invade Africa and South America in an all-out attempt to crush the guerrilla units. Doktor Kurt Unruh von Steinplatz, in his four-volume treatise on the Authority Sickness, predicts these latter-day crusades. We will be ready to strike in their cities and to resist in the territories we now hold. Meanwhile we watch and train and wait.

I have a thousand faces and a thousand names. I am nobody I am everybody. I am me I am you. I am here there forward back in out. I stay everywhere I stay nowhere. I stay present I stay absent.

Disguise is not a false beard dyed hair and plastic surgery. Disguise is clothes and bearing and behavior that leave no questions unanswered . . . American tourist with a wife he calls "Mother" . . . old queen on the make . . . dirty beatnik . . . marginal film producer . . . Every article of my luggage and clothing is carefully planned to create a certain impression. Behind this impression I can operate without interference for a time. Just so long and long enough. So I walk down Boulevard Pasteur handing out money to guides and

shoeshine boys. And that is only one of the civic things
I did. I bought one of those souvenir matchlocks clearly
destined to hang over a false fireplace in West Palm
Beach Florida, and I carried it around wrapped in
brown paper with the muzzle sticking out. I made
inquiries at the Consulate
"Now Mother and I would like to know."
And "MOTHER AND I WOULD LIKE TO KNOW"
in American Express and the Minzah pulling wads of
money out of my pocket "How much shall I give
them?" I asked the vice-consul for a horde of guides
had followed me into the Consulate. "I wonder if you've
met my congressman Joe Link?"
Nobody gets through my cover I assure you. There is no
better cover than a nuisance and a bore. When you see
my cover you don't look further. You look the other way
fast. For use on any foreign assignment there is nothing
like the old reliable American tourist cameras and light
meters slung all over him.
"How much shall I give him Mother?"
I can sidle up to any old bag she nods and smiles it's all
so familiar "must be that cute man we met on the plane
over from Gibraltar Captain Clark welcomes you aboard
and he says: 'Now what's this form? I don't read
Arabic.' Then he turns to me and says 'Mother I need
help.' And I show him how to fill out the form and after
that he would come up to me on the street this cute
man so helpless bobbing up everywhere."
"What is he saying Mother?"
"I think he wants money."
"They all do." He turns to an army of beggars, guides,
shoeshine boys and whores of all sexes and makes an
ineffectual gesture.
"Go away! Scram off!"

"One dirham Meester."

"One cigarette."

"You want beeg one Meester?"

And the old settlers pass on the other side. No they don't get through my cover. And I have a lot of special numbers for emergency use . . . Character with wild eyes that spin in little circles believes trepanning is the last answer pull you into a garage and try to do the job with an electric drill straightaway.

"Now if you'll kindly take a seat here."

"Say what is this?"

"All over in a minute and you'll be out of that rigid cranium."

So word goes out stay away from that one. You need him like a hole in the head. I have deadly old-style bores who are translating the Koran into Provençal or constructing a new cosmology based on "brain breathing." And the animal lover with exotic pets. The CIA man looks down with moist suspicious brow at the animal in his lap. It is a large ocelot its claws pricking into his flesh and every time he tries to shove it away the animal growls and digs in. I won't be seeing that Bay of Pigs again.

So I give myself a week on the build-up and make contact. Colonel Bradly knows the wild boys better than any man in Africa. In fact he has given his whole life to youth and it would seem gotten something back. There is talk of the devil's bargain and in fact he is indecently young-looking for a man of sixty odd. As the Colonel puts it with engaging candor: "The world is not my home you understand here on young people."

We have lunch on the terrace of his mountain house. A heavily wooded garden with pools and paths stretches

down to a cliff over the sea. Lunch is turbot in cream
sauce, grouse, wild asparagrass, peaches in wine. Quite
a change from the grey cafeteria food I have been sub-
jected to in Western cities where I pass myself off as
one of the faceless apathetic citizens searched and
questioned by the police on every corner, set upon by
brazen muggers, stumbling home to my burglarized
apartment to find the narcotics squad going through
my medicine chest again. We are served by a lithe
young Malay with bright red gums. Colonel Bradly
jabs a fork at him.
"Had a job getting that dish through immigration. The
Consulate wasn't at all helpful." After lunch we settle
down to discuss my assignment.
"The wild boys are an overflow from North African
cities that started in 1969. The uneasy spring of 1969
in Marrakech. Spring in Marrakech is always uneasy
each day a little hotter knowing what Marrakech can
be in August. That spring gasoline gangs prowled the
rubbish heaps, alleys and squares of the city dousing
just anybody with gasoline and setting that person on
fire. They rush in anywhere nice young couple sitting
in their chintzy middle-class living room when hello!
yes hello! the gas boys rush in douse them head to foot
with a pump fire extinguisher full of gasoline and I got
some good pictures from a closet where I had prudently
taken refuge. Shot of the boy who lit the match he let
the rank and file slosh his couple then he lit a Swan
match face young pure, pitiless as the cleansing fire
brought the match close enough to catch the fumes.
Then he lit a Player with the same match sucked the
smoke in and smiled, he was listening to the screams
and I thought My God what a cigarette ad: Clambake
on a beach the BOY there with a match. He is looking

at two girls in bikinis. As he lights the match they lean forward with a LUCKYSTRIKECHESTERFIELD-OLDGOLDCAMELPLAYER in the bim and give a pert little salute. The BOY turned out to be the hottest property in advertising. Enigmatic smile on the delicate young face. Just what is the BOY looking at? We had set out to sell cigarettes or whatever else we were paid to sell. The BOY was too hot to handle. Temples were erected to the BOY and there were posters of his face seventy feet high and all the teenagers began acting like the BOY looking at you with a dreamy look lips parted over their Wheaties. They all bought BOY shirts and BOY knives running around like wolf packs burning, looting, killing it spread everywhere all that summer in Marrakech the city would light up at night human torches flickering on walls, trees, fountains all very romantic you could map the dangerous areas sitting on your balcony under the stars sipping a Scotch. I looked across the square and watched a tourist burning in blue fire they had gasoline that burned in all colors by then . . . (He turned on the projector and stepped to the edge of the balcony) . . . Just look at them out there all those little figures dissolving in light. Rather like fairyland isn't it except for the smell of gasoline and burning flesh.

"Well they called in a strong man Colonel Arachnid Ben Driss who cruised the city in trucks rounded up the gas boys took them outside the walls shaved their heads and machine-gunned them. Survivors went underground or took to the deserts and the mountains where they evolved different ways of life and modes of combat."

The Wild Boys

"They have incredible stamina. A pack of wild boys can cover fifty miles a day. A handful of dates and a lump of brown sugar washed down with a cup of water keep them moving like that. The noise they make just before they charge . . . well I've seen it shatter a greenhouse fifty yards away. Let me show you what a wild-boy charge is like." He led the way into the projection room. "These are actual films of course but I have arranged them in narrative sequence. As you know I was with one of the first expeditionary forces sent out against the wild boys. Later I joined them. Seen the charges from both sides. Well here's one of my first films."

The Colonel reins in his horse. It is a bad spot. Steep hills slope down to a narrow dry river bed. He scans the hillsides carefully through his field glasses. The hills slope up to black mesas streaked with iron ore.

"Since our arrival in the territory the regiment had been feted by the local population who told us how glad they were the brave English soldiers had come to free them from the wild boys. The women and children pelted us with flowers in the street. It reeked of treachery but we were blinded by the terrible Bor Bor they were putting in our food and drink. Bor Bor is the drug of female illusion and it is said that he who takes Bor Bor cannot see a wild boy until it is too late.

"The regiment is well into the valley. It is a still hot afternoon with sullen electricity in the air. And suddenly there they are on both sides of us against the black mesas. The valley echos to their terrible charge cry a hissing outblast of breath like a vast WHOOO? . . . Their eyes light up inside like a cat's and their hair stands on end. And they charge down the slope with incredible speed leaping from side to side. We open up with everything we have and they still keep coming. They aren't human at all more like vicious little ghosts. They carry eighteen-inch bowie knives with knuckle-duster handles pouring into the river bed above and below us leaping down swinging their knives in the air. When one is killed a body is dragged aside and another takes his place. The regiment formed a square and it lasted about thirty seconds.

"I had prudently stashed my assets in a dry well where peering out through thistles I observed the carnage. I saw the Colonel empty his revolver and go down under ten wild boys. A moment later they tossed his bleeding head into the air and started a ball game. Just at dusk the wild boys got up and padded away. They left the bodies stripped to the skin many with the genitals cut off. The wild boys make little pouches from human testicles in which they carry their hashish and *khat*. The setting sun bathed the torn bodies in a pink glow. I walked happily about munching a chicken sandwich stopping now and again to observe an interesting cadaver.

"There are many groups scattered over a wide area from the outskirts of Tangier to the Blue Desert of Silence . . . glider boys with bows and laser guns, roller-skate boys—blue jockstraps and steel helmets, eighteen-inch bowie knives—naked blowgun boys long hair down their backs a kris at the thigh, slingshot boys, knife throwers, bowmen, bare-hand fighters, shaman boys who ride the wind and those who have control over snakes and dogs, boys skilled in bone-pointing and Juju magic who can stab the enemy reflected in a gourd of water, boys who call the locusts and the fleas, desert boys shy as little sand foxes, dream boys who see each other's dreams and the silent boys of the Blue Desert. Each group developed special skills and knowledge until it evolved into humanoid subspecies. One of the more spectacular units is the dreaded Warrior Ants made up of boys who have lost both hands in battle. They wear aluminum bikinis and sandals and tight steel helmets. They are attended by musicians and dancing boys, medical and electronic attendants who carry the weapons that are screwed into their stumps, buckle them into their bikinis, lace their sandals, wash and anoint their bodies with a musk of genitals, roses, carbolic soap, gardenias, jasmine, oil of cloves, ambergris and rectal mucus. This overpowering odor is the first warning of their presence. The smaller boys are equipped with razor-sharp pincers that can snip off a finger or sever a leg tendon. And they click their claws as they charge. The taller boys have long double-edged knives that can cut a scarf in the air screwed into both stumps."

On the screen the old regiment same canyon same Colonel. The Colonel sniffs uneasily. His horse rears and neighs. Suddenly there is a blast of silver light reflected from helmets knives and sandals. They hit the regiment like a whirlwind the ground ants cutting tendons, the shock troops slashing with both arms wade through the regiment heads floating in the air behind them. It is all over in a few seconds. Of the regiment there are no survivors. The wild boys take no prisoners. The first to receive attention were those so seriously wounded they could not live.

The Colonel paused and filled his kif pipe. He seemed to be looking at something far away and long ago and I flinched for I was a snippy Fulbright queen at the time dreading some distastefully intimate *experience* involving the amorous ghost of an Arab boy. What a bore he is with his tacky old Lawrence sets faithful native youths dying in his arms.

"As I have told you the first wild-boy tribes were fugitive survivors from the terror of Colonel Arachnid ben Driss. These boys in their early- and mid-teens had been swept into a whirlwind of riots, burning screams, machine guns and lifted out of time. Migrants of ape in gasoline crack of history. Officials denied that any repressive measures had followed nonexistent riots.

" 'There is no Colonel Arachnid in the Moroccan Army' said a spokesman for the Ministry of the Interior.

"No witnesses could be found who had noticed anything out of the ordinary other than the hottest August in many years. The gasoline boys and Colonel Arachnid were hallucinated by a drunken Reuters man who became temporarily deranged when his houseboy deserted him for an English pastry cook. I was myself the Reuters man as you may have gathered."

Here are the boys cooking over campfires . . . quiet valley by a stream calm young faces washed in the dawn before creation. The old phallic Gods of Greece and the assassins of Alamout still linger in the Moroccan hills like sad pilots waiting to pick up survivors. The piper's tune drifts down a St Louis street with the autumn leaves.

On screen an old book with gilt edges. Written in golden script *The Wild Boys*. A cold spring wind ruffles the pages.

Weather boys with clouds and rainbows and Northern lights in their eyes study the sky.

Glider boys ride a blue flash sunset on wings of pink and rose and gold laser guns shooting arrows of light. Roller-skate boys turn slow circles in ruined suburbs China-blue half-moon in the morning sky.

Blue evening shadows in the old skating rink, smell of empty locker rooms and moldy jockstraps. A circle of boys sit on a gym mat hands clasped around the knees. The boys are naked except for blue steel helmets. Eyes move in a slow circle from crotch to crotch, silent, intent, they converge on one boy a thin dark youth his face spattered with adolescent pimples. He is getting stiff. He steps to the center of the circle and turns around three times. He sits down knees up facing the empty space in the circle where he sat. He pivots slowly looking at each boy in turn. His eyes lock with one boy. A fluid click a drop of lubricant squeezes out the tip of his phallus. He lies back his head on a leather cushion. The boy selected kneels in front of the other studying his genitals. He presses the tip open and looks at it through a lens of lubricant. He twists the tight nuts gently runs a slow precise finger up and down the shaft drawing lubricant along the divide line feeling for sensitive spots in the tip. The boy who is being masturbated rocks back hugging knees against his chest. The circle of boys sits silent lips parted watching faces calmed to razor sharpness. The boy quivers transparent suffused with blue light the pearly glands and delicate coral tracings of his backbone exposed.

A naked boy on perilous wings soars over a blue chasm. The air is full of wings . . . gliders launched from skis and sleds and skates, flying bicycles, sky-blue gliders with painted birds, an air schooner billowing white sails stabilized by autogiros. Boys climb in the rigging and wave from fragile decks.

Boy on a bicycle with autogiro wings sails off a precipice and floats slowly down into a valley of cobblestone streets and deep-blue canals. In a golf course sand pit hissing snake boys twist in slow copulations guarded by a ring of cobras.

The legend of the wild boys spread and boys from all over the world ran away to join them. Wild boys appeared in the mountains of Mexico, the jungles of South American and Southeastern Asia. Bandit country, guerrilla country, is wild-boy country. The wild boys exchange drugs, weapons, skills on a world-wide network. Some wild-boy tribes travel constantly taking the best cannabis seeds to the Amazon and bringing back cuttings of the Yage vine for the jungles of Southern Asia and Central Africa. Exchange of spells and potions. A common language based on variable transliteration of a simplified hieroglyphic script is spoken and written by

the wild boys. In remote dream rest areas the boys
fashion these glyphs from wood, metal, stone and
pottery. Each boy makes his own picture set. Sea chest
in an attic room, blue wallpaper ship scenes, copies of
Adventure and *Amazing Stories,* a .22 pump-action rifle
on the wall. A boy opens the chest and takes out the
words one by one . . . The erect phallus which means in
wild-boy script as it does in Egyptian to stand before
or in the presence of, to confront to regard attentively
. . . a phallic statue of ebony with star sapphire eyes a
tiny opal set in the tip of the phallus . . . two wooden
statues face each other in a yellow oak rocking chair.
The boy statues are covered with human skin tanned
in ambergris, carbolic soap, rose petals, rectal mucus,
smoked in hashish and burning leaves . . . a yellow-haired
boy straddles a copper-skinned Mexican, feet braced
muscles carved in orgasm . . . an alabaster boy lights up
blue inside, piper boy with a music box, roller-skate boy
of blue slate with a bowie knife in his hand, a post card
world of streams, freckled boy, blue outhouses covered
with morning glory- and rose vines where the boys jack
off on July afternoons shimmers in a Gysin painting . . .
little peep shows . . . flickering silver titles . . . others
with colors and odors and raw naked flesh . . . tight
nuts crinkle to autumn leaves . . . blue chasms . . . a
flight of birds. These word objects travel on the trade
routes from hand to hand. The wild boys see, touch,
taste, smell the words. Shrunken head of a CIA man
. . . a little twisted sentry his face cyanide blue . . .
(A highly placed narcotics official tells a grim President: "The wild-boy thing is a cult based on drugs,
depravity and violence more dangerous than the hydrogen bomb.")
At a long work bench in the skating rink boys tinker

with tiny jet engines for their skates. They forge and grind eighteen-inch bowie knives bolting on handles of ebony and the ironwoods of South America that must be worked with metal tools . . .

The roller-skate boys swerve down a wide palm-lined avenue into a screaming blizzard of machine-gun bullets, sun glinting on their knives and helmets, lips parted eyes blazing. They slice through a patrol snatching guns in the air.

Jungle work bench under a thatched roof . . . a ten-foot blowgun with telescopic sights operated by compressed air . . . tiny blowguns with darts no bigger than a mosquito sting tipped with serum jaundice and strange fevers . . .

In houseboats, basements, tents, tree houses, caves, and lofts the wild boys fashion their weapons . . . a short double-edged knife bolted to a strong spring whipped back and forth slices to the bone . . . kris with a battery vibrator in the handle . . . karate sticks . . . a knob of ironwood protrudes between the first and second fingers and from each end of the fist . . . loaded gloves and knuckle-dusters . . . crossbows and guns powered by thick rubber sliced from an inner tube. These guns shoot a lead slug fed in from a magazine above the launching carriage. Quite accurate up to twenty yards . . . a cyanide injector shaped like a pistol. The needle is unscrewed from the end of the barrel, the pistol cocked by drawing back a spring attached to the plunger. A sponge soaked in cyanide solution is inserted, the needle screwed back in place. When the trigger releases the spring a massive dose of cyanide is squeezed into the flesh causing instant death. When not in use the needle is capped by a Buck Rogers Death Ray . . . cyanide darts and knives with hollow perforated blades

. . . a flintlock pistol loaded with crushed glass and cyanide crystals . . .

Cat boys fashion claws sewn into heavy leather gloves that are strapped around the wrist and forearm, the incurving hollow claws packed with cyanide paste. The boys in green jockstraps wait in a tree for the jungle patrol. They leap down on the soldiers, deadly claws slashing, digging in. Boys collect the weapons from twisted blue hands. They wash off blood and poison in a stream and pass around a kif pipe.

Snake boys in fish-skin jockstraps wade out of the bay. Each boy has a venomous speckled sea snake coiled around his arm. They move through scrub and palm to an electric fence that surrounds the officer's club. Through flowering shrubs Americans can be seen in the swimming pool blowing and puffing. The boys extend their arms through the fence index finger extended. The snakes drop off and glide toward the swimming pool.

A jungle patrol in Angola . . . suddenly black mambas streak down from trees on both sides of their path mouths open fangs striking necks and arms lashing up from the ground. Mamba boys black as obsidian with mamba-skin jockstraps and kris glide forward.

Five naked boys release cobras above a police post. As the snakes glide down the boys move their heads from side to side. Phalluses sway and stiffen. The boys snap their heads forward mouths open and ejaculate. Strangled cries from the police box. Faces impassive the boys wait until their erections subside.

Boys sweep a cloud of bubonic fleas like a net with tiny black knots into an enemy camp.

A baby- and semen black market flourished in the corrupt border cities, and we recruited male infants from birth. You could take your boy friend's sperm to

market, contact a broker who would arrange to insemi-
nate medically inspected females. Nine months later
the male crop was taken to one of the remote peaceful
communes behind the front lines. A whole generation
arose that had never seen a woman's face nor heard a
woman's voice. In clandestine clinics fugitive technicians experimented with test-tube babies and cuttings.
Brad and Greg got out just under a "terminate with
extreme prejudice" order . . . And here is their clinic in
the Marshan Tangier. Laughing, comparing a line of
boys jack off into test tubes . . .

Here is a boy on his way to the cutting room. Brad and
Greg explain they are going to take a cutting from the
rectum very small and quite painless and the more
excited he is when they take the cutting better chance
there is that the cutting will *make* . . . They arrange
him on a table with his knees up rubber slings behind
the knees to keep him spread and turn an orgone funnel
on his ass and genitals. Then Brad slips a vibrating cutting tube up him. These are in hard rubber and plastic
perforated with pinpoint holes. Inside is a rotary knife
operated from the handle. When the ring expands it
forces bits of the lining through the holes which are
then clipped off by the knife.

Brad switches on the vibrator. The boy's pubic hairs
crackle with blue sparks, tight nuts pop egg-blue
worlds in air . . . Some boys red out rose-red delicate
sea-shell pinks come rainbows and Northern lights . . .
Here are fifty boys in one ward room, bent over hands
on knees, on all fours, legs up. Greg throws the master
switch. The boys writhe and squirm, leap about like
lemurs, eyes blazing blue chasms, semen pulsing sparks
of light. Little phantom figures dance on their bodies,

slide up and down their pulsing cocks, and ride the
cutting tubes . . .
Little boy without a navel in a 1920 classroom. He
places an apple on the teacher's desk
"I am giving you back your apple teacher."
He walks over to the blackboard and rubs out the word
MOTHER.
Flanked by Brad and Greg he steps to the front of the
stage and takes a bow to an audience of cheering boys
eating peanuts and jacking off.
Now the cuttings are no longer needed. The boys create
offspring known as Zimbus. Brad and Greg have retired
to a remote YMCA. Zimbus are created after a battle
when the forces of evil are in retreat . . .
The first to receive attention were those so seriously
wounded that they could not live . . . A red-haired boy
who had been shot through the liver was quickly
stripped of bikini and sandals and propped up in a sitting position. Since they believe that the spirit leaves
through the back of the head a recumbent position is
considered unfavorable. The pack stood around the
dying boy in a circle and a technician deftly removed
the helmet. I saw then that the helmet was an intricate
piece of electronic equipment. The technician took an
eighteen-inch cylinder from a leather carrying case. The
cylinder is made up of alternate layers of thin iron and
human skin taken from the genitals of slain enemies. In
the center of the cylinder is an iron tube which protrudes slightly from one end. The tube was brought
within a few inches of the boy's wound. This has the
effect of reducing pain or expediting the healing of a
curable wound. Pain-killing drugs are never used since
the cell-blanketing effect impedes departure of the

spirit. Now a yoke was fitted over the boy's shoulders
and what looked like a diving helmet was placed over
his head. This helmet covered with leather on the outside is in two pieces one piece covering the front of the
head the other the back. The technician made an ad-
justment and suddenly the back section shot back to
the end of the yoke where it was caught and held by
metal catches. Two sections are of magnetized iron
inside the technician adjusting the direction of magnetic
flow so that by a repelling action the two sections spring
apart pushing the spirit out the back of the head. The
flow is then reversed so that the two sections are pulling
toward each other but held apart. This pulls the spirit
out. A luminous haze like heat waves was quite visibly
draining out the boy's head. The dancing boys who had
gathered in a circle around the dying boy began playing their flutes a haunting melody of Pan pipes train
whistles and lonely sidings as the haze shot up into the
afternoon sky. The body went limp and the boy was
dead. I saw this process repeated a number of times.
When the dying had been separated from their bodies
by this device those with curable wounds were treated.
The cylinder was brought within an inch of the wound
and moved up and down. I witnessed the miracle of
almost immediate healing. A boy with a great gash in
his thigh was soon hobbling about the wound looking
as if it had been received some weeks before. The fire-
arms were divided among the dancing boys and attendants. The boys busied themselves skinning the genitals
of the slain soldiers pegging the skins out and rubbing
in pastes and unguents for curing. They butchered the
younger soldiers removing the heart and liver and bones
for food and carted the cadavers some distance from the
camp. These chores accomplished the boys spread out

rugs and lit hashish pipes. The warriors were stripped
by their attendants massaged and rubbed with musk.
The setting sun bathed their lean bodies in a red glow
as the boys gave way to an orgy of lust. Two boys
would take their place in the center of a rug and copulate to drums surrounded by a circle of silent naked
onlookers. I observed fifteen or twenty of these circles,
copulating couples standing, kneeling, on all fours,
faces rapt and empty. The odor of semen and rectal
mucus filled the air. When one couple finished another would take its place. No words were spoken only
the shuddering gasps and the pounding drums. A
yellow haze hovered over the quivering bodies as the
frenzied flesh dissolved in light. I noticed that a large
blue tent had been set up and that certain boys desig-
nated by the attendants retired to this tent and took
no part in the orgy. As the sun sank the exhausted
boys slept in naked heaps. The moon rose and boys
began to stir and light fires. Here and there hashish
pipes glowed. The smell of cooking meat drifted
through the air as the boys roasted the livers and
hearts of the slain soldiers and made broth from the
bones. Desert thistles shone silver in the moonlight. The
boys formed a circle in a natural amphitheater that
sloped down to a platform of sand. On this platform
they spread a round blue rug about eight feet in diameter. The four directions were indicated on this rug by
arrows and its position was checked against a compass.
The rug looked like a map crisscrossed with white lines
and shaded in striations of blue from the lightest egg
blue to blue black. The musicians formed an inner
circle around the rug playing on their flutes the haunting tune that had sped the dying on their way. Now one
of the boys who had taken no part in the recent orgy

stepped forward onto the rug. He stood there naked sniffing quivering head thrown back scanning the night sky. He stepped to the North and beckoned with both hands. He repeated the same gesture to the South East and West. I noticed that he had a tiny blue copy of the rug tattooed on each buttock. He knelt in the center of the rug studying the lines and patterns looking from the rug to his genitals. His phallus began to stir and stiffen. He leaned back until his face was turned to the sky. Slowly he raised both hands palms up and his hands drew a blue mist from the rug. He turned his hands over palms down and slowly lowered them pulling blue down from the sky. A pool of color swirled about his thighs. The mist ran into a vague shape as the color shifted from blue to pearly grey pink and finally red. A red being was now visible in front of the boy's body lying on his back knees up transparent thighs on either side of his flanks. The boy knelt there studying the red shape his eyes molding the body of a red-haired boy. Slowly he placed his hands behind knees that gave at his touch and moved them up to trembling ears of red smoke. A red boy was lying there buttocks spread the rectum a quivering rose that seemed to breathe, the body clearly outlined but still transparent. Slowly the boy penetrated the phantom body I could see his penis inside the other and as he moved in and out the soft red gelatin clung to his penis thighs and buttocks young skin taking shape legs in the air kicking spasmodically a red face on the rug lips parted the body always more solid. The boy leaned forward and fastened his lips to the other mouth spurting sperm inside and suddenly the red boy was solid buttocks quivering against the boy's groin as they breathed in and out of each other's lungs locked together the

red body solid from the buttocks and penis to the
twitching feet. They remained there quivering for
thirty seconds. A red mist steamed off the red boy's
body. I could see freckles and leg hairs. Slowly the boy
withdrew his mouth. A red-haired boy lay there breathing deeply eyes closed. The boy withdrew his penis,
straightened the red knees and lay the newborn Zimbu
on his back. Now two attendants stepped forward with
a litter of soft leather. Carefully they lifted the Zimbu
onto the litter and carried him to the blue tent.

Another boy stepped onto the rug. He stood in the
center of the rug and leaned forward hands on knees
his eyes following the lines and patterns. His penis
stiffened. He stood upright and walked to the four directions lifting his hands each time and saying one word
I did not catch. A little wind sprang up that stirred
the boy's pubic hairs and played over his body. He began to dance to the flutes and drums and as he danced
a blue will-o'-the-wisp took shape in front of him shifting from one side of the rug to the other. The boy
spread out his hands. The will-o'-the-wisp tried to
dodge past but he caught it and brought his arms together pulling the blue shape against him. The color
shifted from blue to pearly grey streaked with brown.
His hands were stroking a naked flank and caressing a
penis out of the air buttocks flattened against his body
as he moved in fluid gyrations lips parted teeth bared.
A brown body solid now ejaculated in shuddering gasps
sperm hitting the rug left white streaks and spots that
soaked into the crisscross of white lines. The boy held
the Zimbu up pressing his chest in and out with his
own breathing quivering to the blue tattoo. The Zimbu
shuddered and ejaculated again. He hung limp in the

other's arms. The attendants stepped forward with another litter. The Zimbu was carried away to the blue tent.

A boy with Mongoloid features steps onto the rug playing a flute to the four directions. As he plays phantom figures swirl around him taking shape out of moonlight, campfires and shadows. He kneels in the center of the rug playing his flute faster and faster. The shape of a boy on hands and knees is forming in front of him. He puts down his flute. His hands mold and knead the body in front of him pulling it against him with stroking movements that penetrate the pearly grey shape caressing it inside. The body shudders and quivers against him as he forms the buttocks around his penis stroking silver genitals out of the moonlight grey then pink and finally red the mouth parted in a gasp shuddering genitals out of the moon's haze a pale blond boy spurting thighs and buttocks and young skin. The flute player kneels there arms wrapped tightly around the Zimbu's chest breathing deeply until the Zimbu breathes with his own breathing quivering to the blue tattoo. The attendants step forward and carry the pale blond Zimbu to the blue tent.

A tall boy black as ebony steps onto the rug. He scans the sky. He walks around the rug three times. He walks back to the center of the rug. He brings both hands down and shakes his head. The music stops. The boys drift away.

It was explained to me that the ceremony I had just witnessed was performed after a battle in case any of the boys who had just been killed wished to return and that those who had lost their hands might wish to do since the body is born whole. However most of the spirits

would have gone to the Blue Desert of Silence. They
might want to return later and the wild boys made
periodic expeditions to the Blue Desert. The Zimbus
sleep in the blue tent. Picture in an old book with
gilt edges. The picture is framed with roses intertwined . . . two bodies stuck together pale wraith of a
blond boy lips parted full moon a circle of boys in
silver helmets naked knees up. Under the picture in
gold letters. Birth of a Zimbu. Boy with a flute charm-
ing a body out of the air. I turn the page. Boy with
Mongoloid features is standing on a circular rug. He
looks down at his stiffening phallus. A little wind stirs
his pubic hairs. Buttocks tight curving inward at the
bottom of the two craters a round blue tattoo miniature
of the rug on which he stands. I turn the page. A boy is
dancing will-o'-the-wisp dodges in front of him. I turn
the page. Will-o'-the-wisp in his arms gathering outline
luminous blue eyes trembling buttocks flattened against
his body holding the Zimbu tight against his chest. His
breathing serves as the Zimbu's lungs until his breathing
is his own quivering to the blue tattoo children of lonely
sidings, roses, afternoon sky. I turn the pages. Dawn
shirt framed in roses dawn wind between his legs distant lips.

The Penny Arcade Peep Show

1. A copper coil going away pulling Audrey's flesh out in a stream of yellow light flash of showers buttocks soap you can see the hair on legs whispering phallic shadows in the locker room . . . "Wanta feel something nice Audrey?" . . . milky smell of phantom sperm.

2. Two copper coils going away peeling layers of old photos like dead skin . . . Tree house on a bluff over the valley. On closer inspection it is seen to be a reconstructed houseboat firmly moored between the branches of a giant oak and secured by anchor chains to an overhead branch. Branches swaying in the wind give the boat a slight roll. Standing at the wheel Audrey looks out across a post card valley stream winding by a village of brick houses and slate

roofs a distant train. Kiki the Mexican boy who lives
down by the railroad tracks helped Audrey assemble
the boat. There is a kitchen and shower. Often the
boys spend weekends there. Kiki rolls cigarettes
from a weed that grows along the tracks. Smoking
these cigarettes makes Audrey laugh and get stiff at
the same time. Flower smell of young hard-ons the
two boys under the shower. Kiki kissed Audrey on
the mouth and slid a soapy finger up his ass whispering the finger's question. After that Audrey used to
bend over the wheel Kiki pumping him out across
the afternoon sky.

3. Three copper coils going away . . . a red-haired boy
called Pinkie came to live in the village. His father
was a painter and the boy made sketches and water
colors. Audrey has invited Pinkie up to the tree house
to spend the night. Going up the ladder to the boat
Kiki gooses Pinkie with his middle finger. The boy
blushes and laughs nervously. In the boat the boys
wash their dusty feet under the shower. They peel
oranges and drink Whistle. Kiki passes around a weed
cigarette. He squints at Pinkie through the smoke
and asks an abrupt question. Pinkie looks down at his
bare feet blushing . .
"Yeah. Sometimes."
"Is the hair around your dick red?"
"Sure."
"Take down your pants and show us."
"You guys too."
"You first."
"All right."
Pinkie takes off his shirt. Grinning he drops his pants
and shorts and stands there flushed with excitement

as his swaying cock stiffens. Kiki and Audrey strip.
Sunlight in pubic hairs red black yellow. Kiki touches
Pinkie's crotch with gentle precise fingers.

"Come up here and steer Pinkie." He leads Pinkie
to the wheel. "Bend over and wrap your arms around
it . . . That's right . . . spread your legs apart."

Trembling Pinkie obeys. As Audrey watches Kiki
parts the buttocks rubbing Vaseline around the exposed rectum. Pinkie sighs deeply and his ass opens
as if a pink mollusk had surfaced in the quivering
flesh.

"All yours Audrey" . . . Audrey, his blue eyes shining,
moves behind Pinkie Kiki would never let him this will
be his first time can see the red ass hairs the soft flesh
sucks him in playing with Pinkie's tight nuts running
his finger lightly up and down the shaft Pinkie
whimpers and wriggles against him Kiki's fingers prying Audrey's buttocks apart as Kiki squirms forward.

4. Four copper coils going away . . . Seen from above
   as a *Saturday Evening Post* cover . . . Pinkie waves to
   a distant train. Audrey laughed in the afternoon sky.
   Was a window of laughter shook the valley.

1. A copper coil coming in spatters Audrey's naked
   body with little bubbles of light that break and tingle
   his ass opens in a stream of yellow light laughter
   jumps phallic shadows sun licks flesh naked legs
   whispering light.

2. Two copper coils coming in . . . "Let's see you naked"
   . . . He licks his lips feeling the locker room pressure
   in his groin out of control knowing drops his pants
   and shorts swaying cock stiffens eyes shining sketches
   and water colors his ass opens a pink wheel soft clinging Audrey has him to the hilt.

3. Three copper coils coming in . . . "Didn't I see you at Webber's Post?" . . . Bleakly clear I am the boy as a child lying naked on his underwear rubbing himself my room and me there faded pink curtains yellow wallpaper three sketches. Flesh opens a silent door.

4. Four copper coils coming in . . . We're going to give you the last boy . . . yellow light late afternoon rubbing himself my room and me there dropped his pants and shorts eyes shining excitement . . . "Didn't I see you at Webber's Post?" . . . Bleakly clear I am the boy figure on the post card road faded down a street of memories blue light frayed sky . . . "You see this?" . . . Dim in on a stained silent door . . . "All yours Audrey" . . . tree house color pictures can see the red ass hairs buttocks carbolic soap in a stream down the shaft two boys laughing makes me think back child rubbing his pants pressure the swaying pink curtains and yellow wallpaper afternoon hills this whispering dust sea shells in an attic room face seen from a train maybe . . . the last boy.

The setting sun lights Audrey's dead burnt-out face.

Colonel Bradly advised me to contact the roller-skate and bicycle gangs operating in the suburbs of Casablanca.
"They are close enough to the regular guerrilla units so you can orient yourself. Through them you can arrange the special training necessary to contact the more inaccessible groups. Some of the wild boys do not talk at all. Others have developed cries, songs, words as weapons. Words that cut like buzz saws. Words that vibrate the entrails to jelly. Cold strange words that fall like icy nets on the mind. Virus words that eat the brain

to muttering shreds. Idiot tunes that stick in the throat round and round night and day.

" 'here me is' 'HERE ME IS' 'here ME IS' 'HERE me is' 'HERE me IS' 'HERE ME is.' "

Ever hear the CIA talking baby talk? Ever see Narcotics Agents hula-hooping to idiot mambo? Ever seen a China Watcher clawing at the words in his throat? It gives you a funny feeling. You need special training to contact those boys . . . When you get to Casa go to the Cafe Azar on Niño Perdido where the old Fell Bridge Hotel used to be. The shoeshine boy is your contact there. He is known as the Dib."

Owing to the shortage of petrol there is no air service and very few cars on the ground. More primitive methods of transport have come back into use: stage coaches, balloons, camel- and mule trains, litters, rickshaws, covered wagons. There are a few steam railways in operation privately owned by the rich who live in feudal splendor on vast estates. When you want to travel you go to the Travel Pool a square surrounded by inns and brothels. You look around. There is always some way of getting where you want to go. Here is a steam truck that looks as if it will explode without more ado. I give it a wide berth. There are several obviously lethal rocket ships, a band of twenty Swedes with rucksacks on their way to the Atlas mountains, a mule train of guerrillas headed for Guillamine. A Commander with yachting cap supervises a lethargic Arab who is sewing patches on his balloon. "We've got a jolly good south wind coming up" he tells me. I decide to chance the Commander's balloon and settle down at a nearby inn for a long wait. About four in the afternoon his Arab wheels out a gas cylinder and by five the balloon is ready and we cast off. The balloon leaks audibly and the Commander reels about in the basket dead drunk smoking a cigar. The leak brings us down fifty miles north of Casa. I leave the Commander there and take a stage coach the rest of the way.

The
Penny Arcade
Peep Show

◄ The Chicago atomic scientists insist that the atom bomb should not be used under any circumstances.

► The atom bomb explodes over Hiroshima spreading radioactive particles.

◄ The old tycoon sat on a high balcony in a deck chair, his dark glasses glinting enigmatically in the afternoon sun. He was obsessed with immortality and spent vast sums on secret research. He didn't intend to share it with any groveling peasants. Serums, replacements of worn-out parts, were only a makeshift reprieve. He wanted more than that. He wanted to live forever. If the speed of light could be achieved or approached . . He was impatient with scientists who said this was impossible. "I don't pay them to tell me what they can't do . . . Why a rocket with enough push behind it . . ." He did not like to hear the word DEATH spoken in his presence and suddenly boyish voices were singing "The worms crawl in and the worms crawl out."

He looked up to see a fleet of gliders drifting toward him on the afternoon wind piloted by youths in skeleton suits. Silver arrows rained from the sky.

▶ Audrey was in an Eastern market. Steep wooden ramps sloped dizzily down like a roller coaster lined with fruit-and-vegetable stalls. He was sitting at the wheel of a heavy wooden cart with iron wheels and bumper. The cart picked up speed, crashing into stalls, spilling fruit and vegetables which rolled down the ramp. Dogs and chickens and children scattered out from under his wheels "I don't care who I run into" he thought. He was possessed by an ugly spirit of destroying speed. He caught sight of a large cobra by the side of the ramp and swerved to run over it. Writhing fragments flew up in his face. He screamed.

◀ Armored cars, sirens screaming converge on a rocket installation.

▶ Too late. The rocket blasts off a mad tycoon at the controls. The earth blows up behind him. As his ship rides the blast he screams: "HI HO SILVER YIPPEEE." He is riding ahead of a posse tossing sticks of dynamite over his shoulder. Sharp smell of weeds from old Westerns.

◀ House of the General city of Resht in Northern Persia 1023 A.D. The General is poring over maps as he plans an expedition against Alamout. The Old Man of the Mountain represented for the General

pure demonic evil. Certainly this man had committed the terrible sin referred to in the Koran of
aspiring to be God. The whole Ishmaelian sect was a
perfect curse, hidden, lurking, ready to strike, defy-
ing all authority . . . "Nothing is true. Everything is
permitted."

"Blasphemy" the General screamed starting to his
feet. "Man is made to submit and obey."

Acting out a final confrontation with this Satan he
paces the room fingering the jeweled handle of his
sword. He cannot return to his maps. Still muttering
imprecations he steps into the garden. Under the
orange trees an old man is cutting weeds stopping
from time to time to hone his knife on a stone, hands
like brown silk unhurried and steady. He has worked
there as a gardener for ten years and the General has
stopped seeing him years ago. He is as much a part
of the garden as the orange trees and the irrigation
ditch flashing like a sword in sun. The House of the
General is built on a high hill. Orange groves, date
palms, rosebushes, pools and opium poppies stretch
down to massive walls. The Caspian Sea gleams in
the distance. But the General can find no peace in
his garden today. The Old Man peers at this through
the orange leaves with laughing blue eyes and stabs
up at him from the irrigation ditch. Forgetting the
presence of his servant the General raises his
clenched fist to a distant mountain and screams:
"Satan, I will destroy you forever."

▶ Squatting in front of the sharpening stone the old
gardener tests the edge of his blade against his
thumb. The old gardener tested the edge of ten years
unhurried eyes seeing the General long ago in a blaze

of white light. He straightens up with all the power of his bent knees thrusting up under the rib cage knife seeking a distant point beyond the general's sagging body, HIS knife flashing like a compass needle straight from Alamout.

The
Wild
Boys
Smile

June 25, 1988 Casablanca 4 P.M. The Café Azar was on a rundown suburban street you could find in Fort Worth Texas. CAFÉ AZAR in red letters on plate glass the interior hidden from the street by faded pink curtains. Inside a few Europeans and Arabs drinking tea and soft drinks. The shoeshine boy came over and pointed to my shoes. He was naked except for a dirty white jockstrap and leather sandals. His head was shaved and a tuft of hair sprouted from the crown. His face had been beautiful at some other time and place now broken and twisted by altered pressure, the teeth stuck out at angles features wrenched out of focus body emaciated by distant hungers. He sat on his box and looked up at me squinting snub-nosed legs sprawled

apart one finger scratching his jock. The skin was white
as paper hairs black and shiny lay flat on his skinny legs.
As he shined my shoes with deft precise movements his
body gave off a dry musty smell. In one corner of the
room I saw a green curtain in front of which two boys
were undressing. The corner was apparently at a level
below the café floor since I could not see their legs
below the knee. One of the boys had stripped to pink
underwear sticking out straight at the fly. The other
patrons paid no attention to this tableau. The boy
jerked his head toward the two actors who were now
fucking in upright position lips parted in silent gasps.
He put a finger to one eye and shook his head. The
others could not see the boys. I handed the boy a coin.
He checked the date and nodded. The Dib checked the
date of nettles feet twisted by the altered disk.
"Long time nobody use jump" he said leg hairs covered
with mold. The gun jumping, crumpled twisted body,
his face floating there the soldier's identification card
and skinny in picture.
"I was too." He pointed to his thin body. He picked up
his box. I followed him through the cafe. When I walk
with the Dib they can't see me. Buttocks were smooth
and white as old ivory. The corner of the green curtain
was a sunken limestone square two steps down from the
café floor dry musty smell of empty waiting rooms a
worn wood bench along one wall. Embedded in the
stone floor was an iron disk about five feet in diameter
degrees and numbers cut in its edges brass arrows indicating N. S. E. W. This compass floated on a hydraulic
medium. In the center of the disk a marine compass
occupied a teakwood socket. Two pairs of sandals worn
smooth and black mounted on spring stilts eight inches

in height were spaced eighteen inches apart so that two people standing in the sandals would be one behind the other the center of the disk and the marine compass exactly between them. The springs were bolted to pistons which projected on shafts from the iron disk. The sandals were at different levels. Evidently they could be adjusted by raising or lowering the shafts. At a sign from the boy I stripped off my clothes smooth hands guided by film tracks I was to bend over and brace my hands on my knees. The boy reached in his box and took out a tape measure that ended in a little knob. He measured the distance from my rectum to the floor. With a round key which fitted into locks in the support shafts he adjusted the level of the two pairs of sandals on the spring stilts. He stood up and stripped off his jockstrap scraping erection. He mounted one pair of spring stilts and strapped his feet into the sandals poised on the springs nuts tight and precise as bearings his phallus projected needle of the compass the disk turned until it was facing the green curtain which moved slightly as if it might cover an opening, ass arrows indicating N. S. E. W. feet a taste of metal in the mouth 18 penis floated I stepped in the sandals from behind knees his skinny arms and I was seeing the take from outside at different levels soft machine my ass a rusty cylinder pearly glands electric click blue sparks my spine into his I bend over and brace vibrating on the springs iron smell of rectal mucus streaking across the sky a wrench spurting soft tracks a distant gun jumping the soldier's identification disk covered with mold his smile across tears of pain squinting up at me snub-nosed hands at the crotch worn metal smell of the gun as my feet touched the iron disk a soft shock tingled up my legs to the crotch. The penis floated. I

stepped onto the stilts in front of the boy and he adjusted the straps from behind. I bent over and braced
my hands on my knees. He hooked his skinny arms
under my shoulders leg hairs twisted together a slow
greased pressure and I was seeing the take from outside transparent soft machine ass a rusty cylinder phallus a piston pumping the pearly glands blue sparks and
my spine clicked back into his then forward his head
in mine eyes steering through a maze of turnstiles. Stop.
Click. Start. Stop. Click. Start streaking across the sky
a smear of pain gun jumping out trees weed-grown
tracks rusty identification disk covered with mold.
Click. Green Pullman curtain. Click. "You wanta see
something?" Click. Penis floated. Click. Distant 1920
wind and dust. Click. Bits of silver paper in a wind
across the park. Click. Summer afternoon on car seat to
the thin brown knees. Click. His smile across the golf
course. Click. Click. Click. See on back what I mean each
time place dim jerky faraway. The curtain stirs slightly.
Click. Sharp smell of weeds. The curtain was gone. The
feeling in my stomach when a fast elevator stops as
we landed in a stone kiosk by an abandoned railroad
dried shit urine initials

KILROY JACKED OFF HERE   B. J. MARTIN   D & D
    BUEN LUGAR PARA FOLLAR   QUIÉN ES?   A.D. KID

We unlaced our feet and stepped down from the
springs. The disk was rusty and rust had stained the
stone around its edges.
"Long time nobody use jump" the boy said pointing. I
saw my clothes in a corner covered with mold. The boy
shook his head and handed me a white jockstrap from
his box.
"Clothes no good here. Easy see clothes. Very hard see

this." He pointed to his thin body.

Then I felt the thirst my body dry and brittle as a dead leaf.

"Jump take your last water Meester. We find spring."

Above the kiosk was a steep hillside. The boy made his way through brush that seemed to move aside for him leaving a tunnel of leaves. He dropped on his knees and parted a tangle of vines. A deep black spring flowed from a limestone cleft. We scooped up clear cold water with our hands. The boy wiped his mouth. From the hillside we could see a railroad bridge, a stream, ruined suburbs.

"This bad place Meester. Patrols out here."

The boy reached into his box and brought out two packages of oiled paper tied with cord. He undid the cord and unwrapped two snub-nosed thirty-eight revolvers the hammers filed off, the grips cut short, the checked walnut stocks worn smooth. The revolvers could only be used double action. The grip came to the middle of my palm held precisely in place by two converging mounds of hard flesh like part of my hand. The boy pointed with his revolver indicating the path we were going to take into the town under the bridge along the stream. There was no sign of life in the town ruined villas overgrown with vines empty cafés and courtyards. The boy led the way. He would move forward in a burst of speed for fifty feet or so then stop poised sniffing quivering. We were walking along a path by a white wall.

"DOWN MEESTER!"

A burst of machine-gun fire ripped into the wall. I threw myself into a ditch full of nettles. Pain poured out my arm like a fire hose gun jumping. Three soldiers about forty feet away crumpled twisted and fell. The boy got up blowing smoke from his gun barrel body covered with red welts. In a burst of speed his feet reached the bodies. I had fired twice. He had fired four times. Every bullet had found a vital spot. One soldier lay on his back legs twisted under him a hole in the middle of his forehead. Another was still alive twitching convulsively as blood spurted from a neck wound. The third had been shot three times in the stomach. He lay face down hands clasped over his stomach, his machine gun still smoking three yards away white smoke curling up from the grass. It was a subdivision street, lawns, palm trees, bungalows built along one side vacant lot opposite could have been Palm Beach Florida empty ten years weeds palm branches in the driveways, windows broken, no sign of life. The boy went through pockets with expert fingers: a knife, identification papers, cigarettes, a packet of kif. Two of the soldiers had been carrying carbines the third a submachine gun. "No good Czech grease gun" the boy said and kicked it aside after unclipping the magazine. The carbines he propped against a palm tree. We dragged the bodies into a ditch. The pressure of pain lent maniac power and precision to our movements. We rushed about dragging palm branches to heap on the bodies. We couldn't stop. We found a Christmas tree bits of silver paper twisted in its brown needles and heaved it over onto the dead soldiers. We paused panting shivering and looked at each other. Spots boiled in front of my eyes blood pounded to neck and crotch feeling the strap tighten hot squeezing pressure inside stomach intestines a muffled explosion as scalding diarrhea spurted down the backs of our trembling thighs the Boy Scout Manual floated across summer afternoons the boy's cracked broken film voice seeing the take from outside the shelf I rummaged

in the shelf knew what I was looking for along a flagstone path feet like blocks of wood trailing black oily
shit this must be the kitchen door open rusty electric
stove moldy chili dishes food containers silver paper
knew what I was looking for rummaged in the shelves
fingers numb wet-dream tension in my crotch and I
knew there was not much time found a can of baking
powder emptied it into a porcelain fruit bowl painted
roses no water silver pies choking in a red haze not
much time out into the ruined garden fish pond stagnant water green slime a frog jumped the boy was tearing at his jockstrap I sat down and slipped my strap
off strap halfway down his thighs cock flipped out stiff
he lost balance fell on his side I pulled the strap down
off his feet he turned on his back knees up body arched
pulled together spurted neck tumescent choking I
dipped water and green slime into the bowl with both
hands mixed a paste slapped the paste on both sides of
his neck and down the chest to the heart ejaculated
across his quivering stomach I dipped more paste held
it to the sides of my throbbing neck then down the
chest I could breathe now easier to move more paste
down the boy's stomach and thighs to the feet turned
him over and rubbed the paste down his back where
the nettles had whipped great welts across the back he
sighed simpered body went limp and emptied again. I
stood up and rubbed the paste over my body the pain
was going and the numbness. I flopped down beside
the boy and fell into a deep sleep.

"Five Indian youths accompanied us from the village in
the capacity of guides. Actually they seemed quite
ignorant of the country we were traversing and spent
much of their time hunting with an old muzzle-loading

shotgun more hazardous to the hunters than the quarry. Five days out of Candiru in the head waters of the Babboonsasshole, they managed to wound a deer. Chasing the wounded animal in wild excitement they ran through a patch of nettles. They emerged covered from head to foot with pulsing welts whipped across red skins like dusky roses. Fortunately they were wearing loincloths. Pain seemed to lend fleetness and energy to the pursuit and they brought the deer down with another shot. They closed on the dying animal with shrill cries of triumph and severed its head with a machete. Quite suddenly they were silent looking at each other and with one accord were seized by un-controllable diarrhea. They tore off their loincloths in a frenzy of lust, faces tumescent eyes swollen shut, threw themselves on the ground ejaculating and defe-cating again and again. We watched powerless to aid them until the Chinese cook with rare presence of mind mixed baking powder into a thick paste with water. He applied this paste to the neck of the nearest youth and then down the chest to the heart. In this way he was able to save two of the youths but the other three perished in erotic convulsions. As to whether the nettles were of a special variety or the symptoms resulted from an excess of formic acid circulated through the blood by exertion I could not say. The prompt relief afforded by applying an alkaline paste would suggest that the symptoms resulted from some form of acid poisoning." Quote Greenbaum early explorer.

When we woke up the sun was setting. We were smeared with a dried paste of shit, baking powder and green slime as if anointed for some ceremony or sacrifice. We found soap in the kitchen and washed off the crusted paste

feeling rather like molting snakes. We dined on vichys-
soise, cold crab meat and brandied peaches. The boy
refused to sleep in the house saying simply that it was
"very bad place." So we dragged a mattress to the garage
and slept there the carbines ready a snub-nosed thirty-
eight by each hand. Never keep a pistol under your
pillow where you have to reach up for it. Keep it down by
your hand at the crotch. That way you can come up
shooting right through the blanket.

At dawn we set out through the ruined suburbs no signs
of life the air windless and dead. From time to time the
boy would stop sniffing like a dog. "This way Meester."
We were walking down a long avenue littered with
palm branches. Suddenly the air was full of robins
thousands of them settling in the ruined gardens perch-
ing on the empty houses splashing in bird baths full of
rain water. A boy on a red bicycle flashed past. He made
a wide U-turn and pulled in to the curb beside us. He
was naked except for a red jockstrap, belt and flexible
black shoes his flesh red as terra cotta smooth poreless
skin tight over the cheekbones deep-set black eyes and
a casque of black hair. At his belt was an eighteen-inch
bowie knife with knuckle-duster handle. He said no
word of greeting. He sat there one foot on the curb
looking at the Dib. His ears which stuck out from the
head trembled slightly and his eyes glistened. He licked
his lips and said one word in a language unknown to
me. The Dib nodded matter of factly. He turned to me.
"He very hot. Been riding three days. Fuck now talk
later."

The boy propped his bicycle against the curb. He took
off his belt and knife and dropped them on a bench. He
sat down on the bench and shoved his jockstrap down

over his shoes. His red cock flipped out stiff and lubricating. The boy stood up. Beneath thin red ribs his
heart throbbed and pounded. The Dib peeled off his
jockstrap scraping erection. He stepped out of the strap
and tossed the boy a tin of Vaseline from his shoeshine
box. The boy caught it and rubbed Vaseline on his cock
throbbing to his heartbeats. The Dib stepped toward
him and the boy caught him by the hips turning him
around. The Dib parted his cheeks with both hands
leaning forward and the red penis quivered into his
flesh. Holding the Dib's hips in both hands the boy's
body contracted pulling together. His ears began to
vibrate lips parted from long yellow teeth smooth and
hard as old ivory. His deep-set black eyes lit up inside
with red fire and the hair stood up straight on his head.
The Dib's body arched spurting pearly gobs in the
stagnant sunlight. For a few seconds they shivered together then the boy shoved the Dib's body away as if
he were taking off a garment. They went to a pool
across a lawn washed themselves came back and put on
their jockstraps.
"This Jimmy the Shrew. He messenger special delivery
C.O.D." They talked briefly in their language which is
transliterated from a picture language known to all wild
boys in this area.
"He say time barrier ahead. Very bad."
The Shrew took a small flat box from his handle-bar
basket and handed it to the Dib. "He giving us film
grenades." The Dib opened the box and showed me six
small black cylinders. The Shrew got on his bicycle and
rode away down the avenue and disappeared in a
blaze of hibiscus. We walked on through the suburbs
heading north. The houses were smaller and shabbier.
A menace and evil hung in the empty streets like a haze

and the air was getting cold around the edges. We rounded a corner and a sharp wind spattered the Dib's body with goose pimples. He sniffed uneasily.

"We coming to bad place, Johnny. Need clothes."

"Let's see what we can find in here."

There was a rambling ranch-style house obviously built before the naborhood had deteriorated. We stepped through a hedge and passed a ruined barbecue pit. The side door was open. We were in a room that had served as an office. In a drawer of the desk the Dib found a thirty-eight snub-nosed revolver and box of shells.

"Whee look" he cried and popped his find into the shoe-shine box. We went through the house like a whirlwind the Dib pulling out suits and sports coats from closets and holding them against his body in front of mirrors, opening drawers snatching what he wanted and dumping the rest on the floor. His eyes shone and his excitement mounted as we rushed from room to room throwing any clothes we might use onto beds and chairs and sofas. I felt a wet-dream tension in my crotch the dream of packing to leave with a few minutes to catch a boat and more and more drawers full of clothes to pack the boat whistling in the harbor. As we stepped into a little guest room the Dib in front of me I stroked his smooth white buttocks and he turned to me rubbing his jock.

"This make me very hot Meester." He sat down on the bed and pulled off his jockstrap and his cock flipped out lubricating. "Whee" he said and lay back on his elbows kicking his feet. "Jacking me off." I slipped off my strap and sat down beside him rubbing the lubricant around the tip of his cock and he went off in a few seconds.

We took a shower and made a selection of clothes or rather I made the selection since the Dib's taste ran to loud sports coats wide ties and straw hats. I found a

blue suit for him and he looked like a 1920 prep school
boy on vacation. For myself I selected a grey Glen
Plaid and a green fedora. We packed the spare gun and
extra shells into a brief case with the film grenades the
Shrew had given us.

Fish smells and dead eyes in doorways shabby quarters
of a forgotten city streets half-buried in sand. I was
beginning to remember the pawn shops, guns and brass
knucks in a dusty window, cheap rooming houses, chili
parlors, a cold wind from the sea. Police line ahead
frisking seven boys against a wall. Too late to turn back
they'd seen us. And then I saw the photographers, more
photographers than a routine frisk would draw. I eased
a film grenade into my hand. A cop stopped toward us.
I pushed the plunger down and brought my hands up
tossing the grenade into the air. A black explosion
blotted out the set and we were running down a dark
street toward the barrier. We ran on and burst out of a
black silver mist into late afternoon sunlight on a suburban street, cracked pavements, sharp smell of weeds.

THE PENNY ARCADE PEEP SHOW

Naked boys standing by a water hole savanna backdrop
a head of giraffe in the distance. The boys talk in growls
and snarls, purrs and yipes and show their teeth at
each other like wild dogs. Two boys fuck standing up
squeezing back teeth bare, hair stands up on the ankles,
ripples up the legs in goose pimples they whine and
whimper off.

In the rotten flesh gardens languid Bubu boys with
black smiles scratch erogenous sores diseased putrid
sweet their naked bodies steam of a sepia haze of nitrous
choking vapors.

Green lizard boy by a stagnant stream smiles and rubs

his worn leather jockstrap with one slow finger.

Dim street light on soiled clothes boy stands there naked with his shirt in one hand the other hand scratching his ass.

Two naked youths with curly black hair and pointed Pan ears casting dice by a marble fountain. The loser bends over looking at his reflection in the pool. The winner poises behind him like a phallic god. He pries the smooth white buttocks apart with his thumbs. Lips curl back from sharp white teeth. Laughter shakes the sky.

Glider boys drift down from the sunset on red wings and rain arrows from the sky.

Slingshot boys glide in across a valley riding their black plastic wings like sheets of mica in the sunlight torn clothes flapping hard red flesh. Each boy carries a heavy slingshot attached to his wrist by a leather thong. At their belts are leather pouches of round black stones.

The roller-skate boys sweep down a hill in a shower of autumn leaves. They slice through a police patrol. Blood spatters dead leaves in air.

The screen is exploding in moon craters and boiling silver spots.

"Wild boys very close now."

Darkness falls on the ruined suburbs. A dog barks in the distance.

Dim jerky stars are blowing away across a gleaming empty sky, *the wild boys smile.*

William S. Burroughs
August 17, 1969
London

Selected Grove Press Paperbacks

62334-7   ACKER, KATHY / Blood and Guts in High School / $7.95
62480-7   ACKER, KATHY / Great Expectations: A Novel / $6.95
17458-5   ALLEN, DONALD & BUTTERICK, GEORGE F., eds. / The
           Postmoderns: The New American Poetry Revised / $9.95
62264-2   ANDERSON, REED / Federico Garcia Lorca / $7.95
62433-5   BARASH, DAVID and LIPTON, JUDITH / Stop Nuclear War!
           A Handbook / $7.95
17087-3   BARNES, JOHN / Evita—First Lady: A Biography of Eva Peron /
           $5.95
17208-6   BECKETT, SAMUEL / Endgame Act without Words / $3.95
17299-X   BECKETT, SAMUEL / Three Novels: Molloy, Malone Dies and
           The Unnamable / $7.95
13034-8   BECKETT, SAMUEL / Waiting for Godot / $4.95
62268-5   BENSON, RENATE / German Expressionist Drama: Ernst Toller
           and Georg Kaiser / $7.95
62104-2   BLOCH, DOROTHY / So the Witch Won't Eat Me: Fantasy and
           the Child's Fear of Infanticide / $7.95
13030-5   BORGES, JORGE LUIS / Ficciones / $6.95
17270-1   BORGES, JORGE LUIS / A Personal Anthology / $6.95
17112-8   BRECHT, BERTOLT / Galileo / $4.95
17106-3   BRECHT, BERTOLT / Mother Courage and Her Children / $3.95
17472-0   BRECHT, BERTOLT / Threepenny Opera / $3.95
17393-7   BRETON, ANDRE / Nadja / $7.95
13011-9   BULGAKOV, MIKHAIL / The Master and Margarita / $6.95
17108-X   BURROUGHS, WILLIAM S. / Naked Lunch / $6.95
17749-5   BURROUGHS, WILLIAM S. / The Soft Machine, Nova Express,
           The Wild Boys: Three Novels / $5.95
17411-9   CLURMAN, HAROLD (Ed.) / Nine Plays of the Modern Theater
           (Waiting for Godot by Samuel Beckett, The Visit by Friedrich
           Durrenmatt, Tango by Slawomir Mrozek, The Caucasian Chalk
           Circle by Bertolt Brecht, The Balcony by Jean Genet, Rhinoceros
           by Eugene Ionesco, American Buffalo by David Mamet, The Birth-
           day Party by Harold Pinter, Rosencrantz and Guildenstern Are
           Dead by Tom Stoppard) / $15.95
17962-5   COHN, RUBY / New American Dramatists: 1960-1980 / $7.95
17971-4   COOVER, ROBERT / Spanking the Maid / $4.95
17535-2   COWARD, NOEL / Three Plays (Private Lives, Hay Fever, Blithe
           Spirit) / $7.95

62371-1   MILLER, HENRY / Sexus / $9.95
62375-4   MILLER, HENRY / Tropic of Cancer / $7.95
62053-4   MROZEK, SLAWOMIR / The Elephant / $6.95
62301-1   NAISON, MARK / Communists in Harlem During the Depression / $9.95
13035-6   NERUDA, PABLO / Five Decades: Poems 1925-1970. Bilingual ed. / $14.50
62243-X   NICOSIA, GERALD / Memory Babe: A Critical Biography of Jack Kerouac / $11.95
17092-X   ODETS, CLIFFORD / Six Plays (Waiting for Lefty, Awake and Sing, Golden Boy, Rocket to the Moon, Till the Day I Die, Paradise Lost) / $7.95
17650-2   OE, KENZABURO / A Personal Matter / $6.95
17002-4   OE, KENZABURO / Teach Us To Outgrow Our Madness / $4.95
17992-7   PAZ, OCTAVIO / The Labyrinth of Solitude / $9.95
17084-9   PINTER, HAROLD / Betrayal / $6.95
17232-9   PINTER, HAROLD / The Birthday Party & The Room / $6.95
17251-5   PINTER, HAROLD / The Homecoming / $5.95
17761-4   PINTER, HAROLD / Old Times / $6.95
17539-5   POMERANCE, BERNARD / The Elephant Man / $5.95
17658-8   REAGE, PAULINE / The Story of O, Part II; Return to the Chateau / $3.95
62169-7   RECHY, JOHN / City of Night / $4.50
62171-9   RECHY, JOHN / Numbers / $8.95
13017-8   ROBBE-GRILLET, ALAIN / Djinn (and La Maison de Rendez-Vous) / $8.95
13017-8   ROBBE-GRILLET, ALAIN / The Voyeur / $8.95
62001-1   ROSSET, BARNEY and JORDAN, FRED / Evergreen Review No. 98 / $5.95
62498-X   ROSSET, PETER and VANDERMEER, JOHN / The Nicaragua Reader / $9.95
13012-7   SADE, MARQUIS DE / The 120 Days of Sodom and Other Writings / $14.95
62045-3   SAVONNA, JEANNETTE L. / Jean Genet / $8.95
62495-5   SCHEFFLER, LINDA / Help Thy Neighbor / $7.95
62438-6   SCHNEEBAUM, TOBIAS / Keep the River on Your Right / $12.50
62009-7   SEGALL, J. PETER / Deduct This Book: How Not to Pay Taxes While Ronald Reagan is President / $6.95
17467-4   SELBY, HUBERT / Last Exit to Brooklyn / $3.95
62040-2   SETO, JUDITH ROBERTS / The Young Actor's Workbook / $8.95
17963-3   SHANK, THEODORE / American Alternative Theater / $12.50
17948-X   SHAWN, WALLACE, and GREGORY, ANDRE / My Dinner with Andre / $6.95
62496-3   SIEGAL, FREDERICK, M.D., and MARTA / Aids: The Medical Mystery / $7.95

GROVE PRESS, INC., 920 Broadway, New York, N.Y. 10010